Falling Angels, Lost Highways.

(The Long Fall of Rudolf Hess.)

Brian Moffatt 2012.

A Loose Cannon Publication.

Loose Cannon Publications is an imprint of Rocking Boat Press.

To "Eddie" and all of the other "Forgotten Soldiers."
This one is for you.

*   *   *

Published by Rocking Boat Press,
Henderson's Knowe,
Teviothead,
by Hawick,
Roxburghshire,
Scotland. TD9 0LF

Published by Rocking Boat Press 2012.

A catalogue record of this book is available from the British Library.

ISBN: 978-0-9544802-4-0

While some of the events and characters are based upon historical incidents and figures, this novel is entirely a work of fiction.

Set in Times, by the author.

Printed and bound by CPI Group (UK) Ltd, Croydon, CRo 4YY

*   *   *

Some of this book is true.
Some of this book is not true.
Some of this book may be true, and some of this book perhaps ought to be true.
There is no Duke of Marchbank, or Marchbank House.
There is no Welldean House.
There is no Despoine Clinic.
And, unfortunately, there is no "Last Chance Cafe,"
All of the characters portrayed, except for the genuine, are products of the authors own imagination, and bear no resemblance to any persons either living or dead.
So don't worry, it's not you.
However, the author wishes to point out, that if you truly believe that you are the original of Captain Anthony Errington Vardy, or Parsa Khan, or even of Master Zhang.Then you are a very sad individual indeed, and ought perhaps to seek psychological counselling.

This book is a work of fiction, and any statements made or opinions expressed by the characters within, are not to be taken as statements of fact, or as the opinions of the author, but merely as devices to assist in the development of the plot.

Falling Angels, Lost Highways.

(The Long Fall of Rudolf Hess.)

A novel set in 2003.

Introducing Eddie Graham.

I said, "Master,..... The Wild Eagle has gone.
He replied. "No.......For the Eagle, ... it is still Here".

Rosalinde Molesworthy

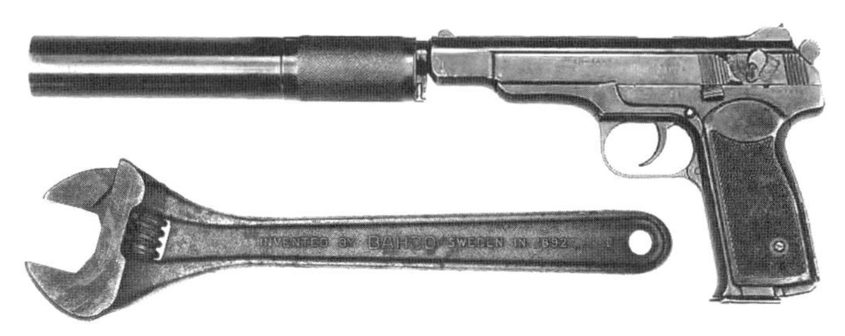

Prologue.

January 27th 2003.

Reb and I were sitting with our backs against the wall, at the long table near the door, chatting idly about nothing in particular, when they entered.

She, and I was only aware of "she," was all long haired, long legged blonde, tall and elegant. Beautiful in old fashioned sort of way. Ingrid Bergmann perhaps, but more young Lauren Bacall.

"Of all the gin joints in all of the world?" I mused. But....a transport cafe in Langholm? And, immediately, unintentionally, but perhaps unavoidably, I slipped on my Bogart persona.

Her companion was small, mousy, middle aged, and overweight, dressed in a tight and rumpled brown business suit, which must have fit her once. Once that is, before she had to join chocoholics anonymous. Terminal dandruff cascaded down her shoulders. Her complexion was pure sugar frosted flake.

She carried an official looking black briefcase under her left arm, and she stared, first at me, and then at Reb.

Then she spoke."Mr. Septimus Higgins?"

"No." I glanced across to where he was wiping down the counter.

"Hey Shorty," I called, "Come on over here."

She looked at me aghast. "You can't call him that, he's just a little vertically challenged."

I caught his eye again. "Lady here, says you're vertically challenged."

He leered over with his gap toothed grin. "Which one said that then, the fat one, or the one with the nice tits?"

The "fat one" pointed over at Shorty a look of revulsion on her face. "Ha! Got you at last Higgins!" She crooked her finger, "Come here." Her beautiful companion said nothing, but caught my eye, smiled, and shook her head slightly.

Shorty raised his right arm in a Nazi salute, "Ja Wohl, Mein Fuehrer," he snapped. He clicked his heels, and a big stupid grin appeared on his face.

Reb muttered under her breath. "Oh God no.... *not* Geordieland's answer to "Benny Hill," He *is* going to say it isn't he?"

Shorty pulled up in front of the spectacular blonde. At five foot nothing, the top of his head didn't even reach the bottom of her chin, and his eyes were directly in line with her ample bosom.
He stared longingly.

My inner Bogart mumbled, "You'll say it for her, and you'll say it for me..... now.....go ahead Shorty......Say it," and Reb mouthed the words, just as Shorty spoke them...."Nice to meet the pair of you."

"Oh Jesus," I moaned, "Who says, the old ones are the best."

Shorty raised his face towards heaven, and peered up into her beautiful blue eyes. Totally unfazed, she smiled back down and extended her right hand. "I'm Miss Abigail Ffanshawe........ that's Ffanshawe with two F's."

"I'll just bet it is." I thought, "This one knows how to play that game." And, right on cue, Shorty muttered, "F's" be buggered. Look like "C" cups to me. Come on and join us pretty lady, and bring your pet doberman with you." He settled himself next to Reb, and crossed his arms defensively.

And there we sat, The Three Not so Wise Monkeys. See all Evil.... Hear all Evil..... and Speak all Evil. Sometimes write all Evil. But of course they shouldn't know that.

They sat down opposite us. The fat one took out a pair of pebble glasses, and placed them on her nose. "I'm Inspector Roselinde Molesworthy."

Boy, if ever a name fit perfectly, then that was it. "Molesworthy," small, brown, half blind, and burrowing after something. But "Roselinde"?

She continued, "Miss Ffanshawe, has already introduced herself." She paused and smiled sinisterly at Shorty. "We represent Her Majesty's Inspectorate of Taxes."

I reached across the table, and shook her hand. "I'm Eddie Graham, I represent Mr. Higgins's interests in both legal and financial matters, but in this instance, at the moment, just regard me as a qualified observer."

She bridled. "*You*, are a qualified lawyer?"

I smiled back, "*I* am qualified in many things." Indicating Reb, I continued, "And this is Lady Rebecca Forsythe-Ingram. Since we need two witnesses to this rather impromptu, and may I say, highly irregular interview, I suggest that she remains, as party to your conversation."

Molesworthy stared in disbelief at Reb's worn down trainers, at the black roots showing through her strawlike beached hair.

"*Lady Rebecca,*" she squawked.

"Oh Indeed," Reb replied, her voice pure Kensington. "Don't be fooled by the appearance. Daddy's a Peer of the realm, and my brother's a merchant banker in the City. Believe me I'm quite the white sheep of the family." She placed her arm protectively around Shorty's shoulders. "Now, what did you what to talk to my husband about?"

Husband! Since when? I thought Shorty was about to explode with mirth. Abigail Ffanshawe, just sat there silent. Smiling. A big cuddly Cheshire cat.

Molesworthy opened her file. "There's been a complaint, Mr Higgins. That is to say a complaint about you. This, is a most serious situation. The allegation is, that you have been openly boasting that you have no intention of ever paying any taxes at all, and when we came to look into the matter, not only have you never paid any taxes, but, it also seems that there is no record anywhere of your very existence."

Something told me she was not telling the truth, so I interrupted. "Can you clarify some of that? Where did this complaint originate?"

She stared at me, expressionless. "I'm not at liberty to divulge that information. However, there was once, it seems, a Septimus

Higgins, of around the right age, but that was in England, over in Blyth, Northumberland. He committed a rather unsavoury crime, and ended up in Durham Prison. He was released in 1998, and no-one seems to know what happened to him."

Shorty grinned evilly, "Oh aye that would be me cousin, Seppy..... confusing isn't it? It's a family name, and me Aunty Ella, couldn't resist calling him it, even though I had it already.

Dangerous little man our Seppy, nice enough, but perhaps a little too impulsive, and it's caused me endless problems."

He paused, leaned back in his chair, and allowed the silence to stretch, a skilled actor patiently awaiting his cue, but was *he* the *only* player in this company? Because with impeccable timing, Miss Ffanshawe raised one elegant eyebrow, and asked.

"Problems.... What kind of problems."

And Shorty, knowing that the spotlight was now fully upon him, relaxed into his role. His face became solemn and he sighed deeply. "Ahh...... Now, do let me explain.....You see, young Seppy's particular problem wasn't his name at all, it was simply that he couldn't stand drug dealers."

Molesworthy cleared her throat, about to interrupt, and Shorty held up a hand to silence her. "Please, do be patient Lady, and I promise that all will be revealed.

Yes....our Seppy hated drug dealers, and he had personal reasons for disliking them.....family reasons. Now, this fact was well known, and so, when one the local cartel's (a.k.a "the Newcastle Mafia's") employees disappeared down on the coast and then, slightly battered and totally deceased, mysteriously floated ashore in Blyth harbour, well.....they suspected that Seppy may have had something to do with it, and they sent one of their "hard lads" down from the West End to Blyth, to stop his clock for him."

"Stop his clock?" Molesworthy interjected.

"Kill him," Miss Ffanshawe whispered.

Shorty nodded his thanks, and continued. "Now, when this guy arrives, Seppy is happily employed building a stand, so that he can comfortably tinker with his bikes, motor bikes that is. You see his hobby is restoring them. He's working at his forge, and there's a sharp metal bar that he's been using as a poker resting in the fire. It's been in there a while, and so it's red hot.

Now, our Seppy, he hears the door go, sees the thugs reflection in the workshop window, and clicks to what's about to happen.

But," and Shorty raised a finger, "Seppy is one cool dude, and calm as you like, he simply carries on working. He let's that villain creep right up behind him, and just when the bastard's gòing to pan him one from behind with a muckle great ball peen hammer, he turns, skilfully trips the guy, and at the same time he gives him a good hard shove. Now.... as luck will have it, he falls forward over the frame Seppy's been welding up. And there he is, sprawled face down, with his backside most invitingly up in the air."

He turned in his seat and faced Miss Molesworthy. "Our Seppy's not big you know, he's the same build as me, and this thug, is six six if he's an inch. I mean..... What should he to do next?"

Slack jawed and aghast, Molesworthy shook her head, and Shorty nodded sagely.

"Exactly.....Well now, it's just as well he's quick, and just as well he knows his history, 'cause he grabs that poker from out of the fire, and taking good aim he "Hot Collars" him......You know just like what was supposed to have happened to King Eddie the Second. Twelve inches of red hot iron right up the Jacksie! "Thuggins,"lets out a horrendous shriek, and collapses completely, with the poker sticking out of his arse. Foul smelling smoke is shooting out everywhere, and Seppy is left doubled up with laughter."

He winked across at Miss Ffanshawe, "All of our family have a funny sense of humour, or at least other folk seem to think so.

However," he continued, "he's wondering at the same time, how on earth can he get rid of six and a half feet of unconscious thug?"

Shorty stared towards the ceiling and muttered, "Christ, It's amazing what goes through your mind at times like these."

Abigail Ffanshawe smiled. "Isn't it just." She gestured with one hand. "Please Mr. Higgins, do go on, pray do tell us more."

Shorty reached across, poured himself more coffee from the percolator on the table, and raised both his mug and an eyebrow to Miss Ffanshawe. She shook her head.

Over in the far corner of the room, the sound system clicked in, and quietly, almost unobtrusively Hank Williams yodelled his way into "Lonesome Whistle," a tale of loss and incarceration. How very convenient!

Shorty savoured the moment, and look of utter sadness appeared upon his face.......Man, was he good!

He cleared his throat. "Well now.....Unfortunately, all of that noise, the screaming, shrieking, moaning, and the laughter, has raised the hue and cry, and in no time at all, the place is crawling with plods, and paramedics. But, despite all of their sterling efforts, "Thuggins," the awkward and inconsiderate bastard, goes and dies, and the unfortunate Seppy is dragged off to clink.

And here's where it all goes sick. Because, despite the fact that it was self defence, Seppy can't prove it, and because of the rather unusual method of dispatch, which it seems has gone a little out of fashion since 1327, the Judge at his trial takes a rather dim view of things, and so, poor Seppy, innocent of everything except self preservation, ends up doing time in "E" wing, where, as a result of both his diminutive size, and his rather unusual pyrography skills he is regarded as something of a legend, and in the rarified atmosphere of Durham Prison he becomes acquainted with some rather interesting, although perhaps illegal skills. He also spends a deal of time in the Prison Library, polishing his rather neglected education, and eventually he leaves Durham, with a Degree from the Open University, of which, I must say, he is exceedingly proud.

Now, he's such a nice little guy, (unless someone tries to kill him that is), that he gets out considerably earlier than anyone expects, and being a sensible lad, he gets both quickly and completely out of Tyneside.

Do you know, the prison doctors reckoned he was half way to being a psychopath, but they said that he was a fine fellow for all of that. They said that he was wonderful material for a Ph.D, but whether for them, or for him, they quite failed to specify.

I haven't heard of him for years, but one thing I do know, is that wherever he is, he's probably best left alone, 'cause frankly...... *I think* he's a complete nutter."

Molesworthy coughed, cleared her throat, and consulted her notes. She nodded....."Yes, That's reasonably in line with what we have here. And of course, you will deny that this "Seppy" has anything to do with you?"

"Oh no Lady! He's got lots to do with me," Shorty retorted, "I told you, he's me cousin."

"But," she continued, "he disappears, just around the time you seem to appear. Rather convenient don't you think?'

"So what missus,.......now't but coincidence."

She gestured with her hand. "Then where do *you* come from."

"Oh Christ, No," Reb muttered in my ear, "Here he goes again!"
"Ahh," Shorty breathed, leaning back in his seat and raising a single finger towards the ceiling. He pointed towards an imaginary moon. A moon visible perhaps, only to the initiated.
We.....the initiated.
His round slightly squashed face took on a look of wonder, his bald pate shone in the light, and a slow smile spread across his visage. He spoke with reverence. His voice full of Awe.
"Awe........ I often ask myself that question! Lady Rebecca and I occasionally discuss it in bed, after a couple of bottles of "Nukey Brown." (Newcastle Brown Ale). He paused..... rain rattled on the window. Gravel crunched beneath wheels, as a car pulled in off the road. Then, he gave a deep sigh and continued..... "Where *do* we come from? .... Where *are* we going to? ..... *Why* are we here at all? *These* are the great questions of the Universe." He stared off into space, then he gave a small start, and continued. "But why ask me?..... I suggest you take a wander up to Eskdalemuir perhaps. To the temple at Samye-Ling. Consult the Holy Llama's."
He should have been on the stage, or in films, the Borders very own Danny de Vito.
Molesworthy was purple, I thought she would explode."*You're* a complete Nutter". she exclaimed.
"Thank God!.... I'm Complete!" he cried joyfully, glancing down. "Some folk have had the audacity to suggest I've lost me Marbles!"
Miss Ffanshawe appeared to be having great difficulty containing herself, and spluttered slightly. Molesworthy shot her a vile look. "Higgins"..... she squeaked "You appear to have no visible means of support"
"Oh God" Reb whispered, "*Is* she just there to feed him his lines"
Shorty looked positively beatific. He smiled knowingly at Miss Ffanshawe's ample bosom. "And I'm not the only one at this table," he crowed. "But" ..... he went on, "with regard to my income. I'm not employed, I'm not self employed, I'm not unemployed, I'm not anything that would fit on your little forms. I does things for people, and they gives me things. I find things, I grow things, I brew stuff. That's it..... End of story. No mystery. No Money, No Income, *No Tax!* I'm not part of your system, and I don't want to be. Work out where I came from if you want. But, not to be rude, this conversation is about finished, so why don't

you just bugger off. Abigail there, can stay if she wants. I quite like her."

Molesworthy bridled. "Don't you dare tell me what to do! You seem to be exactly the obnoxious, violent little liar I was told you were. Admit it! You *are* Seppy Higgins......The one from Blyth" They stared at each other across the table.

And that was when it all came apart.

The door opened, bringing in a cold blast of air, a flurry of fallen leaves, and the biggest ugliest black man I'd ever seen.

His skin was blue black. His flat nose had been flattened even further with some blunt instrument, his head was shaven, it gleamed with rain, and his small ears were oddly pink as if they had been scorched with a blowlamp. He wore a white "T" shirt, loose black cargo trousers, and biker boots. A long black coat flapped around his legs.

He stared at our group. First Shorty, then Reb, and lastly at me. He took a mobile phone from his pocket and consulted the screen, then he nodded to himself, and walked directly to our table.

Totally ignoring, the Miss's Molesworthy and Ffanshawe, he glowered down. "Higgins and Graham?" he grated, in an incredibly thick Glasgow accent. The complete, the original, Tartan Gorilla. His coat fell aside revealing the cut down stock of a double barreled shotgun.

Shorty smiled grimly, meeting that animal stare, and I was aware of his right hand moving slightly beneath the table."You didn't know how lucky you were when you walked in here," he said.

The monster loomed over us as he leaned forward across the table. His breath reeked. Rare spices of the east. Gone rotten overnight. "Lucky Eh?..... More than you two are," and his hand drifted towards the stock of his gun.

There was a horrid meaty thunk, as Shorty's heavy spanner shattered the giant's right kneecap. I would not have believed it possible, but his coal black complexion faded visibly to grey, as he sank down to our level.

"Yeah, Lucky," Shorty replied, "Cause then you could still walk........ Sorry about your arm."

King Kong rolled his eyes, and mouthed... "Arm"?... just as the business end of the spanner smashed his right elbow. He collapsed onto the floor.

Miss Ffanshawe with the two F's reached down, removed the sawn off from beneath the brute's coat, and handed it to me.
" A present from Glasgow." She purred.

And just then, the door opened again.
He was about my height, all in black with a black ski mask. In his right had he carried a Stechkin pistol. An APB 6/P 13. The one with the huge silencer. It's single black "eye" pointed unerringly at me. Christ.... Welcome to Shit Creek....there must have been two of them. Ever so slowly, I placed the shotgun on the table. Moved my hands well away from it.
He took three steps towards us, the gun never wavering, then quite unexpectedly, he dropped his aim, and without hesitation put three rounds into the head of the monster moaning on the floor.
Even with the silencer the sound was as loud as a .22 rifle. Brass rattled across the floor. Pinged off a table leg. The air reeked of burned powder.
He backed towards the door, all of the time covering us with the gun, and Reb exploded.
"You....You..... Selfish.... Dirty.... Bastard... *Look* at him!" She pointed at the floor. "*Who* do you think has to clean up the mess around here!"
He bowed to her slightly, clicked his heels together, and left.
And that was when Miss Ffanshawe burst out laughing.
"You see Molesworthy even violent little liars have their uses." She reached over to Shorty, and shook his hand. "Nice Work!"
"Thanks!"
And I wondered, What the Hell... was a Bloody Russian Assassin.... doing in Langholm?

* * *

Part 1.

Introducing Eddie Graham.

1970 - 2003.

So, Who am I?

Well, as you have already gathered, my name is Eddie Graham.

I'm an Ex-fisherman, ex-policeman, ex-army, and ex-military intelligence.

Military and intelligence? Now, there's two words which should never go together.

I was born and dragged up in Blyth, Northumberland, which is, or I should say was, a coalport, around fifteen miles north of the mouth of the Tyne.You've all heard of "Coals from Newcastle"? Well forget it, it's a myth, 'cause most of the coal came out of Blyth, and way before that, out of a place called Seaton Sluice, just five miles to the south.

Nothing much at the Sluice now, but it's still worth a look. They say that, long ago, the "moorings" there, the long slot cut through the rock, was blasted out with gunpowder, and that it was the first time that had been done. The resulting gash in the rock separated what came to be known as "Rocky Island" from the "mainland".

It was connected only by a footbridge, over and above, of where the ships docked below.

I never did find out if the tale about the gunpowder was entirely true, but it's a good story. (History's a bit of a hobby of mine)

Up until the 1960's, Blyth was the busiest port in the UK, and in its heyday, it was the busiest port in Europe. Eventually, it acquired its own coal fired power station, state of the art for it's time. Coal, shipbuilding, and near full employment, a tough, working class town, and proud of its heritage. Now it's nothing, and one recent survey, even voted it the "least popular town in Britain to live in." What a claim to fame!

So what killed it? Lack of investment? Complacency? Greed? Not exactly...."They," whoever the hell "they" are, (answers on a postcard please), simply found that coal could be imported cheaper from elsewhere, and faster, lower cost shipbuilding abroad slowly strangled the shipyards.

Then in the 80's Thatcher decided to kill the mining industry stone dead, and she and her government did just that......Dead!

It was tragic. It was Evil. There was no lack of coal, and mining was not just a job, it was a way of life. "The Pit," "The Club," "The Community." And "Community", is exactly what they destroyed.

The Tory Government, and its leader were just spoiling to bring down the Unions, and a way of life which had lasted for generations just disappeared. Now, years later, we need the energy, but of course our coal isn't green, and there's no one left to mine it anyway. So we get all of our "dirty" work done in China, a "Communist" dictatorship where the power stations are still coal fired, and no-one cares about human rights, or "saving the planet." What's worse, is that the developed nations of the world, are quite prepared to sell China all of the raw materials they need to produce those cheap goods. Which is the equivalent of selling the assassin, the iron, to make the knife, that will stab you in the back!

No coal for our politicians, they're all wind and water now, (and not just to generate power!) so that Britain can meet its obligations. Retain its "Green credentials."

But, whatever the causes, and you could write a book on them, by the time I was born in 1970, Blyth was heading for the rocks.

My folks had been "Army," killed in pub bombing in Belfast, and I lived with my dear, fat, kindly old Auntie 'Bella, in a run down flat above an empty shop in Sussex Street, just back from the Quay. I had my own room way up under the eaves.

My mate Shorty, who was only a couple of months younger than me, had his home just over the road, next to Alison Horn's builders yard, and the derelict "bonded warehouse" where all the tobacco and whisky used to be stored. So, I've known him virtually all of my life.

Shorty claimed to be descended from Borderers, Higgins's, somehow, quite inexplicably, associated with the Armstrongs of Gilknockie, and me being a Graham, with ancestors harking from up in the Debateable Lands, just south of Langholm, it seemed sort of natural that we become allies. Freelances! The Two Musketeers! All for one, and one for all! ....The Last of the Reivers!

"Schooling" in Blyth was more about survival than education. Rudimentary rather than Elementary, and Shorty and I ended up at what used to be called "Newlands" school up in "The Avenues." 6th Avenue to be precise. Sounds very "New York" and sophisticated? Well......It wasn't!

We survived there, until we were thrown out at sixteen, onto the great heap of the unemployed and perhaps, the unemployable.

Even so, quite a few of our contemporaries did manage to go on from there to Durham..... The Prison that is, not the University.

So eventually did Shorty, and indirectly, it was drugs, that's what did it.

For, Septimus "Shorty" Higgins, achieved nothing at all at school, other than a realisation of life's cruelty. If you're only five foot tall, it's perhaps inevitable that you're going to get called "Shorty." But if they think you're not the brightest bulb in the illuminations? And so, on one fine, happy day, a prize day at that, (although, one in which he was most definitely not a recipient), Shorty, most amusingly he thought, broke wind vastly, in front of the entire school, just as the universally hated, "Creepy" (I'll tell you who did it Sir) Sumpter, was about to take hold of his first prize for Snivelling, (actually it was Gardening, incredibly, a subject well taught at Newlands, and Sumpter, just loved his Sweet Peas). And, one insensitive bastard of a teacher, driven to despair, yelled out. "Higgins! You're as thick as two short planks."

That was it. That was all it took. Everyone screamed with laughter. And "Shorty Two Planks" was born.

They might have called him it behind his back. They may have called it out, and then run away, but no-one ever said it twice.

Because, quite unwittingly they had created the most violent little lunatic known to Geordieland. For Shorty, driven to despair by the constant taunting, acquired a large and heavy spanner, "Just so that he could Fix Things." He carried it in a pocket sewn into the leg of his trousers, and boy, did he know how to use it.

Shorty developed an alternative persona. That of a complete lunatic. Being so small, he claimed, it helped to redress the balance. Also, he thought it was quite good fun!

He would deliberately plan out and execute his various scenarios, and his enemies came to believe that he was totally unhinged.

All around Shorty, Terror reigned. He was the Geordieland's very own Inquisition, and in the immortal words of Monty Python, "No one expects the Spanish Inquisition!"

And so it came to pass, that on dark nights, in back alleys and in other lonely places, his tormenters, one by one, painfully realised the errors of their ways. Shorty kept entire Casualty Departments in employment, and by the time we matriculated from the decrepit educational establishment that we had, for so long called home, he was referred to by only one word.

And that word was......"Sir!"

Which is all a pity, because, in fact, in his own way Shorty was something of a genius, and left to his own devices he was a kind and considerate man. He believed in Equality! Freedom! and Liberty! All of which set him totally at odds with the rest of Society.

Shorty simply hated authority, he couldn't stand the "system." Couldn't stand any kind of authority. Any "system" at all.

If he'd been born a different era, Victorian perhaps, or if someone had taken an interest? If he'd lived an age of self improvement? But he didn't. He lived in Blyth, in the 1980's, and Thatcher was Prime Minister.

She should have loved him. He could have been the perfect entrepreneur. Give him anything mechanical, anything broken, and he would take it apart, find suitable materials from the vast store of scrap he kept in the back yard of his home, manufacture any new parts he needed, (sometimes even he'd invent small improvements), and give it back better than new. He simply couldn't stop himself, he had to fix things.

So, he made a small income, nothing much, but a base to build on. I, on the other hand, had an empty shop, and an easy going aunt. So we decided to put Shorty's skills, and my "premises" together. We decided that we would repair engines and the like in the front shop, and use the large single storied outhouse out back, to house a boat. Because, living in a Port, a hundred yard from the river, almost inevitably, we wanted a boat. We reckoned we could make a few quid with line fishing and lobster pots, and with a bit of luck, in season, licensed or not, we would net a few salmon.

Our outhouse had large double doors to the rear, and we could manoeuvre around a 25 foot boat and trailer inside of there.

Our first was an old ship's lifeboat that we converted. Shorty fitted a decent inboard engine, I scraped the old paint off, repainted, built on a small wheelhouse, and off we went.

Right off of the official radar.

We shivered our timbers. Cap'n Eddie, and Bo'sun Shorty, sometimes Cap'n Shorty and Bo'sun Eddie. Cash only, no books, no bank, no records. And life was just perfect for almost three years. We sold our first boat, and it made us a good profit. So we "did up" another. Bought two and kept one, and suddenly we had a business. Strictly a cash business.

We opened a joint bank account. No questions asked back then, you had some money, you put it in a bank. You just put the money in, that was it. They liked you! The manager used to call us "Sir", until we told him not to.

Then, just as things were going well, Shorty's cousin Billy, came to work for us. He was about our age, and had been kicked out by his parents who lived inland a bit at Bedlington. I didn't like the idea too much, but he was Shorty's kin, and I mean, I was living with my Auntie, so how could I refuse? The kid had no job, and no prospects. But Billy always seemed to me, to have just a bit more money than we paid him.

And then, when things were shaping up just fine, right out of the blue, everything came unstuck.

In January of 1989, on a dark and freezing cold winters afternoon, Auntie 'Bella, shopping bags in hand, waddled off a pavement at the bus station, right in front of a coal wagon. The driver stood no chance of stopping, the road hadn't been salted, and was freezing over, and with the lights of oncoming cars in his eyes, I doubt he even saw her. She died instantly.

Tragic. Worse than tragic. A Bloody coal wagon! And she used to be married to a miner. I really hoped it was local coal. Bates's pit coal, and not imported, because, God! I mean, she would have hated that!

Knocked over by cheap Polish Coal!

I'd always thought that she owned the flat and shop above it. I had never imagined living anywhere else. But it was not so, she didn't, and the owner, a right dodgy builder from North Shields, gave me notice at the funeral, just before we put 'Bella in the ground. He wondered why I hit him. Why I knocked him into an open grave. Why Shorty threw dead flowers from a jam jar onto him.

If a funeral can have a highlight, then that was it. She had a sense of humour, did 'Bella, and I think that we added to the sort of send off she would have wanted.

But now we needed new premises, and I needed somewhere else to live, so we put the two boats we had in the water, and we motored south along the coast to Seaton Sluice, where we found a decent cheap mooring, and a decrepit corrugated iron shed alongside the old lookout post on Rocky Island. It was on the way to being derelict, and we bought it for next to nothing. The owner seemed convinced that we were mad.

We moved in everything we had. The shed had a enough height to put in an upper floor and create a small flat. The view from the lookout post was second to none, and it became our tiny cramped "lounge." There was always plenty of driftwood on the beach, so we installed a big woodburning stove. Plumbed in a couple of radiators. We had mains water and drainage, two pubs within close walking distance, and life, we thought, wasn't going to be too hard. But, all in all, with all of our workgear around, there was really just enough space for two.

I got along fine with Shorty, but then Billy got thrown out of his lodgings back in Blyth, and he moved in as well, "just until he could find somewhere else" he said, and from then on, things just weren't the same.

By now we'd three boats. Two converted lifeboats, and a large fishing coble, a fine example of what is perhaps the most beautiful small scale fishing boat in British waters. It was unique, an expensive indulgence, and we kept it purely for enjoyment. We built on a covered in wheelhouse, and a bit of sheltered storage foward, or "For'ard," as us Salty Sea Dog's like to say.

Cobles, (pronounced co-ble in the North East), are unique to the Northumbrian Coast. There are a few to the north and the south, but they are generally migrants. They have been built there since time immemorial. No proper plans exist for their construction, they are simply built by genius craftsmen, to the clients own specification. Their history goes back to Scandinavia, and the Vikings. They are deep and wide at the bow, and taper and curve beautifully to a sloping and chopped off stern. They are designed specifically for the North Sea, launched from the beach forward, and brought back ashore stern first.

The full bosomed look of the coble, and Shorty's long term devotion to Country and Western music caused us to name her the "Miss Dolly Parton,"resulting in many a ribald comment from the local fishing community, who joked that it was about as near as we would ever get to climbing aboard the original.

Our other craft, the converted ex-lifeboats, were the "Miss Patsy Cline," which we had converted ourselves and balanced up to handle reasonably well at sea, (for an old lifeboat that is), and the "Leadbelly," named after Huddie Leadbetter, the old blues man, but also because she wallowed in anything but the slightest swell. Since she still needed more work and a bit of "trimming" here and there, we never took her out in heavy weather, or it really might have been "Goodnight Irene." A little bit of adjustment though would easily have cured her problems.

We more or less gave Billy the Leadbelly, so he could work on her, put her right, and then trade up to something better, but he was a lazy bugger and the boat was always a mess, paint peeling, green with moss below the waterline, and still wallowing like a whale, months after he got her.

On good calm days, he "worked" a few lobster pots just south of Blyth, and he went out regularly enough. We had a decent pair of old "U" Boat binoculars, so Shorty kept a close eye on him from the lookout, just to make sure that he was okay. He seemed to get along well enough, but he landed everything he caught in Blyth, and never brought anything back in with him to the Sluice. He even left the boat at Blyth most of the time, which should have struck us as odd I suppose, but he said all of his mates were there, and he liked to keep in touch.

He was a bit too keen on the drink, and would roll in, in the early hours, waking the entire house. You'd hear him coming miles away on his old Triumph 500, and I reckoned it was only a matter of time before the Police caught up with him. Bikes and booze are a bad combination. Worse, I could smell it on him......Cannabis, shit, splifs, call it what you will.....drugs. Shorty tried to shrug it off, but I knew he could see bad times ahead as well.

Frankly by now, I'd had enough of Billy. I needed a change, I needed to broaden my horizons, to see life outside of the North East, and so,...... I did the stupidest thing in my life. I applied to join the Metropolitan Police....Sheer bloody lunacy!

Shorty tried to talk some sense into me. Told me, "Everyone hates coppers," but by that time, I'd told "everyone" that I was off, and being young I didn't want to lose face. Off, I intended to go.

And that's how Shorty and I split up. I insisted that he keep the boats, he insisted that we left the bank account in both of our names. So, I just took out a couple of thousand to get me set up in London, and then we both got gloriously drunk.

Shorty said I'd come back up North, and in the long run he was right.

Lunatic day, 23rd of September 1989.... Etched into my brain forever. The day I arrived at Hendon Police Training College.

Generally Londoners don't join the Met. There are simpler, easier, and better paid jobs down there, and most have more sense anyway, and so the force which patrols Britain's great Metropolis, runs on a strange mixture of idiots from the more deprived areas of Britain. Scotsmen, Welshmen, Yorkshiremen, ethnic minorities, and inevitably, Geordies. All of whom know no better. But that mixture is perhaps its greatest strength. It helps everyone get along.

In my humble opinion the Met. is still the best Force in Britain. The Regional ones are just that...... Regional.... Local.... Joined by local lads. Result?......Far too many officers know far too many local Dignitaries, Businessmen....and Villains. They drink with them, play golf with them, join their damned Masonic Lodges, and do them far too many favours.

Promotions, "favours" and "cushy numbers", all are doled out in line with membership of certain little cliques. Little forces, quite literally, run by little men pulled up by their apron strings.

I'm not saying that the Met is perfect, or that such things don't exist within its ranks. They do. That's just an unpleasant facet of human nature. But it's to a far lesser extent, and because almost everyone comes from somewhere else, friendships tend to develop within "The Job" itself, and the Met. has an internal cohesion, which makes for a far better working environment. In the Met. you don't shop your mates, and that is a very "Geordie" attitude indeed. The workload is greater and more varied than elsewhere. Stay there long enough, and you'll see all of lifes rich pageant.......And its Arsehole.

Try to tell any outsider what you've seen, and they simply won't believe you. I stayed there for five years, and I once tried to write it all down, everything that occurred, but when I read it back even I didn't believe it all myself, so why should anyone else?

Two years "Probation," then in the next three, I carved myself my own little niche. Accidently ending up in what is today the Art and Antiques Squad.

My first "beat" after training school covered Portobello Road, and its antique market. Now, all of my life I'd had an interest, more perhaps, an obsession, with antiques. Mostly swords and armour. Back home I'd collected, then bought and sold a few pieces, starting off with bayonets as a kid, things my schoolmates Grandad's had brought back from the war, then moving on, to the odd Japanese sword or two. But down in London I saw quite a few folk making serious money out of dealing. So I dealt. Unofficially of course, glorified collecting really. In my free time, I'd take myself off to the major Auction Houses, Christie's, Sotheby's, Phillip's, either attend in person, or leave a bid or two. I got to be quite well known in "the trade."

I built up my own collection, and continued on, "trading up." I set an upper limit on how many pieces I would keep, and for every new item I bought, I sold something of my own. Not easy, and the number of pieces I kept, gradually increased over time. Usually, because I'd done all of the research and restoration myself, when I sold, I made a substantial profit, and the more I bought, researched, and restored, the more I learned.

Inevitably however, my little sideline came to the attention of "Sir," and one fine morning, I was summoned to the head "Sir's" office.

As a police officer I was not supposed to run a business, and so I explained that I, in fact, was merely a collector, indeed, almost an academic, for by this time I held membership of a couple of

Learned Societies, and had even contributed an article or two to their journals. So, I insisted I'd done nothing at all out of order. Incredibly, and much to my surprise, he agreed. I'd got totally the wrong end of the stick.

The antique trade, perhaps quite rightly, mistrusts the police, and in general, dealers are reluctant to approach the "Law," but my hobby had made me something of an expert on the machinations of the business, and my knowledge, quite unusually for a police officer, was from the inside. So what I had, was a job offer from Art and Antiques. And, that should have been it. Perfect, set for the rest of my career, in a job I could have designed for myself. But it wasn't to be, for two years later, I left both the Antique Squad and the Met, and I went home.

Because Shorty had been arrested...... For Murder!

You see, the story that Shorty told the Miss's Ffanshawe and Molesworthy with regard to his cousin, was true in its essentials, and quite rightly they'd concluded that Shorty himself was the central character. But what he failed to communicate, was the reason behind it all.

Whilst I was off enjoying the delights of London, the Police, and the Antique Trade, Shorty had continued to develop the business. He'd used a bit of our money to add a small additional workshop complete with a forge to his home. Then he began systematically to buy up old and interesting motor cycles, for where my interest was arms and armour, Shorty's was old British bikes. He bought them, restored them, and sold them, but always, he kept the best for himself.

I used to come up and stay with him, when I had a bit of leave, and we'd ride around the old "Border Marches", on vintage Nortons and Triumphs. Tracing the steps of the Reivers.

We fantasised about moving up, living in some ancient Tower, and running some small business. But we both knew that really, it was unlikely to happen.

Billy had moved back to Blyth by now, the old lookout felt like home again, and in some ways I wished I had never left. But being away had expanded my horizons, and Shorty was doing more than o.k.

Billy worried him though. We had given him the "Leadbelly," and at long last he had done some decent work on it, but times had changed. The Soviet Union collapsed in 1991, and all manner of exotic goods were for sale. Fishing boats go way out to sea, for days on end, and notoriously, some, admittedly a very small number and not always entirely crewed by fishermen, were bringing in more than just fish.

Back in those days anything could be had from Russian trawlers, drugs, guns, "immigrants." Huge money, not too much risk, and perhaps inevitably, Billy drifted in that direction. He kept the "Leadbelly," and continued with his "official" occupation, but he also had a share in a much bigger boat. His "partners" were from Newcastle and knew nothing about fishing, but a lot about crime.

Billy was sailing in dangerous waters indeed, and so it should have been no surprise at all that around four a.m. one spring morning, the police came knocking on Shorty's door.

The "Leadbelly" was bottom up, and half submerged around two miles south of Blyth, she was holed as if she'd struck rocks, and Billy was missing. Two days later they found his body at low tide, stuck amongst the pilings of a derelict jetty in the South Harbour. His body was so knocked about that it was impossible to tell exactly what had happened, or how he had ended up in the water, but death was definitely due to drowning.

Shorty was devastated, and of course, he blamed himself for ever giving Billy the boat. There was an inquest, but the findings were inconclusive. There were traces of both alcohol and drugs in Billy's body and it was a case of "Death by Misadventure". No suggestion of foul play.

Billy was buried on a rainy morning back in Bedlington, and that should have been that. But around a month later, an half witted low grade thug called Alfie Devlin, got drunk down in the "Dolphin," a fishermans pub in North Shields, and he started mumbling into his pint, about how he'd got rid of a lad from Blyth, for the Newcastle Mafia. And Billy's name came out.

The fishing community is small and tight knit, and so, within the hour, word was back to Shorty. And quite miraculously, ten days later, Devlin's body floated ashore, in the exact same location that Billy had been found. He'd a few odd bruises on him, and a note in his pocket, thoughtfully written in waterproof ink, and on strong paper. A note, admitting that in a fit of rage, after a drunken argument over cards, he'd knocked young Billy unconscious. Admitting that he'd put the body aboard the boat, holed the hull, and set her adrift. He was mortally sorry. He begged and prayed forgiveness from the family. Now, full of remorse, he believed that he was nothing but worthless trash, and could no longer bear to live. He would welcome the End. In fact, he'd decided to end it all himself...... By Drowning......Goodbye Cruel World ....

And the Tide, like God himself, had moved him in Mysterious Ways.

Shorty took a three day break down to London, and told me the real story. Interviewed with Mr. Spanner, Alfie had admitted to killing Billy, after stunning him with a claw hammer. He had been paid £1,000 for the job by "that lot from Newcastle that Billy sailed with." Billy and his "crewmates" had been dealing both guns and drugs, and Billy being the greedy little sod that he was, had decided to keep back just a little bit extra for himself, and of course, since a couple of them could actually count, they found out, and for the princely sum of £1,000 his "shipmates" got rid of him. Then they spent an extra fifty quid advertising for a new skipper.

Alfie, drunk again, Shorty claimed with a wink, conveniently fell off the quay on his way home. It seemed that everyone on the coast had a fair idea of what actually had happened, but no-one would be saying anything, and with two nuisanceful idiots dead and gone, the police had little interest in the matter.

I tried to warn Shorty, that no good would come of it, that the matter couldn't just end there, but the little lunatic just laughed, and said that come what may, he was ready for it. And of course he was. His inventive use of a red hot poker, put him in Durham for five years.

Shorty's conviction for murder, and his subsequent imprisonment, had a profound effect on me. I had a good job, good prospects, and absolutely no confidence in the legal system.

Art and Antiques was a fine thing, and necessary, but it was well outwith of conventional policing, and I found that I could no longer face being part of a system that turned "Nelson's Eye" to the major problems of society, i.e. the so called "drug culture," with its ever increasing lobby for the legalisation of soft drugs, and the escalating use of the police as quite simply a tool of the State. So, not without some regrets, I resigned.

I moved back up North. The old bank account was still in both of our names, and the house was too. So I became the sole permanent resident of Rocky Island, quite the Lord of the Manor.

I'd put together a decent amount of both cash and goods during my sojourn in London, so money was not a problem, at least for the time being, but I didn't see myself as a fisherman any longer.

I pottered about for a month or so sounding out the antique trade, but frankly it was as dead as the dodo. Folk in the North East simply had never had enough money in the first place to acquire fine pieces, and with a few exceptions, nothing good was going to turn up on a regular enough basis to make dealing in this part of the country interesting enough to keep me occupied full time.

I paid Shorty as many visits as I could. He trusted me, and we came to an agreement that I could more or less do what I thought best with the "business," although calling it a business even, was probably more than a little inaccurate, since it was all pretty much off the official radar. I suppose it had always been part of the North Easts ever growing "Black Economy," and Shorty had kept it that way. We had plenty of money in the bank, and as I've explained there was no problem with me drawing on it.

As fortune would have it, I wasn't the only one getting out of the Met. An acquaintance of mine, Joe Bertram, who hailed originally from Backworth, a small colliery village not far west of Whitley Bay, had done his 30 years, mostly in C.I.D., and was due for retirement. His wife had long since divorced him, mostly due to him having worked constant shiftwork, and now, he just wanted to come back North, and take it easy. So I rented him the lookout, on a long lease, for next to nothing. The condition being that he kept it in order, and looked after the "Miss Dolly," 'cause she was just too good to sell. He bought the "Patsy Cline" off me for a fair price, and intended to take a few tourists out fishing just to keep himself occupied.

I was still only 24 years old. I had no attachments, but now I had nowhere left to live. So, since by now I was finding life perhaps a little too peaceful, I made my next crazy career choice, and on the 1st of December 1994, I joined the King's Own Scottish Borderers.

I did my basic training, and discovered I had a hitherto unrecognised ability with both rifles and handguns. But, being both young and still a bit daft, I wanted to test myself still further.
I fancied something that little bit different, and so, at the first opportunity that presented itself, I applied for the SAS.

I did the basic training, the "Fan Dance" in Wales, the Jungle training, and survived the interrogation ordeals, but still they failed me. It was something in the psychological profile I believe.

They like them independent, but not it seemed as freelance as me. I was disappointed, but not surprised. However, ten days later, just after I got back to the regiment, I got the job offer.

There are some pretty shady outfits in British Intelligence. M.I.5. and M.I.6. are the two which you've all heard of, but to be honest, even I'm a little uncertain of exactly who I ended up working for.

Officially I was still with the Regiment. Except that I wasn't. My orders were given in the back of scruffy little pub's by men and women I'd never seen before, and who certainly didn't look as if they'd ever worn a uniform. But then, by that stage, neither did I.

I'm typical Border stock, 5' 11", bony, long faced, stringy, dark hair. I tan very easily, and since I spend a lot of time outdoors, I can pass if I wish to, as being of middle eastern origin....That is, 'til I open my mouth.... pure Geordie. There's just nothing I can do about it. I can get by in a number of languages, pass for a native of several countries, but the accent? It always lets me down.

After a few "jobs" in Europe to sort of "test me out," mostly surveillance, and nothing too messy, I was moved out East. And so, I ended up in the 'Stans. Part of the hunt for Bin Laden and Co.

It is a little spoken of fact, that the network which today is known as Al Qaeda, grew out of the Arab volunteers who fought the Soviet puppet regimes in Afghanistan in the 1980's. Much of the training and finance, was supplied courtesy of the good old US of A.....via the Central Intelligence Agency. And in many folks view, the word Intelligence ought to be dropped from that title. Bin Laden was even able to set up recruitment offices in the US under the name of "Al-Khifah," and worked out of the Farouq Mosque in Brooklyn's Atlantic Avenue.

Needless to say the snake which the CIA had hatched, eventually turned around and bit it in the leg. So now the security services of the West, spent years and small fortunes chasing Bin Laden about the Middle East, as he flitted from country to country, taking a break occasionally to go hawking with his rich friends in Afghanistan.

And that was how I came to be there, and that was where, in the spring of 1998, I first met Viktor. He, was my opposite number, although we were most certainly not supposed to know each other, and without doubt, we were never authorised to meet.

I was sitting enjoying a cold beer, out in the back of nowhere, up near the Pakistani border. It was one of those surreal places, built by an opportunist known as "Abdul" or at least that was what he answered to. But then everyone up there answered to Abdul.

The bar was built of old metal shipping containers welded together, and in those parts it was a haven, the height of luxury. A noisy chinese generator drove air conditioning and a couple of neon adverts for American beers. There was nothing else for miles.

It had been a long hot and dusty day, and I was feeling none too sociable. The place was near empty, but still, much to my annoyance, he sat down next to me. I was wearing a "bush shirt" loose outside of my trousers, and I moved my right hand across my body, close to the butt of my Colt 45 automatic.

I'm rightly suspicious of strangers. They don't usually bring good news, so I just ignored him, and didn't speak. But he was in my space, and he didn't move.

Five minutes passed, and then out of the blue he turned and faced me. "Debateable Lands."

Bloody Russian accent? I turned, and looked directly at him for the first time, and it was almost like looking into a mirror. He could have been my twin. Same height, same dark complexion, same big bushy beard. What I call a real badmash (scoundrel). We could both have passed for locals. Brothers even, but he would be 10 years or so the elder.

"What about them?"

He smiled, "These here," he waved his hand, "Are......No man's lands, outlaw country, yet to be finally divided...... Bandit Territory."

He had my interest now. "You could put it that way." I paused, "What of it?"

He grinned, and his next words shook me. "Fifteen Fifty Two".

I admit I was taken aback, because the original Debateable Lands, are today unmarked, and pretty much forgotten, but they once straddled the Anglo-Scottish Border just to the south of Langholm. Or to the North of Longtown, depending on your nationality and perspective. Around 100 square miles belonging to no nation, they were once home to every outlaw, thief and murderer, including my own family, the Graham's, and also inexplicably, to Shorty's, the Higgins's, who he claimed were associated with the Armstrongs.

The Debateable lands were divided in 1552. Split between England and Scotland. Or Scotland and England, once again depending on your personal perspective. The French Ambassador did the job, drawing the line that neither Nation trusted their own to do.

Now, as Michael Caine may have exclaimed, "Not a lot of people know that." And yet here, out on the Borders in the 'Stans was one who did. I turned to face him fully. "Who the Fuck are you?"

He held out his hand, and laughed. "Viktor Ivanovich.... Good evening, Eddie Graham." He looked at my waist, and nodded, "Relax,...... you won't be needing the gun. I would call you Comrade, but regrettably, those days are long gone. I think however, that we may be of use to each other?"

I'd heard this sort of line before. "Can't think why I should be of use to you, so whatever it is you're peddling, drugs, guns, or little boys, bugger off and sell it to someone else". But, when he spoke again, there was no trace of Russian. He was pure "Geordie."

"Aye, well, even if I can do now't for you, I can still get yer little mate out of Durham."

Now......He really did have my attention. I *was* impressed. "Wow, A master of the vernacular. And what would you be knowing about "E" Wing?"

"Have another beer." He signalled the barman, "Two Bud's Abdul......Cold."

We waited, silent, until the bottles were on the counter, and "Abdul" had gone back to his seat in the corner.

"Like you, Eddie I'm a collector. No, don't get excited, nothing sharp, no armour."

This guy knew too much.

"I," he continued, "collect information. Files are my speciality, and I've lots of rare pieces. I never sell, I never trade. It's sort of my own personal, and rather private "pension fund." You see, as far as our little profession goes, I'm old school, ex. KGB, and in confidence Eddie," he laughed, "I'm still a believer, an endangered species these days, an old style Communist....Spare me a little time, and I'll tell you a story?"

It was said as a question, a request almost, and I thought it only common sense to at least hear him out. "O.K. "Viktor," if that is your name. Go ahead."

There was a small table in the corner of the bar, well clear of any other company that was likely to arrive, and also out of earshot of Abdul, so Victor and I took our drinks across, and settled ourselves in two battered bar chairs cut from redundant barrels.

"O.K. Convince me."

He leaned forward, and rested his right arm on the table. "Well, my friend..... You don't mind if I call you that do you?" I shrugged, and he continued. "You could say that things really began, back in the autumn of 1962, before you were even born, and when I was just a small boy. "The Confrontation in the Caribbean," what you in the West call the "Cuban Missile Crisis." When Khrushchev and Kennedy, brought the world to the brink of nuclear disaster, as near as we ever got to them actually pushing the button. Publicly, Khruschev backed down to Kennedy, but behind the scenes, it was a quite different story, because both sides were suddenly faced with the very real prospect of M.A.D.....You know the acronym? .....Mutual Assured Destruction. No winners. Nuclear Winter. No more Science Fiction.....For Real.

And so they reached an agreement, Khruschev withdrew the missiles from Cuba, and dismantled their bases. The US agreed to dismantle all US-built Thor and Jupiter IRBMs deployed in Europe and Turkey. ....End of problem?"

I shrugged, and he shook his head. "Well no, not quite. We still wished to expand our spheres of influence, and we are a patient people. What we thought, would a generation be to such a patient Nation?

And so the Soviet Union developed a long term plan. We would cease to totally depend on what today are known as "weapons of mass destruction," and we would work to bring about the downfall of the "Capitalist West" from the inside.

And it was all so simple!.....For in those free and easy days of the "Swinging Sixties," those days of drugs and "free love," we found fertile ground. Fertile ground that is for future blackmail.

We began a huge recruitment campaign.

The youth of the West were becoming increasingly disenchanted with their Governments, and within your universities, with surprisingly little difficulty, we were able to convince significant numbers to become our allies, and to enter your political system as our willing agents.

In time, when they had achieved high position for themselves, we promised those recruits huge rewards, and using every means at our disposal we paved the way for them, eased them along. You would be amazed, perhaps horrified at the names of some of those individuals.

We placed other agents in the media, in the music industry, in the law. Within the Police, and your so called Security Services."

He laughed, "We even placed agents within the Church. It was our little joke, I mean... imagine that!...an Atheist.... Communist.... Bishop! Ha!....How dare anyone say that the Russian has no humour!

And all of our agents were co-ordinated, all worked together. We assisted with the invention of your "Liberal Society," your permissiveness, your ever more "relaxed" attitude to drug abuse, and we also "helped" considerably, with the import and distribution of those drugs.

Our agents within your Government, encouraged the growth of the financial sector, at the expense of your own industries.
Oh yes.....we did a wonderful job. We built a marvellous machine, pressed the button, and found that it worked perfectly.

And then we invented "Perestroika." Friendship with the West, and in 1989 we even opened the Berlin Wall. In 1990 Germany was reunified. ....And we just walked into Europe."

Viktor paused, and tapped his beer on the table.

"But then my friend, came Tragedy.....In 1991, disaster struck....Unbelievable! Incredible! The Soviet Union collapsed! Everything, simply fell apart. And only then, far too late in the day we realised that there was no way to switch off the machine!
Our Agents were up and running. They were still true believers. We had created a Monster. And now.... We couldn't stop it!

By that time, I had been a KGB agent for over 10 years. I was "Old School".....Trusted..... but I was also prepared, and as soon as the cracks began to appear, I implemented a plan. I copied every sensitive document I could get my hands on, in particular every document relating to Great Britain, which was rather privately, my special field of interest.

Believe it or not Eddie, I'm actually something of an Anglophile, and one day perhaps I may even come and live there?" He paused, smiled to himself, and continued. "Others of my colleagues simply stole huge numbers of files. Some sold them on, some offered the subjects of the files the chance to destroy them, for a fee of course. Others, uncertain of the future, obtained information on their own countrymen simply as insurance."

His voice took on an almost religious fervour. "Then, in 1993, the European Union was created, and the final barriers to travel simply collapsed. Many inhabitants of the old Soviet Union, seized the opportunity, and unnoticed, invisible, almost unheeded, they took up employment in the West, and you are grateful to them, for they work hard, and for low wages.

Some who travelled, were "ours," ex. KGB, longing for the old ways to return. Most are doing the jobs which are beneath the dignity of your "educated" young people, and their labours will allow the countries of Europe to continue on their hedonistic "Party to Destruction".

A helicopter clattered by overhead, and Viktor ceased speaking. Slowly, the noise faded into the distance.

I must have looked sceptical, and he gestured with his beer in my direction. "Eddie, the future belongs to my country. You have been invaded, and you don't even know it. If all of our people wore little grey caps with red stars you be would shocked, but they don't, and so you never notice them at all." He took a drink from his beer, wiped his mouth on his sleeve, and continued.

"Now....Through all of this, in the Service, a small number of "believers" have kept the faith, for although the KGB has been reorganised, first into the FSK, and then into the FSB, it still needs experienced officers, and I and a few others have managed to stay within the organisation.....Ultimately, I believe, that they will be the ones to put our country back on track.

I found it interesting that he that he had said "they," and not "we."

"But for now Eddie, my country is in turmoil. Our "Government" has sold off huge portions of our industries for next to nothing to those men you call "The Oligarchs." Men who many see, simply as unworthy, opportunists, adventurers, even perhaps criminals. Yet, even a few of them are our people, financed, and placed by us. They are trustworthy, ex.KGB, and with them perhaps, and in the possession of our files lies the salvation of Russia. "

For" he exclaimed... The Phoenix *will* arise."

He paused regained his composure, and continued. "Privately, I've kept up my interest in Great Britain. My "Official" field, is

"Islamic Terrorism," and in particular, like yourself...... Osama bin Laden."

The air conditioner clattered ineffectually, and a trickle of sweat ran down my back. God it was hot! I signalled to Abdul for two more beers, and we waited until they arrived.

"Nice guy Abdul," Viktor observed, as the beers were placed on the table. "He's one of mine you know."

"Christ!" I exclaimed, "And here's me been paying him for years, thinking that he worked for us." Abdul smiled guiltily, and then we laughed together, because the truth was that we all knew that "Abdul" worked for anyone. Anyone who paid him that is.

He sidled off, back to his place at the end of the bar, well out of earshot.

Viktor, circled his beer on the table, leaving wet marks on the battered surface. Then he took a deep breath, and resumed his conversation, serious, intense, all fervour now gone from his voice.

"So......Now......to the crux of the matter, and the necessity of this meeting.

Eddie.... I need insurance, a safety net, what you could call a "Plan B." All may not transpire as I would wish, and in that event, I need a place of refuge, some means to live "off the radar" as it were. Now, the documents in my possession, give me certain leverage over some highly placed members of the British judiciary, and furthermore my influence extends into the press, the media, and even into the seat of Government itself. Your friend "Shorty," he paused. "I do love his methods of disposing of his enemies by the way."

Enemies plural, I thought. How much does this guy know?

"Shorty," was I do believe, quite wrongly convicted of murder. And given the right "encouragement," I have not the slightest doubt that my friends in England will commence both a vigorous, and ultimately a successful campaign for his release."

He stopped and looked me in the eye. "Go ahead.......Ask."

He allowed the silence to stretch, a faint smile on his face.

I breathed in deeply. "Okay, ... I want Shorty out,......So what's the price?"

He smiled again, the regular sodding Cheshire Cat.

"Nothing, not a bloody thing Eddie. You'll come out of it a rich man, and so by the way will I. You've heard of Ariana Airlines?"

Jesus! So that was what this was all about!

And at that point, I began to think that I might actually be starting to like this guy.

It seems to be a little known fact, even today, but by 1996, Osama Bin Laden had virtually taken control of Ariana Airlines, Afghanistan's official airline, and was using it to convey arms, cash, gold, drugs, and personnel around the Middle East.

So open a secret.....its amazing that it could have continued.

As soon as he spoke the words,Viktor could tell I was hooked. So he told me his story.

He'd been planning this for over two years, but always, up until now that is, there had been problems. Too many guards, no-one to help, routes too busy. He had blackmailed his information out of a double agent, using one of his "appropriated" KGB files, and now, at long last, after all of the false starts, and disappointments, what he had was close information on the movement of a large amount of gold and currency, from Afghanistan, over the Border into Pakistan. And he didn't just know where, he knew when, and exactly which vehicle.

It was a "Jingle Truck", one of those flatbed lorries used throughout Afghanistan and Pakistan to transport everything from firewood to livestock. They also smuggle just about anything in amongst their loads. They take their name from the variety of chains and colourful ornaments dangling from every available part of the vehicle, they "jingle" as they travel along, and the name is army slang, given to them by generations of servicemen stationed in the region. They look like glorified "Carnie's" (showman's) caravans and wagons in the UK.

This one was picking up its load in Jalalabad, delivering it to a compound in Abbottabad in Pakistan, and it would make the crossing at Arandu, on the Jalalabad to Drosh Road, at dawn on May the first. One driver and one passenger, neither of whom would have any idea that amongst their huge load was hidden a fortune in gold and American dollars. Viktor intended to hijack the truck, but he couldn't do it alone. So he'd found me, researched me, and found out about Shorty.

What could I say? I wanted Shorty out, I liked the idea of hitting Bin Laden, and I didn't mind keeping the haul for ourselves and becoming outrageously rich. After all if we turned it in, our governments would only waste it! So I agreed, on one condition.

"No unnecessary killing."

He looked at me as if I was mad. “What is unnecessary killing?”

“If they shoot at us, we shoot back, but otherwise we leave them alive. After all they’re non-combatants, just drivers.”

He was aghast. “You’re just too squeamish, how do we stop them raising the alarm?”

So I explained, and together we worked out a plan.

I was owing a months leave, so I took it. I had no close family, and no-one remarked on the fact that I was not going home to the UK. As far as the army was concerned, I was on an “archeological holiday,” just touring about. Viktor was in a similar position. Both of us were off the official radar, and both, due to our rather covert occupations, possessors of multiple identities.

On Thursday the 30th of April we drove out to our ambush site, still in Afghanistan, just south of the border crossing into Pakistan. We pulled off the road, and parked up for the night. Walpurgis Nacht, the Eve of May Day. Right on the border of Nangarhar and Konarhar provinces. I’d driven up in an old, decrepit, and camouflaged Landrover Defender, and Viktor in a decent but deliberately scruffy black Toyota twin cab. We were dressed as locals, and we looked the part. It’s an appalling place of rocks, rivers and mountains, freezing cold at night. Rusted and toppled lorries littered the banks of the road, tumbling into the river below, testaments to the numerous accidents and breakdowns.

Our target vehicle was camped for the night in a gully just off the road, about three miles below us, we could see their campfire. We watched them through night glasses, and at five in the morning we set up our ambush. We jacked the Landrover onto its side, over the edge of the road and onto the rocky slope, set incendiary charges, and pulled two dummies dressed in army fatigues out of the Toyota, and into the road. Our “casualties.”

We threw boxes and luggage into the roadway. Radios and electronics, rubbish really, but it looked valuable. There were no other vehicles for miles. Sensible folk did not travel this road in the dark.

In the distance a helicopter passed, travelling south....Too far off to bother us.

Fifteen minutes later, way below, we heard the wagon start up and begin to grind up the road. We poured petrol over the Landrover, and then watched and waited until it they were just half a mile south, barely out of sight around a bend. Then we triggered the charges. There was no real explosion, just a great whoosh of yellow flame, and a roiling column of black smoke.

The lorry rounded the corner and stopped. It stood for five minutes. I could see the driver and passenger out, surveying the scene through field glasses. When nothing moved, they climbed back on board, and slowly drove towards our "accident". They squealed to a halt in a cloud of dust, and just sat there for what seemed like an age, just watching. Then the driver cut the engine.

The flames had died, and the wreck of the Landrover was barely smouldering, when the two men climbed down. We lay in the rocks thirty feet away.

In addition to two AK47's, we were both armed with heavy air rifles of the type used by veterinary surgeons. Both were loaded with sedative darts with a more than usually powerful tranquilliser, and at this range we couldn't miss. In fiction, there is always a problem, always a firefight. But have a good plan, and on most occasions things ought to go smoothly. And thankfully, this time around, they did.

We fired together, just as the two men bent over the "casualties." Air weapons make little noise. I took the man on the left and Viktor the one on the right. Simultaneously, our darts struck each of them in the side of the chest. Both knew that they had been hit, and both cried out in alarm. Cried out, but there was no one to hear, nothing to be done. Thirty seconds later and both were unconscious, they would be out for around two hours, and neither had seen any sign of their attackers.

We broke cover, and went through the load of that wagon at high speed cutting ropes, dragging sheets aside, and throwing goods out into the roadway. Viktor knew exactly what he was looking for, three wooden cases marked "drill bits," in Cyrillic. And there they were, in the centre of the load.

Gold does not take up much space, but it is heavy, very, very heavy, and we had 50 bars of it. What is known in the trade as "non good delivery" bars. Which does not mean they are no good, but just that the official markings are not quite in order, usually due to odd stampings, and so they are stamped NGD to show that. Each bar measures around ten inches, by three, by two, with variations, thinner, longer, wider, but they are all .995 pure, and weigh around 400 ounces each.

It was all in two cases that together only made up the volume of one good sized suitcase, but a suitcase that no one man could lift. So we brought the Toyota out of its hiding place in the rocks, parked it alongside the lorry, and as quick as we could, we transferred those bars into the rear cab. One at a time, one of us on the lorry, and the other in the Toyota. Then we loaded on the empty cases. and repacked them.

The third case was lighter but larger, and we could carry it easily between the two of us. The cash. We loaded that in as well, we could count it later. We needed to get out of there as quickly as possible.

We dragged the dummies out of the road, poured petrol over them, and burned them. Then we simply drove off south, back down into Afghanistan. 50 miles later we pulled off the road into a gully, and organised our loot. We removed the rear seat, and packed the gold into a space Viktor had prepared below. Crude hiding place, but we did not intend to be searched. Then we opened the third box. American dollars, all high denomination bills! Stacks of them! We both burst out laughing with relief. We packed the dollars around the gold. There was rather a lot of cash, far more than we had imagined.

So there we were. 1st of May 1998......May Day!....May Day! Certainly "May Day" for Al Qaeda!

We were two rather rich men, and hopefully......untraceable.

Viktor had planned this journey for years. Smoothed the way, bribed, blackmailed, and cajoled tribal leaders and officials over thousands of miles. So, over the next three weeks, using both fair means and foul we drove that Toyota west, back through Afghanistan, sometimes using my various papers and multiple identities for convenience. Then on up north, via Herat, and up again into the old Soviet territories, where Viktor's papers took us west, right across the old Soviet Union.

In different circumstances it would have been the adventure of a lifetime, but I can remember little of it. Day and night we drove, through appalling landscapes. We took it in turns, one of us driving, the other sleeping across the two back seats. We carried enough fuel in jerry cans strapped to the insides of the truck body to take us thousands of miles between stops. We had shovels, tools, emergency rations.

Viktor's cover story was that I was a high ranking "observer" on a covert fact finding mission, with a view to bringing financial aid to the regions we passed through. He changed the detail to suit whoever asked. He was multi-lingual, and was the most amazing and inventive liar. It all cost us a fortune in bribes, but then, we had a fortune.

Eventually we made it into Switzerland, where bankers still had a relaxed and extremely confidential outlook with regard to strangers wishing to deposit large amounts of cash and gold in the safety of their vaults.

We sold the Toyota, booked into a decent but anonymous hotel, and slept for near on 24 hours. And Viktor was true to his word. We split both the money and the gold equally.....We were rich.

I flew back to Army Intelligence, and Afghanistan. A week later Viktor went back too.

* * *

In December of 1998, Shorty Higgins walked out of the front doors of Durham prison, a free man. It had been achieved in record breaking time, after a very intensive campaign by an extremely high ranking politician, who had support from several senior members of the judiciary.

He was, moreover a free man with a degree in the history of popular music, a good grounding in British history, and a certificate from the prison psychiatrist saying that he was not criminally insane, or indeed insane in any other way. He was proud of that degree, but even more proud of his certificate.

I was home on leave, I was there to meet him, and it was the happiest day of my life. Despite the time of year, I hired a car, and we drove up to the Borders, to Langholm.

I'd spent a lot of my time in Afghanistan online, researching, and looking at property, so I knew about the place for sale just north of town, where the road from Copshawholm joins the A7.

"The Road End Cafe," had a little bungalow, a workshop, and a field behind. It was just perfect. Shorty and I were still business partners, with a joint bank account, that place was ripe for development, and quite mysteriously our account had received a substantial loan from an anonymous investor in .... Switzerland, of all places! Enough money to buy the "Road End." In fact, enough to renovate it as well.

What a surprise!

I'd also earmarked a small parcel of land for sale just west of Teviothead. Around six acres, with an old quarry in the centre. A real "Reivers Retreat." (Although some folk do say real Reivers never retreat!). It lay way out in forestry, but with good access roads, and I found it because of the name. "Merrylaw"....... You just had to love a place called Merrylaw.

We talked it all over. Then I told Shorty about my adventures in Afghanistan, about Viktor, about how he came to be released. I asked him if he would renovate the cafe, and look after Merrylaw while I was away. He said nothing.....he just sat there, I thought he would never speak. Then he looked up at me....

"Jesus.... Eddie....That's some story. A Bloody Russian spy got me out! I wondered how it happened." He paused again and looked reflective. "We're a long way from Blyth Eddie, a long way from Newlands.... A very long way... Thank God!....Well, as they say, "Ain't got nothing else to do". Then he held out his hand, and we shook. "Thanks Eddie,....It's perfect. All we need now is some bikes."

I looked down at him. "Thank *you*, Shorty, I'd call you a lunatic for getting into this, but I can't, not now that you've got that certificate."

He laughed, "I'm going to frame it an' put it on me wall".

So the business bought the Cafe, and I bought Merrylaw with its quarry for myself. Over the next couple of years I intended to dig myself in.... Literally! And now that I had private means, I thought perhaps I should be out of the Army, and enjoying myself a little. Because, I'd got myself a project, something which had been working away at the back of my mind for years. Something that needed to be brought out into the light of day.

Back in 1941, my Grandfather had been up south of Glasgow, and he was one of the few people who actually saw Hitler's Deputy, Rudolf Hess bale out, and fall from his plane. He never told anyone, so there was never any official record that he was there at all, but he wrote it all down in his diary, and that diary came down to me when my folks were killed. The whole business of the Hess flight was shrouded in mystery, and I'd always promised myself that I'd have a closer look at it. Perhaps I'd write

an article, or even a novel about it?
And now.... I had both the time, and the money to do just that!

*   *   *

I went back to Afghanistan, but my heart wasn't in it anymore. I knew now where I wanted to be, and what I wanted to do with my life. I was free of the need to earn a living, I didn't need to scratch around for money, but I couldn't think of how to leave in the right circumstances.

As it turned out I didn't need to worry about it, the decision was made for me, and the Army was more than pleased to let me go. Not because I was no good at what I did...I was. But in July of 1999 I took a bullet in the right leg during a firefight in Helmand province. I was just collateral damage, it was nothing to do with me at all, or in fact with the British Army.

Bloody AK47's, everyone's got one! Just two bunches of local badmashes shooting it out in the village square. Probably only a family argument, but there I was, wrong place, wrong time.

As wounds go, it wasn't that bad. Through the back of the right thigh, and by a miracle it missed the arteries and bone. But, it took a while to get me to a decent hospital, and an infection got in, which caused complications. In fact it was touch and go for a while as to whether I would lose the leg, but eventually, by the end of the year, I was more or less back on my feet.

Ever since my trip with Viktor though, the army had been wary of me. I don't know how, or why, but there were sideways looks, veiled comments, "Too close with the locals," "Enjoy your leave did you?" asked with just that note of sarcasm. So I knew that the writing was on the wall.

I was sent for a medical, and then interviewed by a rather senior officer, who suggested that my "wound", may disqualify me from returning to my covert role in the Middle East, and gently hinted that if I wished to resign from the army, perhaps now may be a good time to do it.

He even told me that it had filtered down to him from above, that certain questions had been asked in high places about me and my "friends." Eventually, I worked it out. Some bloody politician had put the spoke in.

Viktor had got Shorty out okay, but the "old boy system." What we in intelligence referred to as the "Eton Disorder," was still operative, and I could forget any advancement of any kind in the forces, or in fact in any branch of life remotely controlled by H.M. Government.

So I took the hint, and I left the employ of Her Majesty forever.

* * *

I left the Army on the 1st of January 2000. New Millenium, New year, New beginning.

All that the army had given me for my years of service, was a slight limp in my right leg. But I didn't care.

The cold back in the UK bothered the wound, and I hoped that would go away, but I still limped a bit, and carried a stick to rest on. A crappy ash stick I'd picked up in at a shop in the West End of London. I'd replace it with a good blackthorn when I got the chance. Nothing like a good blackthorn for style, and for whacking idiots. Always walk wary of a man who carries a blackthorn. There's probably nothing at all wrong with his legs, but if you're not careful there may be something wrong with yours.

I got back to Langholm on the 5th of January. Shorty had picked me up in Carlisle in his red Toyota truck, and he took me back to the Cafe.

He'd been busy. We weren't open yet, but most of place had been painted, the bungalow out back was pristine.... new wallpaper, central heating, double glazing, and the tiles on the roof fixed.

Another Toyota twin cab, a dark green one about four years old was parked outside. He handed me the keys and the registration documents. "Know from your letters how much you like them. I've been and fenced your land out at Merrylaw. "Deer fencing," an' it was dear an' all," he joked. "Big double gates, just like you asked for on the road in. We'll nip up in the morning and you can take a look at it. There's some good fish in that burn up there at the end of the year Eddie, no keepers either." He laughed. "We don't need to do it any more do we? Out with the old lamps at night. But it'll be a bit of fun anyway." Shorty just loved poaching fish.

So off we went the next morning in my new Toyota. Up to

Teviothead, off over Caerlanrig, and down to Merrylaw.

I love these little quarries out in the hills. It's where they dug out the stone to make all of those dry stane dykes that divide up the Border landscape. They say those walls took three cartloads a yard to build, and there's mile after mile of them.You run out of paved road at Merrylaw. There you cross a small ford over the Teviot, and then you're on forestry road for the rest of the way.

My place was in a little side valley just off the left of the track where the Rashie Grain runs out into the Teviot. Just up the track on the right, dug out of the south facing slope of a small hill called "Cockplay."

You couldn't make it up could you? What an address!

Eddie Graham, Esquire,

Cockplay,

Merrylaw,

TD9 0LK

Some folk pay a fortune for a personal reg. and I wondered how much would they pay for an address like that.

You can't see the quarry from the track, its hidden by trees. In fact all of my land was planted with trees, but I had plans for that. I'd leave a good stand around the perimeter, to keep out prying eyes, then fell the rest and create a clearing around the quarry itself. Let some sun in.

It would all have to go eventually, it was that bloody awful sitka spruce that the forestry folk love, and get huge grants for growing. Eventually though, I'd plant decent hardwoods, and do a bit of landscaping, but for now I was just happy that no-one could see in.

We unlocked the gates, drove through, and closed them behind us. The track curved to the right, and a hundred yards later we turned into the quarry itself. This was to be my home, quiet, sheltered, accessible, and right off of the radar. We sat in the Toyota and just looked at it, and then I explained to Shorty what I had in mind.

I'd ordered a dozen of those steel containers that are used by shipping companies and road transport businesses to move just about everything about the world. They also double up as temporary accommodation and offices, and no-one takes a blind bit of notice of them.

One would go just inside of the main gate, and as far as any outsider was concerned, it would be a sort of "gatehouse," used by me for accommodation when I was up here "shooting." For convenience sake, it would also act as my mailbox. The rest of the containers I intended to weld together, and build into a two storey complex at the back of the quarry. I'd cut connecting doors through, and windows in the upper elevation on the front. The top storey would be visible, but the lower one, I would simply bury, stone facing the front so that it would look exactly like a bit of the landscape. Totally secure. Access to the lower level would be through a steel trapdoor. My storage and Armoury.

Shorty just laughed. "Knew you wouldn't just go off and buy a house," he said. "Don't do anything straightforward do you?"

I started work on it two days later.

First I installed a decent heavy duty generator, housed in a small shed. Water was no problem, plenty of that. I tapped into the burn upstream, and installed a decent collection tank to give a bit of pressure, later, I would add proper filtration and UV treatment. Drainage would be via septic tank.

* * *

It took me the best part of 12 months to get it liveable.

Shorty helped when he could, but he was usually working on the Cafe project.What he wanted was more than just a small "greasy spoon". His long term aim was for a place that would be a destination in itself. An American style "Honky Tonk," complete with live Country and Western music.

Merrylaw was mostly my own project. A sort of "unofficial home," disguised as a shooting lodge. I hired an excavator, and levelled the site myself. I poured 12 inches of reinforced concrete onto a rock base, ditched around it to give drainage, and built up the back and side walls of the quarry with those heavy wire cages filled with stones. Then Shorty came over, and we installed the containers, stacked in two layers.

On the top, I added a sloping roof covered with thick pondliner, and a heavy layer of topsoil seeded with grass and wildflowers. I built up the front of the lower level with more wire cages, and heaped rocks against them before once again covering the whole lot with more pondliner and soil.

By the end of that year, when you entered that quarry, all you could see was the front of the containers on the upper level, apparently standing on a mound of grassy bankside.

Entry was via stone stairs, to a centrally placed doorway, and I'd cut four large windows, two either side of the door. They faced south, taking advantage of the all day sunshine. It was warm, it was dry, and in the winter it would be heated by a large woodburning stove, and a solid fuel AGA. For everyday use I had a propane cooker. I had no doubt that women would hate it, but it was exactly what I wanted.

Best of all no-one really knew it was even there. I had a private income, a very private house, and time to do a bit of dealing, a bit of collecting, a little journalism. In fact just about anything I fancied, and in my spare time, of which I had rather a lot, I would set to work on my Hess project.

And so, on one beautiful sunny afternoon, quite appropriately, April 1st 2001, I dug out my Grandfather's old diary, opened it on the table in front of my living room window, put a blank notepad and pencil alongside it, and started work.

I didn't know it then, but what I was about to do, would change our lives forever.

* * *

VJ OQ

10th May 1941

The bike howled as he came out of the corner.......beautiful. Nothing else equalled the sound of the Scott. He'd looked forward to this for months. The thought of it had kept him going, sustained him through all of the long nights back there, in the rear gunners turret. Kept him from going insane as the searchlights swung across the sky, and tried to pin the plane against the inky blackness, like a moth pinned to a setting board.

He had used up most of his stash of fuel for this trip. Pure indulgence, maybe even illegal.

The bike had been locked away in store since '39. There was no way he was having this machine commandeered and ending up as emergency transport for some fifteen stone copper, with an arse the size of a carthorse.

It was a 1929 TT replica, about as good as it got. 596cc's of water cooled two stroke twin. Black, the big TT tank with its cream coloured sides filling what was normally an open frame. He'd had a small pillion seat fitted, 'cause back before the war, Jeannie used to come out on the back with him. The bike was supposed to be good for 75 or 80 m.p.h, but his had been "breathed on" a bit, and he reckoned on more like 90+, if that is he ever found a decent bit of road. Not today though, he had to take it easy to conserve fuel, and the bike was a bit out of balance anyway, since he'd fitted panniers to take a couple of extra cans, and strapped his haversack onto the tank.

He had come away from Rowanburn that morning, and was now somewhere just south of Glasgow. It was late, dusk, and really he ought to be looking for somewhere to hole up for the night. He didn't need anything fancy. Barn maybe? Too early for haystacks.

Some of these farmers out here had it cushy. What with all of the chickens, pigs, and things, and he reckoned he could scrounge a bit of food in exchange for a couple of packets of black market fags, if that is, he got the chance.

He pulled off the road into the cover of a couple of sycamore trees. Out in the field over the fence, he could see two young lads, crouched by the side of a stream. Too early in the year for salmon he thought, could be after brown trout maybe? Late for kids to be out though.

He cut the engine, and took off his flying helmet. Great stuff this flying gear. He had on a heavy Arran style sweater. He smiled, Jeannie had knit that for him, to keep him warm in the turret.
On top of that he had his leather flying jacket. He also had on heavy corduroy trousers, his flying boots, a decent pair of leather gauntlets, and thank God, his R.A.F goggles, hard to ride far without them. Everything was getting to be virtually unobtainable these days.

He leaned on the fence, and breathed in deeply. Beautiful night, stars just starting to show.

His hearing was muffled from the constant noise of the bike, but still he heard it long before he saw it. First, the drone of heavy engines, not British engines either.....Daimlers, two of them! Coming in from the west. Perhaps a Messerschmitt? A bf 110?
But what the hell was it doing out on its own, way over here?
And now he could make out its outline, black against the darkening sky. It was coming in low, engines throttled right back. Heading straight for him! The two kids in the field had seen it too, and were pointing upwards now.

And then quite incredibly, unexpectedly, the pilot put the plane into a sharp climb. Christ! That was impossible, at that low speed. And, just as the plane began to climb, just as the nose rose upwards, something small fell away, fluttering, tumbling, spiralling down towards the ground.

Now the plane was standing on its tail, and he thought he could see that the canopy was open. Then it was completely over on its back, and it was at that point that he realised that the pilot intended to bale out.

He saw the figure fall away, and as he did so, the man's foot caught on the tail of the aircraft, and he spun away. Seconds later, a parachute bloomed, and the pilot began to descend. He guessed that he would land a couple of fields away.

Pilotless, out of control, the plane completed its loop, then it dived away spinning crazily towards the earth. Ten seconds passed before the sound of the impact reached him.

Now the boys in the field, were running towards him, one of them carrying something. A leather briefcase of some kind? They spied him beside the trees, he heard a warning yell, and immediately they changed direction and ran off towards a small wood. He leapt the fence, chased after them, but by the time he reached the trees they were long gone.

He could hear shouting, several voices to his east where the pilot had landed, so he made his way over in that direction, but when he reached the edge of the next field it was obvious from the number of folk about, that no extra help from him was needed, and why get involved in something which was not his business anyway? Could keep him tied up for hours.

So he made his way back to his bike, started up, and slowly headed off down the lane. Hard to see now, and it would be fully dark soon. Half a mile later he found a farm cottage. He turned in through the open gate, cut the engine, and heaved the bike onto its stand. A dog barked loudly, and the curtains twitched in the back window.

It was the best breakfast he'd had since 1939. Big pot of tea, two eggs, two rashers of bacon, two big pieces of home made black pudding, and two thick slices of fried bread. Home baked bread. Then toast with real farm made butter. Unbelieveable!

It had been the bike that did it. Old fellow who worked the place, had owned a Scott back in the early 20's, in fact it was still outback in the barn. That, plus the fact that his son was out in the Western Desert, in Iraq of all places, with No.1. Armoured Car Company RAF.

Nice folk, they'd even let him stay in the spare room.

Of course all the talk at the table that morning was about the plane coming down the night before. All manner of rumours were flying about. Some even said that Hitler's Deputy, Rudolf Hess had been the pilot. Typical country area, full of crazy rumours, but frankly, no-one would believe that one!

"Those two lads out in the field got the best view," he said.

The farmers wife looked puzzled, "What two lads," she asked.

"Oh, there were two boys about ten or eleven years old, fossicking about by a stream. I thought they must be after fish."

"Newts," the old fellow stated. "It would be newts they were after. It's not actually a stream down there, more like a long pond. All manner of beasties in there. Frogs, toads, all kinds of newts, including those big black ones with the orange bellies, the ones they call "salamanders." They're collecting them, stocking a pond down at the village school. Those would be the Stuart lads, Calum, and Rory, their folk farm just down the road, next place west of us."

He left it at that. No need to cause the lads trouble by mentioning the case that fell out of the plane. None of his business anyway, he'd just end up having to make a statement, and then he'd have to explain what he was doing riding around the countryside on a fancy bike. So, he thanked them for the night's accommodation, left a few packets of cigarettes for the old boy by way of payment, and set off for home.

He hadn't gone half a mile, when he came upon the accident. The road was almost completely blocked. A long black car was slewed across the carriageway, front end smashed into the side of a rusty old coal lorry. Loaded sacks had cascaded off the back of the wagon onto the bonnet of the car, and coal was strewn across the highway. Four men, three in fancy black overcoats, and the other, obviously the driver of the coal wagon, were arguing loudly.

He braked to a halt alongside. "Anything I can do?"

"Oh Shit!," he heard one of the men drawl, as he turned towards the bike.

"Posh Bastard" he thought, and then he recognised him.

Jesus! The Duke! Bloody Hell! What was he doing out here? The story was that Buccleuch was confined to his Estates. Too fond by far of Germany, or so they said, and this was well outside of Buccleuch land. Then another of them turned to look, and that was even more impossible. Because he looked just like the King's brother, the Duke of Kent. The third one? The slim fair haired one with the ruddy complexion, and the pointed jaw? That one he knew well enough. The Duke of Marchbank, he'd seen him a couple of times down in Longtown, at the cattle market.

Buccleuch eyed both him and his bike with disdain.

"No problem here," he drawled, "It's just a nudge, no real damage done, nothing *you* can do to help. We'll get it sorted out"

But then the "Duke of Kent," turned to Marchbank. "Peter old chap, in view of the "circumstances," and he emphasised the word, "We really don't want to hang about here too long. It's imperative in fact, that I be in Glasgow A.S.A.P....Now, it'll take us a while to get that wing pulled back off of the tyre, and to settle up with the driver of this lorry, so why don't you just grab a lift with this good chap on that rather nice bike. Perhaps he could get you to a train station or something? Walter here can get the train down from Glasgow. Don't really want to be seen travelling together do we?"

"Circumstances?" he thought. In view of what circumstances? And why *not* travel together?

The Duke of Marchbank, walked across to the bike and extended his hand. "Any chance of a lift then? Where are you heading?"

He explained that he was going to Rowanburn, down on the Border, and was amazed when the Duke asked if he could travel with him the entire way. He opened his wallet, and held out a five pound note.

"Take me to Marchbank House, and I'll give you another. Plus, you can refuel that bike, I've a tank of decent fuel for my estate vehicles."

What could he say? Aside from anything else, £10 was a small fortune to him. And a tank of fuel? So he undid the straps of the haversack he had tied to the top of the tank, and handed the Duke his set of waterproofs. "Keep the wind off you, sorry I've no spare goggles, and I'll need these ones to ride the bike."

Buccleuch, and the "Duke of Kent" seemed amused to see their companion reduced to riding pillion on a motor cycle, but so what, he thought, do the idle bugger good to see how the other half live.

It took him two and a half hours, stopping only to top up the tank from one of his spare cans, and by the time they reached Marchbank House, the Duke was shivering with cold. Even before they reached it, the door of the house was opened by a uniformed butler.

The Duke ushered him inside, "Come in, come in, my good fellow. Christ, I don't know how you stand it on that thing. My backside is numb, my knees are frozen solid, and I'm half deaf".

"It's heaven after a gun turret at 10,000 feet," he replied.

"Jackson!" The Duke bawled at the butler who was standing only three feet away. "Throw some decent logs on that fire, bring us a bottle of the best malt, and have cook prepare something hot. And be quick about it."

"Jackson" caught his eye, behind his Dukeship's back, shrugged, and raised his eyes to the ceiling in exasperation.

"So," the Duke resumed. "What do you do, when you're not tearing around on racing motor cycles rescuing Dukes in distress?"

"Tail gunner in a Wellington, home on leave, go back in a couple of days."

"Well, my good fellow, and I really *don't* want to know your name, what you stumbled upon today, was by way of being a clandestine operation." He tapped the side of his nose confidentially. "Know what I mean?" He nodded. "I mean," he continued "that it never happened at all, you have no idea who we are, in fact you never actually saw us at all."

"Fine with me,",he replied, unease stirring in his mind.

"Jackson", returned with a tray, upon which was a bottle of Glenmorangie, a crystal jug of water, a bowl of ice, and two large cut glass tumblers. By now, flames from the fire were roaring up the chimney.

The Duke collapsed into a huge leather armchair, and indicated another. "Have a seat." He poured two massive measures of malt, added ice and a little water, and passed one over. He took a huge swallow of his own. "Feel free to help yourself when you finish that, you've earned it today."

He reached into a pocket, extracted his wallet, and handed over another five pound note. "There you are.... See, I keep my promises. Find Jackson when you leave, and he'll top up your tank, and those cans of yours. You got me out of a difficult situation today." He finished his drink in one more gulp, and poured himself another. He pointed at the glass, "Drink up, there's plenty more where that came from."

Jackson, returned with two big bowls of soup on a tray, and several large buns, torn in two, and thick with butter.

"Cook has some game pie Sir, but only peas, carrots, and a few roasted potatoes. She says it's all she can provide at short notice. I shall be ready to serve it in five minutes Sir.....Will that be in order?"

The Duke laughed, "Oh well, we'll just have to struggle by I suppose. Mustn't grumble, after all there is a war on. Just bring it through when your ready, and plonk it down on the side table there, I don't feel like leaving this fire."

He was half way down his second glass by now. "So", he resumed. "You're a tail gunner, in a what, a Wellington. That's some sort of a bomber isn't it?

"Aye, that's right." he replied.

The Duke raised a finger and pointed at him. "Bloody awful business this war, you know, and so unnecessary. Fine young fellows like you, tearing about the skies, killing each other. And for what, I ask you?" He finished his whisky, and poured more, spilling a drop or two onto the tray. "Drink up old chap, you've barely dented that one...... Old Jerrie's not that bad really, once you get to know him. Orderly lot the Germans, best of Europe really. Don't know how we got into this situation, I blame bloody Churchill, can't see that there's enough of the world out there to share. Let them have Europe I say, who the hell wants it anyway. It's the Russians we ought to watch out for. Join Germany, and sort *them* out, that's what we should be doing."

He was slurring his words slightly. "Even Adolf's not such a bad chappie you know, I met him at the '36 Olympics. Went over there with a few others, and they really did us proud. Met him again.... Special invitation to his 50th birthday party. What a celebration that was!"

He rose unsteadily to his feet, and began to walk across the room. "Come on, Come along," he beckoned, leading the way to a closed door.

He rose from the chair and followed.

The Duke took out a key. With some difficulty he inserted it in the lock, and opened the door. He flicked a light switch, and pointed. "Have a look at those pictures"

It was a small office, with one window looking out across the valley. The walls were decorated with photographs, mostly family groups. Family and friends shooting with Royalty,photos of the young duke in military uniform. But in pride of place were a series of photographs, beautifully taken and printed, of the Duke in the company of Adolf Hitler and the Nazi Hierarchy. Some had obviously been taken at the 1936 Olympics. The others at what he assumed to be Hitler's 50th birthday celebrations. And they were signed, "To my Dear Friend Peter, may our association be long and lasting.......Adolf Hitler." On the desk by the window was a silver paperweight in the shape of a swastika.

"Oh Jesus"...he thought, "What have I stumbled into".

Then Jackson called through from the other room that the food was served, and the spell was broken.

But the Duke did not leave it at that, and after they had eaten, as he made to leave, he took him by the arm. "Look," he said, "No-one knows how this war will end. We may make peace with Germany, or we may win. But should we not, if Germany were to prevail, then make your way here, and find me. I owe you a favour for today, so rest assured that if ever this country comes under German control, then you will have at least one friend in high places. He grasped his hand. “Goodbye, and May God Protect you.”

“Jackson” accompanied him to the door. They refuelled the Scott, and filled the extra tanks.

“He’s not a bad old guy,” Jackson commented. “But he does rather go on about Adolf. Get him into bother one day, that will, if he’s not careful.”

As he walked back to his motor cycle, he realised, that on his next leave he had no choice but to track down those Stuart boys and find out exactly what had dropped from that aircraft.

He must find out what three Dukes were doing on that lonely road. He turned out of the long drive of Marchbank House, and rode sedately back to Rowanburn.

He wheeled the bike back into the shed, heaved it onto its stand, and locked the door behind him. He opened the back door of the little colliery house,

“Hi Jeannie, I’m back he called.”

She tore into the kitchen and threw herself into his arms.

“Have you heard the news,” she cried. “Rudolf Hess crashed his plane up by Glasgow last night!”

“Oh Christ,” he thought, “*Now* what am I going to do?”

I put down the diary.

Because he never got to do anything. Because God did not protect him. Because two weeks later his plane disappeared over the North Sea.

And no wreckage was ever found.

* * *

Reb.

Shorty sat on the grass down by the river, fed the ducks with the remnants of his sandwiches, and watched the crows wheeling above the ruins of the old castle. The tame heron was behind him, sitting in its usual place on one of the picnic tables. He would save the last piece of bread for her.

Eddie was out at Merrylaw, and the smell of fresh paint in the cafe had been so strong it was giving him a headache, so he'd made his sandwiches, and decided to walk along here to the car park, for a breath of fresh air.

He heard the bike come in behind him, Harley by the sound of it. He'd glanced around, a "bobber," probably an old sportster. Nice bike, but all he could see of the rider, was a figure in black leathers, with a black helmet, and a cut off denim jacket, so he just went back to feeding the ducks, his mind working away on modifications for the cafe.

Five minutes passed, and then he noticed that the biker behind him, seemed to be having problems getting started. So Shorty turned round to watch.

And that was the first time he saw her. She was half turned away from him, and the brass studs in the back of her cut off denim gleamed in the sunlight. R.E.B., "Reb,",beneath the old C.S.A. flag.

She was tall and slim. Thin featured, turned up nose, and that slight overbite typical of the best girl singers. Just a touch about her, perhaps, of a young Jenny Agutter. Her long blonde hair hung, damp with sweat upon her shoulders, the black roots showing.

"Oh God," Shorty thought, "I just love *sweaty* biker girls with *black roots!*" So, he waddled on over.

"Hello Pretty Lady. Need a hand?"

She turned and stared down at him. *Badly applied mascara!*

Oh Christ!....He loved *sweaty* biker girls with *badly applied mascara* and *black roots*.

She stared down at the strange, squashed little figure beside her. Her pale ice blue eyes shone in the sunlight, and then she spoke.

“Bloody thing, just wont start.”

Oh, What a beautiful *posh accent!* And Shorty just adored *sweaty posh* biker girls, with *black roots*, and *badly applied mascara!*

It was love at first sight.

But, try as they might, and on Shorty’s part he didn’t try too hard, the bike simply would not start. “Tell you what,” he said, “my place is just up the road, “The Road End Cafe,” I’ve got a proper bike workshop there. How about we walk along, get my truck, then come back for the bike, and we’ll take it back to the workshop?”

And so, off they trotted, the long and the short of it.

“Where’re you from”, Shorty asked.

“Oh, I stay at Welldean House, up off the Yarrow Water.”

“What?” Shorty exclaimed, “That hippy place some old weirdo, what’s his name? Mister Fang or something runs. Didn’t know they let bikers in there.”

“It’s Master Zhang,” she laughed, “And he’s not really an old weirdo. His full titles are, “Zenji,” as in Founder of a Zen School, “Behdin,” as in “baptized” follower of Mazdaism, Zhang Wenming, after a 7th Century Chinese monk,......Bates,” she concluded.

“Bates!” Shorty exclaimed. “Bit sort of commonplace, after all of the rest isn’t it?” She laughed again, and Shorty’s spirits soared, he loved her laugh.

“Bates was his mother’s name. She was English, but his father was Chinese. It’s quite tragic. You see, he never actually married Zhang’s mother. In fact, he abandoned them before Master Zhang was even born, and then his mother died, and he was brought up in a horrendously cruel Chinese orphanage until he escaped, and ran away at the age of eleven. Ever since then, he’s had the most amazing adventures, and he’s entirely self educated. He sometimes sits up late into the night, regaling us with tales of his early travels. He is the last “Keeper of the Seven Sacred Bowls,” and Welldean has the oldest set of Himalayan “singing bowls” known to exist. He studied as a Yaqui Shaman and Medicine man. He was a friend of Carlos Casteneda. He’s a member of the Native American Church. And, he’s the actual founder, the original Master, of the “Ancient Forest” school of Tai Chi and Qigong. Oh” she added, “And, he also studied Kung Fu at the Shaolin Temple.”

“Impressive,” Shorty replied. “Does he make everyone learn that lot?”

"Oh no, I'm just fascinated with it all. I wrote to Daddy and my brother, asking if they would maybe put some money into a television programme about him. Perhaps finance a film or something. Of course they refused, said it was just another of my stupid ideas, and they've pretty much disowned me anyway. But it didn't matter because Zhang, simply wouldn't hear of it. Said such things were against his beliefs. You see, despite all of his achievements, he's actually rather a modest and retiring sort of gentleman, and that place out there does so much good. It brings so much peace and enlightenment, and it costs him such a huge amount of money to run.

I had terrible problems before I went to Welldean, I was running quite wild. You know, bad relationships, experiments with illegal substances. It was Daddy who first heard of the place, from one of his friends in the music industry. I think he must have told him about my problems, and he suggested that Welldean may do me good. And he was right. Because most of that's behind me now. Master Zhang, supplies me with a small amount of Chinese medication, and that is all I'm on now."

Chinese medication? Shorty mused. Don't care too much for the sound of that.

"Really I ought to move on," she continued, "but I'm staying there for a while longer. I've lent the Master a little bit of money, and he allows me to sleep in one of the student cells. And that's how a biker like me ended up at Welldean.

It was less than half a mile, from the car park to the "Road End," but by the time Shorty arrived, she had told him her entire life story.

He was shocked to find that he was in fact talking to Lady Rebecca Forsythe-Ingram, ("But please call me Reb."). That her Daddy was a peer of the realm, and that her brother was a merchant banker. But he was horrified to learn, that the "little bit of money," that she had loaned to Master Zhang, amounted to no less than £50,000. Her entire savings.

He held out his hand to her as they entered the "Road End".

"Welcome to our humble abode Reb. I'm Septimus Higgins, ex convicted murderer. Did five years in Durham Prison, before being released with an apology, a complete pardon, and a letter from the prison psychiatrist to say that I am in fact reasonably sane. Just call me Shorty, everyone does, I can't think why."

"Ooohh.....Wow," she cried, "A genuine Geordie Badass! I've always wanted one of them, Daddy will be pleased!"

When I pulled up in the Toyota three hours later, Reb's bike was parked outside, on the sound system Dwight Yoakum was "A Thousand Miles from Nowhere," and the pair of them were sitting, covered in splashes of paint, sharing a bottle of Newcastle Brown Ale.

"Reb," Shorty said, "Meet Eddie, he's my partner. Eddie, this is Reb, I suspect you will be seeing her around now and again."

And he was right, because two weeks later, she moved in with him. She brought with her a selection of rare electric guitars, and a drum kit.

They described themselves as "The perfect ill matched pair." "A happy accident which had just been waiting to happen". For how likely was it, in a remote part of the Scottish Borders, to find two total misfits with shared interests in playing vintage Country and Western, and rebuilding old and ailing motorcycles?

Reb fell in love immediately, with both Shorty, and Shorty's workshop. Shorty couldn't believe his luck. This woman could play the electric guitar, sing like Emmy Lou Harris, and..... she could weld to perfection. Even better. Despite her background, she seemed to harbour a secret ambition to run a biker's cafe, and incredibly for a "modern woman," she knew the basics of how to cook. Happy just being together, they selected suitable dishes for a straightforward working menu. And far into the night, they practiced their music. Thank God, there were no near neighbours.

By the time the cafe was finished, they wanted to be accomplished enough, to provide at least part of the live performances. Reb, had received a classical training, Shorty had developed his guitar skills in Durham Prison.

Eat your heart out Johnny Cash, 'cause Shorty Higgins was the real deal, "The Merle Haggard of the Borders." But, they needed a catchy name. "Shorty and Reb," was okay, but not memorable enough.Every known variation incorporating the word "Reiver" had been totally used up, as had "Tarras" and most of the other "location" names.

I knew Shorty loved to sing Willie Nelson songs, and had performed on stage in Durham, as "Wily Nelson". And he didn't want to use that again. But the pair of them now sounded heavily electric, and late one night, after a couple of beers when they were pounding out "City of New Orleans," I called across, "You sound like "Electric Willie."

Reb collapsed with laughter.

"That's it!" she cried, "I just love "Electric Willie".

Then, she flushed bright red, clamped one hand across her mouth, and we all collapsed into helpless laughter.

And that was the night that "Lady Rebecca, and the Electric Willie Band," was born.

* * *

We were sitting in the sunshine, on the bench outside the door, just watching the world go by. All of the painting was finished, and in a week or two we would be open for business. Reb was back in kitchens perfecting one of the recipes.

Shorty took a sip from his can of Budweiser, and nudged me with his shoulder.

"Reb's not going back to Welldean Eddie, I think this is it, we're an item, the two of us."

I shrugged, "Hmm, Yes, I'd noticed that. I'm pleased, she's a nice lass".

"What do you know about Welldean, and this guy Master Zhang," he asked.

He had my attention now. "Nothing much, and little more than rumour, Why?"

"Well," he continued. "Reb seems to think the sun shines out of his arse, and she's lent him quite a bit of money, all of her money in fact. And you know me, suspicious bastard, always thinking the worst of folk....I'm just not so sure about him."

"As I said Shorty, all I have is rumour. From what I hear, "Master Zhang," arrived around '94, or '95, up at Welldean House. That was back in the days when old Lord Kershope had the place. He stayed out there, helped out or something, and taught the old guy Tai Chi, and Qi Gong. But he must have been well fixed, 'cause when his Lordship died, it seems that Zhang had the means to buy the place, and from then on, he's just gone from strength to strength. Being in with the local nobility helped I suppose, and all manner of the upper classes go out there for little "holidays." Quite a few of our "rock nobility" as well, plus of course the odd so called "celebrity." I hear his rates are sky high.

In addition to his regular staff, he has a workforce of "acolytes," students who do most of the work, look after the grounds and the like. Some of them are on benefits, and just sort of "work for their keep." All very philanthropic. The local Council thinks the world of him, he's got charitable status, and there are rumours of all manner of tax concessions. But in certain quarters, there are dark whisperings. Rather too many attractive young ladies seem to form attachments to "Master Zhang," and there are quite a few young kids up there with "absent fathers." The official line seems to be that he is doing a good job, so let's just leave him alone. But as I say, it's really all just no more than rumour, and you know what the rumour machine is like out in these rural areas. Do you want me to ask around?"

"Nah", he replied, "Just let it be, I'll think about it. But I'm not so sure that he'll take well to Reb leaving."

* * *

Eaglesham.

"Fancy a trip up by Glasgow," I asked.

We were clearing up, after a day cutting down trees out back of my house at Merrylaw.

"Aye," he replied, "That would be nice. The Cafe will be open in a day or two, and we'll not get much spare time after that. Not until we can find some decent reliable staff that is...Why do we want to go up there?"

"Aye well, you know me Shorty, can't leave things be. Ever since I read my Granda's diary, I've been itching to see if anyone can remember those two boys I told you about, the ones that ran off with the case from Hess's plane. I've read every report I can find about the crash, and there's no mention of them, or of it, anywhere."

He looked up at me. "Eddie.....Mate....It's what, sixty two years ago? They would have to be over 70 by now, retired, could even be dead. If that is, they stayed in the area at all. You know that most kids in these rural parts simply move away, emigrate or something. But," he continued, "I'm easy with it. A day off would be nice. Can we take off early though, and go the long way 'round? I'd quite like to go out by that Welldean House, just get a bit of a feel for the place."

I gave him my curious look. "Any reason why?"

"Oh no" he replied, all innocence. "Just sounds like a nice bit of the world. We could swing by "Tam Lin's Well," and you could take a photo or two on the way?"

Shorty knew that would get me going. Tam Lin's Well is one of the near forgotten places in the Borders, where the eponymous hero of an ancient ballad, was carried off by the Queen of Faerie. Once it was famous, they even made a film about it as late as the 1960's, Ian McShane, and Ava Gardner, believe it or not. But now, like most of the old Border Tales, it had almost passed from memory. But the well still does exist, at a place called Carterhaugh, and one of my pet subjects was Border myths and legends. Fabulous stuff, and Shorty knew that I was compiling a file of photographs of relevant locations, and that I intended one day to publish them. So what could I do but agree?

"Fair Enough, We'll get an early start, and go 'round that way then."

Seven thirty the next morning we set off in the Toyota, two big flasks of black coffee on board. We arrived in Hawick, about eight, fuelled up at the supermarket, and grabbed a couple of Ginsters pasties, and a packet of Snickers bars. Iron rations.

I judge all of my long drives by pasties, short to medium journeys, one pasty, long journeys two pasties....real long distance, three pasties. Now you may laugh, but find yourself stranded out in the middle of nowhere, and you'll be thankful for Mr Ginster and his products.

I'd packed my Sony camera and its kit. It's a decent thing, six million pixels, and I've a couple of good extra lenses for it too. It'll do anything from landscapes to documents.

No-one's quite caught on to the document thing yet. Even libraries who won't let you copy their old books, seem to take no notice at all of a camera. I've a home made stand and lighting set up. Just pop the page or book on the little mount at one end and attach the camera to a bar at the other, and off you go. Download it all when you get home, then just print it out, or burn it to a disc. I'm no expert photographer, but it works just fine for my requirements.

If you're going to do any serious writing, invest in a decent digital camera. Trust me, you can't do without one. Use it right, and it'll save you a fortune.

It was raining, in fact it had been raining all night, and all of the rivers and burns were in full spate, the water stained brown with peat from up in the hills, the waterfalls full of creamy white foam. They looked just like rivers of frothy brown ale.

Just before we entered Selkirk the sun broke through, bathing the entire valley below us, and out towards Galashiels, with yellow light. It was like the invention of Technicolor, the hills, and the trees, glowing with every shade of green, and over it all, the most magnificent rainbow.

We drove into town past Sir Walter Scott's Courthouse, out the back of which lie the ruins of Kirk of the Forest, where once, long ago, William Wallace was declared Guardian of Scotland. We turned left off the Market Square, and a mile or so later left again, onto the A708, past the site of the battle of Philiphaugh. Three miles further, and yet another left, sharp this time, across "The General's Bridge," doubling back, along the opposite bank of the Yarrow Water.

Now, we were right on the southern edge of Bowhill Estate, the home of the Duke of Buccleuch. Odd really, to think that sixty two years ago, Rudolf Hess flew past just to the south of us. Coincidence?.... Maybe. But if the Duke knew what I was after up by Glasgow, he'd probably have us run off.

In fact, I was only here today, to take a few photo's, because this is where Tam Lin's Well is located. The light was just about perfect, and I fiddled about for ten minutes or so with the camera, taking shots from all manner of angles, (I told you I was no expert), and then deleting the worst of them. At last I was happy with the results, so we took off again, back up the road, and turned north west for Yarrow.

A mile and a half later I stopped again, this time to photograph the cottage where Mungo Park the explorer was born. Almost directly opposite were the ruins of Newark Castle. I already had decent photo's of that, but not taken in light like this. This morning, the Borders were an artists dream. Then we climbed back in and set off for Yarrow, and there just on the right was the turn for Welldean House.

"That's it there then Shorty. There's the drive. Nothing to see."

"Ahh, come on Eddie, let's just take a run up and suss the place out".

I was none to sure about that, but just to keep the little guy happy, I turned and headed uphill.

* * *

Henry Partis, "Chief of Security," at Welldean House, patrolled his perimeter with military precision. That is to say he walked alone, around the bushes and flowerbeds on the outer edges of the Estate. It was the job he had always dreamed of.

"Chief".... of Security. At last a job to suit his abilities.

Gone was the ignominy of his army career, ten years of his life confined in a warehouse in Germany, dispatching components to units all over the world. And all because of his name, and the cruel military sense of humour. For no sooner had he completed initial training, than some wag had christened him with the nickname "Spare."And where could the Army possibly send a man with a name like "Spare" Partis? Why....would he not be just perfect, for small arms component stores. And so, for ten long military years he had been condemned to answering the phone.

He'd tried various subterfuges. "Hello".....“Can I help you".....“Yes?" Even, "What you want," in an angry Chinese accent. But always, the voice on the line would ask, "Sorry,..... Is that...... "Spare" Part'is?"....Followed immediately by gales of helpless military laughter.

His only relief from the torment, was his delight in German Oompah Bands, busty barmaids, and long evenings spent quaffing litres of good German Lager.

He left the army twice the man he had entered it, but unfortunately, the second man seemed to have taken up residence about his waist, and this caused him to walk with an exaggerated military gait, head thrown back, chest and belly thrust forward, his back ramrod straight.

But on very the day of his release from the bosom of Her Majesty's Forces, he had seen the advertisement :-

Chief of Security Wanted.
Must be prepared to live on premises.

"Chief," he thought, booting up his computer. "Live in." He tapped the keyboard ..."Welldean House," and a picture appeared on screen..... Oh, Just Perfect!

He began his application. "Henry Partis. Ex Head of Military Weapons Distribution, Europe."

One month later, and he was nicely settled into a small but comfortable Norwegian style bungalow at Welldean.

And, on this fine morning, Henry stood on his favourite vantage point on the high North East corner of the estate, gazing out over his domain.

Ohhh... he thought, If only I could interest "The Master" in installing high, military style fencing, perhaps topped off with razor wire, just to keep the inmates.....Ooops sorry!....the guests, feeling safe......And a decent guard house? A main security gate? Floodlights perhaps? In Germany they had done this sort of thing so well! And then he could have a couple of dogs, Dobermans, Rhodesian Ridgebacks?

But, Master Zhang would have none of it. He said it would ruin some strange and mysterious oriental "Thing." What was it that he called it?........Ah yes....."Ambience."

A few staff would also be nice. For although Henry was Chief of Security, Henry was quite alone.

Something irritating, disturbed his reverie. Far below a battered pick up truck was turning off the highway and beginning the long climb towards Welldean. Scruffy looking thing, bloody scrap men or something. No chance of them getting in!

And, with military precision, he marched off through the undergrowth in the direction of the main drive.

* * *

I slowed and asked Shorty to look out for Old Deuchar Tower. What remained of it ought to be on our left. But if it was, then it appeared to have been built into a later cottage. Perhaps we could come back another day and take a better look. We drove further, onto the long gravel drive up to Welldean House itself.

The track climbed steeply, high banks of rhododendrons on each side restricting the view. But we never actually reached the house, because, just as we approached what appeared to be the last bend, a tall red faced man in the uniform of a security guard, burst breathless from the bushes, and raised a hand signalling for us to stop.

His small porcine eyes, stared malevolently from beneath the savagely slashed peak of his cap. He had built up the front of his headgear with heavy card, but the effect was somewhat spoiled by the sight of his huge belly straining against the belt of his uniform trousers. He stared with utter disdain at our battered old Toyota.

"Ah Zo", Shorty muttered, "Ze Eagle, perhaps it hass landed. Obviously, they don't let in just any old Tom, Dick, or Eddie."

I wound down the window, and he leaned in. Last nights beer wafted over me. He had a name tag on his uniform jacket, "Henry Partis." I smiled to myself. The badge on his shoulder read."Chief of Security." I greeted him.

"Good afternoon Lance Corporal." He flushed. I'd guessed his old rank correctly!

"We're Shut!" he snapped. No admittance today. You," he pointed a grubby nailed finger in my face. "Can turn around in that gap." He smiled wickedly, and indicated a muddy space between the bushes."Gypo and an effin' dwarf" I heard him mutter. As I've said before, I am kind of dark.

"Oh God," Shorty mumbled. "A Racist, and dwarfist with it."

It occurred to me, that he hoped we would get bogged down in the watery pool he'd indicated. But, if so, he obviously didn't know Toyota 4x4's.

"Okay, fair enough "Chief," I called as pleasantly as I could manage. "Just watch me in, could you, this tracks a bit tight?" He nodded, and stood there, an amused grin on his face.

I spun the wheel and pulled into the space, front end forward. Henry Partis was now directly behind the vehicle.

I hit the accelerator hard, spinning the wheels in the mud. A huge spray of filth and water fountained from beneath the rear wheels, and I lost sight of Henry completely. The truck broke through the stand of rhododendrons, and entered an area of open grass. I put the wheel hard over, hit the gas, and we slewed through 180 degrees, earth fountaining. I came back out of that same gap in the bushes, and swung out onto the drive.

Henry was busy. desperately brushing mud and water from his uniform. Shorty wound down his window.

"Ta Ta," he waved, "Have a nice day."

Henry was still screaming obscenities in the distance as we rounded a bend in the drive......Oh! I do love an informed student of Anglo Saxon!

Jesus, I thought, that had been plain childish. I must learn to behave myself. But Shorty wasn't finished, for no sooner had I turned back onto the main road, than he asked me to turn sharp left onto a tiny side road. He said it led to the Ettrick Valley. We climbed for about five minutes, and then he asked me to stop, so I turned the truck onto the roadside grass, and out we got.

"Lend us your camera, and stick the telephoto on?" I reached back into the cab, opened the case, assembled the camera, and passed it to him. From here, there was a perfect view of Welldean on the opposite hillside.

"This place is called Witchie Knowe," he said.

"How do you know," I asked.

"Been studying it. All sorts of history around here you know. Standing Stones, Dark Age Warrior's Graves, I must be taking after you, thought I might do a bit of writing" But I noticed that all of the photo's he was taking, were of Welldean House, and its grounds. He turned and climbed back up into the cab.

"That's about it, fancy a cup of coffee and a pasty, and then we'll get under way?"

He stuck a Hank Williams CD in the player, and selected "Lost Highway.".“Me and Reb's thinking of making that our signature tune for the group. You know, the old A7 is sort of Scotland's "Lost Highway."

I laughed. "Then I suppose that makes *us* sort of, "The "Lost Highwaymen." He quite liked that.

We listened to Hank, munched our pasties, and drank our coffee in companionable silence.It was a beautiful morning. Sometimes life can be just great.

Ten minutes later we were back on the road. Out past St Mary's Loch, and the waterfall they call "The Grey Mares Tail," then back on down to Moffat, where we joined the M74, and turned north for Glasgow.

I've never really liked the M74. Okay, I know, it's the fastest way from Carlisle and the M6 to Glasgow and Edinburgh, but it's a road without a soul. Worse, it lures the unwary into Gretna, with its kitsch "Welcome to Scotland."

You See....You can't just draw a line on a map and call it a road. Motorways aren't roads. Roads have to evolve over the centuries.You can read them just like a book, and a good road has absorbed the nature and the character of the people who have lived and travelled upon it. And it should tell you their stories.

Our own A7 dawdles through the Borders. But it is 100% authentic. No tartan, no shortbread, no fake weddings. Just, if you're prepared to look for it, the plain, ungarnished, and brutal history of a place that managed to be a both a war zone, and the cradle of British Christianity. And it's all still visible on the Borders landscape.

George MacDonald Fraser, who wrote "The Steel Bonnets," and all of those "Flashman" novels compared the old Borders to Afghanistan, a land fought over so often and for so long that the inhabitants knew no other way of life. And yet those old "Reivers" also managed to gift to the world one of the greatest collections of ballad poetry ever. And the oddest sense of honour and loyalty on the planet.

Ours is the part of Scotland that "they," our politicians up there in Edinburgh, don't want you to see, because "they" want both you and your money up there in their cities, and then off up into the Highlands.

And that's why.......exactly as Shorty claimed. The A7 is Scotland's "Lost Highway."

End of Sermon.

Of course we weren't going as far as Glasgow, and we turned off at junction 8, onto the A71, and so down to Strathaven, where we took the A726, north west for Eaglesham.

Hess's plane had crashed just north of there. I wasn't quite sure what we were looking for, and of course, the landscape had changed over the last 62 yrs, but in the event, it didn't prove too difficult at all. I just found the general area of the Hess crash, and then started knocking on doors and asking if anyone knew a Calum or a Rory Stuart.

Fifth go, and I was in luck.

Farmers.....they simply don't easily give up the land, and Rory Stuart still lived in the same farmhouse where he had been born. He was 73 yrs old. Old enough to have retired. But old farmers just don't do that. Lord knows why, but they're out there in all weathers, red faced and healthy. Eternally plodging through mud and shite, until presumably they just keel over.

Maybe then, like in those old Native American Corn Mother legends, they just plough them back into the earth to regenerate nature. Shorty, ever the realist, says that most of them are just too mean to give up on the Government Grants.

"Goodman's Croft," was an ancient grey sandstone pile, complete with turrets, and crow stepped gables, it even had a couple of gun loops either side of the door. Strange name for a farm, because in Scotland, the "Goodmans's Croft," is the old name for a small piece of uncultivated land on a big estate, a bit of land which has been set aside for the Devil. I wondered if they knew?

But Rory Stuart was no Devil. He was a tall muscular man, ruddy faced from the wind. His thick red hair was speckled with grey, and his blue eyes twinkled. He wore the uniform of the Lowland farmer, blue overalls tucked into green wellies, worn and stained tweed jacket, and a cap stuck on the side of his head. His deodorant of choice?..... "Eau de Silage,".... by Diesel of course.

We found him out front of the house, bending over the bonnet of an ancient Massey Ferguson tractor.

"Lost the way have you," he asked.

I held out my hand. "Rory Stuart?" He looked at my had but didn't take it.

"Who's Asking?"

"I'm Eddie Graham." Amongst other things, I'm a journalist, and occasional Private Investigator. Ex. Metropolitan Police and Army Intelligence, and this, is my associate, Mr. Septimus Higgins."

Shorty extended his hand "I'm just Ex. Durham Prison. You can call me Shorty, for some reason most folk do."

Rory Stuart smiled, then took Shorty's hand and shook it.

"Okay, Gentlemen..... What have I done to deserve a visit from "Ex Police, and Army Intelligence."

"10th of May 1941. You saw Rudolf Hess crash. My grandfather was watching you. He wrote about it in his diary.....I have the diary."

He paled slightly. "He was the man on the motor cycle?" He paused, then, "Oh Shit .... You're another one of "them." Come on, let's go on in the house." He turned, and without a backward glance, he marched off.

Another one of what? I wondered.

It was a large kitchen with a stone flagged floor, a huge AGA cooker, and an ageing sheepdog fast asleep in a shredded wicker basket. No sooner had we sat down than his wife, who he introduced Alice, plonked two huge mugs of almost orange tea, on the table in front of us.

"Strong and sweet," she declared. I assumed she meant the tea, but she was looking at her husband. I prefer mine weak, and without sugar, but I decided to suffer in silence. Having come for information it was better not to upset the natives.

"Right," Rory commenced, "How much do you know?"

"I know my grandfather watched Hess bail out, and heard the crash. I also know that before he baled out, something fell from his plane, and that you and your brother Calum retrieved that “something,” and ran off with it. I also know that no report of that object has ever appeared in any written account of the Hess incident, either official, or unofficial. From my grandfather’s account it was some sort of leather case.

“Right,” Mr Graham. “I’ll confirm that. But before I go any further. tell me what you know about the Hess business in general.”

It took me a few moments to arrange my thoughts. The background to the Hess flight is not that easy to summarise. But, needs must I thought.

“Okay then”......I commenced, “This is my personal take on the situation.

I can’t help but feel that the public has been considerably misled over the past half century regarding the situation in Britain in the 1930’s.

The popular view is that almost alone, plucky little Britain stood up to the growing menace of Hitler’s Germany. This viewpoint has been re-enforced by a huge number of books, films, and television series. It has even been graphically illustrated in childrens comic books. It comes therefore, as a surprise to many, to find that there was in the 1930’s, amongst the “Establishment” of Britain a high degree of admiration for the Nazi’s.

By the Establishment, I mean the aristocracy, the right wing politicians, and even members of the Royal Family itself, the Duke and Duchess of Windsor, being perhaps the most notorious of Hitler’s admirers.

As it became apparent that war with Germany was a very strong possibility, these elements, whose horror was not in fact Nazism, but Bolshevik Russia..... our Nobility, who feared the loss of their lands and position, formed themselves into a number of organisations prepared to negotiate a peace with Hitler.

These groups included the Nordic League, which was originally established by Nazi agents in 1935. Closely associated with the Nordic League were the “White Knights of Britain,” a secret society, complete with ritual initiation based upon Freemasonry. They, were also known as “The Hooded Men,” and have been compared to the Klu Klux Klan.

Both the White Knights, and the Nordic league shared the same headquarters.

Then there was "The Link", an Anglo-German "Friendship Group, and the notorious "Right Club," founded by driving force behind both "The Nordic League" and the "The White Knights," Archibald Maule Ramsay, Conservative M.P. for Peebles."

And there were others. Even the National Party of Scotland the forerunners of the SNP, appear to have been willing to at least discuss peace terms with Germany. Indeed, because of his activities, their future leader, Arthur Donaldson eventually had his home raided in 1941. Subversive literature, and a large cache of weapons were allegedly found, and he was detained for six weeks in Kilmarnock and Barlinnie Prisons.

Shorty laughed. "That's not what the SNP say today though is it? Peace with Nazi Germany?.... Never!... It was all a terrible mistake. But I've read the C.I.D. report of Donaldson's ramblings, on the web. Don't know why anyone should make that lot up!
But these days, the SNP is much more cuddly, so they're editing their early history, and now they put the Donaldson business down to evil minded policemen, plus too much beer and wishful thinking on the part of "the man" himself. Next thing they'll claim is that the "Polis" who wrote the report was English! Pity the buggers ever got a Parliament to shout their mouths off in. ...If that bloody Australian midget Mel Gibson hadn't painted his face blue, and shouted "Freedom," it would never have happened."

Rory guffawed, "Midget" coming from Shorty, sounded hilarious.

I paused, and took a sip of tea before continuing.

"The Dukes of Westminster, and Buccleuch, were particularly prominent pro-Germans.

In 1936, a number of aristocrats attended the 1936 Olympics, and socialised with the German Hierarchy. One of their number was the Duke of Hamilton.

Hamilton was monitored by M15 during the late 1930's, and was believed to be sympathetic to both the Nordic League, and the Right Club.

On the 18th of April 1939, Hitler celebrated his 50th birthday, King George V1 no less, sent a letter of congratulation, and much to Hitler's personal delight, the Duke of Buccleuch, and Lord Brockhurst, together with Major General John Frederick Charles Fuller, actually attended the ceremonies as honoured guests.

In September of 1939 War was declared between Britain and

Germany.

In 1940, the Prime Minister, Winston Churchill, removed the Duke of Buccleuch from his position as Keeper of his Majesty's household. Removed him on the grounds that he was suspected of being a "Fifth Columnist." He was replaced by the Duke of Hamilton! One would have thought that given the circumstances, it was perhaps an odd choice.

By 1941, the war was not going well for Britain. And that was when the incredible happened.

On May the 10th 1941, Rudolf Hess, Hitler's second in command, made a solo flight to Scotland. His flight was in all probability made with the direct knowledge of Adolf Hitler. All manner of reasons for the flight have been put forward, and all manner of conspiracy theories have been advanced, but what is virtually certain is that he brought with him plans for a negotiated peace, with Great Britain. A peace in which Germany would withdraw from the territories in Europe that had been occupied. The condition being that German Police would remain in control of those territories.

Great Britain would be allowed to retain her Empire, and Germany would be free to turn the full might of the Reich against Russia. And that, would have been a result well in keeping with the wishes of both Royalty, and the Aristocracy.

Hess appears to have been intending to make a landing at or in the vicinity of Dungavel House the home of the Duke of Hamilton, whom he claimed to know.

When interviewed after his capture, Hess insisted that Hamilton could put him in contact with King George V1, with whom he appeared to believe, he would have been able to carry out peace negotiations.

The Duke of Hamilton always denied the fact that he knew Hess at all. But whatever the reason, the fact is that Hess bailed out of his plane here, not too far from Hamilton's home, Dungavel House.

There was a small airfield at Dungavel, and rumours abound of runway lights switched on and off on the night of Hess's arrival, of Messerschmitt drop tanks delivered, and of a reception committee waiting at the airfield.

On the morning after the Hess crash, a car containing both the Duke of Kent, and the Duke of Buccleuch, was involved in a collision with a coal lorry in the near vicinity of Dungavel House.

I have reason to believe that the Duke of Marchbank was also present.

There has always been the strongest suspicion that those peers formed part of the "reception committee,",and had been waiting for Hess the previous night.

As everyone is aware, Hess's mission failed. He was incarcerated for the remainder of the war, faced trial at Nuremberg, and was sentenced to life imprisonment.

You could write a book about it, in fact, quite a number of people already have. But in a nutshell, that's about it."

Rory Stuart stared at me for a very long time. Finally he sighed. "Frankly Mr. Graham, I'm sick and tired of the entire Hess business. I wish me and Calum had simply handed that briefcase in. Your grandfather was right, that's what it was, a briefcase. We knew he'd seen us, and for years we thought someone would come looking. But no-one ever did."

"He intended to," I replied, "but he never got the chance. His plane was lost over the North Sea, a couple of weeks later."

He nodded slightly, "Sorry to hear that," he paused, "I don't have the briefcase any more, two of your old associates from Military Intelligence came and took it away back in 1988. You see, I never told a soul about it, but my brother Calum? ......Now he's a different matter altogether. He can't keep shut up. Likes his drink too much. When he drinks, then he starts boasting, and he must have been overheard talking about the Hess business. And word travels. Because like I said, two hard looking men turned up here back in 1988. Threatened me with all sorts of things. "Treason," they hinted, "Security of the Realm," they kept saying. Could have me and my family locked away for years, and just throw away the key. They said that they could even make me disappear permanently. One of them had his jacket unbuttoned, he was carrying a gun in a shoulder holster. They made me and the missus sign the Official Secrets Act."

"Are you certain they were ours," I asked. "What were they driving?"

He looked startled. "What do you mean, "Were they "Ours?" They said they were. They were driving a fancy silver Porsche, can't remember the model."

Shorty could tell something was wrong. "What is it Eddie?

"Can't be certain, but no Department I know of operates exactly like that, and no one I knew ever had the chance of a sports car to run 'round in. Plus, Military intelligence leaks like a sieve. Quite a few folk knew my granda saw Hess come down, and Hess is old news, not exactly top secret anymore, no threat to the Nation. So I'd be surprised if anything new that had come up, didn't filter down to me. And to be honest, I've sort of "unofficially" accessed all of the Hess files that still exist myself, just out of curiosity. Right old dog's breakfast, but nothing relevant in there. Nothing that isn't already out there in the public domain.

Rory Stuart spoke quietly. "You're wrong there"

"Pardon" I asked.

"Threat to the Nation."....."That briefcase *is* a threat to the Nation. It's a threat, because it contains a list collaborator's, all of those people who were prepared to form a new government in the case of a Nazi occupation. All of the people who had been personally approved by Hitler. A list of who would run the country, who would rule, and exactly who would have to be "removed." Contracts and agreements, all signed by those persons. Countersigned and sealed by the Fuehrer himself. The ultimate list of traitors."

He rose from the table and left the room. Five minutes later he was back. Back with a thin manilla folder under his arm. He slapped it down in front of me.

"I'm not stupid you know, they may have got the briefcase, but in that folder are good copies of everything that was in there. Do what you like with it, I just want rid of the thing. I told you I was sick and tired of this business? Well, It's haunted me for 62 yrs. All of my adult life I've watched the great whitewash job that has been done on those names, and the names of their descendants. All of that time knowing what they had really contracted to do. All of that time knowing I could call a halt to it, tell the world exactly what had been planned, bring it all tumbling down. But never quite able to bring myself to actually do it. So there it is, take it...... But be warned, that's a poisoned chalice you have there."

And I opened the folder.

Jesus Christ! but he was right. Some I'd suspected, some I'd never have guessed. There were other names, prominent ones which I had expected to see, but which were quite notably missing.

Still, he was correct, publish this, and Britain, would never be the same again. But this was just a copy. I may now know the truth, but there was nothing much that could be done with it.

Now....I wondered, Where the Hell, was the original?

Shorty was browsing the folder. "You know, the weirdest thing about the whole business Eddie, is simply this....I mean, why Rudolf Hess? Old Adolf wants peace with Britain so that he can turn around and hammer the Russians right? But, why send his most senior and trusted aid? Almost anyone would do surely? Any brave, expendable lunatic, and the Nazi's had loads of them.

Now....think on this. No-one knows squeak about this business with the briefcase. So that part of the scenario has never been explored? You know.....To me this whole business stinks. In fact the choice of Hess as the messenger always did. I mean its obvious to me, that Hess is defecting. He's thoroughly pissed off with Adolf and the Third Reich. So....he talks Mein Fuehrer into allowing him to go. Then, he packs this list," he held it up, "of all the British traitors, personally signed and sealed by his buddy Herr Hitler.

Hitler thinks its a guarantee, an assurance to his loyal followers in Britain, that they'll be on the Third Reich gravy train, when he decides to sashay across the Channel. But it's not. Because Rudi intends to shop the whole lot in return for safe conduct.

Then, it all goes sick. Because, the briefcase falls out of the plane without him, and it never turns up. Rory and his brother Calum see to that. And so Hess is forced to go ahead with the proposals for a peace plan, and ends up in schtuck, and then in Spandau.

You've just got to have studied the criminal mind like I have to understand it properly.....What do you think, Eddie?"

I thought it through. "Certainly, it sounds as plausible as any other explanation."

Rory was looking uncomfortable. "That would mean that Calum and me buggered the entire plan up then?"

"Who can tell what would have happened." I replied. "It's all just hypothetical".

But it had disturbed him. "It's always bothered me you know. I mean, I know he was a Nazi, Hess that is. But whatever he was, he must also have been a brave bastard to put the plane on its back like that, and parachute out into enemy territory. These days you're not even supposed to say that sort of thing. You're judged to be guilty by association. You know, over the years, various attempts have been made to erect a marker where that plane crashed. But always someone has smashed them. Last one was some civil rights lawyer from Glasgow. “They,” refused to prosecute him for criminal damage. So, how they got round it was to divert the new road, when it was built, the A726, right over the top of the site. “To stop the Neo Nazi’s coming in,” they said. But no matter what. Surely that site is part of our history? God knows, I’m 73 yrs old, and no-one cares what I think. But it looks to me like maybe we are just trading up to a different kind of Nazi these days. Just like them, they’re editing our history. In this case, my history.”

He held out his hand. “And if that’s all gentlemen, then I must get back to mending my pet tractor.” We shook hands, and a minute or so later we were outside.

Shorty looked up at him. “Why “The Goodman’s Croft” Rory?”

“You know what it is then?”

“Aye, It’s the land set aside for the Devil.”

“Well, One of my forbears was a bastard son of the 5th Earl of Bothwell.”

I remembered. “The Devil of North Berwick?” But he was a Stewart, not a Stuart.”

“Pure bloody conceit, that was. The family got mixed in with the Jacobites, and fancied a posh spelling. But way back in the 1600’s they thought it a bit of a joke to give the old place that name. Not only that but we all have the middle name Nicholas. So I’m Old Nick! and in taking that document you’ve just done a deal with the Devil.”

He roared with laughter, and there came a huge clatter from above.

A small red helicopter swept in over the old building, pivoted around and settled in the next field.

“My son Donald” Rory yelled. “Got more sense than me. He runs his own aerial survey and pilot training business”

“He’s a qualified instructor?” I asked.”

Rory nodded. “Why? fancy flying do you.”

“Oh Aye,” I replied, “Ever since the Army I’ve fancied trying my hand with helicopters. That’s a Schweizer 300 C isn’t it? Mind if I stay on a bit, and meet him.”

A couple of minutes later, the pilots door opened, and a tall man, a younger version of Rory, climbed down, and walked over to join us. He glanced at the battered folder under my arm.

“Getting rid of it at last are you,” he asked his father. “Not before time."

"This is Eddie Graham, Donnie, and Shorty Higgins. Eddie's grandfather was the man on the motorcycle I've told you about. The one who saw me and your uncle Calum pick up the briefcase." We shook hands. "Eddie is ex Military Intelligence. Maybe it's better him having it than me." He turned to me. "Don't worry Eddie, Donnie knows all about the Hess business, we've no secrets, me and him."

"You know Mr Graham", Donnie began. "Eddie", I insisted. "Okay then ... "Eddie." Well.....Eddie, the oddest aspect of the Hess flight, to me at least, is that no matter what the truth is, after the War, none of the British "Establishment" suffered at all for their actions. Take the 8th Duke of Buccleuch, for instance, who was a very prominent member of the pro German lobby in the 30's? Everything I've read suggests that he was in some way connected to the Hess landing. He was removed from his position in the Royal Household by Churchill, and virtually confined to his estates for the remainder of the War. Not a very good C.V you would imagine? Low profile from then on?....But not so. In 1949, King George V1 made him a Knight of the Order of the Thistle, and the King went even further, he wanted "Johnnie Dalkieth," the Dukes son, to marry Princess Margaret! It never came about, allegedly because the King died. But, I mean what was all that about?

And the Duke of Hamilton. The Hamilton's are still high up in Politics. Just have a look at any of the names associated with Fascism in the 1930's. As far as I can tell, none of our noble admirers of Fascism, come in for even the mildest criticism. And if you believe the popular press, why then, even the Duke of Windsor, gave up his throne for love."

I couldn't help but smile. "It's ever been so Donnie, history is mostly what we today call "spin". It's written by the rich, the powerful, ...and the winners." Scratch the surface, and there's a very different tale. And "modern" history is even worse. Just watch what happens in Iraq, now there's "history" in the making!

Shorty cut in, "Christ, don't let him get started on Iraq and the Middle East, he'll go on all day! What he wants to ask you Donnie, is do you do flying lessons. I hope you do, 'cause lately, he's spent ages out at his place putting in a landing pad, and I'd hate to think he's been wasting his labour."

"What?" he asked. "You've a landing pad, and no plane?"

"Aye, Well," I mumbled, embarrassed, and with an evil glance at Shorty, who just stood there grinning, "I'm a quick learner, at least I hope I am, and a helicopter licence would be a useful asset. History's a bit of a hobby of mine, so I'd also like to photograph a few unrecorded sites, down about Liddesdale?"

He reached into his pocket, and handed over a card. "I'm busy for a week or two, but give me a ring after that, and I'll see what we can arrange. I've decent cameras, and aerial photography is part of what I do anyway."

Shorty was almost jumping up and down with excitement. "How many can get in that thing Donnie?"

"Just two, It's got dual controls though, I do quite a bit of pilot training.

"Aww....That's a pity, I would love a trip or two in that."

Donnie laughed and nodded. "Don't worry, if it's okay with Eddie, I'll take you up sometime, and you can direct me to these sites he wants photographing

I nodded my agreement.

Five minutes later, we were back on the road. Straight down the M74, and then across from Gretna. Past the Army base, and out at Longtown.

I turned south instead of North.

"Where are we off to." Shorty asked.

"Can't wait, I'm hungry. Guess where?"

"The Border Cod." Great....I fancy some fish and chips an' all. Just don't tell Reb, she'll think somethings wrong with her cooking.

We parked up in the layby opposite Arthuret Church to eat. It was a beautiful evening, and as usual, there was no-one about. Weird really, because..... If there ever was a "King" Arthur, then there's a good chance that his head is buried there. Brought there after the "last battle" at Camlann. And, around fifty years after that, in 573 A.D. a major battle took place on this site, and one of the combatants was the original of "Merlin." He's buried out at the back of the church at Drumelzier, just out of Peebles, where two rivers meet.

Rhydderch Hael also fought at Arthuret, and his sword, was one of the "Thirteen Treasures of Britain," and the possible origin of Excalibur. In addition, he is also said to have possessed another of the treasures.... "The Dysgil," a wondrous platter, which never needed replenishing. Some sources associate that with "The Grail".

But, why have you never heard of any of this you ask? And I really don't know the answer to that.

Maybe Indiana Jones, or whatever they call him in this area, has simply kicked the bucket. I told you the A7 was worth the drive. You've just got to know the places to look.

"I could do with one of them Dysgils," Shorty grumbled. "I've finished me fish and chips. Have you got any more pop?"

I reached back behind the seat, opened the cool box, and extracted a couple of bottles of beer "No pop, but have a beer."

He grinned, "You sly bugger, you never said you had any "Hooky"!

I removed the caps with the opener on my key ring. "I'm off for a stroll."

I climbed out, crossed the road, and entered the churchyard. The sun was low on the horizon, and the old tombstones cast long shadows. The mason's marks on the wall of the church tower stood out dark against the stone. In most lights you can't see them.

Usually, there are only one or two scattered about a building, but at Arthuret, there's almost a complete wall of them. I've no idea why. I've heard it said that it's some kind of code, but then folk love to make a mystery out of things.

This was home ground for me. Back in the old reiving days, my own family, the Graham's used to collect their "blackmail" money in the porch of this church on Sundays. In return for which they would provide protection from raiders.

I walked on into the midst of the gravestones, to the old broken Dark Age cross. It glowed red in the setting sun. I raised the bottle, took a long pull, and then in salute to them all, I poured the rest at the foot of the cross.

Archie Armstrong, King James V1's Court fool is buried in an unmarked grave just about there, and God knows who else. The main battle grave is just to the east under the layby on the A7, where the "Burger" stall parks and the lorry drivers sleep overnight in their cabs......"Sweet Dreams".

Then I walked back to the truck.

"Still doing it then?" Shorty asked, remembering. I just nodded.

"Me too now and again" he confessed.

It was a small ritual we had developed years ago, when we used to come up to the Borders on our bikes. Any place the old reivers were, any place we knew our kin had been. Strange I suppose, since neither of us were believers in the conventional sense of the word.....Agnostics really.

He pointed to the tree covered mound in the field, with the crows swirling above, black against the pale blue of the evening sky.

"Reb and me come down here on the bikes now and again. Walk up that track into the trees. Up there, is one of the oddest places I know. Feels like someone is watching you. Creepy, but in a nice sort of way."

I knew what he meant. "Back down where we were brought up Shorty, everything has been destroyed by industry of one kind and another. Whole landscapes remodelled by centuries of mining. Then came the opencast, and the rest. Now there's almost nothing left to see. Up here in the Borders, most of the land is still untouched, and so you get these sort of places. But even here, as you well know, forestry is wrecking a lot of the landscape, and right under where we are standing, there's coal, a hell of a lot of coal, but deep down. So, God knows what will happen over the next few years.....Come on Mate, let's get back on the road. We'll pass Marchbank House on the way back. One of these days I'd like to take a look at that, but it's way back, and not visible from the A7. Don't suppose the current Duke would welcome me either, asking questions about his family and the War!"

"Funny bugger, him," Shorty replied. "He must be the grandson of the guy your granda gave a lift to on his bike?" I nodded.

"All sorts or weird rumours," he continued, "You know, the usual story....drugs,.. drink,... girls,.......parties." He paused reflectively. "Not that I mind girls and parties.

I've heard he has a right bastard of a manager, virtually runs the place for him.

I suppose one day, he'll either kill himself, overdose on something, or they'll trot him off somewhere to dry him out. Bloody so called Nobility! Even his Granda at least had the energy to help bring Hess over." He paused, raised his bottle, and finished the last of his beer. "Roll on the Revolution! What are you going to do with those papers Rory Stuart gave you?"

"Not much I can do, considering they're just copies. I'll stick them in the safe out at my place with the rest of what I have. I'd love to write a book, but unless I can come up with something actually fresh, then I'll be wasting my time. It's all been said already, many times over."

"Pity no-one listened then isn't it ."

I started the engine, and we drove off.

Behind us the sun dropped below the horizon.

* * *

Donnie Stuart was a good as his word. Two weeks later I phoned the number on his card, we arranged for the first of my lessons in the Schweizer, and I proposed that we combine my instruction with a bit of aerial photography.

A lot of our historic sites down on the border, are unrecorded, and as a result many are under threat, mainly from farming, forestry, and lately windfarms.

You see there's a marked reluctance on the part of the big landowners to record these sites. They don't see them as national assets, they see it them as an interference to future development. In other words, our history, the history of the Borders, stops them making more money, and since no Council wishes to upset these powerful folk, very little ever gets done.

In a sad sort of way, it's almost funny, because with monotonous regularity, not just here, but throughout Britain, new, freshly qualified "Regional Archeologists" turn up for work, bright eyed and bushy tailed, itching to boldly go forth and record our historic landscape. Ready..... Trained.... to translate cryptic runes, discover lost Kings...Templars...Burials. To find for themselves.......Fame! Only to be told that "their job," is actually to "sit in that office," drink coffee, and sign off on contracts saying that there is no archeological reason why major developments should not go ahead.

After a year of two of that, they just shuffle off elsewhere. Depressed. All of that time, all of that study, all.... for nothing?

A month later a fresh one arrives, and the cycle resumes.

Archeology must be the only occupation with a higher rate of alcoholism and suicide than Sweden.

Meanwhile, "out on the ranch," a veritable army of the retired, and the unemployed, have equipped themselves with metal detectors, and are out there regardless of weather, making finds that are re-writing the history books and filling the cabinets of our National Museums with magnificent artifacts in gold and silver. And the vast majority of research into both history and archeology is also being pursued by private individuals. If you don't believe me, have a look at the books that get published by those amateurs. Even the academics are using them. It all adds up to lifetimes of unpaid work by self financed enthusiasts. And now, I intended to join them, for I had long cherished plans, to photograph as much of the Borders as possible, from the air, in the correct light conditions, and then to publish a decent book on the subject in order to protect our hidden history.

"They" would hate me for it. I wouldn't be surprised if "they" even tried to stop me.But so what? I was a private individual. And.....It is still a free country.....Isn't it?

* * *

I was a man with two homes. My "official address" was at the cafe. Shorty and Reb had the bungalow, but I had a small flat over the top of the workshop where they restored the bikes.

I had installed an old bank safe in there, and that was where I kept my "official firearms," rifles mostly, and a couple of shotguns. The safe was so big, more of a small strongroom, that I would have no problem with security.

I shot occasionally, over the Border at Otterburn, out on the Army ranges. I held membership of a small private club there. But I was negotiating a bit more land out at Merrylaw, and I intended to landscape a small shooting range into it. That was unofficial of course. The law doesn't easily allow for private shooting ranges. Blast away at the deer, if you've the money, but shoot at a target? All sorts of barriers will be put in your way.

I wanted a safe 800 yards. Private, just for fun. I'm an ex sniper amongst other things, and own some quite exotic modern rifles, but I just love the old stuff, and in particular, old black powder rifles. I'd bought and sold a few, and had kept a couple, but I've always been reluctant to shoot with a genuine antique.

I had a particular fascination with the Sharps, the 50/90. It's the kid in us I suppose, far too much exposure to Westerns.

Shorty was the same. He could name you any actor in any western, quote you lines from most of them. His favourite ever was "High Noon." He said, and he certainly wasn't the first, that the western is the modern morality play. You know where you stand with it. Well, at least you did, until Henry Fonda in "Once upon a time in the West," but then that was just playing about with the format.

I had space on my certificate for a couple more rifles, and so, one fine day, I went online, E.mailed the Shiloh Rifle Manufacturing Company, way out in Montana, and ordered myself a Sharps Rifle, a replica 50/90 with a 34 inch barrel. A legend in shooting circles.

One day I'd buy an original, but not today. This one I just wanted to shoot, and originals really are too rare for that.

* * *

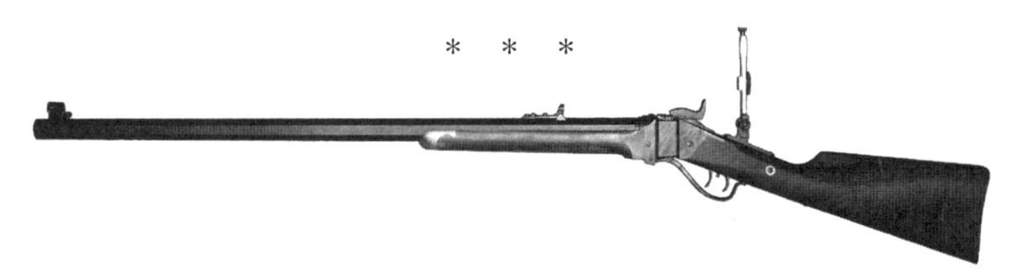

I took the rifle out of its wrapping, and the aroma of gun oil filled the small room. Shorty looked stunned, awestruck.

"It's the Billy Dixon gun isn't it Eddie? That's a Sharps 50/90, 34 inch barrel? What is it, a Shiloh replica?" I couldn't believe it. Where did he get his information?

"How do you know about that?"

"Know? Everybody knows that! Texas, June 27th 1874, second battle of Adobe Walls,Billy Dixon knocked an Indian off his horse. 1538 yards, when they measured it, came to be known as "The Shot of the Century." That shot ended the siege, and Billy got the Medal of Honour."

(Note. Shorty appears to be in error. Billy Dixon in fact received the Medal of Honour for his actions at the Battle of Buffalo Wallow, Hemphill County, Texas, in September of 1874, when he and an "Amos Chapman," were working as scouts for the army. Together with four troopers from a dispatch detail, they were surrounded and besieged by a large combined band of Kiowa's and Comanche's. They held off the Indians for three days with accurate rifle fire, before a storm broke the siege. One trooper was killed, and every man was wounded. All subsequently received the Medal of Honour.)

"No-one really believes it today, they say 1538 yards is just not possible. But then just last year, some scientists with proper radar tracking and all of that, together with some folk from Shiloh tested one of these 50/90's," he caressed the stock lovingly. "They found, that with black powder mind you, they got Billy's range at four and a half to five degrees elevation. At 35 degrees they got 3600 yards. So much for impossible!

This.....has a muzzle velocity of around 1300 feet per second if I recall rightly, and a terminal velocity of near on 700 at maximum range. There's not much quite like it. You must have seen Burt Lancaster in "Valdez is Coming?" I see that you've got the double set trigger? Pull the rear one to set the forward one to a lighter pressure. Nice touch that!

I was starting to feel that it wasn't my gun after all. I looked at him in disbelief. I mean how did he remember it all?

"O.K. Eddie, when can I shoot it!"

"What do you mean "Shoot it" Shorty? You're my best friend, and I hate to bring this up, believe me, but you did do time for murder, even if it was a gross miscarriage of justice. You'll never get authority for a water pistol, let alone a gun, and if Plod ever finds you with one then they could well put you back inside, and simply throw away the key."

He grinned up at me, "Aw, go on Eddie, no-one will know."

* * *

I carried the rifle back through to Shorty's workshop, laid it on an old blanket, and carefully dismantled it. Then I wrapped the octagonal barrel in cloth, and set it up in one of the big bench vices with the top flat upwards. I went upstairs, rummaged around for my toolroll, grabbed Oakshott's "Records of the Medieval Sword" from the bookshelf, and came back down.

We're a superstitious lot, us ex-soldiers, always touching wood, carrying lucky charms or talismans of some sort, even finding hidden omens in odd little events. My own conceit when I was a sniper had been to decorate the barrel of my rifle in some hidden place with a couple of those symbols used by warriors since time immemorial to add mystic power to their sword blades. In my case had I used both the "Hand of God," the open palm with the wrist terminating in a spiral, and the "Circle and Cross," the ancient "Sun Wheel," the absolute origin of the "Celtic Cross".

Old habits are hard to break, and so I intended to decorate my Sharp's in the same fashion, but now, of course, since I was a civilian, there was no need to hide the decoration. So I took a fine hardened steel point, copied the designs from my book onto the top surface of the barrel, and then I carefully engraved them into the steel. I worked a little longer, deepening the channels I had engraved, opening them out to provide undercuts. Then I took a little roll of 18 carat gold from my workbox, and carefully inlaid it into the designs.Then, I examined the work with an eyeglass.

Perfect! Yellow gold, deep blue steel.

I thought of the old Border blade inscription. "God guide the hand that I instand."

Then I re-assembled the rifle, and locked it away in my safe.

* * *

21st April 2001.

Mrs Kang.

It was raining. Well not exactly raining, but not exactly not raining either. The sky was like lead, the cloudbase down on the top of the hills, there was no wind, and Langholm was suffering one of those heavy drenching mists which are unique to the Borders.

Some call it a Liddesdale Dreek.

There's even an artist who captured it to perfection. Tom Scott of Selkirk. He painted stirring watercolours of the Reivers, (If he'd just known a bit more about armour, then they'd have been just perfect), and miserable landscapes of rain soaked, near unidentifiable hills. Brilliant though, fantastic technique, no other watercolourist comes anywhere near him for the sheer beautiful misery, of cold, misty, damp, and unnamed valleys

Farmers, especially hill farmers, love them. They pay crazy prices, and if it's of their own rain sodden farm then they'll break the bank. Amazing really, 'cause usually they're as tight as duck's backsides, (and they're watertight). I've heard it said that the only way to get a drink out of a Border hill farmer, is to stick your finger down his throat. But if you've got a Tom Scott, then keep it, it's better than money in the bank. It'll cool you down on hot summer days, but in winter.... just turn it to the wall, or your heating bills will go through the roof.

It was mid morning, quiet, and we needed a bit of fresh air, so Shorty and I left Reb in charge of the Cafe and walked off up the hill opposite, on the road which led to Tarras, and Copshawholm.

If we were going to develop the business, and still have our bit of freedom, we really needed to find some staff to help out.

The road climbed steeply, winding through trees and hairpin bends. The air was heavy with the smell of damp leaf mould and fungus.

It was still quite early in the year, spring comes late up north, and the larches were just showing green buds. Catkins, what we used to call "lambs tails," still hung in the branches of the hazels.

The blackthorn was in bud but had not yet burst into flower. I just love the weeks when it blossoms.

Folk debate the term "blackthorn winter." What they ask, does it mean? But anyone who's seen complete hedgerows of the stuff, or those tiny miniature valleys in the Borders filled with it, can be in no doubt at all. The bushes look as if they are loaded with a heavy fall of snow.

Shorty joked that blackthorn never grows very high because it is slow (sloe) growing. It was an old joke, and all the better for it.

Was the time that folk gathered sloes, the bitter black berries which are a sort of plum, in the autumn, soaking them in gin and sugar to make "sloe gin" to fortify themselves with in the winter. But in these more affluent and wasteful times, its just easier for them to buy cheap booze at the supermarket, and so the sloes just wither on the branches.

Blackthorn and hazel both make first rate walking sticks, and not just sticks for walking. Back before World War 11, when folk still knew what "Single Stick" was, good blackthorn sticks were collected, dried, and straightened, and the resulting "walking sticks" doubled as unobtrusive weapons for personal defence. And ones with a good "legal reason" for carrying them.

"Poor old bugger walks with a stick"....Poor dangerous old bugger that is.

"Single stick," was the last remnant of the old British form of broadsword fencing. "Breaking a man's head," referred to the drawing of blood with a blow to the head, and thus winning the bout. It went on at country fairs, but like many other things, it never revived after the war.

The very best sticks, if you can get them, grow elliptical in section instead of round, giving a better striking edge. Shorty and I, had spent many a happy hour "fossicking about" in hedgerows in search of our "holy grail," "the perfect stick." A simple pleasure for sure, but a frustratingly dangerous one. For the perfect stick, like the grail itself, is unattainable. You see it in the centre of the bush, straight, elliptical. faultless. But try and reach it? And, if you do succeed.....then you'll find that it wasn't straight after all, and that some random branch had concealed the bend or the flaw.

Blackthorn has the most vicious thorns known to mankind,which is why it is also called the "Devil's wood." It doesn't just prick you, it impales you, and there must be some sort of poison or irritant on those spikes, because the small punctures turn red, and they hurt like hell. You cut the spikes off the stick, and leave on the large knobbles that they grow out of. It's a bloody good weapon.

Shorty and me had some good sticks, and we were always on the lookout for more. Just for fun. We'd also whiled away many a dark evening re-learning the art of using them.

One day I was going to plant a blackthorn grove of my own, and try to grow them just perfect. Then all I'd have to do is re-invent single stick as a sport!

Perhaps we should have lived in the 16th century. Me and Shorty.

We continued on up the hill, passing a low stone cottage on the right of the road. A tall muscular lady of indeterminate age was at work pruning fruit bushes in the garden.

"Hello boys" she called out, "Nice weather for a walk, for those with enough time for it." I just nodded, smiled back, and we walked on.

When we were out of earshot Shorty asked. "Who's that?"

"No idea, I haven't seen her around before. I always thought the place was empty. Must have just moved in."

Fifteen minutes later, we reached the rusted iron monument near the hilltop.

I've always wondered just why Langholm held that man in such high regard. "Hugh McDiarmid" Actually Christopher Murray Grieve..... Poet, Communist, and Founder of the National Party of Scotland. All well and good. But as late as 1941, about the time Hess landed, McDiarmid made no secret of the fact that he considered that Scotland would be better off under the Nazi's than under the British Government of the day, which, when you consider that WW11 was in full swing and British troops and civilians were dying on a daily basis, was a pretty stupid view to express, and one that you would imagine would have killed good and dead any chance of a memorial ever being erected in his memory.

He also listed "Anglophobia" as one of his hobbies. I wonder if perhaps he just hated his Dad, who was the village postman. Because the origin of the surname "Grieve" is usually accepted as English, and like folk with the surname "Inglis," they just sort of strayed across the Border.

I mean, this guy was born and lived just north of the Debateable Land. He wasn't really "Scottish" in the "genetic" sense, or in the way most folk see it at all. He ought to have been a Borderer, and he ought to have been proud of it. But there it stands, just the same. No notice on the entry into Langholm announcing that the engineer Thomas Telford was born just up the way, or that this is the site of the battle of Arkinholm, the battle that brought the Buccleuch family to power, and "Buccleuch" still owns a great chunk of Britain. Another son of Langholm, Sir Pulteny Malcolm, was partly responsible for the burning of Washington in the War of 1812. The oldest whisky distillery in Scotland once stood, and in fact still does stand, unremembered, on the south of the town.

But all the sign on the approach to Langholm says is that Langholm, was the home of Hugh McDiarmid......Weird!

Shorty looked up at the monument. "Me, I think they should put up an iron string vest beside it. Give everybody something to smile at."

Because, Langholm was also home to Gregor Fisher, better known perhaps as "Rab C. Nesbitt," the eponymous central character of a comedy series about a "working," or more like "shirking" class Glasgow family. He was renowned for his sartorial elegance, famously wearing a string vest, and a scruffy headband. Alongside Hugh McDiarmid, another classic image of a true Scotsman.

We started off back down the hill. The view from up here was amazing.....but we couldn't see it for the mist. Downhill's faster, and five minutes later we arrived back alongside the cottage. The same lady was still working in the garden.

"Enjoy yourselves boys? A walk's just what you need, to build up a thirst and an appetite."

She seemed a friendly sort, if a bit on the grim side, but that wasn't unusual about these parts, so we stopped and leaned on the wall.

"Just moved in? I asked.

"About a week ago, I used to live over by Hermitage, but I lost my husband, and the house was too big for me, so now I've got this".

I tried to look sad. "I'm sorry to hear that," I thought I'd cheer her up. "You look to young to be a widow."

She burst out laughing. “Oh, he’s not dead, he buggered off with the barmaid from the “Liddesdale.” Bloody good luck to her, she’s welcome to him, useless idle sod! It won’t last! She’ll sharp find out what he’s like, good for now’t, no jobs good enough for him. But let’s not stand about here in this weather, would you care for a cup of tea and a bit of apple pie? Fresh baked, still warm?

Shorty looked up at me and nodded. We opened the gate, and walked through. My, but she’d been busy, a mountain of weeds, twigs, and branches had been piled into a mound ready for burning. All of the bushes were neatly trimmed, and the soil of the garden was newly turned over. A robin hopped amongst the damp black earth, happily collecting worms.

Our hostess held out her hand, “Mary Kang, best cook in the Borders, “Famous for my jams and jellies.” She laughed. “Family joke, someone used it in my Grannies obituary in the “Advertiser,” (The Eskdale and Liddesdale Advertiser), so we had it carved onto her gravestone, and it sort of stuck with the ladies in our family. There’s pictures of it in one those books the “Graveyard Bunnies” write. (people who like tombstones) I used to be Mary Armstrong, but I’m going back to my maiden name since ”Useless Bugger” left.

She led us through into the house. A large hot fire was burning in the hearth, but the room was just warm.

“Takes an age to warm these places up, it’s been empty for years. The Estates hung onto it even though they couldn’t get a tenant, so I made them an offer, and for a change they sold it, instead of just letting it fall down like the rest of them about here. Have a seat, and tell me who you boys are.” She indicated three high backed chairs, grouped around a small table near the fire.

We sat, and I held out my hand. “I’m Eddie Graham, and this is Septimus Higgins, his friends call him Shorty. Can’t think why.”

Shorty just laughed and shook her hand.

“Shorty and his partner, have the cafe at the road end, so you’ll probably see quite a lot of them since you’re just up the road.”

“Partner?” she frowned. “Would that be a lady, or........are you of some other persuasion?”

He laughed again, “She’s called Reb, no doubt you’ll get to meet her. I think she’s a woman, but I’m not all that knowledgable about these things, so she might be having me on.”

Mrs Kang smiled. She looked relieved. “Make yourselves comfy, tea, apple pie, scones, cream and strawberry jam okay?" she asked. We both nodded enthusiastically, and she left the room for the kitchen.

He looked across at me. "Nice lady?" I nodded. It was pleasant sitting there in front of the fire, the steam rising from our damp clothes.

Five minutes later and she was back. Big pot of tea, two mugs, dinner plate sized apple pie, scones, the thick kind with sultanas in them, whipped cream, strawberry jam, and butter. And she was right, she must be the best cook in the Borders. I looked up.

"Aren't you having any."

"Oh no, I never eat with my guests! You two just enjoy it, finish it all up, I've got a bit to do out in the kitchen." She left the room again.

We sat there in front of the fire, toasty warm, and sure enough, between the two of us we managed to scoff the lot. Pie, scones, cream, jam, and two big mugs of tea each. We sat back, full, warm, and content. The thought of going back out into the cold and wet outside was not a prospect we relished, but really, we had left Reb on her own long enough.

The minutes ticked by, and no sign of Mrs Kang. I thought I could hear her clattering about out in the kitchen though, so I called out. "Sorry Mrs Kang, but we have to get going, I must say that is the best pie and scones, I can ever remember".

She appeared in the doorway dusting flour off her hands, and smiling shyly, "Why thank you Eddie, its very kind of you to say so. Do call by any time for more......That'll be £11.56.

My jaw must have dropped, "£11.56?"

"Why yes,.... You silly boy, you didn't think it was free did you?"

Shorty burst out laughing, and reached into his pocket for the cash.

"Lady," he took both of her hands in his, and looked up into her eyes, "You're just perfect! Do you want a job?"

She smiled down at him. "Doing what?"

"Working." He said. "For money. I'll pay you a percentage of the takings. You'll make a fortune."

And that's how we came by Mrs Kang.

* * *

Chuck.

But Mary Kang did not come cheaply, for she did not come alone. Yes, She would work for us, but if we took her, then we also took her nephew. Her live in nephew......Chuck!

Even in the depths of Liddesdale, film and television had made its impact, and none more so than the films and television featuring Chuck Norris.

Chuck's mother was perhaps his biggest fan. Chuck's dad was an American martial artist, and master of Kung Fu, or at least that's what his Mum said. No-one knew for certain.

She left Chuck at his Auntie's one day, and never came back. The next Christmas a parcel arrived from America, a parcel containing every episode of "Walker Texas Ranger," and so, Chuck fantasised that Walker was his Dad, and no-one dared to disillusion him.

Why......?

Perhaps because Chuck was young and sensitive, and no-one wished to hurt the lads feelings?

More likely because Chuck was huge. He Towered..... He Loomed..... He Lurked in Dark Corners. Folk looked at him, and thought...... Fay Wray....the Empire State building. James Whale would have loved him. For Chuck was to Karloff, what I am to Shorty. Yet he was a gentle soul. At high school, he ought to have played rugby, but everyone was too scared to play with him.

Chuck loved film, and when sports teachers, shunning the wishes of their other pupils, continued vainly to attempt to recruit him, hoping perhaps to use him as a sort of secret weapon? Well, he simply told them to go watch Kubricks 2001.

The opening sequence, he said. Remember?.....

Classic, no other word for it!

Cue....... music!

Also Sprach Zarathustra!

The Ape! ..the Bone! ....the Satellite!

Chuck claimed that there were once two tribes of great apes. The one depicted by Kubrick, picked up the bone, learned the use of tools, and his tribe evolved.

But the others........?

The others simply learned to play rugby.

The teachers looked at him glowering down at them, laughed nervously, swallowed the words they would like to have said, and left him alone to practice his golf swing.

They didn't actually teach golf at Chuck's school, but they left him alone anyway, to teach himself. He asked if he could take his "A"levels in it but they wouldn't let him. How about some kind of a scholarship?

"No chance big boy. Take up rugby or American football, and we'll talk."

Ah,........the system, no room for the individual. Much too dangerous.....Make him into a team player.....Control's the thing!

And so Chuck learned to cook. Auntie Mary taught him. He was brilliant!

We taught him single stick, (a simple weapon) in deference to Kubrick and his ape. He'd be World Class, if only there actually were a World Class.

Chuck though, came with an additional bonus.

Girls!

From September onwards depending on inclination, and the height of the farm above sea level, Border farmers "put the tups in."

For the uninitiated, this is the ritual of introducing the ram to the ewes. The little boy sheep to the little girls. You take the "tup," that is the male sheep, and strap a sort of ink pad to his chest.
Most use red dye, a few prefer blue.....Which is strange since most border farmers vote Conservative.

The sheep don't mind, for although they actually outnumber the human population of the Borders many times over, they don't have a single vote between them.

Don't tell the animal rights activists!

The poor old tup has been starved of feminine company for almost a year, and his balls have swollen to the size of small water melons. Then you just let him loose into a field full of ewes, and you can tell which ones have been the object of his affections, by the red or blue spots on their backs. It's Tup Heaven!

A month or so later, a stupid smile on his face, barely able to walk, they lead, or carry him back out through the gate, and start feeding him up for next year.

Well, if Chuck had been kitted out in the same fashion......Every other young lady in Langholm and surrounding district, would have red or blue bums.

The lad was a machine, and the machine worked all year round, 24 hours a day. He was a giant, but there wasn't an ounce of fat on him. We kidded him that he should patent it as a weight loss system. Get his own programme on one of those odd television channels. "Let's Fuck, with Chuck" perhaps!

In the small circle of our cafe, we nicknamed him "monkeyglands." Every time the postman called, we claimed he was delivering Chuck's vitamin pills.

And Chuck revelled in it all!

Irate fathers used to rush in the door of the cafe, take one look at Chuck, and settle for a cup of coffee and a Penguin Biscuit, before leaving to tell their wives what a tough time they'd given him.

What it did mean in practical terms though, was an endless supply of nubile young waitresses, all delighted to come along when times were busy, and all strangely nervous about the journey home late at night, without Chuck along to chaperone them.

By now, Shorty, Reb, and a few others, had started singing Country and Western in the evenings, and our place was gaining quite a reputation. Chuck's girls came along as well, for the music and entertainment. And pretty girls are always good for business.

Altogether, we had the makings of a first rate Honky Tonk, and, we were now a team.

We also were collecting our own growing band of motorcyclists. They came from both sides of the Border, Geordies, Cumbrians, Scottish Borderers, all united by a love of motorcycles, and Country and Western Music. Many with old Border surnames.

We designed our own badge. It was circular, two hands locked in friendship, above an old "Steel Bonnet." Below the simple words, "Border Alliance," Many folk before, had tried for cross border co-operation and had failed.

Perhaps we would succeed.

We decided that we couldn't just keep on calling it the Road End Cafe. We had a good place, and it needed a suitable name. Shorty thought "The Roadkill Cafe" sounded about tough enough, and the bikers would like it, but Mary Kang ruled that out, insisting that there was no way her cooking was ever going to be associated with "poor wee things knocked over by lorries."

We tried "Desperate Dan's" in homage to the eponymous pie eating hero in the "Sunday Post." We all liked that one, but then we worried about copyright problems. Could be we became famous, and then someone might object to us stealing the name. Look what MacDonald's do to competitors?

Eventually we settled on "The Last Chance." Suitably Country and Western, and also the "Last Chance" of good food before Edinburgh going north, or Carlisle going south.

* * *

Of course it is impossible think of 2001 without remembering the events of September 11th. 9/11 as it is now known. Because the entire world changed that day.

In the Cafe, we all sat stunned watching the television almost in disbelief, as the planes slammed into the World Trade Centre. Footage repeated hour after hour.

That was the day that the "War on Terror" and the hunt for my old adversary Osama Bin Laden, really began in ernest.

Even in the Borders we weren't immune. No-fly zones were created around our local nuclear power stations, down at Sellafield in Cumbria, and at Chapelcross just to the west of us at Annan.

Annan was considered particulary vulnerable to attack, being one of the oldest nuclear facilties in Britain. Not built to withstand much damage, and due to be phased out in the next few years.

9/11 also saw hugely reduced numbers of visitors from the United States, as a morbid fear of flying, became America's latest phobia.

* * *

2002, was a busy year for all of us.

Out at Merrylaw, I constructed a large farm shed, with a huge sliding door. Hopefully it would eventually be the hanger for a helicopter, but in the meantime, a friend of mine, an R.A.F. Harrier pilot had use of it. He's called Archie Armstrong, same as the man buried down at Arthuret Church, and he was in the process of building a fixed wing aircraft of his own. A Vans Aircraft RV6. He brought it over in pieces, a bit over half built. It was a fascinating project, and when we had time, Shorty and I took to working with him, late on into the evenings. When it was completed, he intended to name the plane "Jester," after the original "Archie."

Assuming we ever finished the job, in return for our labour, he'd promised to give me a few lessons, and Shorty a flight or two.

Archie was away abroad a lot of the time, but seemed content to let us work in his absence. It was good to be trusted, and Shorty was in his element, precision work being his special forte.

Meanwhile the "Last Chance" was beginning prosper.

I purloined a recipe from back down in Newcastle, for genuine Geordie "Stottie Cakes." It's a delicious flatbread cooked on the bottom of the oven. There's a secret to making them, and good ones are virtually unobtainable outside of the North East, but now we had a contract with one of the local bakeries to produce them. We told them we had a patent on the method, and swore them to secrecy.

For those wanting a take out meal, we provided "Stotties" filled with either ham and "pease pudding," pork and stuffing, or still warm, with fresh butter and filled with fried bacon.

Word quickly spread, that we were reliable, we were open, and it wouldn't break the bank to come dine with us. We catered for everyone. Businessmen, lorry drivers, bikers, and tourists.

We also had the most eclectic and eccentric background music around, courtesy of Shorty and his new acquisition, his I Pod.

Mary Kang, and Chuck had put together a good, innovative, and substantial menu, and supplemented it with a rotating selection of daily "specials".

The big surprise, was that we were getting an increasing number of requests to cater for evening functions, even the odd wedding. That wasn't quite the way Shorty and I had planned for things to work out. So, we had a meeting one night, Mary, Chuck, and the three of us, and we more or less decided to let things take their own course, and to split the profits equally five ways. The actual property however, would still belong to Shorty and me.

Reb had discovered both a liking and a talent for cooking, and with Mary's guidance, she was now quite capable, if necessary of running the kitchens alone, with only a small amount of assistance from either Shorty, or from one or other of Chuck's girls, a couple of whom we now seemed to employ on a semi regular basis.

Already, Shorty was talking about plans for extending the place. He still worked out back on his bikes when he got the chance, only now they were more of a hobby than a business.

But, despite how well things were going, Shorty occasionally seemed rather "out of sorts."

"Of course," I thought, Reb and him are now a permanent "item." I mean......Women are strange, irrational, and moody things, and he'd always been used to living the life of a batchelor. So I said nothing at all. None of my business really. But it kept on happening, right up until winter, and one night out at my place, when we were working on Archie's plane, I couldn't help but ask.

"Everything okay with you and Reb?"

He'd been installing the instrument panel in the cockpit. He put down his screwdriver and turned to face me. "Aye, She's a great lass," ....He looked a bit uneasy though, "Why, What's wrong?"

"Oh, You know, sometimes you just don't seem to be your usual happy self. You're brooding about something. She's not expecting or anything is she?"

He laughed, "Christ No! ......More's the pity."

I was quite taken aback by that. Stupid really, but until then, I'd never actually considered Shorty and Reb as potential parents.

"There is one thing though Eddie," he continued. "You remember I told you she lent that Master Zhang a few quid?" I nodded. "Well it wasn't just a few.... it was fifty thousand of them."

I must have gasped.

"Aye,.......And she's written to him more than once, asking for him to return it, and had no reply. Now, she's had a solicitor's letter, Zhang's claiming that she gave him the money, and the upshot is, that now she's got now't at all of her own left. She used to be a bit wild you know, and Lady Rebecca Forsythe-Ingram or not, her Dad simply kicked her out, and near enough disowned her. He's a bloody multi millionaire, but he gave her that fifty grand, and told her never to come back for any more. So the Cafe is all she's got at the moment, and she worries about it all of the time, says she's living on charity being with me, and she's scared that I think she only stays with me to keep a roof over her head. Just the other week, I found out that she'd advertised the Harley for sale, just to help out. Of course, I sharp put a stop to that. She's the best thing that's happened to me for years Eddie, and I don't want to lose her. God, I wish she was pregnant."

He picked up his screwdriver, and went back to work.

Christmas came, and we served more turkey dinners than I could ever have imagined.

Brian, another ex.polis, and old mate of mine, who once ran the Museum of Border Arms and Armour up at Teviothead, and who now writes books, had also become a bit of a regular, sitting in the corner with his laptop and a cup of coffee, just tapping away. His wife Maureen has some rare recipes, and Mary and Reb, had somehow managed to talk an ancient family secret for the making of Christmas pudding out of her. It took weeks to prepare, and we made a lot, but we didn't make anywhere near enough.

Everyone kept asking for "seconds." Mothers loved it. Their kids ate mountains, then went home and slept for hours, giving their parents time for some well deserved R & R. As a result of which, next September, we anticipated a small population explosion.

We thought about changing the name from Christmas pudding to something else, and serving it all of the year round, and the three of them were now talking about marketing it commercially.

Maureen has another receipt for Christmas cake, said to be just as good. She's holding back on that one, but I can tell she's weakening. Her grandmother acquired it from an ancient chef, who once cooked for Queen Victoria. Her grandma, worked at one of the "big houses" in Northumberland when she was young. Royalty visited frequently, and with a full entourage. That's where the pudding recipe came from too.

New Year came, and we officially closed for the night. But we had our own staff party. Chuck, who had by now sprouted sideburns, and did a fair impression of "The King," crooned out a number of Elvis songs, backed by a trio of his of lady admirers. Shorty and Reb, rocked through every Christmas song we could remember, and then they all joined forces, and "Lady Rebecca, and the Electric Willie Band,",belted out Auld Lang Syne.

We hugged each other, and raised our glasses..... Happy 2003.

And so, it was. Until January 27th. When a giant black hit man from Glasgow tried to kill us, and was shot in turn, by an unidentified masked man.

A very professional Russian assassin.

Part 11. 2003.

January 27th.

Parsa Khan, swore vilely, and kicked the cat.

The cat shrieked, shot across the grubby threadbare carpet of the living room, and flung itself into the protection of Shabaz's arms.

"Bloody....Stupid....Black....Glaswegian....Gorilla! Parsa yelled, pointing at the murky picture on the ancient television.

"Keep it down," Shabaz hissed. The landlord downstairs was out, but Parsa could perhaps be heard through the walls.

"A thousand, that cost me!" Parsa moaned.

"But not of your money" Shabaz thought.

"All the bloody idiot had to do, was walk in through the door, shoot the bastard, and walk back out."

Shabaz comforted the cat. "You always said, "If you want a job done, do it yourself." Pity you didn't follow your own advice then isn't it."

"Then," he thought, "You would be lying dead on the floor of that cafe."

Parsa looked shocked. "Just you remember who is running this operation. You," he pointed, "were nothing Shabaz Galzai. You'd be an idiot of a herdsman, if I hadn't dragged you out of your village, and arranged for a proper education. A fortune was spent on you. You should be more grateful!"

"Education"..... Shabaz thought.... "More like indoctrination." And it hadn't worked properly. But he mustn't let that show.

"You never let me forget. But think on this, my good "friend". The problem now, is not your Glaswegian. The problem now, is this.... Just who shot him, and why? And, does that person know about us? Because, if he does".....he put two fingers together, aimed them at Parsa, and fired an imaginary shot at his head...... "Phshew!

He was delighted to see Parsa flinch.

"No-one knows about us, my little falcon." Shabaz hated that nickname, and Parsa knew it. "I have taken every precaution. You need have no fear, and I will be back tomorrow."

They'd been together for months now, the last two weeks in this grubby little flat in Carlisle. Aglionby Street, just five minutes walk from the main line railway station. Couldn't be more convenient. They kept open rail tickets, north to Glasgow, or south to London or any of the connecting stations on the way. Fast rail service too, now that Sir Richard Branson had equipped the line with the latest tilting trains..... what were they called, "Pendulinos?"

Shabaz loved railways, and the new 125mph trains were a delight. They were designed for 150, but the British rail system wasn't up to it. How could that be? he wondered. The British had invented the train.

Parsa was on one of those trains now, heading south for Preston, then Manchester, and on to Leeds. To report on his, or rather he thought, "our," failure to eliminate Eddie Graham.

He was pleased he was staying in Carlisle. Their contacts, those fanatics in Leeds.....They scared him. Such intensity.....Such hatred! Why did they hate so? They were British! What could they know of "his" Afghanistan?

The cat purred contentedly, warm on his lap. He wondered who the cat belonged to.

Perhaps it belonged to him.

But Parsa did not return the next day. In fact, he did not return for two weeks.

Shabaz didn't care. He wasn't short of cash, and he preferred to be alone anyway.

First, he cleaned the flat. He scrubbed down all of the surfaces in the kitchen, poured disinfectant down the toilet, and scraped the layers of ancient grease from the cooker.

The decrepit vacuum cleaner failed to start, so he walked into the city centre, found an electrical store, and bought new fuses. He stripped down the plug, replaced the old one, and was in luck, the machine actually worked! He removed the paper dust bag, and emptied it with the utmost care, because if it split he didn't have another. When he had finished using the machine he checked the bag again. It was more than half full, mostly with cat hair.

Next, intending to wash all of the sheets and blankets, he stripped down the beds in both of the rooms. And that was when he found the magazines. Stuffed under his "Uncle" Parsa's mattress.

Shabaz was shocked. He had always suspected that Parsa was

not a good Muslim, but these stained and dog eared magazines, contained photographs more shocking than anything Shabaz could ever even have imagined.

That people could do such vile things to one another!

That anyone should take such photographs!

And many of the girls were Asian. Women with no shame. And it was obvious that his Uncle looked at them for his pleasure.

Shabaz replaced the magazines, remade the bed and left the old sheets in place.

Then he went into the bathroom and washed his hands many, many, times.

He tried to watch television. Television, turned out to be mostly rubbish. Idiots, on banal game shows, animations where only the mouths of the characters moved, and stories with daily episodes....Soaps they called them, where all of the characters seemed to do nothing but shout at each other.

He loved cartoons, and before his parents died, he had possessed a large collection of early classic Disney, on video tapes.....Snow White.... Bambi....Fantasia.....Works of Art!

Probably they had been illegal, certainly they would be now.

He found a strong cardboard box, bought an old blanket at a charity shop, and made a bed for his cat. He liked the cat, and the cat seemed to like him. It might cover everything with hair, but at least it was friendly

He had to get out of the flat, he needed some fresh air, and so he walked back into the city centre, located a decent bookshop, and bought guides to the area. Then he sat and read for a day or two, mostly in the coffee shop which formed part of the book store. Sometimes in the flat.

Parsa phoned, and said he would be away for ten more days ....Good!

He took to walking around the City. He walked the ancient walls, visited the Cathedral, the Castle, the Museum. He bought a rusty old mountain bicycle, from another charity shop, there seemed to be a lot of them, and despite the cold, he ventured further afield, out west along that strange, lonely road on the south side of the Solway Firth, where his guide books said the Roman Wall once ran. A road that the sea sometimes flooded.He found an odd monument out there, to an old King of England who had died in that place, fighting the Scots.

What a bleak place he thought....For a King to die.

His books told him that this was once a war zone, that it had been a war zone for hundreds of years. No-man's land between Scotland and England, where the only way to live was to fight.

One writer even went so far as to compare it to Shabaz's own homeland, back in Afghanistan.

Shabaz thought that he quite liked that idea.

Parsa had lied. He would never have been a goatherd. He came from an educated background, and his parents had been teachers, fluent in English. It was they who had taught him to both read, and write that language. But his father and mother had died. Not as a result of war, or terrorism, but in a simple automobile accident.

After the death of his parents, Parsa, who was not really an uncle, but his father's much younger cousin, had taken him in, and at first Shabaz had been grateful, but then slowly he came to realise that it was not in fact an act of kindness, but merely in order to recruit him for the fight against the West.

Shabaz suspected that he, his "Uncle" as he insisted on being called, was paid for recruits, and that with his knowledge of English, Shabaz was a rare commodity. Within weeks, he was sent across the Border into Pakistan, to a "religious school," and there he remained for three long and arduous years. Receiving his "Education."

"Education" he thought? There had been very little learning, just two years of chanting, and of constant repetition. Two years of "programming." Preparing him for the task now in hand.

Programming which had not been completely successful.

Parsa had been gone for eight days, when he met the girl.

Unlike most British cities, Carlisle did not really have an Asian population, and so anyone with a dark skin was obvious.

She was very beautiful, but his teachers would have condemned her as brazen. Her skirt was so very short, and her breasts....She wore a white blouse with a low cut neckline. He couldn't help but look.

He had seen her in the bookshop several times, and he thought that perhaps, she had been looking at him, when his back was turned. But, all of the time he had been watching her reflection in the window.

That happy day he had been browsing the bookshelves, for more information on the ancient warriors they called "Reivers," when he felt a presence beside him. He'd turned, and she was standing beside him. He swore he could feel the warmth from her body on his arm. Then she spoke, and he thought her voice was like music.

"Hello, are you a student? It's just that I've noticed that you spend a lot of time in the history section."

"Oh no," he stammered. "It's just curiosity. I'm staying in the City for a while, and I thought it would be nice to know a bit more about this area. Are you studying at the College here?" he asked.

She laughed. "Oh no, my father owns a restaurant in the town, on one of the streets behind the Cathedral, I work there part of the time, but when its quiet, I come in here.She held out her hand, "I'm Mehri."

He smiled... "Kind and affectionate." Her hand was warm. He didn't want to let go. "I'm Shabaz."

She paused, thoughtful. "Royal falcon?"

He laughed. "From Girishk, where are you from."

She laughed with him. "Carlisle, born and bred. But my father was born in Bala Boluk."

He was amazed. "Who would believe us, two Afghan refugee's meeting together in a bookshop in Carlisle?"

"And are you a refugee Shabaz."

He felt foolish. And then he remembered his cover story. "Oh no, not really, I'm here with my uncle, he's involved in the textile industry. We're looking to make some contacts in this country, but he's been called away for a few days, and so I've some time on my own." And before he could stop himself, he'd asked. "Would you like some coffee?"

They sat in the window of the upstairs cafe, talked, and watched the world go by.

He arranged to meet her there the next day.

She had a small red car, a Nissan Micra.

They had met that afternoon at the bookshop, and he had told here about this place, the ancient graveyard out at Sark, just over the Border, where the old reiver "Kinmont Willie" was supposed to be buried.

"Willie" had been captured by the English back in the 16th

century. They'd locked him up in Carlisle Castle, and his friends had broken into the Keep in the dead of night, and rescued him.

Mehri knew the story, it was quite famous she said. She even went and found a ballad about it in a book, and read it to him. But she hadn't heard about any grave.

They'd bought a map and located Sark. It wasn't more than half an hour away.

It was a fine, sunny winters day, and had Mehri insisted that she should seek her car, and that they should go and look. She said that they could have a meal together when they returned.

And so here they were on a tiny back road, just across the Border. The map had said "Tower of Sark", but there was no sign of a tower, just a farm on the right hand side of the road, and a battered old Toyota pick up parked on the left.

* * *

I packed the camera and its lenses back into the case. The light had been perfect, and I had some decent shots.

Okay, So....It wasn't actually Willie's stone, it was too late, but there was little doubt that he lay somewhere close by.

I leaned back against the fence, and ate a sandwich. Days like this were rare. It seemed tragic really, a place like this just falling into dereliction. But then who really knew it was here? I took the top from the bottle with the opener on my key ring, and took a long drink. Then I raised the bottle in salute, "Here's to you old fellow, wherever you are," and I poured the remainder into the ground at the foot of the long stone.

I turned, picked up the camera case and tripod, and slung them on my shoulder.

A small red car, a Nissan was parked behind my pick-up, and a young Asian couple were standing on the road beside it watching me. I walked the fifty yards or so back to the road, opened the rear door of the cab, and stowed the camera gear on the back seat.

The couple walked towards me. He was slim, about medium height, and wore a scuffed black leather biker jacket and jeans. She was dressed in tight black jeans, long brown leather boots, and a tan jacket with a fur collar. I thought that she looked rather pretty.

"Excuse me Sir," the girl asked, "Could you tell me, is there an old Churchyard nearby?"

I pointed "Aye, It's over there? Looking for "Reivers" by any chance?"

She looked surprised. "It's true then? Kinmont Willie is buried here?"

I smiled, "Probably, but if he is then his stone is missing. Still, there are stones for his kin. It's worth a look."

She thanked me, and they walked off. As they did so, she took his hand in hers. Lucky lad, I thought. It's great to be young.

And just then, the Border weather played one of its odd little tricks, and quite unexpectedly, a sliver of mist rose from the tiny valley behind the graveyard, and as I stood watching, as they walked off down the track, the two figures slowly faded, until I could barely see them at all, and then they disappeared completely amongst the mist, and the old moss covered stones.

The mist drifted over me, I felt the temperature drop.

And a cold shiver ran down my spine

* * *

The man with the camera had been correct.

There was a William Armstrong there, but the date on the stone was too late. They didn't really care, they were together, and it was a beautiful day. They decided that they liked the place too, even if it was a graveyard. It had that odd air that really old places seemed to acquire. Sad, but nice at the same time.

They tried to imagine what it must have been like 400 years earlier. Not quite so peaceful, perhaps.

By the time they left, the sun was dropping towards the horizon.

She had a small flat, on one of the side roads behind the Cumbria Park Hotel, and she parked her car on the street outside.

"Are you sure it will be alright me being here," he asked. "What will your father think, if he hears of it?"

She just laughed. "Shabaz, This is not Afghanistan. My family have lived in this country for many years. I was born here, educated here, I am a British citizen. Here people may do as they wish. And, I may do as I wish." She smiled up at him, and her lips parted slightly. "Here, you also, may do as you wish."

He wondered if her words may have a double meaning.

She opened the door and ushered him inside. His heart was beating very fast. They were alone together, and it all felt so improper. Improper, yet exciting at the same time.

The flat was immaculately kept, and very well furnished. Everything in it seemed new.

She cooked him a meal of pasta with a piquant sauce. Not "Indian" at all. They ate it in the small kitchen.

He complimented her upon her cooking, and she looked pleased. They cleared the dishes away together, and after dinner, they sat together on the sofa and watched a video on the wide screen television.

She leaned against him, and pulled his arm around her shoulders. Her body was warm against him

Half an hour later, she switched the television off. Neither of them had any idea what the video had been about.....Neither cared.

She took him by the hand, raised him from the sofa, and led him to the bedroom.

They met together three more times that week. They drove out along the Solway Coast, and he showed her the old monument he had found.

They found the ancient village church where the old King's body had lain in State. It was built out of stone from a Roman Fort, and behind the altar, built into the wall, was an ancient Celtic head. The church tower had an iron "yett," and a gunloop protecting the door, remnants of the Border Wars.

They drove along Hadrian's wall, and parked at a small car park, in a place called Steel Rig.

The wind was howling from the North, and they wondered how men from the Mediterranean could have stood it there.

They visited a deserted prehistoric stone circle near Penrith, and a kindly farmer took a photograph of them both embracing beside the stone known as Long Meg.

And he spent each of those three nights in her bed.

Shabaz was deeply in love. But at the end of the week, the spell was broken. Parsa called him on his mobile telephone.

He was returning the next day.

* * *

He awoke that morning to the loud banging of the door. Parsa was back, and he was not alone. The other man was a tall thin middle eastern arab with a shaven head and a pock marked face. He did not stay, Parsa simply handed him a railway ticket and bade him goodbye.

All of the time, Shabaz stood in the doorway of the bedroom, but Parsa made no introduction.

His uncle grabbed him by the arm, and hustled him to the window. He pointed into the street below, at a large white Mercedes van, and behind it a battered green Landrover.

"Behold, little falcon, our new transport! The van and the Landrover. Bought in London, and registered to our clothing company, which of course does not really exist." He threw an envelope to Shabaz. "Documents, insurance, and false drivers licence. That is what took me so long. Keep them on you at all times." He dropped into the battered armchair. "Get some clothes on. There's a couple of cases in the back of that van that need unloading. Be very careful with them".

"But, why have we two vehicles", Shabaz asked.

"Because, we must not be obvious. This man Graham must be watched, but he must be unaware of it. No-one looks twice at a white delivery van, and out there in the countryside many farmers drive green Landrovers just like that one. From now on, you are a driver, a delivery man. The white van is for you." He threw him the keys.

Shabaz immediately thought of Mehri, he must invent a story to tell her, to account for his change of occupation.

"......... Kill Graham."

"Pay Attention!" Parsa screamed.

Shabaz started. He knew his "uncle" had been speaking, but he had heard almost nothing.

"Pardon?.....I'm Sorry, I must still be half asleep, I missed most of what you said."

"Idiot!......What's wrong with you? I said that it is now our task to kill the man Graham. But it must be done carefully.....Subtly. Perhaps he shall die in an accident, or perhaps, he must simply disappear without trace. We cannot afford another "incident" like

the one at that cafe, and so we must watch, we must plan, and then we must act. Osama himself has decreed this. He has spoken to me. He is taking a great interest in you, he believes that you are a most promising young man, and it is his personal wish that our mission should succeed." Parsa smiled benignly.
"If we do this, then your reward will be very great indeed."

Shabaz hauled the heavy cases upstairs, heaved them into his "uncles" room, and dropped them with a slight thump onto the floor.
"Careful!" Parsa screamed, "They're delicate"
"What's in them?" Shabaz asked.
Parsa laughed aloud. "Equipment .....and some nice fashionable new clothes for you! You'll find out exactly what, when it's time for you to wear them. But don't go fiddling with those cases, or you may not live to regret it."
He laughed again.
Something it seemed was funny.
Something, was very funny indeed!

* * *

Parsa Khan was happy. He whistled a little tune as he walked south down Botchergate.
These boys, they were so stupid!
This had been the third time he had used the story that he was a long lost relative. He had always been careful, placing each of the boys in a different school, but even so, he doubted that he would use the same story again.
Shabaz though, was his special project.
Most of his "recruits" had been just ignorant village children, for whom he received reasonable but not especially good payment. But Shabaz.... he was fluent in English, and he could easily pass for someone born and bred in this country.
With a shiver of pleasure, he remembered the astonishment on the faces of the parents as he had pulled his lorry alongside, forcing them over the edge of the road, sending them plunging 200 feet into the bed of the river!
How tragic! But how good. For what right had they to return to

his country with their Western manners and education. They ought to have stayed in the United States.

So they were Teachers!..... Teachers of nothing! Polluting the minds of the young with vile ideas. Bringing back with them their despicable music and decadent films. So called "Culture!"

"Culture," which was an affront to any true believer.

But their son? Now he was an asset, and Parsa had been well paid for finding such a one. Killing the parents had been a small, and not entirely unpleasant price to pay for such a prize.

But Shabaz was proving obstinate, and he may have to remind him of his place.

He reached the door with its peeling paintwork. A bell with a speaker above it was located on the doorframe. He looked upwards, and saw the curtains twitch. Someone was watching him.

He pressed the bell, and a woman's voice answered. He spoke "It is Rashid." A buzzer sounded, the lock released, and he opened the door.

A fat woman with very short dark hair, appeared at the top of the stairs. She wore a tight low cut black dress. A small red heart was tattooed on her right breast. She beckoned, "Come on up Dearie. I've done just like you asked. Got you your special little blonde. Got her all "prepared" for you as well."

He took the envelope from his pocket, and handed it to her. The woman opened it immediately and counted the notes. She grunted, apparently satisfied. "Try not to mark her too much this time."

Parsa laughed. "She knows what to expect, and she's being very well paid for it."

The fat woman just shrugged. She liked to give the impression that she didn't care, but, Parsa thought, she actually does have a heart.

Even if it isn't in the right place.

*   *   *

February 14th 2003.

It was four in the afternoon, on a rare, warm, and sunny winters day.

Mrs Kang, and Chuck, wouldn't be in until around six. Shorty and Reb were out back in the kitchen, so I took my coffee and sat in the booth, almost my booth these days, in the corner.

The windows were open and sounds drifted in from the carpark outside, where two camper vans stood alongside each other.

Four young girls were playing on the tarmac. Skipping, one at each end of the long rope turning, the other two running through, bobbing skillfully in the middle.

Innocent, like a movie scene from an earlier, less cynical age.

I closed my eyes and leaned back, drowsy with the heat from the radiators, and the warm sunshine coming in through the window.

And then the girls outside began to chant.

Miss Lucy had a baby,
She called him Sonny Jim,
She put him in the bathtub,
to see if he could swim,

He drank up all the water,
He ate up all the soap,
He tried to eat the bathtub,
But it stuck in his throat,

They sent for the Doctor,
They sent for the Nurse,
They sent for the Lady,
With the Alligator Purse,

"Dead" said the doctor,
"Dead" said the nurse,
"Dead" said the lady,
With the Alligator Purse.

Out, went the Doctor,
Out went the Nurse,
Out went the Lady,
With the Alligator Purse.

A shadow moved across my face. The bench creaked as someone sat next to me, and a familiar voice spoke quietly next to my ear.

Viktor? Why was I not surprised?

"I love your British skipping songs. Quite Charming. But what could it be that she carries in that Alligator Purse? It may be better if they never find out, Eh?"

He smiled.

"Hello Eddie."

Shorty was back through, back behind the counter, at work on his beloved sound system, so I called over to him, told him to bring a couple more cups, and join us.

A minute later he arrived. I nodded by way of introduction. "This is an old friend of mine, and you really do need to meet him." Viktor reached across the table, and took Shorty by the hand.

"Viktor Ivanovich, Mr Higgins."

Shorty's jaw simply dropped. "The" Viktor? He looked at me, "The Viktor from Afghanistan?" I nodded again.

"Jesus Man, I can't thank you enough, I thought I was in that prison for ever."

Viktor just smiled. "You told him it all then?"

"No secrets here Viktor. Me and Shorty have been friends since we were kids, we both know too much about each other."

He looked wistful. "That, I envy you. I've never had anyone that close myself. Could do with it sometimes. I've always had to watch my own back." He paused. "Speaking of which, how did you like my little performance here a couple of weeks ago?" He pointed at the table by the door.

So it had been Viktor. Perhaps looking back I ought to have guessed.

Shorty looked shocked. "That was you? Well, aside from saving us, you did business the world of good. Loads of folk come in here just to look at the bullet holes in the floor."

Viktor liked that. "Quite some ladies you had with you that night as well. No screams, no hysterics, and your lady," he pointed a finger at Shorty, "she just played hell with me for making a mess on the floor."

"Okay, thanks again. But Why?" I asked "Just why are you babysitting us."

He sighed, "It's been a long day. Any chance of a bite to eat before I start, anything will do.

"ADB Okay, Viktor?"

"What's "ADB?"

"All Day Breakfast," bit of a staple around here. We're still working on our main menu, but don't worry, you'll like the breakfast." Shorty walked across to the counter, and called through the hatch.

"Reb! 3 ADB, ASAP + Tea."

"Five," She called back.

"Reb?" Viktor asked.

"Believe it or not," I replied, "in this, our little closed society, we really are all equal. And, no joking, your chef for today is Lady Rebecca Forsythe-Ingram, AKA "Reb." She's the lady you met last month, the one who complained about the mess.

Shorty walked back over. "Won't take long."

"Viktor" I began. "The police identified the black guy you shot. Some lunatic enforcer from Glasgow. What the hell was he doing down here? I've never had much to do with Glasgow in either of my previous incarnations."

"Think about it Eddie, it's simple. Scottish hit man because, they wanted it to look local. But, its not. The contract came from someone else entirely, a very old enemy of yours indeed. Someone at or near the top of Al Qaeda, perhaps even Bin Laden himself......and that someone, wants you dead."

My blood ran cold. Al Qaeda didn't mess about. I tried not to look shocked....Not very successfully.

"They found out about the gold and the cash?" But Viktor just looked amused.

"Not a chance, I covered those tracks properly. No Eddie, I'm afraid it's your little "hobby." Sixty two years ago or not, your problems originate back in World War Two. To be more specific, your problems originate with Rudolf Hess."

"Hess!" What the Hell can Hess have to do with anything?"

Viktor smiled. "Remember five years ago Eddie, when I explained to you about the agents we had placed within your Society, and about our inability to stop their actions?" I nodded. "Well", he continued, "It appears that you have one of them living right here in the Borders, and I believe that he's still active. An ex-Guards Officer, by the name of Anthony Errington Vardy."

Now, *that* was a name from the past! My own past.

But before he could say any more, Reb arrived with our breakfasts. She placed the plates and the teas on our table, and then she took a very long look at Viktor. She raised one hand horizontally in front of her eyes, and studied the top half of his face.

Viktor simply smiled at her.

She nodded, "I suppose I should say "Thank You." Because.....I know who you are. You see, I never forget eyes. So......Thanks for shooting that bastard."

Viktor gave a slight bow. Then he laughed out loud. "Sorry about the mess."

Reb turned away, back towards the kitchen. "Enjoy your black pudding, it's made with blood." She left us, walked off, and went back out through the door.....Oh, I do love a lady with a dark sense of humour!

He looked down at his plate, and pointed "What's that?"

"Geordie burger." I replied.

He cut into it and tried a piece. "Delicious, I must have the recipe, I've not tasted anything quite like it. What's in it? Quail..... or....perhaps Grouse."

"Could be," Shorty replied. "It's a secret, an old Keelman's recipe from the Tyne".

We finished our meal in relative silence. Shorty cleared the plates away, and then he came back over.

I tapped the table. "Right Viktor, now let's hear it."

"Okay then Eddie, and I'll try and keep this as simple as I can.

Remember I once told you how, back in 1991 at the time of the collapse of the "Old" Soviet Union a number of agents "appropriated" certain files from the archives for their own purposes?" I nodded. "Well", he continued, "since we last spoke of the matter, it has become one of my tasks to try and ascertain just who took what, and exactly where those files have ended up. No easy task I can assure you, and I won't bore you with the details. But one of those files related to the flight of Rudolf Hess, and all that I could find out was that it was not an archive file. It was still marked as active.

I now know that it was taken by a high ranking officer who subsequently disappeared. It was one of a number of files he removed, and the interesting thing is that some of others contained both detailed information, and outlines of operations which have subsequently been implemented......Implemented that is, by Al Qaeda! So.....I am now virtually certain, that all of the files removed by that particular man, including the Hess file, were sold on to either Bin Laden, or to one of his close associates.

Now, since our little escapades of five years ago, I have felt obliged to keep a bit of an "eye" on your activities. To watch out for you. We keep files on all British Intelligence agents, both active, and "retired" So I checked further, and your own file is nowhere to be found."

"My file? Why the hell would anyone want my file?"

"Because, Eddie," he tapped himself on the chest, "I was your case officer. I kept that file updated, and I ensured that nothing untoward was entered. I was very careful, but it appears, not careful enough. Because one thing I did enter, was the fact that you had an abiding interest in the flight of Rudolf Hess.You may remember that we had long conversations about it on our drive across Europe?....Well, it seemed an innocent enough notation to make, the Hess crash was very old news, and it helped bulk the file out, but now I'm not so sure. I now believe that it was that Hess comment which has brought trouble to your door. And that the fault lies with me."

"You can't blame yourself Viktor, you couldn't have known."

He smiled wryly. "Eddie, you may not realise it, but you have been making a few waves here the Borders with your questions about Hess. In Britain it's still a touchy subject in "High Places".......Very High Places indeed.

So.... The Hess file is missing, perhaps sold on to Al Qaeda. Your file is missing. Our sleeper agent, the man Vardy, now works as Estate Manager for the Duke of Marchbank, and Marchbank's grandfather was without doubt a Nazi sympathiser.

I don't believe in coincidence Eddie, so I kept on digging.

In January, of this year, two Afghan assassins, men who had been trained by Al Qaeda, made their way Britain, and subsequently on to Glasgow. They hired the man I shot here in the Cafe. Since then they've simply dropped off the radar, and currently I have no idea where they are.

So, here I am. Because, eventually, I believe they will come after you directly. I want them, and I want to know what was in the Hess file. Whatever that plan was, I do not want it implemented. Because, if it is to be implemented, then it appears that you must die. He paused, and gazed out of the window, at the children still playing outside.

"The world is changing Eddie. Things have moved on, since our time in Afghanistan. In my own country various factions now jostle for supremacy, and although at the moment it is difficult to say just what the end result will be, on one thing almost all are united, and that is our eventual integration with, and domination of, the rest of Europe. For, ultimately the aim of Russia, is control of the entire Continent,.

As a result, certain "old" policies have been allowed to continue. Perhaps of course, this was inevitable, since, as I once explained, the agents we placed long ago within Western Society, cannot easily be stopped. They are zealots, believers, fanatics. And whilst you and I were busy in Afghanistan Eddie, hunting Bin Laden, a series of events were taking place here, in this country. Events which my countrymen were able to use to their advantage.

It was perhaps inevitable that the most successful of what I will refer to as our "sleeper agents," were located in your own Labour Party. However, the Labour Party, was out of power in the first half of the 1990's. But then, in 1997, in a kickback by your electorate against the sleaze which appeared to have infected the Conservative Government, "New Labour" swept to power, and this gave our agents within that Party a real chance. Real freedom for the first time, to manipulate national policy exactly as they wished. And those agents, had been programmed to destroy the very idea of "Great Britain."

Their first step along this road, was to attack the actual concept of "Britishness," the last vestiges of your "Empire." And so, quite subtly, they began to direct their "Party Leadership" towards a new policy, a bright new dream, an ideal, of a "Multi Cultural Britain," and frankly that wasn't too difficult.

Little was to be left in place which offended against that vision. And over the last several years, the process has been most carefully orchestrated.

It was initiated in the main by the policy known as "Political Correctness." Nothing must be allowed to offend against the aims of the State, against the views of your "new and open society."

Quite memorably it was decided that Britannia should be "Cool."

"Cool Brittania!" Shorty interjected, "What a load of Bollocks that was!"

Viktor just smiled.

"Almost unnoticed, within your museums, within your galleries, curators were "encouraged" to remove certain "unsuitable" British artifacts from their displays, and to replace them with objects more in keeping with the new image of Britain.

Paintings which were now seen as "nationalistic," or "Imperialist," were gradually removed from the walls of institutions, and placed into storage. Your folklore, and your mythology was carefully "watered down," and British history was slowly and quietly, almost phased out of the school curriculum.

Ever so carefully, ever so gently, the press, the radio, and television, were brought under control. Certain programme themes were encouraged, whilst others were rejected.

Even the most banal of television series have become organs of state propaganda.

And it was done so perfectly, with the very lightest of touches, that few if indeed any, have noticed it at all."

I must have been shaking my head in disbelief, and Viktor held up a hand to silence any comment.

"Trust me Eddie....Your Culture has been "Edited."

I told you once we were masters of blackmail, and had files on many prominent members of you establishment?" He shook his head ruefully, "You would be amazed at the number of entertainers, scriptwriters, and newsmen who didn't want their murky little secrets leaked to the press. Those are the people we have been able to "encourage" by fair means or foul.

Those who bravely refused to go along with our wishes... were "exposed" ... or to use the more modern term, "outed." And after a few rather high profile cases?....Well, then the rest simply fell into line.

On another front, different forces were at work, convincing the public that Britain was the financial powerhouse of the world. A veritable Giant.....The City of London was everything!

No longer was there any need for your country to rely on manufacturing. International Finance was the way forward! And Britain, would lead the way!

Britain would save the planet. Your industry would cease to pollute the environment. Your new "green credentials" would be a beacon, lighting the way for the rest of the world.

Anything slightly dirty you needed, you would have made both easily and cheaply elsewhere.

The culmination of these policies has yet to be initiated, but when it is, it will cause total disaster. Financial Collapse. Perhaps even global financial collapse.

And so, your Nation, who less than one hundred years ago possessed an "Empire upon which the Sun never set," has almost ceased to exist as a cultural entity. Before too long, it will cease to be a financial giant.

If you don't believe me,... just take a good look around."

He paused, and took another sip of coffee.

Shorty stared at him. "Christ..... Viktor, but that's a black picture, and frankly it's kind of hard to believe. I mean, I know things have gone downhill, but to believe that it's all been deliberate?"

Viktor tapped the table. "What I have told you is only part of the plan. The part which affects Britain. We have also been hard at work elsewhere. But ultimately, it is intended that Britain will provide the trigger for what is to follow.

That's not all of it, and from your personal point of view, its not the worst. As I've told Eddie in the past, it was our policy from the 1960's to infiltrate, and to bring down Western Society, and I do believe that those policies have been "successful," if indeed such horrendous destruction can be deemed success. But for Britain, that was only the first part of the plan. My countrymen have destroyed your image, corrupted your society, and only one thing remains."

"And what's that?" Shorty asked.

"The Aristocracy, and the Monarchy." I answered

"Correct Eddie," Viktor replied. "And that I believe, is where the Hess File comes in."

Shorty leaned back in his chair,

"So Viktor, What's your angle on all of this? I mean until today, apart from a few hints from Eddie, I thought that the world came apart on the day Dylan went Electric. And suddenly here we are, two Geordie lads, being told by a one time KGB agent, in a Cafe in Langholm, that the Ex Soviet Union has destroyed the very fabric of our society.That the ruling classes are about to be brought down by something brought into Scotland 62 years ago by the second in command to Adolf Hitler, and that two Al Qaeda assassins are out to kill us!

You expect us to believe all of that? You know, coming out of the blue like this, it all seems rather far fetched don't you think? I've no doubt that some of what you say is correct, and I'm quite sure that you believe that all of it is. But".....he went on. "Perhaps you are giving your "agents" a little bit too much credit.

Because....By God!...We're British!......And, personally I think that the British are quite capable of engineering their very own downfall, without any outside interference at all!

Currently, we even have a Prime Minister who believes that a stupid grin, and the ability to play the guitar badly, are suitable qualifications to be a world leader!"

And frankly, despite Viktor's story, I couldn't help but agree with Shorty on some of that at least.

He nodded. "Fair enough, if I was hearing this for the first time I would be sceptical as well, but whatever the causes, the results will be the same. The Hess plan is certainly active, witness the attempt on your lives in January?"

Shorty resumed. "Look, Me and Eddie, we're long time Socialists. Old Fashioned Socialists. We're from a *mining* background. You're talking about our Aristocracy, for God's sake! Our very own Class Enemy! What do you expect us to do? Help you to bring them down? Or help you stop it?"

Viktor shrugged, "Some years ago, I told Eddie that I was something of an Anglophile. That has not changed. Frankly, having lived my early life in the Soviet Union, I came to admire Britain. You had what we lacked, you possessed individuality, you were a nation of eccentrics, of adventurers, of innovators. You had National Identity, and moreover you were proud of it.

The old USSR, was a fine ideal, and it ought to have worked, but it was grey, it was soulless, and it lacked romance.

I still do admire your country, and perhaps I regret the part I have played in bringing about it's downfall. Neither am I certain that whichever faction should ultimately come to power in Russia, that they will necessarily have the interests of the common man at heart. But, whatever happens, whatever the outcome of the next few years, it is perhaps possible that I may decide to stay here, and make my home in this country.

You are still an island, you may yet find it possible to retain some of your identity. And a grey nation stretching from France to Russia is perhaps not a place where I would wish to live.

He turned to me, "Eddie, You and I have a common shared experience, and I like to think that we are perhaps friends? I could not stand by and watch, whilst you were hunted down by Al Qaeda. I believe in the case of Hess, that with your own background, you are perhaps the best qualified person, and the best placed, to decide what action should or should not be taken.

Therefore let us combine our talents, and investigate this together."

He reached across the table, and we shook hands, but I didn't think that I was ready yet to tell him that I already knew exactly what it was that Hess had brought with him to Britain.

"So where are you staying Viktor?"

We were standing together, out in the car park. It was dusk, and the camper vans had left.

Now I could see a third van, dark green, and much larger, parked under the trees at the far side. Not quite a Winnebago, but big just the same. A mountain bike was strapped to a rack on the rear.

Viktor pointed towards it. "What the well equipped spy is driving these days, come on over and take a look. In this country, no-one looks twice at a camper van. Just some crazy mountain biker, taking a few months of unpaid leave to see Scotland. I move it around regularly, and I've found a couple of decent places out in the forestry. The bike gets me around short distances, and keeps me fit at the same time." He laughed. "I just tell everyone I'm a freelance writer, researching for a novel about the old Borders, that I've got Border ancestors, and that I'm also researching my family history. I say my grandmother was a Graham actually, hope you don't mind? I mean that's what we're talking about if anyone asks."

By now we'd reached the side door of his van. He took a key ring from the pocket of his jacket, opened the door, and ushered me inside. He flicked a switch, and the lights came on.

Impressive. He had a small bedroom, a galley kitchen, and a bathroom. His main lounge was at the rear of the vehicle. He'd a comfortable arm chair, and a desk with a swivel chair, all bolted to the floor. Plenty of lockers.

Viktor closed the curtains. "It's amazing the amount of equipment you can store in a vehicle like this Eddie, know what I mean? Should have thought of it years ago. Anything you need, just ask." He opened a cupboard, took out a bottle of vodka, poured two glasses, and passed one to me.

"But I brought you a little present anyway." He reached further back into the drinks cabinet, there was a slight click, something slid aside, and his hand came back out holding a package wrapped in plastic and sealed. He handed it to me. "It's an old friend, No numbers, no record."

That familiar smell greeted me when I broke the seal......Gun oil.

It was a Colt 45 Automatic, complete with three loaded magazines. Just like the one Viktor knew I had carried in Afghanistan. He passed me an extra box of ammunition.

"I don't doubt you have something of your own already, but that one's untraceable. Any "unfortunate incidents," and you'll be in the clear, at least as far as the gun's concerned. But if you do have to use it, try and keep one of them alive, because I really do need to ask them a question or two."

Of course I knew that he was right. They'd tried once, and they probably would try again. So I didn't argue, I took the gun, and I raised my glass in salute. "Thanks Viktor.... So you're going to babysit me?"

"Not exactly, but like I said, where you are, they will be. Eventually. And I want them. I want to know what they have. Don't worry, I won't get in the way, in fact most of the time you'll not be seeing me at all. You won't mind if I drop in at the Cafe, now and again though I hope?"

"No problem there, "The More the Merrier." Tell you what, why not park up here for a day or two? There's caravan parking round the back, Shorty and Reb won't mind, and the food's good.

It can get quite lively in the evenings. Bit of music now and again. There's just one thing you ought to know."

He had been re-arranging the cabinet, and turned to face me. "What?"

“The two women who were sitting with us when you shot the black guy. They’re some sort of investigators. Possibly even intelligence officers?”

He just laughed, “Oh, don’t worry, I know all about them. No doubt they’ll tell you what they’re up to in due course.”

And so Viktor joined our happy little band.

* * *

February 28th 2003.

Zhang.

In his private sanctum, in one of the highest chambers of the ancient tower of Welldean, “Master Zhang,” that is........ Zenji, Behdin, Zhang Wenming Bates, Yaqui Shaman and Medicine man, One time associate of Carlos Casteneda, Member of the Native American Church, Shaolin Master of Kung Fu, Founder of the “Ancient Forest” School of Tai Chi and Qi gong, and Keeper of the Seven Sacred Bowls.........Closed his eyes, reclined back upon the crimson cushions of his gilded throne, relaxed his plump little body, and prepared himself for meditation.

The corners of his oriental eyes creased with little crows feet of happiness. His neatly trimmed white beard, shone with aromatic oil. His still-dark hair gleamed, brushed back from his high forehead, and held in the shortest of pony tails.

The great gilded throne with its dragon arms, was the gift of a grateful American acolyte.

Ahhh..... She had been a wonderful student, amazingly endowed, gifted, and most generous. He would miss having her around. However, it was time for his renown to spread across the Atlantic, and she was now his emissary, launched upon her missionary voyage to spread word of the Gospel of Welldean.

In due course she would return to his haven. They always did. The stresses of the world were many, and, no doubt she would bring more lovely ladies back with her. All wishing to partake of the benefits his learning. All willing to contribute towards the progress of his mission.

Strange, but fortunate, that so many beautiful women found life so stressful. Such a fine thing that he could assist them towards inner peace. And in the meantime, until she returned, there were others, in fact, quite a lot of others, all of whom came to find the true path to enlightenment. All of whom left .....Satisfied.

Life, Zhang thought was good.

All of those years spent in his lonely cell, the constant study, the strict regimes, the exercises. All had been to a purpose. Lonely roads which needs must, he had travelled. All to reach this....the ultimate.... state of perfection.

So many years of work and contemplation, to achieve his goal, but now with the Welldean Centre, he had perhaps received his true reward.

He remembered the day when he stumbled upon his greatest treasure. Surely, his feet had been guided on the path? Others claimed to own similar relics, but most were mere fakes or copies. Welldean stood far above them all, for his seven sacred Himalayan singing bowls, were the oldest in existence. Perhaps even meteoric in origin. Unbelievably old......their existence long thought to be no more than rumour.

Powerful..... For, beyond doubt they were imbued with the spirits of the earliest masters.

They had been brought to Britain by George Bogle the 18th century Scottish adventurer, diplomat and explorer. Bogle, the man who first brought knowledge of Tibet and its mysteries to the world.

Following his death they had lain, unrecognised, near discarded, in the possession of his descendants, who lacking facilities to display of all their treasures in appropriate and secure surroundings, loaned the bowls to the Gulbenkian Museum of Oriental Art in Durham, where they were fully and correctly recorded, classified, and inventoried. Then, due once again to lack of space they were consigned to storage, "pending further study, prior to publication."

And, in storage, they were quite simply...... Forgotten!

Just seven old metal bowls from Tibet.

But the ways of the universe are indeed mysterious, and so in the fullness of time they came to reside at Welldean, where they served their true purpose, bringing peace and tranquility to all who heard their song.

A slight draught disturbed his reverie. The door to his sanctum had opened. Soft footsteps approached. Faint perfume drifted to him. He opened his eyes.

Fragrant Lotus stood before him. Young, dark, full bosomed.

Oh God, she was Beautiful!

He gave all of his female students exotic names. They seemed to like it.

He spoke, his voice soft, soothing.

"Yes, My child, how may I help? You appear troubled."

She bowed her head, and knelt before him.

"Master, I am so sorry to disturb your meditation. Forgive me, but I am puzzled. Last night I overheard two of the older students. They spoke of a legend. They claimed that certain men, holy men, men who have studied the ancient arts and sacred texts in solitude for many years, claim to have the ability to create Tulpa. And, I know, that you, are acknowledged by all here to be," she paused, and then continued, "The most Holy Master in all of this land. Therefore, Master Zhang, may I most humbly request your honoured opinion upon the concept of Tulpa?"

Careful.... thought Zhang, who had no idea what on earth she was talking about.

He sighed, and raised his eyes to heaven. "Ahhhh......The Tulpa. It has been many, many years since that question was last asked."

He was silent for minutes on end. Then he looked back, and stared straight into her eyes. "This involves the secret teachings. Teachings far, far above your present status. I ought perhaps, to leave your question unresolved,...... until that is you reach further enlightenment.

He paused again, then smiled reflectively.

"However, once, I was young like you. Young, and curious....... Perhaps, it is good that you have this thirst for knowledge, and therefore," he raised his finger, "I believe that I shall attempt to assist you to proceed further along our sacred path. Who knows....you may have the makings of a great Master.

I shall retire now and meditate....For the Tulpa requires a great deal of thought. a great deal of preparation." (he laughed inwardly, ...and a great deal of bullshit!)

"The process may tire me, but tomorrow evening, when we meet again for the laying on of hands. I will perhaps enlighten you further, for now though, Fragrant Lotus, leave me to ponder."

She lowered her head. "Thank you Master, I am most grateful that you spend your time in the instruction one so unworthy." She rose, backed to the door, bowed, and silently left the chamber.

Zhang climbed to his feet. Oh, He adored Reiki! ...He'd even developed his own variations....And ....Wow! .....Did he look forward to that laying on of hands.

He turned, took a key from his robe, and walked to a door in the corner of the room. The chants of the novices, the faint scent of incense, drifted from the chambers below.

Tulpa.....? He must consult the Holy Texts. In fact, he must consult the oracle itself.

He opened the door. Eerie blue light suffused the room. There was a barely audible humming. He stepped within. Seated himself before the oracle. And prepared to ask the question.

He logged on to Wikipedia. And murmered

"Oh",...."Apple of my Eye"....."Great God Macintosh,"

"Now"... "What the Fuck...." He tapped the keys, "....is a Tulpa?"

He laughed aloud.

Zhang just loved the Internet.

* * *

A full moon was rising, a deep yellow, an almost orange moon, still low on the horizon.

It was well after ten, the shutters were up, and we were closed for the night.

Shorty had finished clearing up, and was sitting quietly in the corner booth. Unusually, Reb was nowhere around. Something was wrong. He was dressed in dark green cargo trousers, and his old camouflaged combat jacket. He just sat there, saying nothing, cutting something up with his fixed blade bowie. It looked like an egg.

Worse still, Creedence was thudding, muted from the Wurlitzer. Appropriate....."Bad Moon Rising." Shorty's battle song.

"Where's Reb? He looked up from his work.

"Gone off home to do some knitting."

"Knitting?" I thought, she despises knitting.

"Hope you don't mind, I borrowed your camo paint, the green stuff you paint your face with."

I strolled across and sat down opposite him. Now I could see what he was actually doing. It made no sense. He was carefully cutting a ping pong ball in half.

"What's that for."

"Oh, just a little idea I've had in mind for years. Thought on a nice night like this, there might be a bit of hunting, ...rabbits and stuff."

Rabbits, Okay, but what I wondered, was the "Stuff?"

He stood up, put the two halves of the ball in his pocket, walked over to the door, and threw me the keys.

"Have some supper Eddie. There's beer in the fridge, I'll be out till late, so just lock up when you leave.

"Where are you really going?"

He shrugged. "You know what they say, "Ask me no questions, and I'll tell you no lies."

He walked out of the door without another word. Trouble, for certain.

The track on the jukebox changed."Blue Moon," from Shorty's "American Werewolf" selection.

Boy, that man just loved a soundtrack to his life.

* * *

Tulpa! A being brought into existence solely by the willpower of a yoga master. How cool was that!

As his American students, would exclaim.... Wow.... Gee.... Neat.... Cool........Awesome!

If only ....If? ... Could I do that? Zhang giggled. One could but try. And if it didn't work, then perhaps he could create such an illusion.

Humming quietly beneath his breath, he descended the spiral of the tower. He walked the path through the Zen garden, with its white raked gravel and stones. Indeed, he thought, the shadows were beautiful in the moonlight. He crossed the ornamental garden, to the corner of the Estate, to the door of his private bungalow.

He entered. Ahh....The automatic heating had come on. He loved comfort. Must be all of those years in his cold cell. Still, a student must suffer to learn the Mysteries.

He drew a warm bath, added a little of the sacred lotions, whipped up a froth of bubbles, poured whisky from a cut glass decanter, and luxuriated for half an hour in the soothing waters. Then, he dried himself, threw the towel on the floor for his servant to replace in the morning, and made his way to his sleeping quarters.

From a golden loop on the belt of his silken robe, the gift of another acolyte, he selected an elaborately pierced key. Crossing to a fine lacquer cabinet in the corner of the room, he inserted the key into the lock, and turned. The well oiled mechanism clicked open.

Now,.......He must meditate.......He must attempt to summon the Tulpa. So.....How to proceed? How to create the right mindset? Thoughtfully, he began his selection from the cabinet. A few pipes of the sacred herbs........ a wafer or two of the magic sacrament?..... A mushroom perhaps?......He poured another tumbler of Glenmorangie, just, he mused, to add a small Scottish variation. He gathered his materials, dimmed the lights, and made his way over to the great four poster bed with its satin sheets. He sat crossed legged on the bed, and prepared his mind for meditation.

He clicked the remote control. Ever so softly, his favourite meditation music commenced, and from the Bose speakers, Annie Lennoxs' voice crooned............

"Sweet Dreams are made of this"

Who was he to disagree?

How he loved those lyrics.

An hour later he was collapsed insensible upon the bed, a wondrous, stupefied smile fixed upon his face.

* * *

Above Welldean House, far far above, the bowl of night was purple black, a dark jewelled vessel, within which sailed the silver moon.

Below, in the valley, the road was a slender luminous ribbon, undulating through the hills. The river gleamed like molten quicksilver.

3.a.m "The Midnight of the Soul." Nothing disturbed the silence.

Well, almost nothing. Almost silence. For along the winding road, came a small green gnome, mounted on a strange grey, and silent steed. A steed that carried no lights.

They had never caught on, Shorty thought, these LE Velocettes. Expensive in their day, no real power, 55 miles an hour if you were lucky and there was no headwind. But the plods had liked them, 'cause they were reliable, did 95 to the gallon, and best of all, they made almost no noise.

"Noddy bikes." "Silent LE's," they called them. So Mr. Plod

bought enough of them to keep the model in production. Shorty loved this bike. It could have been designed especially for him.... nice low seat. His was a mark 111, 1961, a 192cc water cooled four stroke. An opposed twin. In original Met. Police grey.

Hard to see at night. What was it they said, "at night all cats are grey?" Well this cat was grey....and green. He laughed gently to himself. He rode by moonlight.......Ill met by moonlight?

He thought of his "equipment" in the panniers.

He had almost reached the hamlet of Yarrow. "Hamlet of Yarrow?" He chuckled ....old joke.

"Tae be, or no tae be, Aye......that is the question."

.....Oor Wullie.

The turn for Deuchar came up on the right, and he swung onto the side road. He passed the site of old Deuchar Tower, and reached the turn for Welldean. The tyres barely swished as they moved from tarmac, to the gravel of the long drive.

Now, high above, he could see the silhouette of the house and its tower black against the sky. No lights showed.

The drive rose, and climbed steeply. Five minutes later, he pulled to the right, through a gap in the tall rhododendrons lining the drive. He was in luck. Bedrock surfaced just behind the bushes.

He put the bike onto its stand, and opened the panniers. From one he took a military haversack, from the other he removed a camouflage net. He covered the machine, then stepped back and examined his work. Near invisible, but a faint aroma of hot motorcycle hung in the still air. He'd just have to risk that, the chances of anyone on foot out here at this hour were remote indeed. Most of this lot were scared of the dark anyway. He walked off into the bushes.

Slowly, silently, he made his way towards the corner of the Welldean Estate, his passage marked only by the slight tremor of a branch, the quiver of a leaf.

No more disturbance than that made by any other small hunting animal.

* * *

The Tulpa!

Master Zhang stirred.

God, He felt rough. He must have gone a bit too heavy on the old herbs and sacraments.

He tried to breath deeply. It was difficult. A heavy weight was pressing on his chest. He struggled to open his eyes. Slowly the room came into focus.

Arrrggghhhh!.........."Something"..... was sitting on his chest.

Something small, something green, heavy, and...... Horrible!

It was balding. It's large head glowed in the diffused lighting. Dark hair straggled down either side of its squashed face. Great bulbous shining white eyes stared down at him.

The Tulpa!

He had achieved it!

By the power of his mind alone, he had created it. A being of pure thought. With only his mind, and of course the sacred herbs.

But wait!.... Why was the Tulpa singing quietly?

"Dem bones, dem bones, dem dry bones?" The singing ceased.

"AAAhhhh......Grasshopper," it intoned.

Those words! From his early days back in his cell. What was this, some kind of weird peyote flashback? That had never happened before.

Then ever so slowly, the horrid creature reached up, wrenched the white eyes from it head, and placed them in the pocket of its combat jacket.

Ugghhh.... revolting!

But...For God's sake....... Why was the Tulpa wearing a combat jacket? Worse...Why was it wearing surgical rubber gloves? His fuddled mind searched for an answer.

The creature spoke again. "Greetings Master Zhang." And there was something strangely familiar about that voice.

A dreadful truth formed in his mind. *This* was no Tulpa. *This* creature was far more dangerous. And he screamed.....

"Seppy Higgins!"

The creature started, it peered down into his face for what

seemed like an age, and then... It spoke......!

"Blooody Hell! Oswald... "Ratty".....Hanratty!

Well,....That explains a lot. Haven't seen you since '94, when they let you out of Durham.The old cell was never quite the same without you. You always were a bundle of laughs. In a pathetic sort of way."

Shorty paused, and stared off reflectively, humour in his eyes. "Remember that time in the showers, Ratty, when you dropped the soap, got all annoyed when you slipped on it, and shouted out....."Oh Bugger It!" in front of Big Stevie the Poof? We laughed about that for years. Stevie was only 5' 6", I wonder why they called him Big? Any idea,.......Eh Ratty? Quite the legend you made for yourself that day! I'll have to E.Mail Big Stevie..... Maybe put you two back in touch."

"Zhang" was starting to recover now. Starting to panic. He remembered the rumours about Septimus "Shorty" Higgins, and his methods of dealing with his enemies.

He was sweating. He tried to raise his right hand to wipe his brow. It wouldn't move. He tried his left. It was stuck fast.

And that was when lucidity returned, his mind finally cleared, and he realised that he was spreadeagled, bound hand and foot to the bed, with a violent, psychopathic, green painted midget killer astride of his chest.

"Seppy" reached behind his back and produced a very large, very shiny bowie knife. It's honed edge gleamed wickedly.

"Now, "Master Zhang," I've got hours to play our little game. This is a nice set up you have here. I had no idea who you were "Master Zhang." I mean ...Ratty,.....I guessed you were a fraud, but this really is a surprise. You....An Oriental Master.... Do tell me,.....how did it all come about?"

He paused, thoughtful. "Hold on, though, I remember now. The prison library? You took out every episode of Kung Fu! That's where I got "Grasshopper," you drove me mad, day in, day out watching it. And when you worked in the kitchens you burned your forearms trying to carry hot pans. Then you blackmailed the barber into giving you a haircut like David Carradine. Got yourself the nickname "Kwai Chang" Hanratty. You used to go down to the Gym, and make everyone laugh. Said you were going to China to study when you got out.

But I remember you from the old days back in Blyth. That's why they put us in the same cell. Remember? 'Cause we came from the same place".

Shorty waved the knife, and then pointed it at Ratty. "But in those days, the furthest East you'd ever been was on a glorified dirty weekend, a Pit outing from Bates's Colliery. Three days to Rosse Burt in Amsterdam.

And as far as I recall, the only Temple you ever entered, was Angela Temple from Cambois. And when her Dad found out he hoyed (threw) you off the ferry, and you had to swim back to Blyth. We all thought that was great. You came out of that river a proper little drowned Ratty."

Shorty rose from his position straddling Zhang, and wandered about the room. He opened a cabinet alongside the widescreen television and its DVD player. Chronologically arranged on the shelves was every episode of Kung Fu. Next to them were the Master Carradine's instructional DVD's on Tai Chi, Qi Gong, and Kung Fu.

But Wait..! ...What was this doing here... Hand labelled in black felt tipped pen...."Bambi!".... Ahhh...."Ratty" likes Classic Disney! Hold on though... Shorty looked closer at small print on the cover... "Bambi Woods"...in..."Debbie does Dallas" ...1978! .....Ha!.... Vintage Porn!

He waved a couple of the Carradine DVD's in the direction of Master Zhang. "Oh,.....Ratty, you've kept the faith."

He rummaged through the rest of the cabinet. Simple instruction in Reiki, decent DVD's on Yoga. Tantric Sex. couple of books by Carlos Casteneda, Teachings of Don Juan and all of that hippy rubbish. Sheafs of print outs from the web.

"Okay.....Most of it's obvious. I mean it's what you are Ratty. A Con Man. That's how you ended up in Durham. Fiddling savings and pension money out of old ladies at that old folks home in Cowpen. After you got your redundancy money from the Pit.

Of course!..... You call yourself Bates! In memory of Bates's Pit, where you used to work! Nice to know you've a still got sense of humour. Now, just tell me about how you came by this place, how you acquired these magic singing bowls, and where you got those slanty eyes......Then we'll get down to business."

Ratty started.... Business? What Business? His mind raced.

Shorty resumed. "I've been told you've a Chinese father, but the nearest your Dad got to China was the Sun Sun Restaurant in

Waterloo Road, and they even banned him from there."

Ratty twisted his head, in the corner of his vision he could just see Shorty at the cabinet. He had a military looking haversack open, and was carefully removing cables, what looked like a clock, and a box with an aerial. Zhang really began to panic.

"For God's sake, Seppy......Shorty......What are you doing?.....What do you want?"

Shorty, stopped what he was doing, and walked over to the bed. He looked down on Ratty, quite a novelty he thought, for a man of his height to be able to look down on someone.

He said nothing, he just stared into Ratty's face with his eerie pale blue eyes. The silence stretched, and the icy fingers of terror clutched at Zhang's bowels.

"Seppy,....Shorty....,whatever it is you're planning....... Please ......Stop.....Don't!" he whimpered. We were best of mates in Durham, nearly a year in the same cell. This is a good little number I've got here. I'm respected. My student's are rich, generous, I get pop stars, politicians, famous folk."

He simpered, "Always lots of pussy too."

Shorty smiled. Ratty hesitated, Shorty he thought, liked that bit about pussy.

"I'll cut you in on it. Introduce you as a Master. Say you've lived for years in China perfecting your Art. It's dead easy, just say nothing and look inscrutable. I'll even put you in touch with my surgeon, and get your eyes done up like mine. I could do with a bit of company, someone to reminisce with about the good old days back in Blyth".

Shorty laughed out loud. "Good old days back in Blyth.....With you! So that's what you think, Eh Ratty? That you can buy your way out of this, with a job offer and promise of a bit of spare pussy?....."Wronngg!" he intoned his voice ringing like a bell. "Now this is what this is about Ratty....This is the "good news, I..... Septimus "Shorty" Higgins.....am about to become betrothed!"

God! Ratty thought, he's completely unhinged.

"But," Shorty resumed. "Here, for you, is the "bad news." The Lady of my choice, the Lady who has captured my affections is a Lady indeed. In fact, the Lady Rebecca Forsythe-Ingram. Known as Reb to me, and to you, I do believe, as "Little Hibiscus Blossom." A student of yours, now residing permanently at my humble abode.You have perhaps noted her absence of late?

She chooses not to return here to your seat of Celestial Enlightenment."

Ratty started to relax, and Zhang took over once more.

"Ahhhhh......Little Hibiscus Blossom," he breathed, "a fine student." With a very rich Daddy and Brother he thought......

"No problem at all Shorty, may I offer you my congratulations in advance. You are blessed with the greatest of good fortune. And as the Lady Rebecca is aware, all of my students are free to leave whenever they wish. Now, just release me, and I promise I'll forget all about this little temporary unpleasantness that you've caused me."

Shorty cast a benign eye upon Zhang. "I fear the purpose of this little interview has not yet registered with you Oh Master, for there remains to be settled the little matter of the Lady Rebecca's dowry. Around £50,000 pounds, entrusted to her by her father. A sum which I believe you may be holding for her in safekeeping? And have in fact been holding for these last several years. With compound interest, and a small fee for my services, I estimate that her investment ought now to be in the region of,"......he removed a notebook and a calculator from the pocket of his combat jacket, tapped keys, scribbled on a page, tore it out, and placed it on the bedside table.

"That reads, Sixty nine thousand, three hundred, and fifty five pounds, and ninety nine pence. But since I know you, knock off the ninety nine pence, and"....Shorty paused for effect .... "You're going to transfer exactly that amount of money to the account number on that paper."

Zhang screamed. "She gave me the fifty thou! The silly bitch needed my help. She was grateful......They all are!" He stopped immediately. He'd said too much.

"Hmmmmm".... Shorty mused. "That's about what Reb and me reckoned. "They all are." How much have you fiddled Ratty? What's your miserable skin worth do you reckon?

£69,355.......I think you're getting off cheap.

Now, this is how it's going to go down. Do you remember, how much I love music? Got a B.A. in "History of Music" in Durham I did. You hated the noise I made, all of those old CD's.

You remember the "Delta Rhythm Boys?" You particularly hated them." And he began to dance around the room, spinning and leaping into the air, a tiny green imp, waving a huge and glittering blade.

"Dem bones, Dem bones, Dem dry bones!
Dem bones, Dem bones, Dem dry bones,
Dem bones, dem bones, Dem dry bones,"

Shorty ceased dancing, and pointed with the great knife.

"Now!...........Hear the word of the Lord!

You,....... Oswald "Ratty" Hanratty have sinned most grievously, and needs must make confession to Father Higgins. And, Who knows......? If the confession be truly, completely, and faithfully given, and an appropriate penance be received, to wit £69,355, then in the fullness of time, you may yet receive absolution for your sins."

He began laying out equipment on the bed. Lengths of electrical cable, a two socket plug, a time clock, the transmitter with the aerial, a microphone, an ugly looking pair of alligator clips, and a roll of duct tape. Zhang stared, wide eyed. and whimpering.

"Don't fret now Ratty, just follow my instructions and you may even survive."

May....Survive? Zhang thought. Now, the little lunatic was singing to himself, quietly......

"Ohhhh........The cable's connected to the time switch,
The time switch's connected to the terminals,
The radio's connected to the microphone."

Then he took up the knife again, and with one stroke he cut Zhang's flowing silk pyjama's from his navel to his groin.

"Uuggh....Revolting! Shorty exclaimed, peering down.

All of the colour had drained from Zhang's face.

"Don't worry, I'm a fastidious little fellow." He held up his gloved hands. "Just avoiding any unpleasant bacteria which may be present." Not to mention avoiding any fingerprints, he thought.

He picked up the alligator clips. "Its okay, I've blunted the jaws, and weakened the springs. You'll be safe for an hour or two. Nothing will rot and drop off later." There were two clicks, and Zhang went rigid.

"Swanicles" Shorty intoned, "that's what the Great Milligan christened them, and that's where the electrodes are now attached".

He picked up the tape, tore off two strips, and applied them over the clips. "That's it then. Wriggle you may, but those clips won't come off." He took a third piece of tape from the roll, and covered Zhang's mouth.

"Now Ratty, Remember "Allo Allo?" All those repeats we watched in the television room at Durham? Ah,....How we laughed.

"Vell".......he giggled. "As ve say in Ze Resistance, "Leesten Carefulley I veel say zees only vonce."

And.......This is how it all works. You are now incapable of releasing yourself. Your "swanicles" are wired to the mains. But," he raised a finger," there is a time clock preventing the current reaching your family jewels, and that clock I will set for one hour."

"This," He held something aloft, "is a microphone attached to a small radio transmitter, I am placing it next to your head. Any words you speak will be transmitted to a recording machine in my pocket. I'm going to leave you now, and, as I leave I will switch on the power to this little system.

Exactly one hour later, the alarm on that clock over there will ring, the connection to the electrodes will be made, and.......

"ZAP!" he yelled. "Sizzling sausage time!

"Oh...How I wish I could be here to see it! But", he raised his finger again......"ZAP!" It need not be.

IF..... five minutes after I leave this room, you begin to talk into that microphone.

IF..... you truly and accurately, confess all.

IF......you tell of your time in Durham, and how from there you came to be Master Zhang,

IF......you explain how you have been systematically gathering wealth ever since.

IF......I get all of your confession on my recorder. And, I mean all......."

He paused. "Oh, and add on a bit about how you came by those magic bowls I've heard so much about.

Then, and only then, I will make a telephone call.

And then, VOILA! You will be rescued!

If not...... "ZAP!".....he screamed.

Of course,.....Your rescuers may require an explanation for your unusual predicament. Tantric experimentation perhaps?"

He laughed insanely, ripped the tape from Zhang's mouth, walked to the door, bent down, and switched on the power.

He waved, "Ta Ta For Now!" And the door closed behind him.

"SSHHOORRTTYYY." Zhang screamed.

But there was no-one there to hear him.

Five minutes later Shorty lay in the grass alongside his motorcycle. The Moon had set, and he gazed into the fathomless depths of the Universe glittering far, far, above him.

Another fine performance. What a pity no-one had witnessed it. He had missed his vocation, he really ought to have been on the stage.

Then, through his headphones began the full, and tearful confession of Master Zhang.

In his pocket his mini disc recorded it all,

It made fascinating listening.

* * *

The Confession of Master Zhang.

Heavy breathing sounded through the headphones, a muffled shuffling, a light sobbing, and courtesy of the wonders of digital sound, clearer than if he had been in the room, Shorty heard Zhang begin to speak.

"Okay, You win.......My name is Oswald Hanratty, I was born in 1960, and brought up in Blyth, on the North East Coast of Northumberland.

I am not a good man, I have sinned. My early life was spent working at Bates's Colliery, but in 1985, I was made redundant. I invested my redundancy money, but it was not enough to live on, and so I took a job as a male nurse tending old folk, at a home in Cowpen. And that was when temptation crept up on me.

It began simply enough. Old ladies seemed to like me, and I was happy enough, letting them stay up late to play their Daniel O'Donnell tapes in the lounge, and fetching them illicit fish and chip suppers, when no-one was about. But they always told me to just keep the change, for a beer or a night out, and I realised that the old dears actually had more money than they could ever use.

So, gradually I started, just taking a pound or two extra here and there, nothing that would be noticed. Half of them were so forgetful that they wouldn't have known anyway.

Then I began to seek their pensions for them, and sometimes I would forget to pass it on. It didn't feel like real theft. I mean...Nobody actually got hurt.

Of course, it got worse, and then one day there was a complaint that money was missing.

I had five bank accounts, and the Police only found one, but what was in it was too much by far, and to cut a long story short, I ended up doing time in Durham Prison.

Three years I was in there, and it showed me the light, for in Durham, I found my true path, and all because of Master Carradine.......Tai Chi, Qi gong, Kung Fu, and....Mysticism.

I got out in 1994, with four of my bank accounts still active. I didn't report to any probation officers, I didn't go back to Blyth, I went straight from the Prison to the railway station, and took the first fast train to London.

Destiny called.

Money talks. So off I went to Harley Street, and had my eyes done Oriental.

I holed up in a cheap hotel until the bruising cleared up, and then I bought myself a new identity. Passport, driving licence, the works. You make good contacts in Durham, so I knew where to go.

I came back to Durham as Zhang. Went to the Gulbenkian Museum of Oriental Art. You see I'd done my homework in Prison, and I knew all about Mr. Bogle, and his acquisitions in Tibet. All about the "Singing Bowls" he'd brought back, and with my new oriental eyes, and the right story, there was no problem getting a job as a volunteer, and doing a bit of classification work.

I bought seven replica bowls on the web, made a good job of oxidising and ageing them,and then one day, just as I knew it would, my opportunity arose. A bit of work on the Bogle collection. So, out with the old, and in with the new.

Then, with the greatest regrets, I had to leave the Gulbenkian, to go back east to study. And off I did go, but not east. North.

I bought myself a light tent, some equipment, and got on the train to Edinburgh. It might not be exactly out of the country, but it was a long way from Blyth.

For three weeks, I walked south into the hills, finding quiet spots, doing a little Tai Chi, fishing, just enjoying the quiet.

Then, I came up the Yarrow valley, turned right past Deuchar

Tower, and walked right up into this place. I pitched the tent, made a meal, had a beer, and that evening I did a little practice in a clearing.

I didn't know it but I was being watched, and when I was finished this old guy came out of the trees. Tall, white haired, and sprightly enough it seemed.

"Tai Chi"? he asked. So I spun him the yarn. Chinese father. Parents dead. Been studying for years. Master and all of that. I thought he believed me.

He owned this place, Welldean House and its Tower. Lived up here all alone. He asked if I'd like to stay on and teach him a few simple forms, and he let me stay in this bungalow.

He was alone, no family, wife dead. So I thought, what the Hell, its a cushy number.

He learned well, fast, and we got along. But he was ill, and he knew it. Not long to go, and he was grateful for my company.

Then like a bolt from the blue, one day he came down to the bungalow, and told me he knew I was a fraud. I was shocked. I thought I was better than that. I thought that no-one could see through me.

He said he didn't care, and as long as I told him the truth, he would see me okay. So, I told him it all. Durham, the lot. When I finished, he was silent for a long time, I thought he would never speak, but he did. He said there was still a chance for me, and that if I would promise to do nothing but good, he would name me as his heir, and leave me the house and estate. I couldn't believe it.

Why, I thought, Why me? So I asked him.

He had no-one, nothing, and when he was gone it would be the end of a line stretching back a thousand years. I was his last hope. So he made a will, naming me as his heir. In my proper name.

A month later he was dead.

That's how I got this place.

And this place is genuinely, the property of Oswald Hanratty.

He was Lord Kershope. This was my chance, I'd gone from nothing to everything. From Durham Prison to Lord of the Manor.

And now I've gone and blown it again. It's women, I can't help myself. They trust me so much. I teach them, bring them harmony....and then they just seem to give me things.

Lots of them are rich. They like to give me money, just to contribute to the running of this place. Sometimes quite a lot of money. How can a man like me say no.....?

And some of them, quite a few really, are a bit lonely, and one thing leads to another. I can't help it you know.

I truly believe that all in all, I'm on the side of the Angels, helping in some small way to make the World a better place. Doing something to right the wrongs that put me in prison.

If I were to get another chance, I'd change. I'd struggle to be a truly great Master. I'd fight to resist temptation.

Please...........Help me be a better person.

A good person."

Zhang's voice faded to nothing......Silence.

Man.....Shorty thought, he was good....he'd almost believed him.

* * *

30 minutes had passed since Shorty, had left Zhang. Perfect timing.

He packed up the camouflage net, replaced it in the panniers, and put his receiver and headphones in his top pocket. No need to worry about the electronics attached to Zhang. Untraceable, no prints, he'd never handled them without the gloves.

He mounted the L.E., took his mobile from his pocket, and called the police.

"There's been an incident at Welldean House. Master Zhang, in danger, The enemies are upon us! Men all in black with hoods and long swords. Hurry Please. Come Quick!" All in his best Fu Manchu accent. Christopher Lee would have loved him.

He kick started the bike, and purred off down the drive, no more than a grey shadow. He reached the A708, turned right, instead of left, which would have taken him back the way he had approached. He then took the left turn over the Yarrow, onto the tiny road to Kirkhope, and the Ettrick Valley.

His night vision was excellent, and like an ancient reiver, he rode by starlight. He stopped the bike on top of Witchie Knowe, and sat there, waiting, looking back across the valley at Welldean and the A708 far below.

The minutes ticked by, and then the police must have phoned the house, because every light in Welldean came on. Floodlights bathed the grounds. A searchlight wavered outside of Zhang's bungalow.

There was a slight flicker of light in the corner of his vision, and a convoy of emergency vehicles burst into view below. Blue lights travelled west along the road. Sirens echoed through the hills.

He took a small pair of binoculars from one of his pockets, and examined the scene in detail. He checked his watch, 57 minutes had passed. He turned on his receiver and put on the headphones. Minutes drifted by, and then came a shuffling, and muffled voices.

"Get them off of me for Gods sake! Turn the power off.......hurry!

A bell rang loudly!

"AAAAARRRRRRGGGGHHHHH!..........YOU BASTARD! ....Zhang cried.

No power had surged through the cables. What a pity.......there was no fuse in the plug that connected the clock to the terminals.

No Sausage sizzled this morning!

Still, confession was good for the soul.

Shorty plugged in his I.Pod, adjusted the earphones, kicked the bike back to life, and headed for home. Mike Oldfield's "Moonlight shadow," trickled into his conciousness. "Beautiful," he thought, "Just beautiful."

The track changed. "The Rolling Stones." Mick blasted out "Sympathy for the Devil."

But the bike barely disturbed the silence.

* * *

March 2nd 2003

Zhang was ecstatic!

The Ninja raid on Welldean was the stuff of legend.

Yes, the ordeal had been horrific. But the benefits..........

And a Master needs must suffer for his Arts.

For hours that morning, the Police had diligently searched the grounds, but no trace had been found of the Ninja who had tried to extract his secrets. .....But of course..... Ninja leave no trace.

The raid was the first item on all of the news channels. Messages of sympathy, and pledges of support for Welldean were pouring in. He'd have to arrange shifts to answer the phones, and reply to the E.Mails.

Television crews were camped outside of the grounds, all vying to interview him. He had received offers, substantial ones at that, to be interviewed on late night chat shows. And not just British Television. It may prove necessary for him to cross the Atlantic. First Class. All expenses paid!......This was the Big Time!

"Oh.....Thank You........Shorty Higgins. You've made my life wonderful!"

Of course, there was still the small matter of the confession.

That very morning, he'd arranged for the transfer of funds from his private and secret bank account, to the number Shorty had left.

Paid in full!

The joke was, that since that time, the offers he'd received and the pledges from students, had far exceeded even that amount. He was actually into pocket, and it wasn't yet dinnertime!

And.....All because of that violent little lunatic. He just couldn't wait to rub his tiny squashed nose in it. When he found him that is.

There was a quiet knock on the door of his bedroom. He called out, and Lotus Blossom entered.

"So sorry, to disturb you Master, but perhaps you may benefit from a light massage with aromatic oils, to relieve the stress of your ordeal?"

Zhang smiled at her. "Most kind my dear. How very thoughtful of you. That would be so welcome.

He lay back and prepared for relaxation."

* * *

March 3rd 2003.

Over two days had passed since Shorty walked out of the door. Off into the night to go "hunting."

I pulled the Toyota into the "Last Chance" car park. It was 9.30 a.m. and the place was busy, alive with tradesmen's vans.

A bright blue "Open" sign glowed in the window alongside American neon. Budweiser, Coors, a Cowboy boot, Lone Star.

Two men were manhandling a 1950's style jukebox through the door, and I squeezed past them.The walls were newly painted, off white, with red trims, but the most striking things in the room were the posters of Country greats. Larger than life size, Dolly Parton, Hank Williams, Dwight Yoakum, and Shorty's favourite, his alter ego, Willie Nelson.

As you know, he'd performed in concert whilst in Durham as "Wily" Nelson, although inevitably due to his size, he'd had to suffer jokes about being a "Half Nelson," instead of a "Full Nelson" like the real Willie.

But in pride of place was a photo I had taken myself of Shorty and Reb. They had been singing together, togged out in full "regalia," Reb standing, Shorty perched on a high stool. Blasting out an electric version of "Wind beneath my Wings" at each other, eyes wet, utter sincerity in their voices. The lighting had been just right, and I thought it was the best photo I had ever taken of him. Not that I'd taken that many.

And, prominently displayed in a small glass case in the centre of the shelving behind the counter was Shorty's "War Hammer," and long time friend, his huge adjustable spanner.

Perhaps, I thought, love was actually changing his disposition.

Shorty and Reb were in the corner booth, deep in conversation. Incredibly, sitting with them, totally relaxed and at ease, were the Miss's Ffanshawe, and Molesworthy.

Shorty called over, "Hey Eddie grab a coffee, there's a fresh pot behind the counter. Come on over and join us, I was just telling Abbie and Ros about our plans for this place."

I filled a mug from the percolator.....Jesus, but Shorty liked strong coffee! I read the notice above the machine....“Wake up in the morning with a “Jumbo” mug of Shorty’s finest. Each cup comes with a voucher towards your first Pacemaker.”

I crossed the floor, took a seat, and nodded to the ladies.

“Abbie and Ros? I thought you and the Tax Office were at daggers drawn?” Shorty laughed, “Don’t worry Eddie, that was just a ruse. They’ve explained. They’re not really Tax Inspectors at all, more sort of “private investigators.”All hush hush, but it’s not us they’re looking into after all.”

I stared at the pair of them sitting there like a pair of basilisks.

“Private Investigators” Eh? I used to be in that line of work myself a year or two back, similar line of investigations perhaps?”

Abigail smiled, her big blue eyes looking up from beneath those long lashes, her honey blonde hair framing her face.

How do they do it, these women? Develop “that look,” that killer look, that just hits you in the pit of the stomach and travels on down? Do they practice it each morning in front of the mirror, or are they just born with it?

“Hi Eddie,” she breathed, but it was “Ros” attempting to be all business like, who continued.

“Good morning Mr. Graham. As you are no doubt aware, it is perhaps inevitable that there be a some amount of overlap in certain forms of private investigation. It is also possible that we may on occasion require the assistance of a third party in order to be able to satisfactorily continue, and ultimately to conclude our enquires. Now, should that be the case, I would be delighted to consult with you. However, in the immediate future it is unlikely that our areas of interest will overlap, and thus we are able to offer you the benefit of our company on a purely social basis.”

I couldn’t help but smile. “My God!....She is fluent in pure Bullshit!” I shook her hand.

“Ever thought about a career in Politics?”

She tried, she struggled nobly, but slowly, the business facade collapsed, and she grinned.

“I did once consider it, but....Politics? ....You know what they say about shite? Well, Bullshit tends to float to the top. Ends up at Cabinet level. Whereas the common or garden variety sinks to the bottom. That’s my summary of the British political system by the way. These days, as far as I’m concerned it’s a case of “Come back

Mr. Fawkes, all is forgiven."

"Abbie,"(I really much preferred Miss Ffanshawe with two "F's") cut in, "She should know, her degree's in Political Science."

"Ros" continued, "I prefer to work behind the scenes, anyway."

I was warming to Ros. Perhaps great minds did think alike....

"Sure you two are in the right line of work?" They glanced at each other but said nothing.

Then Ros, picked up a small package from the table, opened her heavy purse, and placed it inside. "Thanks for this Shorty". He bowed slightly.

She turned back to face me. "Your two friends here have been most helpful to us. However, duty calls, and we really must be off." They rose in unison and walked towards the door.

Catwalk! ..... Wow!..... did that Abigail know how to wiggle. An accomplishment all to rare today, outside of the fashion industry. Feminists.....they just waddle.

Reb watched me, pity, (false pity), in her eyes. She was trying very hard to keep control.

Was it that obvious?

She pointed..."You're Smitten," and the pair of them began to duet "It must be Love."

I tried to look serious, and cut in. "What gives folks? Looks like you've come into money. I've heard you talk about it, but I never thought you'd get around to doing it. Quite a change in the old place."

Shorty grinned up at me, "Yep, we thought it was about time to get this show properly on the road. We're taking out the back wall completely, putting in a little stage and some decent speakers, and going for the full works. What we've talked about ever since we got the place. Good hot food all day, tables in small booths along the walls.

The bar that's "Shut when it's open, and open when it's shut." We'll Close at seven, lock the front door, and then......Private Club.....Country and Western behind closed doors till late. Dancing, live music some nights. Bring your own booze.

Bikers welcome. Strictly no drugs. And out here on outskirts, there's no-one to complain about the noise."

He pressed his remote, and "Wild Side of Life." erupted from the speakers. "We're already the Borders very first, and probably only "Honky Tonk, and now, it's time we upgraded. Who cares if we don't make a fortune, it's what we want to do, and that's all that matters to Reb and me." He reached up, put his arm around her shoulders, and she rested her head on his bald pate.

"So the two of you's permanent?" They grinned up at me, and nodded. I reached over and shook their hands. "Congratulations!

Funny business that, up at Welldean the other night. It's all over the news, Master Zhang attacked and tortured by Japanese Ninja intent on learning his secrets. The police totally baffled. No trace at all of his assailants?"

The pair of them almost doubled up with laughter. Shorty lowered his voice to a whisper, I had to lean down to hear him better. "That's not the biggest mystery though Eddie. Right out of the blue, Zhang returned the money Reb had lent him. With very generous interest". He reached into the pocket of his combat jacket, and took out a small package, a very similar package to the one that Ros had put in her bag. What was going on?

"When you get back home, have a listen to that, then lock it away in that big safe of yours. Insurance you could call it."

They burst into laughter again.

Shorty turned unaccustomedly serious. "Eddie, you know you and me have always been partners. Back in the old days in Blyth, at the "Sluice," and then when we bought the cafe?"

He hesitated, looking worried. "Well, Reb wants to put most of her money into this upgrade. So, if its alright with you, how about a three way partnership?"

I put on my serious face, and looked from one to the other. "No chance!"

They were shocked, horrified. Oh Christ, I'd gone too far.

"Give me a pound".

He looked puzzled, but reached into his pocket, and handed over the coin. I stared at it.

"Well I'll be buggered! ..... Shorty!..... This pounds got two heads! It must be worth a fortune. Tell you what, let me keep it, and I'll pay you all of my share in the cafe for it. Then there'll be only you and Reb in the partnership. One condition though, I want an A.D.B. whenever I ask for it, with black pudding, and all of the coffee I can drink. We'll draw up the papers tomorrow."

Reb grabbed me round the neck and hugged me, and I saw a tear run down Shorty's cheek and trickle through the designer stubble on his chin, before parting company and landing in my coffee mug.

Deal done!

Some folk like a touch of salt in their coffee. But my mug was almost empty so I didnt have to find out.

I stared out of the window. “Ros and Abbie” were climbing into a small green 4 x 4, a Suzuki “Jimny”. A half minute later, the engine started, and they drove off North.

Shorty saw me watching them. “Nice lady that Ros, smart too. She’s a coping quite well considering. She lost her father around two weeks ago, bad road accident or something. He was some sort mine owner, and involved in metal trading. Something to do with Lithium. Abbie says she’s about to become very rich, and has no idea what to do with the money. I thought she looked a bit smarter today didn’t you? You know, better turned out somehow?”

Yeah, that was true, but then I suspected that her appearance when we first met was all just an act anyway. I had a fair idea just what sort of “private investigations” those two involved themselves in. But who for? Or were they perhaps freelancing? And what it had to do with us out here in the back of nowhere, I couldn’t imagine.

“Shorty,”

“What”

“Be careful, Those are two dangerous ladies”. But I knew I was wasting my breath.

Because, he only laughed again.

* * *

The small green 4 x 4 turned off the A708, slowly climbed up past the ruins of Deuchar Tower, and onto the long gravel driveway to Welldean House.

It was a beautiful clear morning, the sun was high in the sky, and the smell of damp foliage drifted in through the open front windows of the vehicle.

In keeping with the ambience of their surroundings, Abbie had chosen an appropriate CD, an old recording of “The Corries,” and their classic version of “Dowie Dens of Yarrow” drifted on the morning air.

Ros made the last turn, out of the tree lined drive, and onto the great sweep of white gravel that led up to the main entrance to the house itself.

The media had gone, and once again peace had descended over the ancient pile.

Welldean House, was set in a hollow of the hills. Unusually, the stone of which it was built, had been quarried from the living rock of Welldean Hill, and the oldest part of the building, the pele tower, which dated from the late 15th or early 16th century, had been built on the forward edge of the quarry itself.

The entire site faced south, and the views, down the narrow valley of the Deuchar Burn, out across the Yarrow Water, and on to Witchie Knowe, were stunning.

Over almost five centuries, the house had been adapted and extended. A barrel vaulted hall with chambers above had been added to the north face in the late 16th century, and this was adapted in the 18th century, when a third story was built on, and a series of bay windows were pierced through the massive masonry of the second floor. All of this work, had resulted in a major enlargement of the quarry, within which the main house stood.

High walls extended north from either end of the main building, ending in a vertical cliff face. some thirty feet high. Fruit trees grew there, and had been trained up against the rock.

Additional accommodation had been built against the east and west walls, housing, for the ever growing number of students. The hillside both above and below the site had been landscaped into terraces, and planted with mature trees of exotic varieties. White gravel pathways wound through the trees, and in the distance, the Zen garden gleamed in the morning sunshine.

Located as it was within the shelter of the quarry, the site trapped the heat and held it. Novices in their saffron robes, worked diligently, pruning, hoeing, and tending orderly rows of vegetables.

The Miss's Ffanshawe and Molesworthy parked their Suzuki in the spacious "Visitors Car Park," and walked on towards the tower. A neatly painted sign directed new arrivals to the public entrance positioned just to the right of the weathered front wall of the ancient pele itself.

A turnstile was located just inside the door. A notice welcomed visitors, politely suggesting that whilst there was no charge for entry, a small contribution of between £10 and £20 per person would greatly assist Master Zhang in the development of this, his chosen path, and would further enable him to assist others along the road to enlightenment.

Ros smiled to herself, picked up a large oriental handbell, and rang it loudly.

A tall florid man in the uniform of a Security Guard, appeared. The beer paunch bulging out over his too tight belt, rather detracted from the impression he obviously wished to project via the fiercely slashed peak of his military style cap, which extended so far down over his forehead that it almost obscured his small piggy eyes.

"Sorry Ladies, we're shut for an hour or so longer. The Master is instructing students in Kyudo. "That", he paused, looking down his nose at the two women, "is Japanese archery. It is an art which requires the utmost concentration. But do feel free to come back later."

He launched into a well worn monologue. "Perhaps you would care to walk down to the restaurant on the lower terrace, where they serve the very finest vegetarian cuisine. Five star ratings from "Visit Scotland." Their director eats here himself. I can recommend our very own beer, it's brewed on the premises, and we also have a limited amount of wine from our small vineyard, ...The first in Scotland."

"Stop Right There!" Abbie snapped. She produced a small wallet, and flipped it open, allowing him a fleeting glimpse of a gold shield.

Ros, pinned him neatly with her eye.

He stared down at her.

She spoke, "Miss Ffanshawe, and Miss Molesworthy. We are Officers of Her Majesty's Inspectorate of Charities.

As a result of the unfortunate incidents of two days ago, the Minister urgently requires that we carry out an inspection of these premises, with a view to ascertaining your suitability for the continuance of your charitable status. "Ninja raids," she paused, "May not be compatible with such status, and of course there are Health and Safety issues to be taken into consideration."

She pointed to a spot on the floor. "Zhang! Here! Now!

"Security", drew in his belly, and pushed out his chest. Ros noted his name tag. "Henry Partis."

He stared icily down at Miss Molesworthy. "More than my job's worth to disturb the Master when he's teaching".....he paused... "Lady," he added slight condescension in his voice.

"Ahh," Ros sighed, "I feared as much.".... A bloody chauvinist she thought. "Now, Listen ...This can go one of two ways," and she produced a long brown, and official looking envelope from her ample purse. "Either we get to see Zhang ....Now......Or"....she produced a mobile phone....."I phone for Police assistance, they arrive, and together we execute of the terms of this rather lovely warrant. And.....this warrant, grants me full access to search every nook and cranny of this rather salubrious establishment. Much to the discomfort of both your students, and more importantly for you, of Master Zhang himself.

Furthermore," she continued, "The arrival of the law will no doubt coincide with the arrival of a fair number of members of the media, all hungry for more footage for the 6 o'clock news."

She waved the warrant again, and then tapped the envelope with her finger.

In truth, it contained vouchers for shopping at Sainsbury's.

"You look like an intelligent sort of fellow. So, just shuffle off and find your Master.......Now!

Wait though.... on second thoughts... be a good Security Officer, and I'll make a small concession. Don't disturb him after all, just take us to see Zhang instead, I'd quite like to observe this Kyudo thingy."

Together, they walked through the width of the building and out into the courtyard formed by the main house, the east and west walls, and the cliff face. To the left, was a stone arch, where ancient studded oak doors, aged black over centuries, stood wide, secured on massive wrought iron hooks.

"Partis" nodded. "Through there, that's where they practice."

Ros waved a hand in dismissal. "That will be all Lance Corporal".

He stared at her in disbelief. "How did you know".

Outwardly Abbie was emotionless. Her face showed nothing. Inside, she was in hysterics.

Ros looked the "Security" man up and down. "Smart man like you, that bearing.....you had to be Ex-Army."

He nodded, and she continued. "It's elementary my Dear Watson. No-one with your surname, could ever be a Private, and so.... Instant promotion! You see, I know the British Army, and they would never have tolerated a"..... and she paused before declaring ......"Private Partis."

Henry Partis ground his teeth in frustration.....She knew!

Oh...Why was life so cruel? Would he never escape the dreadful joke Her Majesty's armed forces had inflicted upon him?

He turned sharply on his heel, and marched his way back to his post, his polished, studded boots, crunching on the gravel.

Abbie smiled as they made their way towards the gate. How long had they spent with those lunatics at the Road End Cafe? It must be catching, this weird sense of humour. Still, it all seemed to be good for Ros, and she'd had a hard time of it lately.

They walked through the gate together, and out onto the neatly mown grass of the terrace. Immediately to the right, and extending to the west, was a long low oak framed building. It looked newly built. In line with its far end was a grassy space about the length of a bowling green, and then another smaller building with one open side, facing east. There was a low mound inside, mounted upon which were five targets slightly over a foot in diameter. The back wall was lined with straw bales. The bales bristled with long arrows, the targets with few.

Ros snorted, and muttered, "Call that Kyudo? They've better Archers in Ambridge." ("The Archers". A long running British radio "Soap," about a family of farmers named Archer, living in a fictional town called Ambridge.)

Abbie glanced at her, "Behave yourself, let's try and keep this serious. I'm sure there's connections here, but we don't know what they are. And" she continued, "you were a bit heavy on "Fat Henry" back there."

Ros slowed her pace "Sorry Boss, I'll try to keep it under control. It worked though, we're in. Let's call at Sainsbury's on the way back," she waved the envelope, "some of these vouchers are for wine, and we owe ourselves a night off."

Abbie laughed. "I'll warrant you're right! But not unless you go via Edinburgh, that's the nearest. You'll just have to get by with Tesco.

Ros nudged her with her elbow, "Rumour is that Eddie's got a good cellar though!"

They walked on past the end of the main building. Sliding doors had been pulled back, and the west end of the building was open. The polished wood of the floor stood a foot or more above the grass, and served as a platform upon which the archers practiced. But only two figures stood upon that platform. Both were dressed Japanese style in long divided skirts, and white short sleeved jackets. The shorter of the two was Zhang, black haired, white bearded, beard neatly trimmed. The taller was a striking dark haired woman in her early thirties. Like Zhang, she was dressed Japanese style, but in addition she wore a leather breast protector. Her long dark hair was tied back, and cascaded down behind her, but most striking of all, were her dark brown eyes, which were heavily made up with eye liner, mascara, and dark blue eye shadow. She seemed quite out of keeping with her surroundings in what was supposed to be almost a Monastery.

Zhang's voice drifted to his two, as yet unobserved visitors. "No Kathy,....I mean, Lady May Blossom, your release is still not correct. Allow me to demonstrate."

He turned, and caught sight of Ros and Abbie standing there, watching.

"So sorry, This area is private......No Visitors Allowed."

Abbie stepped forward. "Master Zhang?" He nodded, and she continued grim faced. "Unfortunately,.....We".... She indicated Ros, "Are *not* visitors. We represent Her Majesty's Government. We are Inspectors from the Department of Charities, and we have here," she reached over, and took the envelope from Ros, "a warrant to inspect these premises in their entirety, should such action be necessary."

Zhang paled visibly. "Errm" he stuttered, "And why would that be necessary? We at Welldean, are a Charitable Religious Organisation, we are dedicated to the help and well being of others."

Abbie and Ros stepped up onto the platform.

Ros took over. "It's in relation to the unfortunate business of the raid the other night....."The Ninja,".... Our Masters, up in Edinburgh, and indeed, down in London, are not too keen on "Ninja," and are somewhat concerned that the incident may reflect an unfavourable light upon the Department in general. As you know Religious, and Charitable Institutions benefit greatly in terms of exemption from taxes, and rather relaxed, shall we say attitudes towards such matters as health and safety. To wit... I do hope you have full approval for a range such as this. I mean.... Japanese archery? Kyudo is it called? Is such a little understood practice from an official point of view. I trust that you have applied for the proper inspection certificates?

Zhang was thinking quickly. "Of course, our premises are open for inspection by all who wish to see them. Quite a few of my disciples... Oh so sorry, I mean students, are even members of her Majesty's Government. I'm sure all will be found to be in order. Now, what were your names? You seem to have neglected to mention them?"

Careful Ros, Abbie thought, He's not as daft as he looks.

Ros stepped forward, and extended her hand....Body contact. ....Zhang took it. It was warm and dry. She held his hand, while she spoke. "I'm Roselinde Molesworthy, and this, she nodded to Abbie, is Inspector Abigail Ffanshawe."

Zhang's mind spun....Molesworthy......Rosalinde?

The name was strangely familiar. Where had he seen it, or had he heard it?.....Yes! ....The Times Obituaries!....That was it!

His favourite early morning read. James Molesworthy, O.B.E. .....Deceased!....The metals billionaire! ....Lithium! .....Precious metals! Fondly known in the media as "Jimmy the Mole," or "The Golden Mole" from his interests in mining! Survived by his only daughter Rosalinde!

It was even on his "to do" list. Send letter of condolence, and an offer of grief counselling A.S.A.P.!

His facial muscles changed gear. Worried to concerned. "Miss Molesworthy? Not Jimmy's daughter?"

You cunning Bastard! Abbie thought, Now you're for it!

Expressionless, her hand still in his, Ros looked up into Zhang's eyes. "You knew Daddy?"

Zhang clasped both of her hands in his "Careful," he thought, "Play this just right, lot at stake here." He held her gaze....."I met him out in Japan, during my Zen studies. We socialised a little, and I did a bit of survey work for him up in the North of India, plus some rather confidential work during my time in Afghanistan and Tibet. He thought I "blended in" rather well you see. I recall, that he spoke of you often and most fondly. A wonderful man.... So sad....Britain needs more like him, I was devastated to hear of his passing."

Zhang paused, and gazed off into the depths of the hills, apparently lost in thought, then he gave a small start.

"So Sorry.... But really my dear, ought you to be working, at a time such as this? Surely, you ought to take a holiday? I can probably arrange for you to stay here, in the guest quarters if you wish? You could meditate, recover, and we have a grief counselling service if you feel you need a little help. No charge, it's the least I can do for the daughter of a dear friend."

Ros's eyes were damp. Outwardly sad, inwardly she was furious. Show nothing, she thought. "That is most kind of you Master Zhang, but as the great teachers say....."No Work, No Food," and my work distracts me from my grief."

She looked at the bow Zhang had placed on a low table. "I used to love bows and arrows. When I was a girl, I made my own with a branch and some string. I played Cowboys and Indians all one summer, and I once hit the middle of the target with an arrow."

"Oh Christ!" Abbie thought, "What now!"

Ros went on, "But that bow's not much good, its all the wrong shape, the top bit's way too long. No wonder your friend there's having trouble. Robin Hood's bow was the proper shape."

Zhang smiled indulgently, "That my dear is a "Yumi" the traditional Japanese bow. Japanese archery is far removed from European. Indeed, it is an exercise of the mind, more than a sport or a preparation for war. The extra length of the top limb, allows for greater power, and for the archer to use a bow even longer than his own height. Perhaps you would care to give it a try?"

Ros simpered. She looked at Abbie, "Do we have time?"

Jesus, but she was good. Should have been on the stage, but then she had spent five years at R.A.D.A.

"Alright Ros, Go ahead, but we are a bit short of time. And don't forget we've more inspections later today, down near Hawick."

"Just one moment," Zhang turned, and took a leather breast protector, from a shelf on the wall, "better to put this on first. Ladies I'm afraid, are prone to painful accidents without one."

Ros walked over. The tall dark woman joined them.

"This is Kathy," Zhang announced. Kathy nodded, rather curtly Ros thought, "Can you help Rosalinde with the gloves Kathy, and perhaps lend her your bow?".

Kathy gave a small bow, but said nothing. She passed Ros first a thin cotton glove and then another leather glove, both for the right hand.

"Put the thin one on first, and then the leather one," Zhang instructed. "The thin one is simply to protect the leather from the sweat of the hand." He took Ros's left hand, sprinkled powder onto the palm and rubbed it in. "When you release the arrow, try to let the bow turn in the hand." He placed a number of arrows on a table

alongside the shooting position.... This should be fun, he thought.
Ros bent down and scrutinised the arrows. She rearranged them. Then she took two back to the rack, from which Zhang had selected them. Examined the remainder, and chose two others. Satisfied, she smiled, picked up the yumi, and stood on the edge of the platform facing the targets.
Zhang stood to her left.
She spoke. "I always thought of my arrows as little boys and girls, silly isn't it?"
Zhang was puzzled. Why did she say that? Coincidence, or had she heard it somewhere?
She selected an arrow, placed it on the string, raised both bow and arrow vertically above her head, and then brought it back down into the full draw. Her right hand was far back behind her ear.
Zhang was worried, something was very wrong. That draw had been perfect.
Ros turned to Zhang, the bow still pointing at the target. "Master.....Am I holding this thingy correctly?" She look straight into his eyes, and at the same moment released the arrow.
There was a solid thud. The arrow stood in the centre of the left hand target.
Ros repeated her actions four more times, each time turning and looking into the eyes of Master Zhang.
Five arrows now stood in the centres of five targets.
"Oooohhhh Goody, I haven't forgotten after all. Pity you've no proper bows though. Then I could have tried my Robin Hood trick, you know, splitting the arrow? That used to be my favourite."
She replaced the bow on the table, took off the gloves and the breast protector, dropped them on the floor, and turned to Abbie. Her voice was stern when she spoke.
"Come along Miss Ffanshawe we've seen enough here. I'll write the report when we get back." And off she marched in the direction of the exit. Abigail Ffanshawe followed.
Zhang, and Kathy stood on the platform speechless.
Jesus H. Christ! What was that about!
And Master Zhang began to worry all over again.

* * *

Back in the car, Ros turned to Abbie. "Sorry about that Boss. I know I was out of line, but after that rubbish he spouted about knowing my Dad, I couldn't help myself."

Abbie started the car and moved off.

"No harm done, it's not really within our remit anyway. We're just supposed to keep an eye on Eddie, and Shorty Higgins. Can't say I feel too good about it though, in fact, I rather like them. Very unprofessional of me."

Ros looked thoughtfully back towards Welldean House. "Did you notice that girl back there, "Kathy" was it? Wouldn't have taken her for the type for Welldean, too much of a "presence" to her. And that make up.....? Not the usual student. Who on earth was she? Don't suppose we'll ever find out."

But Abbie did not reply.

They reached the main road, and turned left for Selkirk.

* * *

April 27th 2003.

The Hess Run.

"Archie" Armstrong, or to give him his official title, Squadron Leader Johnnie Archibald Armstrong, brought his plane around in a long turn, and headed back in towards the Northumbrian coastline.

It was a clear and cloudless morning in late April. He knew this landscape well, he'd spent many an hour, dodging through the hills of Northumberland and the Borders, down low below the radar, swooping in undetected, on targets at Otterburn and Spadeadam ranges.

He'd logged his flight with the RAF controllers at Boulmer, and also with the civil aviation authorities.

The RAF's a small world, and his mission this morning was an open secret at Boulmer.

No other military flying was taking place, and he had a clear cross country run, to just south of Glasgow, before making the turn back down, south east to Carlisle.

Doing the run, they'd talked about for years, him, Shorty, and Eddie.

The Hess run.

Archie Armstrong was not a rich man, and he drove an old car. In fact not a car in at all, a Toyota pick-up, battered, bashed, but reliable. That truck was so ugly that senior officers often threatened to throw it, (and sometimes him,) off of the base entirely. But Archie's reply was always the same. "Have a look around the Middle East," he would say, "all of those war zones in fact. When times get tough, what do you see bouncing across the desert? BMW's? Range Rovers? Mercedes? ...No!... What you see are Toyota pick-ups. Okay, Toyota's with .50 caliber machine guns mounted, but Toyota's just the same. It's tough, reliable, and if the Revolution ever does come? Then all I'll need is the machine gun.

And exasperated, his critics would simply walk off shaking their heads.

Archie might not drive a flash car, but he had two things his brothers in arms did not have. One was a near derelict stone built house in Liddesdale, out on the hill behind Toftholm, and the other was his very own aircraft. The house he was rebuilding. The plane? He had built that himself, with just a little bit of help.

Even with around 100 years of aviation history, aircraft were normally still the province of the super rich. That is, commercially built aircraft. But build it yourself, and it was possible to own a good plane, for around £40,000. Expensive yes, but many of his fellow officers drove cars that cost more than that. And Archie had managed to build his even cheaper.

Jimmy Dixon, a pilot friend, had brought the kit in from the USA, intending to build it, but then his wife had run off with her girlfriend.

Her Girlfriend!

The guy was devastated....... he'd quite fancied the girlfriend himself. He'd even suggested a romantic weekend away together. But she'd preferred his wife.

His wife left a note recommending a dubious club in the Soho, and suggested he turn gay. The result was a messy and expensive divorce, in the course of which he offered Archie the plane kit, plus his workshop equipment at a bargain basement price.

The plane had taken them 1500 hours to build, Archie, Eddie and Shorty. The deal being that they worked for free, in exchange for flying lessons for Eddie when the plane was complete, and the occasional trip abroad for Shorty.

Most of the work had been done out in Eddie's shed at Merrylaw, and the parts had then been transported down to Carlisle Airport for final assembly.

G-JARC, (G the British prefix, J for Johnnie, and ARC for Archie,) was a Van's Aircraft RV6. One of the best self builds in the world. So good in fact, that it was the only kit aircraft in use as a military trainer. The Nigerian Air Force flew them.

He called it after his namesake, the original Archie Armstrong, who had been Court Fool, and very much more besides, to James the V1, and later to Charles I.

"The Jester" was red and yellow, a low wing monoplane. Pilot and passenger in side by side arrangement. Even with the two crew and a full load, he could take off and land from a 500 ft strip. Alone, and with a light load he could get in and out in a much shorter distance.

The 180 hp Lycoming engine gave him a range of over 720 miles at 75% power, and a potential top speed of 210 mph, but Archie was happy just cruising along at around 160. His day job gave him all of the high speed kicks he needed.

He switched the camera's on, and the screens fitted above the passenger seat came alive....All up and running correctly.

It had taken days to fit the four cameras, two on the port wing, one pointing forward, mounted well out to avoid the blur from the prop, and one off at about 45 degrees to the side. A matching 45 degree camera was mounted on the starboard wing, and a fourth under the belly of the plane, pointing straight down.

Eddie reckoned that configuration ought to give a 200 degree field of vision, and the downward camera was a bonus if he needed it. He would edit all of the footage together on the Mac, and add commentary on the places of interest as they came up.

Archie had set the GPS up with the flight plan in detail, coast to the crash site. They'd talked it all through must be ten times, but he intended to add just a little bonus he hadn't mentioned to Eddie, should it prove possible.

Hess had flown this course low, but Archie intended to keep a constant height of 500 ft above ground level. Any lower, and the field of view of the cameras would be too restricted.

He may do it again he thought, low level, some other day just for the hell of it.

He crossed the coastline. Just off his starboard wing were the ruins of Dunstanburgh Castle, the wildest and most picturesque of the sea castles of Northumberland. Five miles to port the camera's recorded Alnwick, with it's spectacular Castle, home to the Duke of Northumberland.

Bamburgh and Alnwick were better known, more photographed, used as locations and backdrops for film and television, but Dunstanburgh still retained that wild romance, that commercialism and exploitation can so easily destroy. Archie loved the Borders, so much history in such a small area of hill country.

He flew on inland, and directly over the village of South Charlton, he turned north west, and traversed the eight miles to Chillingham Castle, the next point on the SatNav. Over

Chillingham, he made a course change, due west and out over the massive granite dome of the Cheviot, the very hub of Border history.

Historically, everything had both revolved, and evolved around the Cheviot and its foothills, which straddled the Border, forcing travellers and armies alike to take the narrow coastal roads on both East and West.

This was once the edge of the Roman Empire.

Just to the north of his present position, Arthur was reputed to have fought one of his major battles in the valley of the River Glen.

It was also the very cradle of British Christianity. Lindisfarne with its Priory was just off the coast behind him, and off his starboard wing was Yeavering Bell, and the Anglian Royal Town.

Back in the early 7th century, Edwin of Northumbria together with St Paulinus, spent a week baptising Christians in the river at Gefrin, just below Yeavering. Edwin, the near forgotten king, whose Christian Kingdom stretched from Edinburgh in the North, to York in the South, and out West, right to the Irish Sea.

Edwin was the man who brought peace to the land, who actually did, what the legendary Arthur was credited with doing!

Flodden field was also just to the north. 1513......when Scotland lost both its king, and much of its nobility.

Outsiders looked at this place, and imagined that the Border divided the two countries. But once this was almost a land of its own. Three "Marches" on either side, each "policed" by its own "Warden" in an attempt to control a people who referred to themselves as neither English or Scots. Just as "Borderers." Remembered by history as "The Reivers"

And for Archie this *was* the land of the Border Reivers, who had used these hills as a refuge. On the English side, the likes of the Robsons, the Charltons, the Dodds, and the Milburns
On the Scots side the Elliots, the Nixons, the Croziers, and his own folk the Armstrongs. Outlaws, quite literally "freelances," all long since cleared, dispersed.... gone. Spread to the four corners of the earth. Cleared by the very warlords who ought perhaps to have protected them. Cleared from this land that they had fought to protect for generations. Land now owned by the descendants of those very warlords. The Percys, Dukes of Northumberland, the Scotts of Buccleuch, The Kerrs, Lords of Lothian.Families who over the last 400 years, had married and intermarried until now,

the Borders was virtually owned and managed by one large, and extended family, whose branches stretched throughout the British aristocracy, and into the Royal Family itself.

Politics! thought Archie.... What a load of Bollocks!... Doesn't matter who's in Parliament. These same people always had, and always would pull the strings.

Hope they never find out I'm an Anarchist, or they'll take me Harrier off of me!

But strange perhaps, how now, all of these years later, some of the descendants of those old Reivers were drifting back. Here and there you'd bump into them. People like himself, Eddie, Shorty, those Moffatts up at Teviothead, the ones who used to run the Museum. All back. All sharp edged and intractable, after an exile of 400 years. And all aware of their heritage.

An endangered species the ethnic Borderer! He laughed to himself, What was that old expression.... "Shake loose the Border?" Well, if enough of us come back.....then....Why not?

It could do with it.

He crossed College Valley, and then the Bowmont Water.

The old town of Kirk Yetholm, with its tiny gypsy palace, and its twin, Town Yetholm straddled the river off to starboard.

Hownam with its prehistoric camps passed below, and then the land fell away as he approached the ruins of Cessford Castle, which back in the 16th century, was home to the Kerrs, the cunning and notorious Wardens of the Scottish Middle March.

Now he was flying due west, out over Ancrum, with its battle site and reputed connections with the Knights of Malta.

He passed just south of Selkirk, and came up on Bowhill, home of the Duke of Buccleuch. Easily visible, just over two miles to the north.

And the cameras recorded it all.

Ten miles later he crossed the tip of St Mary's Loch, then on west to the peak of Broad Law, and his next course correction, 22 degrees north to a point just south of the village of Sandford, around 31 miles ahead.

Archie knew that Hess had missed his alleged target, Dungavel House, which lay a mere three miles southwest of Sandford, now just ten minutes flying time ahead.

At Sandford, he turned due west for seven miles, and then 30 degrees north.

Hess had been lost, and had looped northwest, then south out over the Firth of Clyde before returning inland on a course which doglegged over West Kilbride, Auchentiber, and Kilmaurs, before intersecting his own westbound flightpath near Ballageich Hill.

Three miles later he had turned due east, and around seven miles later, he baled out over Floors Farm.

Archie followed the flight path meticulously.

He checked the cameras. All were running perfectly.

Flying west, the sun had been behind him, warm on his left shoulder, and he had watched the shadow of his little plane skip across the landscape like a tiny bird in flight. Now the sun was coming in from ahead on his right, and he adjusted the peak of his cap to keep the glare out of his eyes.

Strange, but it felt colder flying this way. He looked behind his rear wing, and there was his shadow darting across the ground.

The shadow looked larger, different somehow? Strange how the sun played these tricks

Christ! he shivered, it *was* colder.

He could see the village of Eaglesham ahead just forward of his starboard wing. Four miles to Floors Farm.

He dropped his airspeed as low as he dared.

He could see the A726 coming up below.

He must be getting nervous, his hands were freezing.

Now for his little gift for Eddie. The GPS showed him just about on the site.

Archie pulled back on the stick, and put the planes nose straight up into the air. He continued to pull on the stick. The plane was now upside down and on its back halfway through a tight loop.

This was the point when Hess would have dropped out of the cockpit. The nose began to drop back down to complete the loop.

Then, inexplicably, the sky turned dark, the sun disappeared, and below him the fields were deep in shadow.

It was terribly......bitterly....cold.

And Archie Armstrong blacked out.

He couldn't have been out for more than a few seconds, the stick was still in his hand.

Incredibly "The Jester" was the right way up, but he couldn't see a damn thing, the cockpit was frosted completely. He checked the instruments, horizon level, plenty altitude, flying due east.

The plexiglas started to clear. He increased power, and came around 50 degrees to starboard. Thank God for GPS. He was on course for Carlisle. Only seconds must have passed, but it felt like hours.

The radio came alive. Aleysha, from Boulmer, urgent, worried.

"Boulmer to Golf Juliet Alpha Romeo Charlie! You dropped off the screens for five seconds, answer please Archie."

Worried? Most unprofessional. Nice girl, bonny too. He must be okay he thought, he was harbouring evil thoughts. "Golf Juliet Alpha Romeo Charlie, to Boulmer. No idea what you're talking about, must be a radar glitch, I'm fine, just turned south heading for Carlisle. Thanks for watching out for me though, I'll ring you from a land line later."

He was shaken, but there was not a trace of it in his voice. That last line was a bit of a give away. Now the gossip machine would go into top gear.

Wouldn't stop him ringing her though.

He tried not to think about what had actually happened, because if "they" ever found out he'd lost conciousness, it'd be "medical time," and goodbye to flying.

He needed to see the camera footage.

The cold, the shadow of the plane, surely he didn't imagine that?

Just keep it normal. He clicked on his mobile phone. Hands free! And, wonders of modern science, a good signal. He phoned Eddie at the Cafe. "Mission accomplished!.... Collect me from Carlisle?" 90 miles and half an hour later, he was on the ground.

Eddie, picked him up in the Toyota twin cab, and by then he'd done all of the post flight checks, parked the plane in the hanger, and unloaded all of the discs from the cameras.

He was still shaken.

For God's sake, just act normal, he reminded himself as he walked towards Eddie in the car park.

He tried not to think about the other time he'd had a "problem."

* * *

I watched Archie, walking briefcase in hand up to the truck. Something was wrong, I'd never seen him like this. Distracted, no eye contact, white as a sheet, silent. This guy was a combat veteran, a little trip across reiving country was a morning stroll for him. He'd been looking forward to it. We'd been planning it for months. He should be happy.

"You okay"?

"Sure, the discs are here," he tapped the briefcase, "Got it all".

But he sounded uneasy to me. He opened the passenger door, climbed in, and said hardly a word all of the way back to Langholm. Back at the cafe, he walked straight through into the office, opened the briefcase, took out the four discs, and spoke almost the first words of the last half hour.

"Run them, I want to see what I got."

"Why now?"

"Wait and see, then we'll talk."

I set up the player, brewed a big pot of coffee, heated some pies and mushy peas, and nodded Shorty over to the office.

"What?" he asked.

"Don't know, something's not right with Archie."

I hadn't all of the equipment I would need at the office, and so I could only play one disc at a time, but each disc had a time display in the right hand bottom corner, so I could easily insert another, and fast forward to the time required.

I started with the forward camera. The quality was first class, high definition, with steady shot technology ironing out any vibration. With the sun from behind, it played like a travelogue of the Border.

Archie just sat there steadily munching through his pie and peas, saying not a word. Then just over half an hour later, the screen showed the west coast, as the plane made the turn out over the Firth of Clyde, and turned back for the short run to the crash site at Floors Farm.

I noticed Archie tense as the plane made its final turn back due east. The light had changed as the sun came in from a forward angle, but oddly the landscape also appeared darker. Must be a trick of the light I thought.

Archie spoke for the first time. "Now watch, I did you a little stunt flying." And as Floors farm passed from below the forward camera, the nose of the plane rose, showing the sky above.

But that sky was no longer blue, it had darkened to near black.

Bloody camera fault, I thought, but then spots of light shot across the screen. I paused the disc and rewound. The dots were blurred, streaked, but the configuration was unmistakable.

The Plough! Utterly, completely impossible in daylight, in bright sunshine.

I started the disk again. The plane completed its loop, and the light returned to normal, but for the next minute or so the picture was blurred. When it cleared, the plane was obviously on a south east course, heading for Carlisle.

Archie spoke again "Run the disc from the belly camera, the one pointing down. Just the section over the crash site, and the minute or two before that."

"What's going on Arch."

"Run it".

It took a minute or two to set up, then I pressed "Play". There was the landscape below, with the shadow of the little plane skipping along, and then the light changed slightly, ten seconds later Archie suddenly shouted.

"Freeze That!"

"What? "It's just the ground".

"Can you zoom in?" he asked.

"On what?"

"The shadow of the plane."

I fiddled with the mouse, clicked zoom a couple of times, and there it was centre screen.

"So?"

"It's too big, I noticed it as I came in for the final run to the crash site, but that's not the point. The Jester's a single engined plane, that's the shadow of a twin."

The hair stood up on the back of my neck. He was right.

He continued, "Run the rest".

I restarted the disc. Floors farm showed below, but darkly, then the nose of the plane rose, climbing, climbing, and the belly camera ought to have shown the A726.

But it didn't. Instead, forward and below was a small country road, just visible in the dark. Then the camera was pointing straight upwards as the plane reached the top of the loop, and once more the stars flashed across the screen, before it went both dark and blurred. A minute later it cleared, showing the main motorway south to the Border in bright sunlight.

Shorty breathed. "Jesus Christ!" I watched Archie carefully. He appeared to be more at ease.

"Thank God the camera's got it! I thought I was going nuts. Get me another coffee, and I'll tell you about it, but I need a solemn promise...... Not one word ever leaves this room, or I'll be off flying forever. In fact, I might just end up in a giggle jacket."

Shorty went off to the counter, and came back a few minutes later with a pot of fresh coffee. We really shouldn't drink so much of this stuff, I thought, as we settled down in the armchairs.

Archie began. "When the plane went into that loop over the crash site....I blacked out.... Bad stuff for a pilot, and before anyone suggests it, it wasn't the G's. I've been through much tighter turns than that without my suit, with no problems at all. When I came to, a few seconds later, I was the right way up again, and my hand was still on the stick. But the canopy was all frosted up. It took about 30 seconds to clear. I'd no idea what had happened, and I thought I'd hallucinated the whole thing. That is, until I saw that footage.

I remember that as I came up to the crash site, I felt dreadfully cold, then I saw the shadow of the plane on the ground, and thought it looked odd. After I came out of it, after the loop, as I say I put it all down to imagination. Now, having seen that footage I don't know what to think. But I'd better tell you that this isn't the first time."

We both just stared at him. "What do you mean," Shorty asked, "Not the first time." You told us you'd not flown that course before."

Archie was quiet for a second or two. "I haven't..... It was "Lockerbie," in the Harrier....But after this, I don't think it's the plane or the place......It's me.....Ever since I was a kid, some places, for no reason I know, give me the creeps. Flodden, a little plateau up on the Eildons, the Edward the 1st memorial, down on the sands on the Solway. I can't abide to be there.

Other places have a feeling so comfortable, that I don't want to leave. My house out at Toftholm is one of those. Eddie's place at Merrylaw, the old site of Gilknockie, this Cafe.

Me Mum used to say I had the second sight, and I just laughed at her. Until Lockerbie that is. And it wasn't actually Lockerbie at all, it was that little box of airspace at 31,000 ft, just to the south, where Pan Am flight 103 blew up..... I just had to go and fly through it.

Silly bugger that I am, I plotted an exercise, on one of the days we were down at Spadeadam. Made sure everyone else was down near the ground, and that there was no commercial traffic, then I flew my jet straight through that little bit of air. Harmless I thought, just a bit of morbid curiosity.

But they were there.... waiting for me, how or why, I don't know, and I heard them, the screams, the aircraft breaking apart....The Falling,....the Long,....Long,....Falling.

And ,in my mind I saw it all. It's the most terrifying thing that's ever happened to me, and up until now, I've never dared tell anyone what I did. I thought it was all in my mind. And I was cold that day as well, so very, very cold. The canopy didn't freeze, but it took me hours to warm up again.

Now that I've seen the footage from those camera's I actually feel better. I've no idea what it is but.......It's not my imagination."

He paused, and took a drink. "I'm cursed with this, and it worries me. Superstition says these things go in three's. And that's two of them out of the way."

He looked from one of us to the other, and I knew that we all had the same thought in mind.

Would there be a third thing?

And what would it be?

We tried, all ways, to dismiss it. Put it out of our minds, tricks of the light, camera faults, overwork. But the doubts remained. We never spoke of it to anyone else, and after a while life returned to normal. Archie went off back down to the squadron, and the squadron went for a tour of duty in the Middle East. He said he would phone when he got back. Come on up to Carlisle and give me a few more lessons in the RV6.

I was looking forward to it.

* * *

May 10th 2003.

Anthony Errington Vardy.

It was a Monday in early May. Around 11a.m. A bright cold morning for the time of year.

Reb was back in the bungalow, Shorty was behind the counter, and unusually, the place was empty.

I was in the corner booth, idly chatting with a mate of mine, Hector "Ecky" Charlton. Known to most folk as Detective Inspector Charlton.......Sir!" He represented almost the entire C.I.D. Department in these parts, and covered most of eastern Dumfriesshire.

Coppers have a strange way of sussing each other out, some secret radar, which allows them to recognise each other on sight, probably even in the dark, and I hadn't been in Langholm for very long, before this guy nodded to me in the street, and asked "Which Force?" From then on we bumped into each other on occasion, had a drink or two together, swapped tall stories, some of them even true, and formed an easy free wheeling friendship.

He was tall, thin, bony, fair haired and blue eyed. He looked like a hill farmer, which most of his folk were, and had been for generations. A rare breed these days, a genuine indigenous, dyed in the wool Borderer. Stick a steel bonnet on his head, and there was your authentic Reiver, and I've seen portraits of that same face, painted near on 500 years ago.

Ecky had also led the enquiry into the incident at the Cafe back in January. He's a good guy, for a cop that is, but as yet I'd never had to put his friendship properly to "The Test,"....My test..... My only test.

It's this.....When you're out there on foot patrol together, find trouble, and turn around to face it?....Well, if he's still there beside you when you look back?.... Then, and only then, he's a good mate. Invariably it works. But I guarantee, that you'll lose your faith in your fellow men, because, fifty percent of the time (or more) they've simply buggered off.

Sitting in the corner, Ecky and I were just about invisible from the door.

I heard gravel crunch, a clatter of pebbles hit the front wall, and a black Range Rover slewed to a halt outside. From what I could see, even the windows were tinted black. A second later the car door slammed shut, and I got that old familiar feeling....trouble.

Don't ask me how you know, I couldn't tell you, but I noticed that Ecky sensed it too. There's a reason that folk where I come from always choose the corner table. Walls on two sides of you, and you can always see the rest of the room. But that's just habit. The feel for trouble comes from experience. Bad experience.

If there's one thing Shorty can't stand, it's guys who wear tweed jackets, yellow waistcoats, and deerstalker hats. "Poncey bastards," he calls them. And if there was one thing worse, it was one of those poncey bastards with a shotgun. And that's just what walked in the door.

Shorty was behind the counter, polishing the cups and glasses. "Poncey," was about 40 yrs old, tall, fair haired, and hook nosed. Whereas Shorty was about 5ft tall, dark haired, and squash nosed. Exact opposites.

He slapped the shotgun down on the counter, and looked down the length of his considerable nose at Shorty.

"I say, "Short Arse," he drawled in an upper class Southern English accent. "Give me a coffee, and a decent pie. I don't suppose you have game, so I'll make do with steak and kidney. And make sure its fresh. I don't usually dine in establishments like this, but nowhere else seems to be available."

Shorty raised up his head, and looked up his short squashed nose at the man.

"Sorry.....Sir...., Business rules, I don't allow shotguns in here unless they're in a gunslip.

The man looked down at him, drew himself up to his full height, and continued. "Do you know who I am? "

Shorty walked along behind the counter, and removed the industrial can opener on its huge iron bar, from its mount behind the counter. He turned and laid it carefully on a shelf.

"Oh Aye, I know who you are. You're the guy's just put a shotgun on my bar, and doesn't want to move it. What is it, a Remington 870?"

The tall man at the counter hadn't noticed us. Beside me Ecky made a move to stand up. I put my hand on his arm, and whispered. "Just leave it for a while, Shorty can handle it." He raised an eyebrow, looked at me quizzically, and sank back into his seat.

The tall man resumed. "I'm Captain Anthony Errington Vardy, Estate Manager for the Duke of Marchbank, I pretty much run the place for him. I often conduct shooting parties around this area, and if you my man, ever wish to see any of our not inconsiderable number of visitors directed towards, this.... rather humble establishment, then I suggest that you keep a civil tongue in your head."

Shorty walked back along the bar, and before "Captain Anthony Errington Vardy etc." could do anything at all, he picked up the shotgun slid the cross bolt safety over to the right, into the "on" position and walked back along the counter. "Bloody idiot" he muttered. "You like these pumps?.... You look more like a man needs a double barrel, to go with that name." he said, and he raised the gun vertically, barrel down, slid it into the socket of the massive can opener, and pulled hard on the stock. The barrel folded neatly in two. In the fashion of an Old Western saloon bartender, he slid the gun back along the counter. It came to rest before Vardy. "There, now you've got one, a "doubled" barrel shotgun." He laughed like a maniac, and picked up the bar of the can opener. It was a formidable weapon.

"You moronic little Dwarf," Errington Vardy screamed. "Look what you've gone and done to my gun"

That did it. Shorty yelled, "I'm not a fucking Dwarf!" and he raised the iron bar like a baseball bat. It gleamed coldly in the fluorescent light. Shorty was armed, primed, and ready to do battle.

Then I spoke, and everyone froze.

"Killed any good rent boys lately Anthony?" Ever so slowly he turned and glared at me."Thought they took your rank away. Naughty calling yourself Captain."

Hatred burned in his eyes. He couldn't believe it. "Eddie Fucking Graham".

Ecky was on his feet. "Mr. Vardy," Ecky intoned, steel in his voice as he fixed him with that look that only policemen have. And Vardy had seen that look before.

"Captain Vardy if you please......Officer?"

"Inspector Charlton, Dumfries and Galloway C.I.D," and that

rank's for real." Ecky paused. He just stared at Vardy. Oh, I love to watch these guys in action.

Vardy was recovering his composure. "Thank God Inspector! How fortunate you were here." He pointed at the tiny menacing figure, still holding the iron bar across his shoulder. "This lunatic has simply wrecked my favourite shotgun, and I fear that his intention, had you not so conveniently intervened, was to assault me with that iron bar."

Ecky, looked from Vardy to Shorty. He picked up the remains of the Remington. He checked the magazine..... Loaded. He checked the chamber....one round in the barrel. He put the gun back on the counter. "Aye, it's lucky that I saw everything that happened. But what I saw, was a man, that is to say you "Captain" Vardy, enter this cafe, place a loaded shotgun on the counter, and demand service. Mr Higgins here, thinking quickly, noticed that the safety was off, and fearing for his life, he took away the weapon, and rendered it safe. Now, I know of you, Mr. Vardy, and you are fortunate indeed that you actually reside on the English side of the Border, because therefore it may be a day or two before my report arrives on the desk of the Chief Constable of Cumbria, recommending that he revokes your shotgun and firearm certificates, and so Mr Vardy, I suggest that you play with your toys whilst you can, since you aren't going to have them much longer." He picked up the gun, and thrust it into Vardys hands....."Now, Sod Off!"

Vardy turned to me, his face red with fury. "I knew it! I knew as soon as I saw you Graham, I just knew that someone would try to fit me up for something. I go shooting with Chief Constables on both sides of this Border!

I ....Have.... Respect!

Jesus Christ!......he burst out. ...."I'm,......I'm......I'm....A....

MASON!" He yelled......"I'll have your guts!"

We all burst out laughing, Shorty and I raised our right legs, put our right hands under our knees, and shook hands.

Vardy rushed out of the door. The doorbell played "Dixie" as he left.

Ecky looked from one of us to the other. "He may be right you know, I'll just bet he gets to keep that certificate."

"Thanks Ecky."

"Least I can do. I used to get bored, but there's never been a dull moment since you boys arrived.

So Eddie.... How do you know him, and what rent boy?"

Shorty poured the three of us another cup of coffee, and we took them back to the corner booth.

"You go first Ecky. I never expected to see that evil bastard again, so tell me what you know about him. Then I'll tell you my story. If you're worried about how long it will take, just count it that you're back on duty, because "Captain" Anthony Errington Vardy, definitely falls into the category of "official business."

He sighed, "Okay, but there's not much to tell from my perspective. I've known Pete Irvine, that is the Duke of Marchbank, for years. We grew up together. His land runs alongside our farm, down near Scotsdyke, and despite being "Nobility," he was a decent friendly sort of a lad.

When we were kids we used to go poaching together, a pheasant or two with catapults, salmon at the back end of the year, always getting into one kind of scrape or another. If he had a fault, it was that he was a bit easily led. Later of course, all of that came to an end, because off he was sent, down south to one of those posh schools where they turn out "Gentlemen." I still saw him in the holidays, but things were never quite the same.

Now they may have once turned out "Gentlemen" at those schools, but "mischief" down there by our time, had come to mean "experimenting" with drugs, and when he came home, his idea of a good night out involved, drink, cannabis, and a snort of cocaine.

Then in 1986 I think it was, his Dad died, and he was flung into the deep end, but of course he was too young, and he hadn't a clue. So what did he do? He hired himself a succession of "Estate Managers," and frankly they simply robbed him rotten.

Vardy was at school with Pete. Eton, I now recall. He must have forgotten me, because I met him once on one of the summer breaks, but then, that was a long time ago. He had a hell of an opinion of himself even then, and it was obvious that the two of them were using drugs, so I kept out of the way.

Vardy, kept well in touch after the death of the old Duke, and about 1995, when the latest "Manager" got the push, Pete offered him the job.

From what I hear these days, he virtually runs the place, and has poor old Pete totally under control. There's rumours of drugs, parties, and girls, all organised by Vardy. And Pete by all accounts does exactly as he's told.

I'd love to sort the bastard out, but although some of the land is in Scotland, the house itself is in England, on the other side of the Border. Cumbria don't seem too bothered, it's on the edge of their area, and you know how some of these guys are about the "nobility" anyway.

I've little doubt Vardy's bringing in drugs, but probably from the South, and no doubt he'll be on his guard about coming over the Border from now on.

But, there's another aspect to all of this. You can drive through that area, the old Debateable Lands, in fact through all of the area starting just south of Langholm, and its beautiful, it looks untouched. You'd never realise that it's actually a landscape under threat.

The coal measures start just around Hollows, and the site of Johnnie Armstrong's old tower at Gilknockie, and they stretch all the way down towards Carlisle and the Solway. Once, way back in the 17th and 18th centuries, there was quite an industry there. In fact at one point, Canonbie was the only place in Scotland where iron was being smelted. Energy being the big issue these days, there's a lot of folk got their eyes on that landscape.

The problem is that the coal, hundreds of millions of tons of it, will have to be deep mined....But whose going to do the mining?" He looked from me to Shorty, and went on. "All of the miners from down your way, are too long in the tooth. Same in the rest of the old British coalfields, so they'll probably have to bring them in from abroad. Ironic eh? Close all of the pits, then find you need the energy after all! There's talk of drilling for natural gas as well.

Pete Irvine knows all about it. A huge amount of it's under his land. I haven't spoken of it with him for a year or two, but he used to be dead set against rampant industrial development.

It'll be interesting if it ever does get under way, 'cause half of it's under England, and the rest of it's under Scotland.

But that bastard Vardy's a total lunatic. As I've told you, my folks's land runs alongside the Marchbank Estates. About nine months ago my sisters laddie was flying his model aeroplane out in the field. Those little planes are marvellous these days, radio control has come on a long way. His was a Spitfire. I flew it a few times myself, fully aerobatic, great fun.

But, one day, it strayed over the boundary and Vardy was in the field next door. He blasted it out of the air with his bloody shotgun. The kid was in tears. Vardy just laughed, and tore off in that black Range Rover of his. Claimed later that it was "scaring the game," and that the lad had done it on purpose. I tried to get his shotgun certificate revoked then, but believe it or not, I was turned down flat. He really does go shooting with certain police officers, all of them "Craft Brothers." So, as I said before, don't expect anything different this time."

Shorty gave a crooked smile. 'Well, at least he won't shoot any aeroplanes down with that gun."

We paused as Chuck walked in the door to start his shift. A car pulled away, and through the window I saw two young ladies waving. They looked like twins.

Twins !.......What next? They should create a category in the Olympics for that lad.

Ecky resumed. "Tell you what. Since I'm on official time, how about a bite of lunch before you tell me what you know about Vardy. My treat, I'll put it down on expenses. Any chance of three plates of Geordie Burgers and Chips Shorty? I don't know what the hell you put in them but it seems to be addictive."

Shorty laughed. "Ahhhh ......Everyone wants to know that. Secret recipe, not me Mum's, she was a bloody awful cook. This one came off a trawler, but that won't help you 'cause there's no fish in it, not today, well, at least I don't think so."

"Hey Chuck," he shouted. Chuck's huge frame filled the door to the kitchen. He grunted.

"I've got the grill going for you, all of the stuffs mixed, so can you do us three "Geordie Delights?" side order of Pinto Beans."

Chuck nodded, grunted again, and lurched back into the shadows. He looked knackered. Must have been a really tough night.

Shorty got up, put on a fresh brew of coffee, and shouted through to the kitchen

. "Hey Chuck,....Go easy on the Monkey Glands, your new supply hasn't arrived yet. And don't let any get into the burgers, they make folk frisky enough already, and Ecky's got three kids."

By now, the place was starting to fill up with the usual lunchtime crowd. Bikers, lorry drivers, the local bank manager, staff from shops in the town.

Don Williams was crooning "You're my Best Friend" from the

sound system, causing an older couple near the door to clasp hands, and look dewy eyed and soulful. Don Williams does that to folk.

Mrs Kang bustled through from the kitchen. She must have come in the back door.

Our plates arrived on the counter. I went over, picked a tray from the rack, and collected them. Mrs Kang was worried.

"Don't know what's wrong with our Chuck today, his eyes look terrible, dark rings and all. What he needs is a tonic, I'll have to sort something out for him, I've got a bottle of me Granny's Recipe, she swore it worked for her, and she should know, she had seven lads, and they all grew up to have big families as well. That'll perk him up again, it usually does, it's difficult for a lad his age you know, all that hormones and growing." She frowned, "Do you know Eddie, I do wonder if some of those lassies that hang around here aren't above trying to take advantage of him, and him such an innocent young lad as well. Then there's that widow lady out on Tarras, the American one. She's always picking him up to do odd jobs for her. He's forever having to go and fix her washer or something. Don't know what the world is coming to."

"Innocent young lad?"..."Fix her washer?" Never heard it called that before. Women are just blind to the actions of their families male offspring I suppose.

I shrugged, "Don't worry Mary, he's just a bit tired, all young lads go through these spells, he'll grow out of it in time"

"Grow," Jesus I hope not, I thought, we'll have to get bigger doors, he already had to stoop to get in. I considered the phenomenon that was Chuck, and wondered,....I mean it must be legal,.....But,.....What on earth was in it,....and could we patent and market "Granny's Tonic?"

We sat and ate our meals in companionable silence, while Willie Nelson quietly rode the "City of New Orleans."

Since the place was crowded, it wasn't possible to continue the discussion about Vardy. So Shorty stood us three giant helpings of Mary's bread and butter pudding poured with maple syrup and cream, and then we took yet another coffee through the arch into Shorty's office.

Ecky grabbed the big recliner, and lay back. "Oh God, I don't know if I can stand doing criminal investigation with you two, I could do with a good kip. It was that pudding that did it. Made with old bread....My Missus won't entertain it, she's gone all

"Nouveau Cuisine," organic veggies and nutburgers, little portions, arranged like some bloody modernist painting. Says the way I eat at work, I'll not live to be old. But I just want to live to be happy. She keeps nagging me to go to the doctors and have my cholesterol checked. She'll have me on statins if I'm not careful. Always muttering about the "Free Radicals." I thought she was going into leftist politics.

Pies are my weakness, I drive her mad, I told her that "Omega Three," was a planet on Star Trek. You know Shorty, you ought to get a licence for this place, get in Some Hook Norton, or Theakstons. I'd never go home, I'd just change my name to "Old Peculiar" (Theakstons finest brew), and park me'self a caravan out back."

He sighed, "Ah Well, Eddie back to business. "Tell me about "Vardy and the Rent Boy." Make a good name for a comedy duo that would."

I thought, "That's the only thing that I miss about the Police Force.....The weird humour."

"Nothing funny about them, though Ecky. Vardy is one of a kind. Con man, liar, probably thief, forger, or at the very least associate of forgers, probable fence, and genuine 100 percent ruthless sadist.

You know a bit of my history. When I was in the Met. I moonlighted a bit, "collecting" and dealing, mainly in antique Arms and Armour. I used to do all of the big London auctions, and quite a few of the provincial ones as well. This would be around '92.

I kept both sides of my life separate, and so very few, if any, in the antique trade actually knew that I was anything other than a dealer. It was quite good fun really, I heard all manner of information that no-one would tell a copper, and I developed a separate persona, so to speak. It was a relief, time away from the "Force," and it helped me keep my sense of perspective. That's one of the problems with "The Job," no-one speaks to you, and so you tend to spend all of your time with other coppers.

I first became aware of him, Vardy that is, when I was paying my bill at Bonham's in Knightsbridge. You pay in the accounts department way down in the basement.

I'd picked up a couple of useful early basket hilts. Nothing fancy, just plain ordinary fighting swords, but pretty much what was in use up here on the Borders, "reiving era" into the 17th century.

I'd noticed him at the back of the room earlier, not buying much, just bidding up some of the poorer stuff. I reckoned it was probably his anyway.

He came and stood behind me. "Don't know why you bought those," he said, looking down his nose and over my shoulder. "You went far too high. Nothing worth having there. If you really want some decent blades, give me a ring. I dispose of a few pieces now and again, trading up you know". And he handed me his card.

"The Honourable Captain Anthony Errington Vardy."

Specialist in Fine and Early Arms and Armour.

Valuations, Collections purchased.

Address in King Street no less. Now it so happened, I knew every premises in King Street, and that had to be a box number, and answering service. So the old radar cut in.

I saw him around the rooms quite a bit, after that. He didn't buy, just sold, and pushed the prices up.

It wasn't possible to say that what he sold was "wrong," it just didn't feel "right." Never any provenance, some nice blades, but the hilts? Perfect....but just that bit too perfect.

Age on metal is hard to simulate. It can be done, and it is done. A good restorer can work miracles. But when that "restorer" steps over the line....then Beware! And when that "restorerer" hails from far off, eastern Europe for example, so far away that no-one over here has ever heard of him?..... Then what's to stop a ruthless bugger like Vardy slipping a few copies through as original?
The answer is ......Nothing! Could be that the actual maker doesn't even know, and sold the piece as a replica in the first place.

Then he started offering some very good Scottish swords about privately, signed hilts at that. Simpsons, John Allans, Walter Allans. Jacobite Swords. The big money ones.

He tried to sell me one. It was in the car park opposite Wallis and Wallis's rooms in Lewes. But it just didn't have that "feel."
Too nice, too clean, and the story he told....?

"Eddie .... You don't mind if I call you Eddie do you......I've got a bit of a problem.....I've been up onto one of the Scottish Islands, can't tell you which one," and he tapped the side of his nose. "Famous you see. Laird's ex. regiment, good old stick, but absolutely impoverished these days.

Well,......the family was out in the '15, and again in the '45, and although the dear old place is falling to bits, and needs a fortune spent on it, the collection's never been touched. Mucky, dusty, but totally intact.

Poor old fellow's in a hell of a fix, his father died, and left a simply horrendous tax bill, and to cut a long story short, he's going to have to sell the jolly old Arms and Armour, all very much on the Q.T., to pay Her Majesty ......Bloody Awful isn't it?

Charles Whitelaw saw the collection, and so did James Mann, but the family didn't want it published. Must be the only untouched Jacobite Armoury left!

Well," he continued, "The Laird and I had a bit of a session on the local malt, and before he went off for the night, he sold me one of the family swords. Just a token so to speak of the quality of to come, and if I can sell it on for good money, then there's another, and another, and so on, much, much, more.

God! The stuff this man has! Huge cabinet of swords, all by the best makers, about twenty Doune pistols. Caddell, Campbell and company.

Would you like a look? Only thing is, due to the circumstances, confidential sale and all that, it has to be cash, and you can't reveal where it came from.

Ha, I thought the perfect con man's tale! And then, he opened the boot of his car.

At first glance I thought it was the real thing. I picked it up. I don't know who made it, but whoever it was, he was brilliant. Up until that point in time, most of the fakes that I'd handled were out of balance. Made from photo's in books, or aged up from those swords used by re-enactors, (Which are almost invariably, way too heavy), but this one was beautifully balanced, the leather liner of the basket was aged and stained with sweat and grease from the hand. There was corrosion visible right up at the top of the blade, just beneath the base of the hilt. And it was signed... I.A S. beneath the wrist guard. John Allan Stirling. Not just good. The very best.

But something was lacking.

You've either got it, or you haven't. And if you haven't, then stay as far away from Art and Antiques as you can. "Feel"...... "Age"..... "Use." It all imparts an indefinable aura to the genuine article.
That can't be faked, and this one didn't have it, so I put it down, made my excuses, and left it. "Sorry Mr Vardy, too rich for me at the moment I'm afraid, but good luck with it, I'm sure you'll find it a home."

He slammed the boot, and turned on his heel. "Stick to your little Border Swords then Graham. I thought you were a collector, I see I was mistaken." And off he stalked.

But he did find a home for it. Three months later it appeared in the "recent acquisitions" section of the newsletter of one of our more famous museums. So now, God help us, I suppose it will be in the text books."

I paused, "That's the Art Market for you Ecky. Long way from Antiques Roadshow.

After that, he tried the same story on a lot of other folk, sold quite a number of those swords too, all with much the same line in patter. Hush, hush, mustn't tell, rest of the Family would go mad if they knew the old fellow was parting with it."

Ultimately, of course the market clicked to the fact that something was wrong. Too much, too quick. Once in a year or two maybe, but far too many collectors were showing off far too many rare and perfect pieces. And so the prices dropped, and everyone became suspicious of good Scottish swords.

But then came the surprise, and I must confess, that until I saw him today, and heard your story, I had no idea how it came about. Vardy, came up with the genuine articles. Beautiful early British basket hilts, Lowland Scots daggers and ballock knives, silver encrusted English Basket hilts. All perfect, and beyond rare. All sold through the best auctions.

I've three in my own collection. All totally fresh to the market, and now I know how.....The Duke of Marchbank. Vardy's into the Marchbank Armoury."

Ecky grunted. "Nothing illegal there though Eddie, he's pretty much got control over Pete Irvine, so what he does really is up to him. But,.....What about the "Rent Boy?"

I continued, "Yeah, well, the Art World is pretty free wheeling when it comes to sexuality you know. I mean it wasn't too hard to work out that, Guardsman or not, Vardy swung both ways.
He used to go off with some rather odd types from Auctions. Fellows rumoured to have a bit of a preference for "rough trade." Occasional woman too. But all of them "professionals."

Not really that unusual in those circles I suppose, and certainly not enough to cause a stir down in South Kensington. But, in the Arms and Armour world, it was a standing joke that Vardy was the man who put the "Buy" into Bi-Sexual.

By this time, 1993, the job had clicked to my little hobby, and I was transferred to the Art and Antiques squad. Very few in the trade knew that, and certainly not Anthony Errington Vardy.

I'd noticed him paying a bit too much attention to one of the porters who worked a few of the London rooms in '92 and '3. Don't know if you go to auctions, but these are the chaps who hold things up and shout "showing here," as the lots are called.

Quentin James was a pretty lad, perhaps a bit too much so, and I asked one of the dealers, "What's with Vardy," and nodded over to where the pair of them were deep in conversation.

"Porters don't earn much, so young Quentin makes a bit on the side," he replied "He's got a little flat off Portobello Road. Quite a lot gets "Shown There." That evil bastard Vardy's one of his regular clients. If you look closely, the lad's using make up to cover the bruises. Trick of the trade I suppose." He shrugged, "Takes all sort's."

Bizarrely, at that moment, through from the bar drifted the sound of Boy George, mincing his way through "Do you really want to hurt me"?

I frowned at Shorty, and he shrugged, "Not me."

Serendipity? I couldn't think of how that got onto the sound system.

I resumed my story. "Then on the 25th of July, I received an urgent call to go down to Notting Hill Police Station. Well out of my normal sphere of operations. The Honourable Captain Anthony, was under arrest, and under investigation, regarding the beating to death with a chain of a rent boy by the name of Quentin James. Because of the Art and Auction connections, C.I.D. required the assistance of someone with a knowledge of the trade. And quite honestly, I was it.

I'll never forget the look on his face when I walked in. He had no idea that I was Police, and there to put him behind bars. He thought that I was the cavalry come to his rescue.

"Thank God you've come Eddie. There's been a terrible mistake, I went looking for young Quentin, you know, the lad from Christie's, we were going to go for a drink together, and he's been horridly murdered. And now these dreadful policemen think I have something to do with it!

I remember smiling at him. "I think you are labouring under something of a misapprehension, Captain Vardy. You see we've never been formally introduced, "I'm Detective Constable Eddie Graham, Art and Antiques Squad, seconded to Notting Hill, for the duration of this investigation."

His jaw dropped, he stuttered incoherently, and I thought he was about to cry.

We had it all. Evidence in spadefuls. All of the neighbours had seen Vardy at the flat on numerous occasions. Some had even seen the lad battered and bruised, and heard noises of violence.

On the day of the murder, one woman had actually seen Vardy and the boy go in, had heard the sounds of sobbing, and then the screams of agony. She'd called the police, and they arrived just in time to catch him on the point of closing the door as he was leaving. His fingerprints were all over the place, and the victims blood was on his shirt.

Bingo! Bang to rights.

But......He had the money, and money talks. He, or someone close to him bought him the best Q.C. available, and at his trial at the Old Bailey, a jury of his peers found him "Not Guilty."

Back in those days, "rent boys" were referred to as just that, "rent boys." No "Sex Workers," no "Victims of Society."

The defence claimed that Quentin James had lured Vardy to the flat, convinced him that it was all nothing but a harmless game, and then things just got a bit out of hand, and the lad turned out to have a weak heart. They trotted in all manner of psychiatrists, who told how the lad was a compulsive and self destructive masochist, who manipulated his clients into beating him for his own gratification.

The upshot of it was that Vardy walked.

The Army wasn't so kind. He was court-martialled, and stripped of his rank.

But he didn't leave London. He simply went back into the Art Market like nothing had happened. Picked up his "rank" as if he'd never been stripped of it, and opened up again for business, financed by the money he'd clicked from the gutter press for his story.

He told everyone that Eddie Graham was the man responsible for fitting him up in the first place. No-one believed him, but he said it just the same. I still saw him around the auction circuit, but if I walked in, then he walked out. We held each other in mutual loathing.

In '94, I left the Police, and joined the Army, and that was the last I saw of him until he walked through that door today. And that, Ecky, is it."

Except, I thought, for what Viktor had told me.

That Vardy was also a long time, and deep placed Russian Sleeper.

"Jesus," Ecky breathed, "Is that all."

* * *

June 15th 2003.

Someone was watching me. Or perhaps I should say, someone else was watching me.

That is, someone apart from, Ros and Abbie, Viktor, and Ecky Charlton.

Al Qaeda?......Huh!..... If it was them, then they'd just have to join the queue!

He, she, or they, were using two vehicles, or at least I thought they were. If indeed I *was* being watched, and not just becoming completely paranoid.

The problem is that some vehicles are everywhere. They are so common that they pass by almost invisible. What criminal worth his salt needs a high powered "get away" car? Just steal a white van, the modern cloak of invisibility.

I've got a thing about white vans. You can't really tell them apart, and there's thousands of them, in particular Mercedes Sprinters. Every delivery man seems to use one, and no-one takes a blind bit of notice of them. But why do they insist on them being white? Why not red, green, or purple? But no.... Henry Ford once said, "available in any colour as long as its black." Mercedes drivers seem to think the same about white, and I kept on seeing them, parked close by, parked wherever I went. Nothing unusual about that you may say? But time is money, and most delivery men are here and gone.

This driver was in no hurry at all. He changed his plates now and again, but I was convinced that it was the same van.

The other one was a green, short wheelbase Landrover. I would see it out in the hills, up on some track. In view, but unapproachable. Out here in the Borders, every second farmer has one, and so it was hard to be sure that it was the same one each time, in fact some of the time it probably wasn't. But someone was using one to watch me.

And occasionally I would catch a glimpse of a lone figure out on the hill, and a gleam of light from what could have been field glasses.

In town, I would feel that familiar prickle down my spine, that told me someone was watching. I just didn't quite know who.
But why, or what they wanted was quite beyond me.

* * *

June 25th 2003.

He strapped the mountain bike onto the rack, then walked to the front of the van and flung his cycling helmet onto the passenger seat.
Stupid looking thing he thought, but good together with the wraparound dark glasses. Good as a part of his disguise
The van had been delivered to him that morning. Left in the car park as he had arranged. A 1970 Volkswagen T2 Combi. Pity to lose it, he'd always liked these old V.W vans.
He drove slowly out to Longtown, just another tourist, doing the Borders in a beat up old camper. He turned off onto the A 607 for Gretna. But *he* wasn't going to Gretna.
He checked his watch......08.45 hrs...... Perfect!
He pulled onto the grass verge, parked, ate a sandwich and drank a cup of coffee from his flask. Five minutes later, he drove on.
He approached Army base on his left, and stopped 200 yards short. There was no-one about. But there may be camera's.
He took a knife from his pocket, and unfolded a steel spike. He climbed down from the cab, kicked the front wheel, and knelt down. Then he drove the spike into the sidewall of the tyre.
Air hissed, and it collapsed onto the rim. He walked back to the rear, removed the bike from its rack and leaned it against the side of the van. He took the jack from beneath the front seat, raised the vehicle up, and removed the wheel. No-one approached.
He strapped on his helmet, climbed aboard the bike, and cycled off. Half a mile later he pulled to the side of the road, and unfolded his mobile phone, 09.05 hrs. He had the number committed to memory. It rang once, and was answered immediately.
"Listen carefully," he began. "This is not a hoax, this call will establish my credentials. I am Malik al-Maut. You will fear me, for I am the Angel of Death. I act in retaliation for the aggression

of the Western Imperialists against my homeland of Iraq. This aggression will cease, or the consequences for you will be extreme. You will receive one more call from me before the end, but today, you must know that I am serious. Today, at 09.11 hrs an explosion will occur in the vicinity of a British Army base. You cannot prevent my actions. It is impossible, for I *cannot* be stopped. For I am Malik al-Maut. The Bringer of Death."

He closed the phone, and checked his watch. 09.09 hrs.

He took a small black box from his pocket, and opened the lid. Beneath the lid, was a red button. He closed his eyes, and in his mind he sang a little song. Oh, this was the bit he always enjoyed. He knew just how long that little song lasted. His song reached an end, and he glanced at his watch.....09.10.55

He giggled. He always got it right.

Captain Martin was furious. "Bloody Hell!" he screamed into the phone.

"What's holding them up! It must be ten minutes since that fucking hippie parked his crappy van there, and just buggered off. They're supposed to be guarding this place, not sitting on their fat arses drinking tea."

But even as he spoke, the Landrover roared into sight. It tore through the front gates, almost on two wheels, slewed out into the roadway, clipping the rear bumper of a huge timber wagon, the first of a convoy of three travelling towards Gretna. The Landrover didn't even slow, and shot away in the direction of the ancient camper van.

"Oh Shit," Martin yelled. "More sodding trouble! What are they, pissed or something? Get them into my office when they come back!"

"Yes Sir," It will be a pleasure Sir," Duty Sergeant Brewer replied with smile.

09.10.56.....57.....58.....59.....

09.11......!

He looked back up the road in happy anticipation, as he pressed the button.

500 kilos of enhanced home made explosive triggered by one

kilo of Semtex, detonated immediately.

The VW disintegrated into metal fragments. Fragments, both large and small. The engine unit was blasted back down the road, where it demolished a low brick wall, most of the windows in the army base were blown out, a huge fireball rose into the sky, and a crater six feet deep was blasted out of the road.

But quite incredibly no-one died.

The second timber wagon in the convoy had been less than a hundred yards past the van when the explosion occurred. It was hurled completely off the road, into the adjacent field where it landed battered and buckled on its side, trapping the driver in the shattered ruin of his cab. Heavy timber flew through the air, and was strewn like matchsticks over both the road, and the nearby fields. But the wagon had formed a barrier between the blast, and the approaching Army Landrover, and it shielded the vehicle, which was overturned, but survived more or less intact. The three occupants also survived, with cuts, bruises, broken bones, and one Army medical pension.

The third timber wagon, approaching from the east, was still some distance away when the van exploded. All of the windows of the cab were blown in, and its bodywork sustained considerable damage from flying debris. The driver was cut about the face and upper body, but both he and his pet Chihuahua, which had been in the cab with him, lived to both tell, and bark the tale.

A huge, black, mushroom shaped cloud hung motionless in the air.

In Captain Martin's Office, the windows were shattered, and he was half deaf from the effects of the blast. Sergeant Brewer helped him to his feet, and together they stared at the smoking scene of devastation.

Martin took stock of the situation.

That van should never have been able to park anywhere near here!

Chain of command, he thought.

When things go wrong, what action should a good officer take?

Years of training clicked into place.

Ah,.....Yes!..... He remembered now!

"Oh Shit! Duty Sergeant," he exclaimed, "How the Hell are you going to explain this?"

Me explain? thought Sergeant Brewer. Where the fuck were *you*?
And in that moment, Brewer realised that he was doomed.

* * *

He paused on the bridge, crushed the transmitter under his foot, and threw the fragments into the River Esk. He'd ditch the mobile elsewhere. Who can tell, they may be able to trace it.

Not bad, he thought as he cycled off up the road.That should give them something to talk about.

They'll be sure to sit up and listen, next time I call.

* * *

June 29th 2003.

It was mid morning, and "Roxanne" was oozing quietly from the sound system when "The Police," in the person of Ecky Charlton walked up to my table. How appropriate.

I was in our "management" booth in the corner. Shorty had even put a notice on the side.

Ecky looked decidedly uncomfortable. He took the seat opposite me. Over at the other side of the room, in the small two person booth, Brian was working on his laptop. He always seemed to be there these days, just part of the furniture, said it was the only place he could work properly. Perhaps he should have a notice on his little booth as well? We wouldn't mind.

But no-one else was nearby. No-one within earshot.

Ecky tried to fix me with his gaze. "Confession Eddie, Confession and absolution."

I smiled over at him, "No chance Ecky, experts have tried that before you. You'll get nothing out of me, at least nothing that I don't want to tell you. I'm agnostic, you need to go turn the screws on some poor wee Catholic. Threaten him with the Eternal Fire."

But levity was lost on him, and he looked even more uncomfortable. "Not you Eddie, It's me".

"Stay there," I ordered. I walked over to the counter, poured two fresh coffees, and asked Mary if she could do us a couple of rolls with sausage. Delicious smells drifted from the kitchen, and she glowered at me.

"Sausage buns is no good for growing lads like you two, just wait half an hour, and I'll have some proper food ready."

"It's okay Mary, this is just a snack." I carried the mugs back over to the booth.

"Right Ecky, What's the problem?"

He frowned. "Basically Eddie, you are.

When you and Shorty turned up here in 2000, no-one took a lot of notice. Just two more crazy "Geordies" sick of the way the North East was heading, coming back to their old family roots. Just like Brian over there," and he nodded to where he was sitting tapping away on the laptop.

Brian caught his eye and waved. "Hi Ecky." Another Ex-Met. from years back.

The track changed, "Every Move" How bloody appropriate. It was creepy, that system, I mean Shorty and Reb were back in the house.

Ecky nodded at the speakers, and looked even more uncomfortable. "That's a brilliant interview technique. "How does it work"

I just shrugged. "Coincidence?...It's certainly not me. Usually, it's just Shorty having a bit fun with his bloody I.Pod. But he's not even here. Now carry on.....?

"Yeah..... Well, as I say, no-one took much notice, until you began asking around, chasing up your little "hobby project."

"What," I asked. "Hess?"

"Aye,.... "Hess," He shrugged. "Almost everyone around these parts has forgotten about Hess, and the younger folk have never even heard of him. But in certain quarters, highly placed and influential people, are still more than just embarrassed about how their fathers and grandfathers were acting back in 1941, and when you turned up in Langholm, joking about the memorial to Hugh McDiarmid out on the hill. Asking questions all over the shop. Asking if anyone was still around who remembered the Hess incident, even taking the odd statement. Well, bells began to ring, and one of them was on my telephone."

I held up my hand to stop him. "Been there Ecky, say no more. You were dragged into "Sirs" office, and told to keep an eye on me. But now that you know that Shorty and I are simply fine generous, and upstanding members of the community with sunny and outgoing dispositions?....Now you feel guilty.... No problem Ecky, I think I'd guessed that much already, so don't let it bother you. It's just the dirty side of your job, and I'm too long in the tooth to worry about that sort of thing anyway. I like to think that we're actually good friends."

It didn't help, he looked worse than ever.

"That's not all Eddie," and he drew his jacket to one side, revealing a Smith and Wesson automatic in a shoulder holster beneath his left armpit.

Now Detective Inspectors in Dumfries and Galloway, simply don't go around armed. So I was suitably surprised. I tried not to show it.

"Okay,......I'm impressed.....So tell me."

"Right." He resumed....."After the shooting at the cafe back in January, I ran a check on you, and as you will no doubt guess, immediately I bumped into a stone wall. All I could get out of your old "Department" was that you had been involved in some very covert work out in the Middle East. It was suggested that "my" shooting may in some way have been linked to the work you did back then, and to cut a long story short, it was further suggested that I write it off in exactly those terms.

They assured me that no further questions would be asked. So I did just that, submitted the file, and, as promised, nothing else was said. But it niggled at me. So I ran a check on Abigail Ffanshawe, and Rosalinde Molesworthy. And my computer just shut down. No warning no nothing, completely buggered, dead as the dodo. I had our local "expert" look at it, not that he's much good, but it was no go. So I went home for the night, had a nice drink of hot chocolate, and then.... off to bed.

3 a.m. it was when they arrived, not quite the boys in the ski masks with the guns, but bad enough. Scared the hell out of the wife. They sat me down in my own kitchen, and started firing questions at me. What the Hell was I doing, running checks on Intelligence Agents? I'd been told to keep out of things, so why had I started up again? I said I'd had no idea that they *were* Intelligence Agents, but they didn't believe me.

The upshot of all of this was, that they decided that I knew more than was good for me, and they told me that they had decided to shut me up. I confess that at that moment my blood ran cold. But I needn't have worried, because all they have done is to temporarily recruit me. Officially, I'm seconded, on "Special Duties." Unofficially, I'm working with Abbie and Ros.... babysitting you."

He slapped a leather wallet down on the table and opened it. M.I.6. I.D.

I had to laugh, I used to have a couple just like it, and not just in my own name.

"Eddie for Christ's sake what is this all about? All they would tell me is that it's got something to do with you looking into the Hess business."

Of course, by now I had a fair idea of what it was about, but there was no way I was going to tell any of them. Let them work it out for themselves.

So I shrugged, and played the daft lad. (some of you may think I don't have to try too hard.)

"Ahh....don't worry Ecky, It'll all blow over, its just the Establishment trying to protect itself.

The Hess business went right to the top of Society. Although some do say that M.I.5 arranged at least part of it. So they're still touchy as well.

You've got yourself a right cushy number, and I'll try and make it last as long possible. All you have to do is sit around in here eating "Geordie Burgers" and drinking coffee, and in a month or so it'll all blow over.

He gave me a dubious look. "If that's true Eddie, then why the hell did they give me this gun? I know how to use it, I did three years in Ireland. But I hate guns. Someone up there must think I'll need it"

The sound system played "Billy's Theme" from "Billy the Kid and Pat Garrett." Shorty was back behind the counter now, and I reckoned he'd seen the bulge of the of the gun under Ecky's jacket. Ecky looked across at him and laughed. Shorty wagged a finger at him.

"You need a tailored jacket for one of them Ecky."

Brian smiled, and continued with his tapping.

"How's the flying going." Ecky asked.

"Great, most fun I've had for years. Hope to get my helicopter licence next year, and if I'm lucky, and Archie can spare the time, my fixed wing licence as well."

Donnie Stuart, and I had been out each day for a week or two, photographing, mostly around the Hermitage Valley, and Arnton Fell. Next, I wanted to do the Ninestane Rig with it's stone circle and related earthworks. I handled the take off's, the landings, and the short flight out into Liddesdale, and Donnie flew over the sites themselves, while I directed him, and worked the cameras.

Donnie brought his wife Janet with him now and again, and she took the Toyota down to the "Last Chance," while we were out. The pair of them were becoming quite part of the family.

If the weather held fine, I hoped to be able to finish photography of area by the end of the summer. It was amazing what showed from the air, that was totally invisible on the ground.

July 1st 2003.

Anthony Errington Vardy was delighted. He had been up to Edinburgh. Business with the Estates accountants, and had called at Welldean to pick up the girl on the way back.

Now she sat there in the passenger seat, silent, but he didn't care, he knew she hated him, and what he was forcing her to do. But they both knew that she had no choice!

It was a wonderful arrangement! He'd tried to get her to work for free, so that he could pocket her fee for himself, but she'd drawn the line at that. Said she was a specialist, and didn't work for nothing...... Quoted the bloody Duke of Wellington at him! "Publish and be damned!"

Cheeky bitch, but he'd have his revenge eventually, and he wasn't paying for her services anyway. He would deliver her to the Duke this afternoon, and that would keep him "tied up" for the rest of the day. If there was time, he may even get to watch them at it, through the mirror, with his camera. Neither of them guessed that the cellar was set up for both sound and video. Afterwards, Irvine could deliver her back home.

Just one little detour left to make.

He drove up the hill into Selkirk, turned right into the car park, and then drove on to the far end and down the slope, where he parked. Fifty feet away, to his right, was an old green Landrover. An Asian man sat in the passenger seat, and another, older, lounged against the front wing. Parsa, and his little friend Shabaz.

Vardy opened the door, and climbed down. "Wait there," he instructed the girl. She stared at him balefully.

He crossed to the Landrover, and Parsa Khan extended his hand in greeting.

Bloody cheek! Vardy ignored it. "You've got them?"

"Of course," Parsa replied. "And the money."

Vardy felt relief. He'd never liked dealing with this man, there was something unclean about him. Like a predator of some sort, a reptile, cold, unblinking, diseased in some way.

How the hell had it happened? This was a Russian operation

from start to finish, an old operation at that. He'd thought it was all forgotten about when the Soviet Union collapsed. That he would have to think of some other way of achieving his ends. And then in January, after all of these years, these two sodding Afghans had turned up. With the plan. Still, the money was good, and the papers were impeccable.

Parsa raised his left hand, and the other one, Shabaz, passed two large brown envelopes out through the passenger window. He took them, and handed them to Vardy. Then he nodded towards the black Range Rover.

"Pretty little chicken you have there. Wife? Girlfriend?

"Business acquaintance," Vardy replied.

Parsa Khan laughed. "Wish I was in that line of business." He turned, walked to the opposite side of his vehicle, and opened the drivers door.

"I'll be back in touch when the remainder of the documents are ready."

* * *

July 12th 2003.

Parsa sat on the grass alongside his truck, the sun warm on his back. The view from up here was spectacular.

Ten days now, he had come to this place. Turned off the main A7 at Castleweary, followed the track out past Phaup, up through the forestry plantations, and out onto the south western slope of Great Moor.

Climb over the fence, walk a few hundred yards to the summit, and on a clear day it was possible to see the sea glinting on both the east and the west coasts. Unique, the narrow neck of Britain, and a wonderful vantage point.

The Landrover was near invisible amongst the trees, and who cared anyway? No-one took any notice of another 4x4 in this area.

For safety though, he carried papers identifying him as a research student from Durham University, studying the habitats of birds of prey.

He poured another cup of coffee from the flask. Too easy to

become drowsy on a day like this. He removed a small notebook from the button down pocket of his green military style shirt, opened his newspaper, and copied down the times and dates.

He smiled. How convenient of them to provide farmers with information on low flying. Such things he had heard, disturbed the livestock. He picked up his field glasses and watched a pair of deer as they crossed the track. Imagined them in the sights of his rifle, and the pleasure of seeing them fall. His mind drifted back to the days when he used to hunt.

He had rarely gone for the clean kill. He liked to see them struggle and kick, to hear their squeals, and see the fear in their eyes as he approached with his long sharp knife. The red blood on the green grass.

The thought aroused him.

It really had been too long.

He must contact the woman, and arrange for the girl again. The blonde, like the ones in his magazines. He lay back, closed his eyes, and savoured the images in his mind.

He would hear it approach anyway, and it wasn't due back for another hour. The sun was warm, the birds were singing, and he allowed his mind to drift further.

He awoke with a start. The sky had clouded over, and he was cold without his jacket. He looked at his watch....13.27.... had he missed it?

A low regular throbbing sound, gradually increasing in volume came from the east, behind the hill. Right on time!

It was amazing really what creatures of habit men were. He climbed into the cab of his Landrover, just as a small red helicopter cleared the top of Great Moor Hill, crossed the valley, and swung left along the long ridge of Caerlanrig.

He watched it diminish in the distance and begin its descent. Ten days now, four flights over those ten days, and always the same pattern. Out at 11.30 back at 13.30. Literally, he could have set his watch by them.

Never follow a routine he told himself. Always appear random. Routines create danger.

Must change my vantage point, he thought, I've been coming here far too long.

Pity really, he quite liked this place.

July 17th 2003.

He had parked on the A7, in the layby below the Mosspaul Hotel, crossed the fence, and struggled with his equipment up to the summit of Wisp Hill.

The climb was worth it. It was a perfect day, and he had a grandstand view. Far below him lay the entire the sunlit valley of the upper Teviot.

Fate decreed that he record his triumph for posterity.

With the utmost care, he set the video camera on its tripod, and adjusted the angle to perfection.

He....Parsa Khan, "The Director" was present, his camera ready to roll.....The long waiting was over......And it was time.....Time to command his cast to appear.

The minutes ticked slowly by.

13.00 .....13.05 .....and finally at last......13.10!

Now, all of the component parts must be brought together. He drew his mobile phone from his pocket, opened it, and dialled the number.

Once again it was answered immediately, and he began.....

"Listen carefully, for this is not a hoax. I have proven my identity in the past.

I am Malik al-Maut. I am the Angel of Death, and today I shall bring death to many.

It is now 13.11. Two minutes after this call terminates, I will enter a small helicopter. A red Schweizer 300C. It carries no other passenger, for it is a bomb, a flying bomb, and it is loaded with 300 pounds of military grade explosive.

I will fly it from the Hermitage valley, in the Scottish Borders. Across the summit of Great Moor Hill. I will follow the line of the river Teviot.

And then.... I will fly directly to Annan, where I will crash the aircraft into the most sensitive area of the Nuclear Power Station at Chapelcross.

I will breach the Nuclear Reactor!

Many will Die!

Your Military will have the pleasure of watching my final flight on their radar screens.
There is no time to stop me.
I am invincible!
I do this in retaliation for the continuing aggression of Western Imperialism against my homeland of Iraq.
Think upon your fate. For you are powerless to prevent this.
For I am Malik al-Maut.
I *am* a Weapon of Mass Destruction.
I am The Bringer of Death!"

Within two minutes, the call was passed to, and evaluated by R.A.F. Central Command, an assessment was made, and a decision was reached.
At 13.18 the Prime Minister was contacted, and permission was given to proceed.
"No time to stop you, Eh, Bonny Lad," Air Chief Marshal, "Geordie" Forster muttered as he picked up the phone. "But why the Hell", he wondered, "has the bastard told us so much?"
It was 13.20

"Up above the Clouds, the Sun is always Shining," Archie thought, as his Harrier broke through high cloud cover over Bellingham.
From five miles up, the Borders looked like such a small place. From five miles up the Borders was a small place.
A mile to the south, off his port wing, his partner, Davy Crozier, was climbing towards him.
An alarm sounded, and an urgent red light began flashing on his instrument panel.
"Emergency! Combat Imminent!"
It was the light which should never have come on in British airspace, and immediately, the voice in his helmet, gave the

co-ordinates and direction of flight of the target aircraft.

"Terrorist attack in progress. Red Schweizer 300C. Give no warning. Terminate without weapons fire. Bring it down with a near miss Archie."

Archie acknowledged, and a lump, like lead, formed in the pit of his stomach.

He had a bad feeling about this.

Davy, now just off his port wing, raised his fist and gave a thumbs up sign, smiling, eager to go.

Archie, set the co-ordinates, put the nose down, and together the two Harriers streaked west for the Border.

It was 13.26

The Harrier has a top speed of over 660 miles per hour. Over 10 miles per minute.

Just three and a half minutes to the target

The two aircraft maintained a height of 15,000 feet. Almost immediately, their target was in sight on radar, travelling west across Great Moor Hill. Then it turned to port, and commenced to travel along the long spine of Caerlanrig.

Archie became more uneasy. Why here? Co-incidence?

Something about this was very wrong.

Target speed was no more than 70 knots, and the two Harriers, descending almost three miles in less than 20 seconds, dropped upon their prey like stones, right out of the sun, their airspeed in the vicinity of 680 miles per hour.

At that speed, there was no time to carry out a visual inspection of the intruder, and Archie realised the mistake just an instant too late.

Could that be Eddie's mate?... Donnie! ...They sometimes flew about the Borders taking photo's.

TURN!

Make another pass!

Force him to land!

He screamed to his wingman to abort the attack, and hurled his own aircraft to port.

But Davy never heard him, and his plane came in just above, and on the starboard side of the Schweizer. He was so close that the armoured tip of his wing sheared one of the rotor blades clean off, and the huge shock wave of the Harrier sent the tiny helicopter, spiralling downwards.

Horrified, his mind reeling, Archie heard the dying echoes of the screams.

He pulled around in the tightest turn he'd ever made, and flew another pass over the crash site. A single tall plume of smoke hung in the air.

On his radio he heard Davy acknowledge the kill.

Archie felt sick. Oh, Jesus! he thought. Lockerbie, Hess.....And this was the third one.

He'd killed Eddie.

* * *

Parsa Khan was ecstatic. The fools had believed him!

In his heart, *he* had not really believed that his plan could work. But not only had it worked, he had it all on film.

Eddie Graham was dead! And not only was he dead, he had been killed, knocked out of the air by his own countrymen.

The Landrover he thought, I must get back. I must return to the flat. Everything must go on disc immediately.

It must go to Bin Laden!

He was a genius. He was made. How they could laugh. The British had gone and killed their own man! And they would know that they had been tricked into it!

Now, with Graham gone, the rest of the plan could go ahead.

* * *

It was 13.30

Shorty and I had spent the morning servicing the generator. The problem had been cured by little more than draining the petrol tank, and cleaning the fuel filters. Water must have got in there somehow, probably condensation, and that had been most of the problem. But Shorty had brought new parts over, and so while we were busy, we renewed the plugs and points, changed the oil, and fitted a new air filter.

It ran sweet as a nut. Nice to have the power back on.

I was sorry to have missed the trip out over the Ninestane Rig. Still, I'd see the photo's soon enough, and there would always be another day.

They'd be back soon, Donnie and Janet, so I started preparing a dinner for four. Nothing elaborate, just four big slices of Mary's Wild Boar and Venison pie, with chips, and mushy peas.

We'd been hearing military aircraft off and on all month, and thought nothing of it. This was an electronic warfare area, and they regularly practiced about here, weaving in and out of the hills to avoid the radar, before popping up and "attacking" the army bases across at Otterburn in Northumberland, and at Spadeadam down in Cumbria.

Sounds like a long way, but at the speed those things moved it was just a matter of minutes.

I'd just finished cutting up some decent King Edwards for chips, when there came the most God Awful roaring. It sounded like some bloody lunatic was trying to land his jet right on top of us. I threw down my knife, and rushed outside.

Shorty had just finished tidying up in the generator house, and was standing in the doorway. Dust, and dirt and debris were flying everywhere, and out behind the house, an RAF Harrier, was hanging there in the sky as if the pilot intended to descend upon my helicopter pad.

I shielded my eyes. I could just make out a Jester's bauble, painted on the side below the cockpit.

Archie?.... Jesus Christ! What the Hell was he thinking of.

Through the dust I saw the pilot raise a hand in salute, and then the plane simply rose on its column of exhaust fumes, moved off along the tiny valley to the northwest, and climbed
rapidly, until it was out of sight.
We waited, outside for fifteen minutes, but he didn't return.

But neither did Donnie and Janet.

* * *

Archie felt huge relief, whatever had happened, Eddie was still alive.

It was just possible that it *had* been a terrorist attack, but his gut reaction told him no.

That had been Donnie Stuart's Schweizer 300. He had never actually seen the plane, but Eddie had talked about it often enough.

Archie turned the Harrier, and made one low pass over the crash site, his onboard camera's recording it all. Way out towards Hawick, he could see the procession of blue lights making its way down the A7. Davy Crozier was circling up at 10,000 feet, Archie climbed to join him, and together the two planes headed south for RAF Cottesmore. Debriefing would be arduous.

And the enquiry would take months.

* * *

I saw the plume of smoke, but thought little of it. Commonplace, just some farmer burning rubbish, or tree trimmings burning out in the forestry.

We waited an hour for the Schweizer to return, but of course it never did.

By now, both of us were uneasy. We told ourselves that they could of just flown direct home, but that seemed unlikely, since they'd intended to refuel from the tanks at my place.

So we set off for Langholm, only to be stopped by the police before we had travelled half a mile. There was no way past. They had a bloody great patrol car slewed across the highway. I pulled to a stop, and climbed out.

He was short, ruddy faced, overweight, and I'd seen him around. "Traffic," what we used to call the "Shiny Arse Brigade," or the "Persecutions Department."

You'd see him hiding in farm gateways, just off the main road, sitting on his fat backside waiting for speeders.

Like most Scottish policemen he'd had his smile removed, and I wondered if the operation had been painful.

He walked towards us. "Sorry Sir, No way you're going along this road."

I stared at him."There is no other road. What's the problem?"

"Crime Scene Sir, that's all I'm able to tell you".

I didn't need to be Sherlock to work it out. Donnie was late, plume of smoke, road sealed off. So I asked him. "Crime scene involving a small red helicopter by any chance? If it's a crash, then why "Crime Scene?"

He coloured. "I've told you, I'm not able to say."
"Jesus man! If it is that helicopter, then they're friends of mine."
He shrugged and reached for his radio.....Calling for backup.
So I turned away, walked back to the Toyota, reversed it onto the grass verge, and went back the way we'd come.
"What's up", Shorty asked.
"Donnie's crashed, or at least I think so. They've got it all sealed off, won't let us through."
"Oh Shit, Eddie.....Why did Archie come by? I mean that's a hell of a coincidence."
I'd already come to the same conclusion.
We stopped at my place, picked up the camera and a pair of binoculars, and then we worked our way out through the maze of forestry roads, northwest alongside the Teviot, and then back down into the next valley. Down through Hislop.
I parked the truck, and together Shorty and I climbed the north west slope of Blackcleugh Rig, the long ridge on the north west side of the upper Teviot. From there we had an unrestricted view of the valley below.
The main wreckage was down almost into the river itself, just below the old British fort on Caerlanrig. Small pieces were strewn over the hillside. One rotor blade was lying a long way from the main crash. It was obvious that there would have been no survivors.
I felt sick. If I hadn't asked him to do the photography, then perhaps this would never have happened. What the hell should I tell Rory Stuart?
I must have spoken aloud, because Shorty looked up at me. "If it hadn't been for the "genny" you would be down there in that plane."
I nodded. "Yeah, I know." And unease began to stir.
A large group of men were standing on the road on the hill opposite, and I scanned them with the binoculars. Police, Ambulance, Fire Service, and a number not in uniform. Volunteers? Probably mountain rescue.
A line of men were making their way down the hillside, apparently searching.
I was looking straight at him, when one of the police officers pointed. Seconds later, I heard his shout across the valley. Two uniforms detached themselves, and began moving in our direction.

But out of condition policemen would take an age to cross this terrain, so I took a few photographs, and then we walked back down to the truck.

Five minutes later, we came down past Falnash, and rejoined the main road at Teviothead. I turned right for Langholm.

The road out to Merrylaw was completely blocked off, and despite the distance from the crash site, police cars lined the A7, and officers were preventing anyone at all from stopping.

Something about all of this was very wrong. We were silent all the way back to Langholm.

It was 15.30.

* * *

Somehow, I believed, the crash was connected to me. And I didn't trust the "Authorities" to handle it.

First, I called Rory Stuart. I hated to do it by telephone, but he needed to be told before the news channels or anyone else put it out.

He was silent for a very long time, I heard him mutter "Oh God," then he simply broke down, and the line went dead. Five minutes later he phoned back.

All he said was, "I should have known this would happen," and then, "I'll come down, be careful, I have to see you."

Then I broke the story. They would hate me for it, but it had to be done, so I called one of my contacts at Border Television, drove to Carlisle, and did an impromptu interview complete with photographs of Donnie, Janet, the plane, and the crash. I explained that we'd been doing survey work around the Borders.

But anyone watching would know that I was still alive.

Shorty said I was Nuts.

Back at the "Last Chance," I left Shorty in the office, went out through the back and up into my flat over the workshop. I booted up the computer, and typed out my statement.

Never let anyone else write down a statement for you. Either do it yourself, or if you're really in schtuck, ask them to state their case, and then say you'll issue a statement via your solicitor, when you've had an opportunity to consult with him. Then say absolutely nothing.

But I'd broken no laws, and so I just typed out my own. Just brief details of my project to record the lost sites on the Borders, and that in order to photograph them, I had hired Donnie Stuart to fly me around. I gave details of the times and dates that we had flown, and also that he was giving me instruction as a trainee helicopter pilot.

I said that because of the breakdown of my generator, I had stayed behind that day to carry out repairs, and my place in the aircraft had been taken by Janet, Donnie's wife.

Then I printed it out, folded it into an envelope, and placed it in my inside pocket.

They arrived a half hour later.

I came through, and met them in the Cafe. Two men in dark business suits, complete with matching waistcoats and watch fobs, one tall, the other short and fat.

Scottish....Some weird Celtic incarnation of Special Branch. Behind them, Ecky Charlton.

I led them through into the office. Ecky took a seat in the corner, and just sat there, with a faint smile playing about his lips.

They didn't introduce themselves. Just stood there trying to look sinister. Then the tall one opened the proceedings.

"Mr. Graham, We require like you to accompany us to the Police Office, to answer some questions."

Always get them to be specific, and always stay on your own ground. Unless they are arresting you, don't even think about entering a police station.

"About what exactly?" I asked.

"It's with regard to an incident at Teviothead this afternoon."

I just shook my head, "Sorry, I don't accompany strange men to police stations. I do however believe that I am aware of the incident to which you refer, and in order to assist your enquiry, I have prepared this." I reached into my pocket, and handed him the envelope containing my statement.

"What is it?" he asked.

"My statement, duly signed and dated."

He opened the envelope, and had the good grace to read it.

"That's it?" he asked. "That's all you have to say".

"Yes, That's all."

"Bloody smart arse, ex Met, ex bloody Army," the little fat one exclaimed, "Think you know it all"

I pursed my lips and blew him a kiss. "You two are a dead give away you know. You should have just sent a couple of low grade uniforms down here, a sergeant, and a plod. Have a cup of tea, and ask a few civil questions. Then it would have looked about right. But *you're* here, so something went very wrong up there didn't it, or they wouldn't have called you lot in......Whoever you lot may be."

He reddened. Bloody amateur.

Ecky's smile broadened.

The pair of them hammered away at me for an hour or so, but it was simply water off a ducks back, and they knew it. So, eventually they gave up and left.

But the little one fancied himself as "Terminator". He pointed his finger at my face and spoke the immortal words.

"I'll be back".

I turned to Ecky as they disappeared out of the door. "Jesus, Will they never think up some new lines. Fancy a bite to eat."

"Wouldn't say no to a coffee and a biscuit." he replied.

We took the management booth, and Shorty came over to join us.

"Still got the gun Ecky" I asked.

"Aye". He looked uncomfortable.

"So you're with M.I.6. and not those two idiots."

He nodded.

"So what do you reckon to all of this then?"

"All I can tell you Eddie, is that it definitely wasn't an accident. I don't know all of the details yet, and even when I do, I doubt that they'll let me say anything. I also know that it will probably go down as mechanical failure."

I snorted. "So who was the target? I doubt that it was Donnie and his wife, so the only sensible conclusion would be that it was me they were after. And that's two attempted hits. First, the black guy in here, and now the crash. Do those two clowns who just left know anything about my interest in Hess?"

He shook his head. "Rumours perhaps, nothing more."

"My problem then is this, Ecky. Were both of the hits from the same source, or is there more than one lot after me? It takes no genius to work out that the helicopter and the Harriers that were about today are connected in some way, but surely H.M.G.

wouldn't go that far to stop me."

No, I thought, They may well wish to stop me, but much more subtly than that.

Ecky just shrugged.

At ten that night, I received an E.mail from Archie.

What he told me would be regarded as "highly classified," and would never under any circumstances be admitted to. He'd taken a risk in sending it, and had sent it from an internet cafe computer. He'd been all day in de-briefing.

Archie gave me the full story. Of the first call made by Malik al-Maut in order to establish his credentials just before the Longtown car bombing, of the second call, warning of an impending helicopter attack by Donnie's Schweizer 300 on Annan Nuclear Power Station. Of the downing of the helicopter, and of to his own appearance with the Harrier, out behind my house.

Pending an internal enquiry, he said, he was suspended from flying.

He confirmed that the official line would be that the helicopter had crashed due to "mechanical failure." The Harriers, it would be claimed had simply happened to overfly the area, where the pilots had both seen, and reported the wreckage.

Officially, there had been no call from Malik al-Maut. There had been no terrorist threat.

And no blame would attach to any military aircraft.

* * *

Parsa Khan sat in front of the television, and wept. He was finished. Graham had made a fool of him. All of his planning, all of the detailed execution of his plans. All had been for nothing.

But far worse. All afternoon he had worked on the computer, transferring his video footage to disc. Then he had packaged those discs, and he had posted them off to his controller in Leeds.By the last post. There was not the slimmest chace of retrieval.

He had made *himself* into a fool.

When he had posted the discs, he had allowed himself to relax. He had bought take away food from a restaurant in the city centre, and had gone back to the flat.

But Shabaz was not there.

At 6 pm he eagerly switched on the television news, just in time to see the face of Eddie Graham, speaking directly to the camera.

It was as if he were speaking directly to him. Eddie Graham! ....Not Dead!....Alive! Being interviewed. Reporting on the crash of the helicopter.

He had flung the food across the room, and now it trailed down the wallpaper, and lay stale and stinking on the floor.

Shabaz could clean it up when he returned.

But it was 10.30 p.m., and Shabaz was not back.

* * *

Shabaz stood outside of the flat, and stared up at the window. The light was still on, and he could guess at the reception which he would receive.

He had spent the day with Mehri.

Quite out of the blue, she had taken him to meet her father, Ibrahim, at his restaurant. He was a tall slim, hawk faced man around 55 yrs old, older than Shabaz had imagined.

He appeared to be delighted to meet Shabaz, and gave him a full tour of the premises, but he had asked many questions, particularly relating to Parsa's "textile business," and how long Shabaz would be remaining in the country. He had managed to answer them all, using only the most general of terms, but now he felt guilty at the deception he was playing on Mehri, and now also on her father. They were good people, from his own country. He knew that he was not behaving honourably, but what else could he do?

And it was then, that he realised with the utmost clarity, that Mehri now meant more to him than his mission. He was trapped, and there was no way out.

Back at her flat that evening, they'd sat together on the sofa, while the Border News played on the television. She cried out when she saw Eddie Graham's face on the screen

"Shabaz! That's the man we spoke with when we drove out to Sark, the man with the camera! Don't you remember?"

It had not been difficult to feign shock, for Graham was alive and well. A simple generator fault, he had stayed behind to repair it, and he had survived, his place taken in the aircraft by the pilot's wife. Parsa's plan had failed, and two innocent people, a man and a woman, had died when the helicopter plunged into that valley, and burst into flames.

He felt sick. He had steeled himself for the death of Graham. Told himself that he was no more than a casualty of war. Even the pilot he had justified as simply collateral damage. But an innocent woman? Allah be praised there had been no children.

There was no mention of any other aircraft being involved.

Next, a grim faced policeman appeared, stating that although it was too early to say for certain, it was being suggested by experts at the scene that the most likely cause of the crash was mechanical failure. There had been photographs of the crash site taken by Graham, but the only television footage was of a crowd of reporters, standing around at the end of a country road.

Mehri nudged him, she had been speaking, and he had not heard.

"I said, I'm pleased he wasn't killed, he seemed to be a nice man, but of course I shouldn't think that, because that poor man and woman died."

Shabaz was confused, because he thought that perhaps he too was relieved as well.

And now they must start thinking of a plan to kill Eddie Graham, all over again.

When would this nightmare end?

Shabaz sighed, took his key from his pocket, and opened the door to the flat. Slowly he climbed the stairs. "Parsa?" he called. An overpowering smell of stale curry filled his nostrils. The door on the landing was ajar. Not sure what to expect, he pushed it further open with his foot.

His uncle lay collapsed, unconscious on the floor in a pool of vomit. An empty bottle of cheap Vodka lay by his side. The glass had rolled across the floor.

Good Muslim or bad, his "Uncle" was unconscious from drink.

* * *

Rory Stuart.

It was around 10 o'clock the next morning when Rory Stuart arrived.

It was a grey damp day, with the cloud sitting low down on the tops of the hills.The road out along Caerlanrig was still blocked off, and looked like being that way for some time, and so I met him at Teviothead. We drove in past Falnash, and then I led him out through the forestry tracks to my place. Coming in from that direction, it must have looked even more remote than it is.

He looked strained, pale, gaunt, and red eyed. It seemed as if all of the life force had been drained out of him.

I opened the gates, and we drove through. He climbed down from the cab of his Landcruiser with a briefcase under his arm, and stared around at the trees dripping moisture onto the ground. There was almost no noise at all.

"Like it quiet, don't you." It wasn't a question, just a statement.

I led the way up the steps, and in through the front door. He collapsed into a chair in the kitchen. I put the kettle on the propane stove, and set up the percolator.

"Like some breakfast?" He shook his head.

"How was the trip." He just shrugged.

"It was my fault Mr. Graham. I killed them."

"Please Rory, look, they're saying the crash was due to mechanical failure, so why not just leave it at that, and see what the enquiry comes up with?" But he just shrugged again.

"You know, and I know that that story's rubbish. The men who came up to see me last night, were no ordinary policemen, and the questions they asked weren't ordinary questions. Something is obviously very wrong. But this, or something like it was inevitable. I knew something terrible would happen, I just didn't expect this, and I don't know how I could have stopped it anyway.

It all goes back to the Hess crash."

I poured the coffee, passed him a mug, and leaned back against the bench.

"Why Rory? Why now? I mean the Hess story is over 60 years

old. You don't even have the documents any more."

He shuffled his briefcase around on the table, then looked up at me. "Back in early January, two men came to the house, two Asian men, one middle aged and one young. They brought the Hess file with them. The original Hess file. They threatened me, at least the older one did, said I must do exactly what they said, or they would kill my wife, and my son, and daughter in law.

He showed me photographs. Horrible photographs, of what he had done to other people, and right there in all of them, there he was, grinning at the camera, a hunting knife in his hand.

He said that some of the people in the photo's, even after what he had done to them, had managed to live, at least for a little while, and then he laughed, as if that were the greatest joke in the world.

He told me that I must give the Hess file to you, and swear to you, that these were all of the documents which fell from Hess's aircraft, and I must never tell anyone the truth, no matter what happened, or they or someone from their organisation would return. He said that he would look forward to that with great pleasure.

He left me a mobile phone number, and told me to contact him as soon as it was done. Then they just walked out of the door.

I was in shock, but then I did the stupidest thing, because I opened the file that he had given me. Even though he had told me not to.

It was the original file that Calum and me took from that field when Hess crashed, but there were more papers in it. A great many more. And photographs.....All of them looked to be authentic, but surely they must be fakes? There were more names, more detail, and in addition there was another file. A very thick one, implicating both the Aristocracy and the highest echelons of the Royal family, even the King himself, in a scheme to assassinate the Prime Minister,.....Winston Churchill. Then they were going to make peace with Nazi Germany. The man behind this plan, the organiser, the leader, was the Duke of Marchbank.

I couldn't believe it, all of the documents appeared to be authentic. But now that I knew what was in there, I couldn't do it could I? I couldn't just give them to you, because you already knew what was in the original briefcase, and so you would know the other documents had been added.....And so I did the second stupid thing.

“What was that?”

“I phoned the number he had given me, and when he answered, I told him that you already knew all about the original Hess documents, that you had copies of them, and that his plan couldn’t work.

I thought that I could put a stop to it, but it didn’t work. He flew into a rage, and simply cut the call short.

Three hours later, he called back. They were coming for the documents the next day. But I couldn’t let them just have them could I? I couldn’t just leave it like that, and so once again, I copied the entire thing.....And that’s it.” He pushed the briefcase across the kitchen table to me..... “It’s yours.”

“The next morning they were back. They said they would leave me and my family in peace, just as long as I never spoke of the matter to anyone. They reminded me of the photographs, and to my shame, I agreed to say nothing.

I hoped that that would be the end of the matter, but in my heart, I knew that it wouldn’t end well.

Then, shortly afterwards, I heard about the shooting at your Cafe. I’m sorry Eddie, when I look back, I realise that I probably knew they were behind it, but I told myself that it was coincidence, nothing to do with Hess at all. And now, Donnie and Janet are dead, and it’s all my fault. I don’t *know* how they did it, but it was you they were after Eddie. That crash was no accident.They need to kill you, because you know the truth, and as long as you are alive they can’t use those papers.

I sat and stared at the briefcase. So, that was it, the entire story.

An ex Russian spy had sold the Hess file, along with my own, to Al Qaeda, and now Al Qaeda intended to destroy the credibility of the British Monarchy, and Establishment, using documents over 62 yrs old, cobbled together with a convincing fake plan to assassinate Churchill.

Perhaps the idea of the fake documents had been in the Russian file all along? Properly handled, I knew it would work. But where were the original papers now, and what could I possibly say to Rory?

He stayed on for another half hour, but then he had to leave to make arrangements for the double funeral.

I led the way back through the forestry. We stopped just short of Falnash, and said our goodbyes.

Just before we parted he shook my hand, and spoke the thoughts that had been in my mind all morning.

"Be careful Eddie, They may try again"

I drove back out to Merrylaw, and sat for a couple of hours reading the copy files Rory had left with me. They had done a thorough job.

But Rory's synopsis had not been quite correct.

What I was holding in my hands, was actually an approval, apparently signed by Adolf Hitler. An approval of a plan, to assassinate Churchill. It named, each and every one of the participants, and contained their signed letters of agreement to their individual parts in the venture. In return the Fuehrer, guaranteed them immunity, and protection from prosecution under any future German Government. Hitler had appointed his second in command, Rudolf Hess, to carry out peace negotiations with Britain on his behalf, and on behalf of the Third Reich.

Churchill was to be lured to a State dinner at Windsor Castle, hosted by the King himself. All of the most prominent Nobility of Britain would be present. At the dinner, he would suffer a fatal heart attack, and would be pronounced dead by the Royal Physician. Death was to be achieved by the administration of poison.

Immediately following the announcement of the death of the Prime Minister, senior elements in the armed forces, would take command of the country, and the King himself would broadcast to the Nation.

Hitler would express his condolences, and once again offer to make peace. The King would agree to hear the peace proposals, and Rudolf Hess was fully authorised to carry out negotiations on the behalf of Adolf Hitler

It was perfect. Today, most, in fact probably all, of the parties named in the documents were dead, and could never speak to prove their innocence.

As far I as I could tell, there was every chance that properly handled, these files could bring down the British Establishment.

I decided that the less folk who knew about this the better. So I took everything down into my cellar, and locked it into my big safe.

The crash of the helicopter cast a shadow of depression over us all, and so after a week or so we decided to attempt to lift it, by throwing a party at the "Last Chance."

It would be a good opportunity for Shorty, Reb and Co. to try out the various arrangements of their band, and we'd make it a Friday night, so that those who worked conventional hours wouldn't have to worry about getting up early the next morning.

I called in at the "Cross Keys" down at Canonbie where Abbie and Ros seemed to have taken up semi permanent residence, and invited them along.

Viktor was still staying out back in his big mobile home, and I found him in Shorty's workshop, servicing his bike. Shorty had found him a ten year old BMW F650, not hugely fast, but good for both on and off road work, and the pair of them had stripped it down and rebuilt it. Viktor had sprayed it a dark matt green. He seemed to spend a lot of time just touring around the hills.

I told him about the party, and warned him that Abbie and Ros would be there, but he just smiled enigmatically.

Ecky Charlton said he might just drop by, and all in all, it looked like being an interesting evening.

Friday turned out to be a beautiful day, so Chuck set up a pit barbecue out back of the cafe, and the smell of chargrilled steaks, floated on the evening air. Shorty had rigged extra speakers up on the roof for the folk outside. Word had travelled, and both the cafe, and the car park were packed. About thirty bikes were in, Reb had invited some of her old associates down from Welldean House, and we had the usual mixture of regulars and locals. Since we still didn't yet have an official license, everyone had brought their own drink.

Shorty had auditioned two of the waitresses in the cafe to provide vocal backing for the band, the core of which was still only himself, Reb, and Chuck on drums, and tonight Brian's daughter Avril and her friend Elizabeth, were also up on stage with their fiddles.

By seven p.m. everyone had been well served with both food and drink, and Shorty and the band were up on stage, ready to start.

As usual they intended to open with Hank Williams' "Lost Highway", in deference to the A7, our very own "Lost Highway"

The original Hank Williams Senior.

into Scotland.

Shorty stood in the spotlight, and introduced the members of the band. Then he began to announce the first number.

"Ladies and Gentlemen, Hank Williams'.....Lost......"

And that was as far as he got. Because, at that moment the door to the Cafe opened, and a tall slim man, with a thin bony face entered. He was dressed all in white. White suit, and white stetson hat. His jacket was embroidered with musical notes and scrolls. And he was carrying a guitar.

He walked through the crowd, leaped onto the stage, and strode to the centre. The entire room was completely silent. The tall man adjusted the mike for height and slung the guitar around his neck. Someone passed him a cable, he plugged the instrument in, and struck a chord.

"Ladies and Gentlemen....This is a little tune of my own, it's called "The Lost Highway."

Whoever he was he was brilliant. He could do Hank Senior to a "T."

He finished the number, and the room and the car park outside, exploded with applause. He did two more songs, "Long Gone Lonesome Blues", and "Howlin' At The Moon". Then he finished up with a barnstorming version of "Move It On Over," a number that Hank had recorded in 1947, and one which many say marks the actual the birth of Rock and Roll.

The audience was ecstatic, but "Hank" just turned on his heel, walked back through the band, and exited stage left.

Shorty came back to centre stage, and took the mike from the stand. "Who the Hell was that" he asked?" And the band went into an impromptu version of "Ghost Riders in the Sky."

Ten minutes later Ecky Charlton joined me, sliding quietly into the booth where I was sitting with Brian and Maureen. I couldn't help but smile. "Never knew you could sing Ecky."

"Oh Aye", he replied, "I can sing alright, I just don't get the chance. I do a fair impression of Johnnie Cash too. Me and the wife, Judy, we're a good duo. Way back, we used to do the club circuit, just for a bit of fun, and to help keep the wolf from the door. But then I joined the force, and you know "the job," they don't approve of anything frivolous, so I was more or less "informed," not officially of course, that if we kept it up I could give up any thoughts of promotion. So we've had to keep it low key. But bugger *them* now, 'cause D.I. is as far as I want to go, and it's time we both had a bit of fun.

Brian raised his glass to him, and we all drank to that.

At eight thirty, the band took a break. Ros and Abbie, had brought two chairs over, and were sitting alongside us.

I was looking directly at Ros, when the door from the kitchen opened, and Viktor walked through. All of the colour drained from her face. She looked as if she had just seen a ghost.

Viktor gave her a little wave, poured himself a cup of coffee from the percolator, and wandered across, an amused smile playing about his lips.

He gave a small "policemans" salute. "Evening All," and he nodded towards Abbie and Ros. "Aren't you going to introduce me to these two lovely ladies Eddie."

What was going on here? I wondered. "Viktor, may I have the pleasure of introducing "Miss Abigail Ffanshawe," and "Miss Rosalinde Molesworthy." Oh, didn't I sound frightfully formal.

Abbie extended her hand. Viktor raised it to his lips and kissed her fingers, clicking his heels together at the same time. Rupert of Hentzau to perfection. Viktor had been watching too much late night television. It was a scenario straight out of "The Prisoner of Zenda."

But Ros did not extend him the same courtesy. All she said was, "We've already met. In fact, Viktor and I are rather old acquaintances." Then, quite unexpectedly she rose to her feet, took him by the hand, and with an abrupt, "You must excuse us, we have rather a lot of catching up to do," she led him off, back out through the kitchen, the way he had entered.

Chuck was back up on the stage, in a white Elvis suit. This was his part of the evening, and much to the chagrin of the biker crowd, most of their "ladies," had gravitated to the immediate front of the stage.

In the process of perfecting his act, Chuck had come to adopt the technique favoured by very many actors as well as singers.

In order not to be overwhelmed by the crowd, he would select one or two members of the audience, and would perform his act directly to them. In Chuck's case of course, the targets were invariably female, and usually rather attractive. Which was just fine.....unless one of the girls happened to be the object of someone else's affections.

And on this evening, although she didn't yet know it, he'd chosen the rather spectacular blonde slightly to the front of stage left, the one wearing the white dress a la Marilyn Monroe and the polka dot hairband, but unfortunately, she had also caught the eye of Lonnie, the huge would be badass from Canonbie.

Lonnie had it all, shaved head, huge bushy beard, tattoos, beer belly, facial piercings, torn jeans, cut off leather jacket, chains dangling from his belt, and huge boots.

All that he was actually lacking was a bike. He usually arrived on the number 95 bus.

He didn't even know you were supposed to pay. He looked so fearsome the drivers had never dared ask him for the fare.

His Mam and Dad, who were Social Workers and Ex Hell's Angels, wondered why he didn't go and buy a Harley or something. But Lonnie was a truly mean biker, and he just couldn't bear to give up on the free transport.

Chuck had worked his way almost through his Elvis repertoire, gazing all of the time into Marilyn's baby blue eyes.

Lonnie could stand it no longer, and just as Chuck announced "Heartbreak Hotel," he forced his way through the crowd to stage centre. I felt Ecky tense beside me, so I nudged him in the ribs. "You're off duty, so don't worry about it bonnie lad, Chuck can handle it. Hank got this sort of thing all of the time you know"

Chuck fixed the blonde with his eyes, and his mouth twisted in an sexy Elvis sneer.

She simpered up at him, her ample bosom heaving.

"Weell, ... Since my baby left me,
I found a new place to dwell,"

"Aye, well Bugger Off and dwell there then!" called Lonnie.
But Chuck never flinched.

"It's down at the end of Lonely Street,
At Heartbreak Hotel."

"Get off, yer Big Jessie! Lonnie yelled.

But Chuck just moved slightly, until he was standing just to one side of him, his gaze still locked with the girls.

"I've been so lonely baby,
"Well I'm so lonely,"

The mike was in his left hand, and he raised his right above his head.
"Well I'm so lonely I could die."

And on the word "die," Chuck's right fist descended, directly onto the top of Lonnie's head.
It was a pile driver of a blow, but he never broke his lyrics.
Lonnie's eyes rolled upwards into his head, and he collapsed like a sack of grain onto the floor. The crowd broke into cheers, two bikers rushed forward, grabbed Lonnie by the ankles, towed him unceremoniously across the floor, and deposited him, propped up against the counter.
Unfazed at all, in fact more animated than ever, Chuck continued his rendition. He even did an encore. His leg shook, his hips gyrated, his pelvis thrust. He ought to have been born in the 16th century, because then the codpiece could have been invented just especially for him.
The audience went wild, the bikers cheered him, and the girls duly swooned.
Meanwhile, over at the counter, Lonnie slowly regained consciousness. He groped his way upwards and just knelt there...... Resting....
Resting face to face to face with Chuck's Auntie, Mary Kang.
"Aye.....Lonnie....And you'll be having a bit of a headache now then won't you?" she asked solicitously
"Yes Mrs Kang," he replied sheepishly.
Mary reached behind her, and removed some Paracetamol tablets from a cupboard.
"These are good. These....would be just what you're needing.... They'd fix it up real quick."
Lonnie nodded.
"Well".....Mary continued. "They sell them at the chemists down by the Town Hall." And she turned, replaced the tablets in the cupboard, and closed the door.
Lonnie staggered to his feet, lurched across the room, and disappeared through the front door.

Ecky had watched the entire performance. He laughed, "So...Jeddart Justice is alive and well!"

Outside of the window, I saw Viktor wheeling his BMW out through the gate. Ros was with him. She was dressed in an oversize leather jacket, and carrying a black helmet. Viktor started the bike, she climbed on behind him, and off they went. North up the A7.

I glanced across the table. Abbie had seen them as well. She shrugged, and held her hands palms upwards......Mystery.

Ten minutes later, I was over at the counter, when Lonnie shuffled back in through the door.

Chuck was beside me, one arm around "Marilyn," who was clinging to him like Ivy.

No I thought, not Ivy, she was last week.

Looming in the shadows behind him was a very tall, very obese biker girl, clad totally in black leather.

Lonnie, edged up to the counter, and looked sheepishly at Mary Kang.

"The Chemist's was shut. Mrs Kang."

"Aye".....she replied, drawing the word out in the way only a Borderer can..... "I ken't that, but the walk in the fresh air would do you good." She turned on her heel, and disappeared into the kitchen.

"Sorry Chuck," Lonnie mumbled.

"Think now't of it," Chuck replied. He turned with his back to the counter, revealing the huge girl behind.

"This is Jezabel Lonnie, and she's been asking after you for weeks now."

Jezabel smiled a huge, gap toothed smile. She reached out, and took Lonnie by the arm.

"Come on out back pet, and have a look at me Kawasaki will you?"

"Ahh"..... I thought, "It's been a long time since I've heard it called that."

A huge grin spread across Lonnie visage, his facial jewellery rang like tiny bells. And arm in arm they walked back out through the door.

It was late, when we heard Viktor's bike return, Shorty and Reb had retired for the night, and I had promised to close the place up.

We were in the management booth, just myself, Ecky, and Abbie.

I had a bottle of Glenmorangie and a bottle of spring water open on the table, and we'd all had more than a couple of glasses by the time the pair of them came in through the door.

Viktor walked over to the table, and helped himself to a glass.

I nodded to Ros, but she held up her hand. "One of us had better remain sober, because we have to get back down to Canonbie. Would you like a lift Ecky? Since you're now "one of us" as it were, I sort of feel responsible for you. You can always pick up your car in the morning."

I couldn't help but smile. "So, now it's all on an official level is it?.... But what about Viktor there? Should you be talking in front of him? I mean surely he's just an innocent bystander?"

The pair of them burst out laughing. "Oh no," she replied. "There's nothing innocent about our Viktor," and she slipped her arm around his waist, "we're old acquaintances."

Viktor nodded. "Met in Croatia years ago, me and Ros. She was supposed to kill me, she's very good at that sort of thing you know."

"But not good enough," she interrupted. "You've no idea what a shock it was when I saw him walk in here tonight. I thought I'd shot him properly with my little gun." And they both burst out laughing again.

Viktor sipped his whisky, and squeezed her to him. "Of course.....I didn't take it personally."

Ecky was watching in amazement, unused to all of this "Secret Agent" camaraderie.

"So where did the pair of you go off to tonight?" he asked.

"Oh, just a little tour around, off across the Hermitage Valley, had a walk around the Castle, visited the Lady's Well, which turned out to be nothing more than a muddy hole in the ground now. Pity that. And then Viktor took me down to see his house out on the Tarras Water."

"What house Viktor?" I'd heard nothing about this.

"Well Eddie, I'm getting a bit too long in the tooth for this exciting life, so I decided that it was about time I found somewhere of my own. Have you ever heard of "Glen Tarras?"

"Only one I know, used to come in bottles like that one on the table," I replied.

He looked pleased. "That's right, the distillery was out south of Langholm, not too far from Gilknockie Station. Beautiful little side valley. You can still see the long mound where the buildings used to stand. It shut around the time of World War One, but there are still a few houses down that way, alongside the river, and one of them was empty. I found it a while back when I was out on the bike. So I made a few enquiries, and the upshot is that I made an offer, and now it's mine. It'll take a bit of doing up, but so what? It's a base, somewhere to call my own."

"So, You're staying here are you." Abbie asked.

Viktor nodded, "Could be.... Who knows?...No objections from the "Senior Management" are there? I mean, we're all friends together these days."

I looked from one of them to the other. "What do you mean, "Senior Management?"

Abbie looked embarrassed.

"Ooops, Sorry," Viktor replied, "I thought you knew." But he didn't look in the least sorry.

"Abbie here is not quite your normal field agent. Quite the reverse, she reports direct to the Prime Minister. Has her own office in Parliament." He laughed. "You know back home, all of you agents have sort of "nicknames," on their files that is."

"Go on" Abbie interjected. "Tell them mine then."

"Well, You see, Abbie there, is always at the Parliament, and you know where that is, so she gets....

"Westminster Abbie" I interrupted.

Everyone laughed, including the lady herself, who was by now, showing the effects of the malt.

"So what's mine," Ros asked.

Viktor looked embarrassed. "Are you sure you want to know?"

"Go on, tell her," Abbie urged.

"Okay, You're the boss.....she's called "Dirty!"

"Dirty!" Ros exploded, "What the Hell for!"

Viktor smiled knowingly. "On account of what you carry in that little alligator purse of yours."

Ros blushed. "Trust you to know all about that."

We sat there for another half an hour, until the bottle simply ran out. What a strange group of friends, I thought. All brought together it seemed by my interest in a senior Nazi, who fell out of his aeroplane up near Glasgow, in 1941.

Each one of us I thought, knew something about the story. None of us knew it all, except perhaps for me, and I wasn't even really sure about that.

* * *

Parsa, was both relieved, and exhilarated.

He was not disgraced! Indeed, he had been complimented on the planning and execution of his plan, and on the crash of the helicopter. He was assured that at the very highest level, it was considered a major blow against the West, proving to them, that the forces of Al Qaeda could penetrate the boundaries of any western country at will, and bring about destruction. And better still, that they could use the very armed forces of a nation such as Great Britain as the instrument to carry out the act of terrorism.

He was promised the highest rewards when he returned to his homeland.

With regard to the matter of Graham, he was instructed to proceed with extreme caution. There must be no more high profile attempts on his life. Graham must simply disappear without trace, and once he was removed, then another method must be found of making the Hess documents public.

And so, Parsa decided to simply watch, and to wait. To wait for an opportunity to catch Graham unawares. Then, he and Shabaz would carry out the execution in person. At close quarters.

He went through to his bedroom, opened one of his cases, and removed a pair of long bladed hunting knives. His favourite weapons. He drew one from its sheath. The blade was blue black, and reflected almost no light, but the honed and razor sharp edge gleamed evilly.

Sometimes, he thought he lived just to kill with the knife.

He caressed the edge with his thumb, drawing a thin line of blood. He put it to his lips, and savoured the taste.

Next time, there would be no mistakes.

He picked up the telephone, and arranged for the girl.

Just one more time, he told himself.

* * *

It had been the most wonderful day. He had left the Sprinter parked out at Kingstown, where Parsa would never see it, and Mehri had picked him up with her car.

He was supposed to be up near Langholm, watching Eddie Graham, but Eddie Graham, could wait for another day.

They drove south on the M6. as far as Penrith, and then turned off onto the A66, and out to Brough Castle. Then they spent the day just wandering back via Appleby Castle, Penrith, and then the little deserted castle at Clifton.

Shabaz liked that one the best. There was no-one there, the door was open, and even much of the original woodwork was still in place.

"Not a place to take children though," Mehri commented. He glanced at her, and wondered why she had said that. Then she took him completely by surprise.

"Don't go back Shabaz."

"Back where" he asked.

She flew into his arms, and hugged him so tightly that it hurt.

"Back to Afghanistan! Just tell your uncle that you don't want to work for him any more. Stay here with me." And now tears were running down her cheeks.

He caressed her hair. "But how could I do that, this is not my country, I would have no work."

She dried her eyes on the back of her hand. "My mother died three years ago, my father is alone, I am his only child."

"I'm sorry," he replied, "I didn't know."

"I have talked this over with father, he likes you, he believes that you like me, and if you wish to stay, he says that he will train you to work the restaurant, as a sort of assistant manager.
And if you and I remain together, then who knows what may happen."

Shabaz was speechless. He just clung to her. The prospect of staying here in this country had never even occurred to him.

He, was not here to become a part of Britain. He was here to destroy it, to bring it down, and if Parsa ever suspected that he was not fully committed to their mission, then he was certain that he would simply send for someone, and have him killed. Or Parsa would do it himself.

He must think, he must plan. He must find some way out, because he knew now that staying here with Mehri, was exactly what he wanted to do. They talked of little else, almost all of the way back to Carlisle.

They turned off the motorway, onto the old A6, and entered the town via Botchergate.

Traffic was heavy, the car moved at a snail's pace, and they hadn't travelled more than a hundred yards, before the traffic came to a complete standstill. Shabaz gazed around. Much of this area was under renovation, and on the left, just ahead of the car, was an empty shop, its murky windows covered with peeling posters.

To the right of the shop was a blue door with peeling paintwork, he supposed that it most likely opened onto to a flight of stairs leading up to the premises above.

Despite the run down appearance of the property, a bright new bell and speaker box were affixed on the right hand side of the doorframe.

He craned his neck and peered upwards. The curtains moved in the upstairs window, and he glimpsed the face of a middle aged woman with short dark hair, looking down into the street.

For no reason he could think of, a cold chill ran down his spine.

Just as the line of traffic began to move again, the blue door opened and a man's head came into view. He peered furtively up and down the street, and then stepped out onto the pavement.

He couldn't believe it. Speak of the Devil.... And he will appear? It was his Uncle...... Parsa! What had he been doing, up above that shop?

Shabaz sank down into the passenger seat. He must not be seen! But inexorably, almost in slow motion, as if dragged by some irresistible force......Parsa's head turned, and he glared directly into Shabaz's eyes

Shabaz was amazed. His uncles face did not register anger, but pure shock, and then he turned quickly on his heel, ran across the road through the slow moving traffic, and disappeared off up a side street.

Mehri, looked puzzled. "What was that all about."

"I don't know, but that was my uncle ..... Parsa."

She was silent for a few seconds. And then....."Shabaz?"

"What is it?"

"That door.....The house that your uncle came out of."

She paused.

"What about it?" he asked.

"Well, that place has an evil reputation. A certain type of girls work there. Not good girls, if you know what I mean. Girls who will do anything for money, and the woman who owns it is well known. Some of the girls who have worked for her are said to have simply disappeared, others have been injured. Most of the business people in the town know about her, and in many places she is not welcome.

Shabaz thought of the stained magazines beneath his uncle's mattress, and shuddered.

* * *

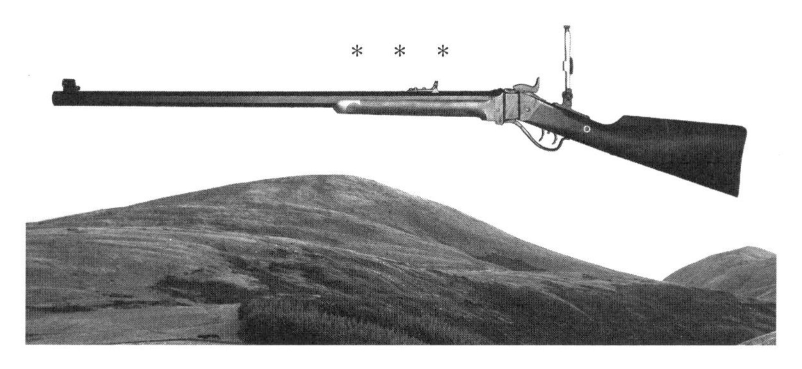

Shorty and Reb lay belly down in the grass, on the summit of Rowantree Hill, and looked down, at Eddie's house and enclosure.

He had calculated the distance exactly, 1540 yards.

The Billy Dixon Shot!

But this would be even more difficult. Downhill. So he would have to compensate for the fact that the bullet would be falling, and that therefore the gravitational force upon it, would be far lower.

For months now, whenever Eddie was away and the weather was good, they came up here, and he practiced with the Sharps.

Just three shots on each occasion.

Shorty knew Eddie had told him not to, but he couldn't seem to help himself.

After each session he carefully cleaned the Sharps and replaced it in the gun safe back at the "Last Chance." He loaded his own ammunition, carefully by hand, and always took care to ensure that there was no discrepancy in the number of rounds that Eddie kept with the gun.

Reb said she thought Eddie knew about it really, but turned a blind eye. Shorty wasn't so sure.

He'd placed a large orange oil drum out on the range at the back of Eddie's house, and if he missed, then the shot would simply plough into the bank of sand behind it.

That sand was carefully raked and smoothed, so that the fall of the shot would be easily visible. So far he had not managed to hit the target. But he had achieved some near misses.

He'd lit a small smoky fire 50 feet beyond the target to indicate the direction and speed of the wind. Crude perhaps, but it might just help. But up here in the hills, the wind swirled around quite unpredictably. Of course, that was what made this all so interesting.

Reb lay upwind of him and off out to one side, with a huge spotter scope, ready to call his hits, or more likely, his misses.

He had the rifle propped up on sandbags. They'd carted the whole lot up the hill on a quad bike he'd worked on rebuilding over the last few months.

He pulled the hammer back to half cock, opened the breech, and selected a round from the cartridge box. The brass gleamed in the sunlight as he slid it home. He closed the breech.

Reb clamped her ear defenders onto her head.

Shorty brought the rifle to full cock, and pulled back on the rear trigger to "set" the forward one. He sighted on the oil drum, made allowances for wind, and the drop of the bullet. Then he rested his finger gently on the second trigger, took a deep breath, exhaled slowly, and at the same time, squeezed gently.

The massive rifle erupted, gouting acrid white smoke, and the buttplate slammed into his shoulder driving his entire body back across the grass.

Even after all of these months, the impact still came as a surprise, and three shots would be quite enough to bruise his shoulder.

Seconds later Reb called."10 feet high, 12 o'clock." Indicating the fall of the shot.

Shit! thought Shorty. He was on the right line vertically, but way too high. It was being up on the hill that was doing it. The bullet was falling at least as fast as gravity was pulling it down.

They repeated the process twice more. Two more misses, one too low, the last one correct vertically but a foot off to the right. Should have been a hit really, but just a puff of breeze from the left, at just the wrong moment, and the shot was carried off line.

It was a Hell of a distance after all, and he was beginning to wonder if this shot was just not possible. Could Billy Dixon's hit at this range, have been no more than a very lucky fluke?

Reb rolled over onto her back smiling. "Nearly got it that last time." she paused smiling. "Shorty?".....You know .... Up here on this hill....in this little hollow.....Well..... no-one can see us, can they?

He grinned. "Aye Pet, you're right there."

"Well" she continued. "It's nice and warm up here in the sunshine. Is there any special little thing you would like me to do for you? A sort of little alfresco treat?"

"Ohhh Aye" Shorty replied, "There is, but I don't like to ask you to do it."

"What is it then," she asked her breath catching slightly in her throat. "I'm very broadminded."

"Well.......It's this......You know how I've got these odd little tastes and fancies?"

She nodded, eagerly.

"Well.....then....Luv..........Pass us one of those stotties with the pork and stuffing. I'm bloody starving!"

She grabbed at him, and they rolled about in the grass laughing hysterically. An hour later, satisfied grins on both of their faces, they packed up all of the gear into the trailer of the Quad bike, and trundled off back down the hill. Best get back to the Cafe before Eddie returned. Just as well this was a quiet area and the neighbours turned "Nelson's Eye." Because that Sharps made a noise like a small cannon.

Next time he might try shooting on a site that was level, and not downhill.

Maybe he would manage it then.

* * *

What was he to do?

Mehri had dropped him off at Kingstown, and he had collected the van. He'd promised to meet her the next morning, at the bookshop. Then with a heavy heart, he drove back to Aglionby Street, and the flat.

The Landrover was parked on the street outside. His uncle was at home.

And so Shabaz began to work on his anger. He thought of the years he had spent in the school in Pakistan, the indoctrination, the training, the hatred of the west instilled in the students.

And then, he thought of the grubby mattress on his uncle's bed, the magazines, the vomit he had been obliged to clean from the floor. And lastly he thought of the face of that woman in the upstairs window above that dirty little shop in Botchergate.

He parked the van, and stamped up the stairs. He inserted his key in the lock, released the catch, and slammed the door open.

It rebounded off the wall.

The cat sensing what was to come, shot out of the door, off down the stairs, and stood back arched and hair bristling on the doormat.

He strode through the doorway. His uncle Parsa sat on the sofa, glass in hand watching some brainless game show on the television.

Shabaz struck the glass from out of his hand, grabbed his uncle by the scruff of his neck, and hauled him to his feet. "Viper," he yelled, "Vile Pervert," I know exactly what you and that woman did today.

Parsa struggled in the grip. He must be bluffing! Things had gone too far with the girl this time, but how could Shabaz possibly know? The colour drained from his face. This was not how it was supposed to be!

"What woman" he yelled.

Shabaz slapped him about the face, threw him to the floor, and strode through to the bedroom. He ripped the mattress from the bed, grabbed the magazines, returned to the front room, and threw them at his uncle.

"Drunk! .....Fornicator," He screamed. "What of these!"

But Parsa was recovering. "Fornicator! What then of you! What of the woman I saw you with today? Who is she, What have *you* been up to?"

He broke away from Shabaz, and pointed a finger into his face. "Sins of the Flesh!" he yelled. "You....Shabaz Ghalzai, who ought to have been out watching for Graham.....You have been rutting with some filthy little whore!"

Shabaz simply snapped. He wasn't even aware of what he was doing. His right fist connected with his uncles jaw, sending him flying across the room and slamming him against the wall. Slowly, Parsa slid down, and lay motionless on the floor.

Shabaz sank into the armchair, and lowered his head into his hands.

Five minutes later the cat slunk back in through the door, went to its bowl, and emitted a loud "Meow."

* * *

Slowly, and painfully, Parsa stirred, and regained consciousness. His jaw ached abominably. He groaned and tried to climb to his feet, but the effort was too much. He slumped back down against the wall and began to assess the situation.

Shabaz was sitting in the old battered armchair stroking his bloody cat! Just as if nothing had happened!

Shit!.... How was he going to resolve this? There was simply no going back, no way out. The entire mission was his responsibility. A fortune had been spent on planning, training, and documentation.

Pull out now, and they would be ruthlessly hunted down and killed. Probably killed messily, and on camera, if for no other reason than to provide an example, and encouragement for others.

This was a two man mission, there was no time to obtain a replacement for Shabaz, and so he must make peace with him, at least until Graham was dead. After that, he would look forward with anticipation to disposing of him. He sat for a minute or two, savouring the methods he would use.

He lowered his head, and sobbed, "I'm sorry, so very sorry, I should never have said it. It was anger, and shock.

You are young, and you have found a girl. Such things happen, they happen to everyone. When I was your age it even happened to me. And these feelings can be so strong".....he sobbed again.

Shabaz ignored him.

Surly little bastard!...... Oh, but you will suffer for this! He thought of his long sharp knives.

"Shabaz?.....The house that you saw me leave. It is my contact point. Why do you think we are living here in this street, in this flat......It is to be close by. Parcels and equipment are dropped off there, documents for the man Vardy, and someone is always there to receive them."

That was actually true, it was how the business with the woman had begun. He should have just left it like that.....Business........ But he had seen the girls, and she had seen the look in his eyes, and had asked him. "Would you not like to stay a little longer?" And so it had begun.

Shabaz was looking across at him now.

"I'm sorry about the drink," he continued. "It was the strain, the planning, the failure of the plan with the helicopter crash. I was so downhearted. But of course, you are right, it *must* cease.

We are bound together you and I Shabaz, by family, by our mission. And our mission must not fail.

We must work together. When it is all over, then perhaps our ways must part. But until then, we must act and think as one."

Painfully, he climbed to his feet, crossed the room, and extended his hand.

Shabaz looked at the hand for a very long time. Then he took it. He hated this man for the words he had spoken about Mehri, and he would believe almost nothing he said, but he knew there would be no way out. The mission must go ahead as planned, and they must succeed.

They must kill Eddie Graham!

But when it was over..... then he was staying with Mehri.

He looked up at his uncle. "So what now? Have you a plan? I want finished with this."

Arrogant little bastard, Parsa thought. He walked from the room, and returned with his hunting knives in their case.

"Remember your training? Remember how to use these?

Shabaz nodded.

"Yes, I do have a plan, and this time it will succeed, because this time we will do it ourselves, and this time we will get in close."

He crossed to the table.

"Come, sit with me, and I will explain."

Half an hour later Shabaz rose from the chair.

"Agreed then. But once this is over, I go my own way?"
"Okay with me," he lied.
Shabaz walked to the door. "I need some fresh air, I'm off out for a while. I may be late back."
Parsa just shrugged. Who did he think was in charge of this?
But slowly, doubt entered his mind, for he knew that his control over the boy had slipped.

* * *

It was 9.30 p.m. when he reached Mehri's flat. Later than he usually called, and she looked alarmed when she answered the door.
"What is it? is something wrong?" He stepped inside, closed the door, and held her to him.
"I've had an argument with my uncle. We're splitting up.
I haven't told him, but I've decided to stay in this country. To stay with you." She clung to him. "But," he resumed, "I must continue to work for him for a few weeks, until he can find someone else. After that, I will be a free man."
"When," she asked.
"At the latest, by the New Year".
They made coffee and sat together making plans. At 10.30 p.m they switched on the television, and caught the local news.
Fiona Armstrong was the newsreader. A photograph of a womans face, with a strange blank look, appeared on screen. It had probably been taken post mortem. She was young, blonde, and had perhaps, once been pretty.
"Police are trying to identify the body of a young woman found today alongside the main line railway track in Carlisle. Although it is possible that she may have fallen from a southbound train, informed sources believe that the police are treating the death as suspicious."
The camera showed officers searching the railway line just south of Botchergate.
Mehri took Shabaz by the hand. A cold shudder ran down his back.
They had driven within a few hundred yards of that very place that day.

August 10th 2003

Kathy Pringle. "Lady Katrina"

We'd been out to my place at Merrylaw, Shorty and I. Putting in a large area of hard standage out on the hillside at the rear of the house, then just playing about with the JCB, draining the ground, doing a bit of landscaping, readying the "Estate" to put in young oak and ash trees, and those hedges of blackthorn I'd always promised myself.

The trees and shrubs would have to wait a little longer though, maybe September or October? Everything was still in fruit just now, and couldn't really be moved about.

The blackthorn hedges would provide a bit of additional security, not the sort of thing the average intruder would care to negotiate, especially in the dark. And a year or two down the line, if I looked after them properly, we'd have a source of good straight sticks. Might even try to coax some honeysuckle up the stems, and produce one or two of those twisted spiral sticks locals used to call "nibbies" back in Victoria's day.

I'd planted a row of sunflowers earlier in the year, along in front of my house, and they were just coming into spectacular bloom.

Jesus! I was in danger of turning into a gardener!

I was thinking of adding a veranda to the exposed "upper" story of my place, so I could sit out at night with a beer and watch the sky. On the nights when the midges would let me that is.

Perhaps I could get the work done by late spring, I mused, my favourite time of the year. Ready for those nice long evenings, still getting lighter. Usually April and May brought the best weather in this part of the world.

Past the summer solstice now, and already I seemed to sense the beginning of that long slide back down into the dark. Never could figure why all of the visitors felt obliged to arrive in the height of the summer.

It was about seven in the evening when we got back down

towards the “Last Chance”.

We were both in fine fettle, and looking forward to one of Mrs Kang’s steak and kidney puddings, and a bottle of cold “Hooky” to wash it down.

Shorty and Reb were due to do a few songs later.

I stopped for the lights at the bridge, then drove over, and down the last quarter mile.

The day’s trade should be about over, and the evening crowd wouldn’t be in for a while yet. There were four cars in the car park, including the little Suzuki belonging to Ros, and Abbie.

For some reason that cheered me up even more. “Watch it Eddie,” I thought, “Careful of strange women”. (I Must’ve developed second sight like Archie. You’ll see what I mean.)

Shorty opened the door, and we walked through. The sound system was low. Dwight Yoakum was crooning “Two doors down,” perhaps my favourite miserable song. Why do we like these miserable ones? I mean I was happy, and it still sounded great.

Mrs Kang looked through the hatch from the kitchen.

“Hi Mary, any chance of two steak and kid’s with the trimmings,” I called. She just grunted and disappeared.

Chuck was behind the counter, “Give us a couple of Hooky’s from the cooler Chuck. What’s wrong with Mary?”

“Auntie Mary? I don’t know, but I think there’s something wrong with me.” He looked crestfallen. Dwight changed gear, and began “Inside the pocket of a clown.”

“What is it Chuck,” Shorty asked with a grin, as he nudged him in the thigh with his elbow. “Shagged out, and out of the old monkey glands.” Chuck looked down sadly.

“I’ve lost it Shorty,”

“Lost what?

“My “Allure.”...... When women see me, you know, I mean, they give me a sort of look, and I know that all of my systems are up and running.” He scratched one of his long dark sideburns and hitched his tight black jeans up a notch. “Then I feel reassured, happy, sort of warm inside. I don’t take advantage of it you know. Well, not all of the time at least.”

“So,” I winked at Shorty, “What’s gone wrong?”

“It’s that woman. Through there,” and he nodded towards the office.

“What woman Chuck.”

“There’s four of them in there,” he replied. “Reb, Ros, Abbie, and..... “Her.” No offence meant Eddie, but its hard enough for a lad like me being around Abbie, without them bringing someone like that in.”

“What do you mean, “no offence meant” Chuck? Abbie’s just an acquaintance, nothing more.”

He looked at me sidelong. “Aye if you say so Eddie, but does she know that?”

“Anyway,” I continued. “What woman?”.

“ “They’re waiting for you in the office.”

I nudged Shorty. “Chuck.....Tell Mary to put the dinners on hold.”

“Come on mate....Let’s go and see what this is all about”.

Shorty picked up the control for his I.Pod. and followed. Dwight was a “Thousand miles from Nowhere.”

She was stunning. Tall....slim,....long dark hair, huge brown eyes, high cheekbones, full lips. She was dressed in a tight black sleeveless polo necked top, black jeans, and high heeled shoes. God knows how she had negotiated the car park in them.

But it was the make-up that did it. Perfect application. Black eye liner, dark blue eye shadow, deep red lips. Hint of ultra expensive perfume.

She sat beside Abbie, and they could have been twins, but like day and night. One blonde and smiling, the other with that dark pouty sullenness.

Now I knew exactly what was wrong with Mary Kang. Boy, she wouldn’t approve of this one.

No wonder Chuck was devastated.

Abbie opened the proceedings. “Hello, Menfolk. Have a nice day?”

She nodded her head in the direction of the dark haired woman. “This is Katherine Pringle”. Rebecca knows her from Welldean. She needs your help.”

“Katherine” took my hand. Her grip was firm and cold. She held on for a fraction longer than necessary, looked up at me from beneath long, dark lashes. It was a professional look, practiced, and it had its inevitable effect. It just stopped me in my tracks. Warning bells began to ring.

“Just call me Kate,” she breathed....... “Eddie.”

Now if any man tells you he's immune to this sort of thing, he's either a liar or he's gay.

Because girls like Katherine Pringle, know exactly what they are doing, and precisely what effect it will have on a man.

So I took evasive action, and looked deep into Abbie's eyes. She smiled at me, and my heart did a flip.

Shorty beat me to it. "Welldean?" he asked. "Not more trouble with Master Zhang I hope. I thought the little bugger was going to behave himself in future."

Ros answered. "No, not Zhang, nothing to do with Welldean at all in fact. Kathy's afraid. Someone's out to kill her. But she insists that she tell you the full story herself, because we think you may know the man ....Anthony Errington Vardy?"

I looked from one of them to the other, "Are you sure it's me you should be talking to? What about Ecky Charlton, he's "The Police" around here.

"Kate" opened her purse, took out two cards, and passed one to me. "No Police," she said.

I shrugged, and read the card.

Dr. Katherine Pringle,
Despoine Clinic for Psychological Research,
Private referrals only.

I laughed. "And you make a "A Fistful of Dollars" eh?"

Ros and Abbie just stared at me.

"I mean," I went on......."Despoine"...... "The Mistress"....I paused for effect..... "With no name." Or with a name known only to initiates? But initiates into what, one might ask. It's clever that, but still an unusual choice of name......At least for a Clinic!"

She shrugged, "They told me you were shrewd Eddie" And she passed me the second card.

"Mistress Katrina,"
Specialist Domination to the highest standard.
Strictly by Appointment.
Contacts by E.Mail only.

I tapped it with my nail. "Ah...Yes...And..."For a few Dollars More?"

I raised an eyebrow, and passed the cards to Shorty. He read them in silence.

"Oh, I see why you might not want Ecky involved. But why come to us?

Ros answered. "Perhaps because you three represent "The Good, the Bad, and the Ugly?" Feel free to argue about who, is which."

Christ, but she'd caught it now!

Reb just laughed. "I'm the Good."

Ros continued. "Eddie, We don't want the police involved. This is a sensitive area in several ways.

Shorty snorted, "Sounds like Kate is good at dealing with "sensitive areas!"

Kate laughed at that, but Ros looked serious. "Just let Kathy tell you her story. Then we'll decide what is to be done.

What could I say? Might as well hear it out.

"Okay Girls, but Ros, sooner or later, you're going to have to explain to me and Shorty just *exactly* what "investigations" Abbie and you are doing. I mean we love having you around, but now you seem to be interested in Welldean and this business with Miss Pringle here in addition to everything else.

"Please, just call me Kate," The dark girl interjected.

Abbie answered, "Fair enough Eddie, I promise that if you help us out on this one, then eventually I'll tell you" She paused. "Almost everything".

"That's some sort of a promise?" I laughed "Tell me *almost* everything? More likely tell me *almost* anything?

I smiled across at Doctor Katherine, "Mistress Katrina," Pringle.

"Go ahead then "Doctor," tell us your story."

But she wasn't in the least embarrassed. "Oh, the "Doctor," is real enough....Eddie. I took my Ph.D at Durham. I'm a fully qualified Clinical Psychologist, and a practicing one at that.

You see, my specialist study was the psychology of sexual behaviour. But, unfortunately, or perhaps fortunately, I found that I had more than a purely "medical" interest in the subject, and that I actually rather enjoyed it.

So after I qualified, I moved down to London, found myself a little flat and office, and then I advertised, rather discretely, for a few clients with "sexually related psychological problems."

I am a real Doctor, and I did do legitimate treatment, but I found after an amount of probing that some of my patients didn't really wish to be cured at all, and that they preferred a little more of a "hands on" approach.

At first I simply referred them to certain "ladies" of whom I was aware from conversations with other clients. But then I thought "Why Not"? I was aware that I had the looks, I could work on the persona, and I knew more about the psychology of sex than almost anyone else. So I decided to adapt my practice slightly.

I took a lease on the flat next door, and equipped it with all of the usual, or perhaps I should say unusual......paraphernalia?
I enjoyed choosing the clothes and the make up, and over the next few years, I developed my alter ego. "Mistress Katrina".

For those requiring it, I provided legitimate counselling, and treatment for their "disorders".

For the others I provided safe, hygienic, and very discreet services in accordance with their needs.

After about five years, I found that I needed larger premises, and since both of my "professions" were rather well paid, I purchased a country house, discreetly walled, in around three acres of woodland, just off the M40 to the north of the M25.

Discreet, not too far out of London, and convenient for clients flying in through Heathrow.

"The Despoine Clinic."

"Private Referrals Only."

I've been in business now for 12 years. I employ three other fully trained, qualified, and experienced staff.

I'm rather proud to think that my clinic is unique in Britain, and that we truly manage to achieve a level of safety and security sadly lacking in most other establishments. I do believe that we really manage to help our clients in more ways than one.

We at the Despoine," she paused, "Quite simply, are the best."

Shorty snorted, "You're just running a brothel!"

"No, Mr Higgins.....Shorty," She paused, "*That* is a common misconception. We provide no actual sexual services. We are not prostitutes. We simply assist our clients to live out their fantasies, or at the very least to come to terms with them. If "sexual services" are required, then we have to bring in a specialist to provide them. But that is quite rarely indeed.

Since we have clients from the very highest levels of both the Government and Society, we manage to maintain a very low profile, and to run without interference from either the Police, or the press. In fact everything is just perfect, or at least it was until Anthony Errington Vardy."

She paused, and took a sip from her cup of coffee.

"Even when I first arrived in London, he was well known in the S & M world as an evil bastard. One who liked to hurt both men and women, but not in a "nice" way. There was actually a warning out about him in the circles I moved in. And when he killed young Quentin James? Well, everyone thought that would be the end of him. But somehow he got off."

She paused again, and then continued. "He came to me when he was acquitted. Asked me if I could help him. Said that he needed to learn to control himself, and naive idiot that I was, I thought that he might just be genuine, that perhaps I could do some good, and foolishly I agreed.

Half way into our first consultation I realised that he was not telling me the truth. That he had no real wish to change. That he enjoyed being as he was.

Help was not what he wanted, he was simply seeking to extract information about my clients. So I told him to get out, and when he wouldn't, I simply had him thrown out of the door.

"How did you do that," Shorty asked, ever interested in the mechanics of violence.

"Oh, my flat at that time was above a gymnasium, and some of the lads "helped out" when necessary. I'd a buzzer down to their office, and I paid them well if they were needed. Plus, the owner was a client, which did help as well.

But Vardy didn't just forget it. He watched me, or had me watched, and about three years ago, we had a break-in at the clinic. A real professional job. They got past the wall, the sensors in the grounds, and the security systems. It was so good, I wasn't even really certain that there had been a break-in, and nothing had been taken, just a few things not quite where they should have been.

This was around the time I discovered Welldean.

I need to get away now and again, and Welldean provides the perfect relaxation. It didn't take me long to realise that Zhang's an old fraud, and in fact Zhang knows that I know. But we both keep up the pretence. I come and do a bit of yoga, a bit of meditation, a touch of martial arts, and we're both content with that. His fee's are high, but no higher than other places.

Now there's a place I love, the site of old Gilknockie Tower, down south of Langholm. I don't know why, but it's got a certain atmosphere, peaceful, but more than that. Slightly creepy but in a nice way. So, one beautiful night in late May, two years ago, I drove down there from Welldean, with a friend, intending to practice a little Tai Chi, and a little Qi Gong in the old earthworks".

I glanced over at Shorty. Coincidence? She might not be that bad after all? He just raised an eyebrow, and shrugged.

Kate continued. "After a while, I became aware that we were being watched. And there he was, Anthony Errington Vardy, standing alone on that bridge over the Esk, the one built from the ruins of the old Tower. He was all in grey tweed, with that revolting yellow waistcoat of his, long brown boots, and he was carrying a shotgun under his arm.

I think he was taken aback to see me, but he didn't take long to recover. He crossed the bridge, and walked towards us through the trees.

He should never have been in that place.

"Hello Doctor Pringle," he said, "Still in the same line of business, running the Clinic?"

Of course I couldn't say much with someone else present, so I just nodded. "Hello Mr Vardy, What brings you to these parts"?

He went on in that supercilious way of his, head back, looking down his nose, to tell us how important he was, how he was Estate Manager for The Duke of Marchbank, how he ran virtually everything for him.

I hoped that he would just go away. But then he asked "What brings you to the Borders,"and my friend who knew no better, blurted out "Oh we're students at Welldean House, up by Yarrow. Kathy's part time, but Master Zhang says she's very talented."

"Interesting," he nodded, "She certainly is that." He looked at me speculatively, and then, right out of the blue.... "Oh, by the way I heard about the break-in out at your place a year or so back, *when all of those files, were taken*, terrible business."

But nothing *had* been taken, and that was when I realised, that he was probably responsible, and that he may have copies of my client list.

"I'll tell you what," he continued, "Why don't we meet up down at the Cross Keys in Canonbie tomorrow night. I'll stand you dinner, and we can catch up with each other. 7 o'clock be okay?"

I was stunned. What could I say. Up until that moment I'd never really believed that there had been a break-in. So I agreed to meet him, and the next night I drove down to Canonbie.

We ate a decent meal in almost total silence. But the food was tasteless to me, and I just waited for him to get to the point.

After we had eaten, he suggested that we sit in his Range Rover in the carpark for a chat about "old times". I thought it would be about sex, I thought it was likely to be unpleasant, but it was not what I had imagined. He was pimping.

Pete.....That is Peter Irvine, the Duke of Marchbank. Vardy has had him totally under his control for years. He's got him hooked on drink, cocaine, and on sex. He's been supplying him with drugs in ever increasing amounts for years, and he's introduced him to escort girls, and a bit of S&M. He's even got a dungeon fitted out in the old tower. That's how he has been keeping control of him.

And he soon got round to the purpose of our meeting. "Thought you had seen the last of me didn't you Doctor Pringle. When you had your bully boys throw me out? But you were wrong.You see I'm a patient man, and I keep the old eyes open, and an ear to the ground too.

I knew you'd moved out by High Wycombe, so I had a friend of mine who owed me a little favour, pay you a visit one night. Everything was almost in order when he left, wasn't it? Just enough out of place so you would suspect someone had been in, but not enough that you'd be sure."

He gave that odd high pitched giggle of his. It chilled me to the bone.

"My man's very good, or at least he was. He had an unfortunate accident shortly afterwards, drunk you know. Fell off the platform on the Piccadilly Line, just as the train was coming in.Messy....but rather convenient, don't you think? Keeps everything nice and secure. So now I can assure you that the only people in this world who possess a list of your clients, and full details of their little "disorders," are yourself, your work colleagues..... and me.

Most unfortunate if that information was to suddenly surface in the public domain. And it won't Kathy.... You don't mind if I call you Kathy do you? I mean I think we may be working together for a little while.....At least it won't surface, if you do precisely as I say. You see, my meeting with you was ever so fortunate, because you're exactly what I need at the moment."

And he went on to explain.

Pete Irvine, is unmarried, he has no close relatives, no heir, and a vast fortune. His estate is considerable, and beneath it are huge reserves of coal and natural gas.

Our mutual friend Eddie," she paused, and looked me in the eye. "The Honourable Anthony Errington Vardy, has convinced him that he should make a Will.

A Will, which in the absence of any legitimate offspring, of which of course there are none, names him as his sole heir.....and Pete has agreed.

Vardy gave me a choice. Either "session" in the dungeon with Peter Irvine once a week, or he would publish all details of the Despoine Clinic. He needs me to help keep Pete happy and under control.

He didn't know it, but at that point he was on very thin ice indeed.

"How's that then?" Shorty asked, "What else could you have done?"

She smiled at him speculatively. "You know, you really are quite famous Mr Higgins, a bit of a legend in certain circles in fact. I think a man with your reputation ought to have a fair idea."

"What, you'd kill him?"

She smiled, "No,....not me..... at least not personally. But, in my line of business, I meet all manner of people. All of whom are rather fond of me, and some of them, have very interesting skills, contacts, and careers. Vardy didn't realise it, but he gave me two choices. I could go along with him, or arrange to have him permanently removed.

I even toyed with the idea. He could perhaps take a trip down to London, and have an "unfortunate accident" on the underground, just like his friend....That would have been nice, and I gave it very serious consideration indeed.

But I decided in the end that I would be wiser not to become an accessory to murder, and that if I did in fact take that course, then I would possibly just be exchanging one problem for another.

So I went along with his "request," and so for the last two years, whilst I have been visiting Welldean, I've also been providing Pete Irvine, with top class dungeon services out at his home.

Shorty's hand was in his pocket. I wondered what was coming.

Out in the Cafe, Jim Reeves faded mid verse on "He'll have to go."

And Hank Williams wept out "Cold, Cold, Heart."

"So.... What's this to do with us"? I asked.

She looked Shorty straight in the eye. "Nice choice of music.... But unfortunately, my hearts just not cold enough. Pete's basically a nice guy, and I always thought I was immune, but I went and fell for him."

Then, she dropped her bombshell.

"I'm pregnant, and Pete's the father!

He's overjoyed. He's promised to come off the drugs, and he wants to marry me.....He *is* going to have an heir.

And Errington Vardy will kill me, when he finds out!"

The four women just sat there, watching Shorty and I.

Shorty spoke first. "You brought Miss Pringle down here from Welldean Reb. What do you expect Eddie and me to do? I know there are obvious problems, but why not just level with Ecky Charlton? He's a good man, and if me and Eddie smooth the ground first, maybe we can keep Kathy's "professional status" out of it.

But it was Ros who answered. "Okay, I'm going to have to tell you a little bit more than I want to. I'm not too worried about Eddie, because like it or not, as a result of his previous occupations he's still covered by the Official Secrets Act."

Unfortunately I thought she's probably right.

"But the rest of you"....she looked from Reb, to Shorty, to Kathy.... "Are going to have to sign it. And no maybes."

"Bugger that!" Shorty exploded "We're signing nothing. Me and Reb can keep shtum when we want to. So go ahead, and say what you have to, it'll go no further"

Kathy Pringle nodded her agreement. "I sign nothing either."

Abbie just sat there, doing her imitation of the Cheshire Cat. I winked at her.

She nudged Ros lightly in the ribs. "Told you so. Let's stop pretending Ros. There are no secrets between those three." She gave an odd little smile. "So Kathy is the only one who doesn't know. Let's just make this a little chat between friends. Because that's what I think we've become."

"Really," I thought, "How nice!"

I looked forward to being Abbie's friend.

Ros sighed, "Well, it was worth a try, but God help you if you tell any of this, because I won't be able to.

Okay....Eddie knows, so probably Shorty does, and therefore no doubt Reb is aware. ....Abbie and I are "investigators," but we are not exactly private investigators. We work for certain Government Departments, under the umbrella of what is popularly known as MI6."

I couldn't, resist it, "See Kate.....More ladies from the "Pleasure Gardens".

Shorty laughed. Kathy and Reb looked puzzled.

So I let Shorty tell them. "MI6 Headquarters at Vauxhall Cross, was built on the site of the Vauxhall Pleasure Gardens. Notorious in its day amongst other things, as a place for illicit sexual liaisons. It used to be said that the pathways were so intricate that a mother could get lost just looking for her daughter. Nowadays there's nothing left down there by the Thames. Nothing that is but the "Spooks".

Nice one Shorty, I thought.

Ros continued. "I can't tell you exactly what we are doing up at Welldean"

"I'll bet" I mused.

"But," she nodded towards Kate, "With Miss Pringle here, and her little problem, we seem to have stumbled into an area which may involve matters of National Security at the highest level."

I burst out laughing. "Oh Aye, haven't you just! Kate's little black books, with all of the records of the misdeeds of the rich, the famous, and the powerful. Tell me, have the pair of you reported any of this back to our good friends down south?"

Ros, had the good grace to look embarrassed. "Not yet we haven't, we would rather just deal with it as part of our ongoing investigation."

I looked back to Kate. "So, Vardy will kill you if he finds out?" She nodded.

"So what are you going to do about the baby?"

She held my gaze. "I'm going to marry Pete. He'll have the legitimate heir he's always wanted, and Vardy will never be named as his successor"

Shorty snorted. "And of course you'll become the Duchess of Marchbank."

She turned and faced him. "Shorty, I know you'll find this hard to believe, but I truly am very fond of Pete Irvine. However, after twelve years in my business I have no need of his money, and less need of a title. The only title I wish for is the one on my card. Pete and I have talked this over at length. The baby was conceived in May, and I'm now three months pregnant. Soon it will be obvious to everyone, including Vardy. We intend to marry at the end of October."

"So what's the problem?" I asked, "I mean once you're married, that will be the end of Vardy's ambitions."

"You can't really believe that Eddie. You know Vardy. My professional opinion is that he's a sadist, he's completely deranged, psychopathic, and highly unstable. When he finds out about the baby, I don't know what he might do. He's killed once for certain, and probably at least once more by his own admission."

Ros cut in. She looked into my eyes, and smiled.

"Oh God, I thought, here we go."

"Eddie,"she purred, reaching over the table, and taking my hand. "Kate needs your help...In fact....We all," she looked from Kate to Abbie, to Reb, "need your help.

You know this area. We need somewhere for Kathy.....Kate, to stay, away from sight, away from Anthony Errington Vardy, just for a couple of months. I'm sure you know some out of the way cottage we could use? Some old friend perhaps, she could stay with?"

Abbie, I noticed was not a happy bunny, in fact she was looking daggers at Ros.

Shorty watched her from the corner of his eye. Then he reached over the table, and took Kate by the hand. With a beatific smile he looked up at her.

"Eddie and I, in accordance with the ancient rules of our chivalric order, are honour bound to protect both fair ladies, and innocent little children. And since from your own admission, you now fit neatly into both categories, please allow me to offer my sincerest assurance that we will assist you to the very best of our abilities....And, we promise, that you may sojourn for the next several weeks, in total safety, out at Eddie's place at Merrylaw!

He paused. "However, may I enquire, when your wedding does take place, as to the exact location of the festivities?"

I was stunned. "Oh Jesus! That little lunatic!.....He'd just committed me to weeks on end with a beautiful, pregnant, dominatrix!...Why?......My life was complicated enough..... Why me!

I thought Abbie was about to explode.

Kate, just looked puzzled.

“The wedding will be at Marchbank House, on the 31st of October. Why?”

Shorty took Reb’s hand. “Because, fair lady....There is a price for Eddie’s protection and hospitality.”

I was speechless, but he just winked at me and continued.

“My partner here, Miss....Sorry...”Lady” Rebecca Forsythe-Ingram, whom you Kate, know as Reb..... is to be my wife. And Eddie’s price, is that there be a double wedding on the 31st, and in the interests of both friendship and economy, I also, believe that it would be advantageous that we combine our celebrations. Further, I do believe that between us we ought to be able to arrange a most interesting and varied guest list.

Kate looked both amused and delighted, Reb leapt to her feet, and hugged Shorty, Kate hugged them both, Ros, congratulated Shorty and Reb.

I stood like a lemon. No-one had asked me anything. But what could I do? It was all cut and dried. Shorty and Reb were to marry. I couldn’t spoil that?

Abbie just glowered at me.

But when everyone had recovered, I took Kate to one side.

“There’s another condition, something you can do for me.”

She looked suspicious, “Oh Eddie...Girls like me hear that one all of the time.”

“No, don’t worry, nothing like that. But you see the big lad out there, at the counter?

Well......he’s a sensitive soul..... So....”

* * *

It was almost eight by the time we finished in the office.

Abbie and Ros took off for Welldean to collect Kate’s belongings. The story they would tell Zhang, was that quite unexpectedly Kate was required back in London, to deal with urgent “logistical problems,” relating the development of her “practice”. She would be out of touch for some time. She may even be out of the UK for a while.

Always be wary of the terms "Logistics," and "Logistical problems." They sound great, sound clever, and are very none specific. Few folk like to show ignorance, by asking exactly what you mean. But, personally I believe that they carry that unmistakable odour.... of pure bullshit.

Reb and Shorty, went back through to the kitchens, to consult with Mary Kang about additions to the menu, and Kate and I walked over to the counter.

There were a few customers lingering over coffee's. A couple by the door, a biker who was a regular, getting back into his leathers, prior to setting off for Edinburgh, and an Asian in the far corner dressed in blue overalls, and reading a copy of the "Sun."
Obviously, an Islamic fundamentalist scholar, studying our media, in order to be better able to condemn the moral decadence of the western popular press.

"God," I thought, "I must stop being so cynical, he's probably just a driver with a load of teddy bears or something, and after all, who didn't like a sneaky peek at page three?"

"Hungry? I asked Kate. She nodded, "Care to try some Geordie Burgers?"

"Geordie Burgers? What's in them".

"Oh, It's an old recipe of Shorty's and mine, secret ingredients. We serve them with Pinto beans, and hand cut chips. Some folk even come back for more."

"That's one of my lines," she joked, "Along with "I'll try anything once." And she looked up at me from under those long dark lashes.

Electric, and she knew it. I could see that this could be the beginning of a long and difficult few weeks.

"Kate," I asked, "If we're going to be living in the same house for a while, could you please stop doing that?"

She smiled, all innocence. "Doing what?" Then she relented. "Sorry, It's just second nature. A bit like you, Shorty, and your friends... Always joking. It's what happens in small and enclosed societies. You develop your own "sub language," see there I go again. We do it all of the time at the clinic."

"It's nothing like joking Kate, it's unsettling for a man. And you know it."

"Okay Eddie"

But I didn't think she could stop, it was just part of her.

Chuck was at the far end of the counter, as far away from her as he could get. But still, Kate caught his eye. She looked surprised.

"Excuse me, but are you Chuck Elliot?"

He ambled over. "Sure, that's me."

"The" Chuck Elliot? The one who sings like Elvis?"

Incredibly Chuck blushed.

"Eh, Well...Yes, I sometimes do a song or two. Just when no-one is about."

"But," Kate breathed, holding him transfixed with her gaze, "They say you do..... "It".......So well".

Oh God! I thought, She's at it again.

"I just love the little stage at the end of the cafe, is that ...where you...."perform"....Chuck?"

"Er....Y...Yes," Chuck stuttered. "S..S...Some....N...nights."

She placed one hand upon her breast, "Oohh.... I just *adore* Elvis."

She was staring deep into his eyes.

Please, I prayed, I know I asked you to do it, but please, go a bit easy on the lad.

But now, there was no turning back.

"Oohh...Chuck," She simpered, "Would you do me a great favour? Would you....Could you... ...."perform".......With me?"

There came a huge crash from the kitchen, Mrs Kang appeared to have dropped a pan or something.

"P P Perform?" Chuck asked. "W....W....With you?"

"Yes..... Up *there* on the stage."

"Up......there...on....the stage....."Perform".....With You?"

"Why yes, A duet perhaps? You do duet Chuck don't you."

Chuck looked relieved. "Oh I could try."

He turned to me. "Did I hear you say you wanted to order Geordie delights? I'll just give Auntie Mary, your order Eddie, and then I'll go switch on the mikes."

He shot away out to the kitchen.

There came the sound of angry whispering, then a loud whacking noise.

Kate laughed. "Auntie Mary doesn't miss much does she."

Chuck ambled back out, rubbing a rather red ear.

"Do you know the words to "Love me Tender?" he asked, massaging his ear again.

Shorty, and Reb wandered back through.

"Mary's not happy," Shorty whispered. "What's up?"

"Oh, Kate and Chuck are going to duet on "Love me Tender."

They burst into gales of laughter. "That explains it," Reb spluttered, "yet another woman setting her sights on poor wee innocent Chuck."

Kate and Chuck climbed up on the stage. The lights came on, the mike whistled, and the sound system cut in. They warbled together a little, as musicians do. Chuck picked up his electric guitar, and made those strange noises, turning keys on the machine head. ...Tuning up.

Eventually they were ready.

The biker had come back in, parked his helmet on a table and decided to stay and listen, the couple by the door looked fascinated, and the Asian in the far corner had even lost interest in the "Sun".

Chuck had always done a fair impression of Elvis. But we were totally unprepared for Kate.

She was brilliant. She stared up into the eyes of her giant partner, harmonising to perfection, and Chuck looked back down at her, sheer adoration on his face.

She crooned.

"Love me Tender,
Love me true,
All my dreams fulfil,"

Chuck warbled

"For my darlin', I love you,
And I always will."

It was beautiful. Sickeningly beautiful. The hair stood up on my back. I'd just wanted to make him happy. But now he was smitten.

A cold draft raised goose pimples on my arms. But it was not because of the scene on the stage.

I glanced around. The door was closing. The biker sat entranced. The couple by the door stared in amazement at Chuck and Kate. But the Asian driver had walked out, and he'd walked out in the middle of a riveting performance.

Leaving behind on the table, his copy of the Sun.

Chuck and Kate finished their song.

Kate came over to my table in the booth in the corner, and a minute later Chuck arrived with our plates, and a pot of tea.

"What did you make of 'Stan over in the corner Chuck? The guy in the blue overalls."

He shrugged, "Not much, but why "Stan?" he asked, "How do you know he's called Stan?"

"Old army joke. You see, they're all called "Stan," Afghani....Stan, Paki....Stan, Tajiki.....Stan, and so on. I don't know which, but I reckon he was some sort of 'Stan. You seen him before?"

He looked puzzled. "Oh Aye Eddie, he's a bit of a regular. Him and his mate meet up here now and again. Lots of driver's do, we're becoming a bit of a landmark. He drives a green Landrover, and his buddy's got a white Mercedes Sprinter. Don't care for the one that's just left too much, but the other guy's okay, always has a pleasant word. I thought you must know them, 'cause the first time they came in, they asked if this was your place."

His brow wrinkled, "Funny thing though, when I think about it, they're never usually around when you're here, but they always ask after you."

"Oh Bloody Hell!" I thought.

We ate in relative silence, I couldn't get the Asian out of my mind. We finished our meal, and Kate sat back in her seat. "That was absolutely delicious, what's in them, Venison?

"Oh, sometimes, It's an old Jacobite recipe me grandfather taught me. Bit of a family secret. One day we might produce them commercially."

But she had caught my mood "What's wrong Eddie?"

"I don't really know, probably nothing. It's just that for a while now I've had the feeling that someone's watching me. Paranoia perhaps. But that Asian guy asking about me? It just makes me uneasy."

I pushed my chair back. "Let's get under way, and we'll get you settled in out at Merrylaw."

I noticed that Chuck was back up on stage, guitar in his hands, the oil on his dark hair and sideburns gleaming in the spotlights, as he sat there, headphones in place, quietly strumming.

Shorty and Reb were working behind the counter, and I waved to them as we made for the door.

But just then Chuck stood up, took off the headphones, switched on the speakers and struck a chord.

Spotlit, bathed in pink light, he towered above us, a giant glowing memorial to "The King."
Then....His hips gyrated, his left leg began to shake in time to an unheard, and unholy rhythm, he fixed Kate with his eye, pointed, and, agony in his voice, a lone tomcat screeching his mating call to the moon, he howled his way into the first verse of "One Night."

"O.....nnnne.....N' Night With You,
Is what I'm now praying for,
The things that we two could plan,
Would make my dreams come true,"

"Juuuuu.....st Ca....all My Name,
And I'll be, right by your side."

SMACK!.....

A wet dishcloth hurtled from stage left, wrapped itself around the right hand side of his face. And cut his performance short.
Auntie Mary had struck again!
But Chuck didn't care. The poor idiot just wiped his face, and grinned, cow eyed.
Kate blew him a kiss, and with a deliberate wiggle, she walked out of the door, waving to him over one shoulder, as she sashayed across to the Toyota.
Mary Kang glowered from the kitchen window.
"Was that what you wanted Eddie?" Kate asked.
"Not exactly."
I climbed in and started the engine.
"What a fool I am," I thought.

* * *

Merrylaw.

And so began, what I look back upon as my "Days in the Wilderness."

I'm just not used to female company. At least, that is to say, not full time female company.

Kate was highly amused when she arrived out at my home.

"Cockplay!" "Merrylaw!" What sort of an address is that?

"Actually its real," I replied. "I mean who could resist it? That out the back is "Cockplay Hill,"and the house we passed is "Merrylaw."

"Thank God no-one knows I'm staying here then, I'd never hear the last of it in my line of business."

Fortunately I had a guest bedroom, but unfortunately only one bathroom, so it would be a bit difficult at times.

Frankly, I couldn't think how we would manage. I was a long time batchelor, when I put something down, it would still be there when I went to pick it up. Everything was in it's proper place.

But I needn't have worried. She was no real trouble, at least not in that way. But, as the days passed, she became rather relaxed around the place, and made herself quite at home.

She loved to sing, and would accompany it with a few little dance steps. She was totally without embarrassment, and often she'd wander about in the mornings and evenings in only her underwear, and it's just not easy for a man to ignore that sort of thing. So I said so. She looked crestfallen.

"Sorry Eddie, I didn't think you would mind."

"Oh, I don't mind, you just carry on doing it, as long as you don't mind my lecherous glances. But it is rather disturbing all the same."

"Mmmm," she mused. "I really will have to be a bit more considerate. I could probably think of something? I mean, I've told you, when I'm working I don't do sex, and being engaged to be married I won't do sex, but if things get too bad, I'm sure I can assist. A little massage perhaps? I'm very good at that, or maybe some other little treat? Not into S&M by any chance?" And she laughed again. "I really ought to keep my hand in."

Then she raised a finger and pointed. "Just kidding, I'll behave myself," she said, a wicked twinkle in her eye.

"Oh Christ!" I thought. "Please God.....Just send me a nice old fashioned demon to torment me, he can offer Money.....Power.....Position.....Something nice and conventional."

"Kate, please, listen. Just cool it slightly. Just a bit.

I mean do you really enjoy tormenting a man?"

She put one hand on her hip and pouted. Her small firm breasts pointed at me provocatively.

"Well, Yes Eddie, actually I do. I mean I even do it for a living."

Suddenly, we both saw the funny side, and collapsed in a heap together, laughing.

When we recovered, I felt obliged to ask, "You know you're quite freewheeling for a girl who's pregnant and about to be married. But you're going to be the Duchess of Marchbank.
What about Pete Irvine?"

And so she became serious. "I am very fond of Pete, and I do intend to marry him."

She went silent, and I thought that was all she would say. But then, she spoke again.

"I have thought this through Eddie. I'll marry him, and I'll have the child, but I can't stay married. I don't belong here, I have my own life, and whatever anyone may think, I do enjoy it. And I enjoy the freedom that it gives me.

I've never really cared what people think of me, so yes I'll marry him, but after the baby is born, I shall divorce him, and go back to London. Back to running the Clinic."

I must have looked shocked.

"Oh, I'll come and see him and the baby on a regular basis, probably every month or so, but not as his wife. No-one owns me, and there is no way anyone could persuade me to become the Duchess of Marchbank. I have no wish to spend the rest of my days, opening fetes, attending the Women's Institute, and acting as a decoration on Pete's arm.

You've seen how Mary Kang looks at me. I couldn't put up with all of the whispering, and Pete shouldn't have to either."

"Does he know?" I asked.

"Yes. We've talked it all over. He actually does love me you know, I wish he didn't. But then, there's nothing I can do about that. He's promised to bring up the baby correctly, and as I've said, he's coming off the drugs.

With regard to his other "little problems," well they really are in my line of country anyway. I'll see him regularly, and I'm happy enough to assist. And that's it, let's say no more about it."

But our mood had changed. And from then on she did try to behave herself.

At least some of the time.

Like most couples who live in close proximity, what we needed, if we were to have any sort of harmony, was some form of "common ground".

The constant teasing and innuendo, was enjoyable enough in its way, but frustrating in the extreme, and wearing at the same time.

Oddly it came about from the most unexpected quarter.

We were down at the gatehouse, rummaging around for some old maps I'd promised to show her, when she noticed the blackthorn sticks drying on the rack on the back wall.

I did most of my work on the sticks down there, drying, steaming, and straightening them. Some still had the thorns on, some I had cut them off, and some were straightened ready to be varnished.

She picked up a light stick, and swished it through the air.

"What's this Eddie, a walking stick?"

"Sort of, it's a blackthorn. Most folk out here use a stick for walking with. Not because they're infirm, it's just good for getting over rough country. But the blackthorn is a bit different.

A couple of generations back they were carried both as a walking stick and for defence. There was once a style of fencing known as "single stick," the last remnant of the old British system of broadsword fencing. Blackthorn makes the very best sticks, it's tough, resilient, near unbreakable, and these days almost everyone is unaware of its true potential. You can carry one around in the rougher parts of our cities, and no-one will know that you are both armed and dangerous. In fact they'll probably think that you're disabled.

A good one, like the one you have there is almost impossible to find. I've been collecting them for years, and I've just two or three like that."

She was looking closely at it now. "Why, what's so special about this?"

"Well," I replied, "It's too light for me, so it's probably better as a ladies stick, but see?.....It's the section of the stick, which makes that one different. It's not round at all, it's elliptical. Better still, its almost egg shaped. Near enough, that narrow edge is like a blade. And it's had a lot of long thorns, I've cut them off, but look at all of the knobbles left behind. Score a hit with that, and your opponent will know about it.

Plus, that one grew on steep bankside, more of a rocky cliff face." I pointed. "You see there, the root is still on it, angled out to one side? You only get that on sticks grown on slopes, and the fact that it was on poor ground, and in the case of that stick, at a high altitude, means that it grew very slowly. Lots of annular rings. That's one tough stick. I'll shape the root into a round ball, something like a Zulu knobkerrie. Then that stick will be perfect."

"I used to fence epee." she said.

"Wow! The tough end of fencing."

"I've even got a medal or two for it," she went on. "I love swords, but I've never had time to collect or anything. Rebecca said you used to deal in Arms and Armour?"

I nodded. "Still do....Listen, I'll show you a few pieces if you like, and perhaps tomorrow we could finish that stick you're holding. You can keep it if you fancy."

And that was when I really took to her. Because she smiled at me. Because I was a bit funny about my sticks, and I knew that she understood. She knew that I wouldn't give that blackthorn to just anyone, and she realised that it was more than just a piece of wood. It had it's own "magic," it had character, it had fond memories woven into it.

"Thanks Eddie, I'd really like that. Then perhaps you could teach me how to use it. Teach me single stick?"

"Fair enough."

And now we were friends. And we both knew it.

We walked back over to the house.

In the main room, I crossed to the to the bookcase, released a bolt beneath one of the shelves, and slid the unit aside, revealing a steel door. Attached to the left hand side of the frame, was a combination lock.

"Ooh Eddie....a secret door. I do love secret doors, I've one or two myself at the Clinic. They give my clients just that little extra frisson of anticipation."

I dialled the combination into the lock, swung the door open, and the lights came on automatically, revealing stairs leading down into the basement.

"Why you dark horse," she exclaimed, placing one hand on her breast theatrically. "Oooh, I'm really Thrilled....I would never have guessed.... You Naughty Boy!....You've got your very own dungeon...... I just can't wait to see."

"Feel Free," I replied gesturing to the staircase, "but its not what you might expect."

"Oh you'd be surprised, there's not much in the way of dungeon equipment, that I haven't seen or obtained already."

And like a child at Christmas, she led the way.

She reached the bottom, and gasped.

"I was wrong, I've never seen anything like this."

"It's both my workshop and showroom," I explained. "I'd be obliged if you kept this viewing to yourself."

"Sorry," I continued, "Force of habit, I tell that to anyone who comes in here. Not that many do come here really, just an occasional client. Folk I've known for a very long time. I do most of my dealing online these days. No address."

I gestured around, indicating the exhibits.

"The armour is arranged both chronologically, and by nationality. The swords, chronologically, and by both type and nationality. The firearms are grouped in a similar fashion.

Anything you see two of, displayed one behind the other, they're the duplicates, and the poorer one is for sale.That's how I trade up.

Really I suppose, I'm not a dealer at all, just an obsessive collector, who sells a few bits and pieces.

Sorry to disappoint you, not your kind of "dungeon" at all perhaps."

She was speechless, walking from one display to the other, her face like a child let loose in a toy shop. I threw her a pair of white cotton gloves.

"Put these on if you want to pick anything up, the sweat from the hand can play hell with polished steel, and having to continually clean pieces can get a bit tiresome."

Then she took me quite aback. She pointed at a small, worn, close helmet.

"That's Greenwich isn't it? First period, before his death in 1547. When they were just making pieces for Henry and his mates. I thought the Royal Armouries, and the Metropolitan had them all. That one looks quite a bit pre 1540 to me, small, close fitting, that low comb. And the visor looks like its for field or tilt. It reminds me of the Genouilhac armour in the Met.

I was amazed.

Brian who writes the books over at Teviothead, his wife Maureen, is the only other woman I know who has a clue about armour. Pity I couldn't introduce them.

"How the hell do you know about that?" I asked.

"Oh, my Dad used to take me to the Tower of London when I was a kid, that was when all of the armour and cannon were there, long before they shifted it up to Leeds, and down to Portsmouth.

Greedy Sods, thought they could make more money that way.

Dad was "Army," well connected, and he knew the Master of the Armouries, Nick Norman... Lovely man, they used to talk for ages.

And that started my interest.

We had some great times. Dad taught me Epee, taught me to shoot pistol too. He had books on armour....catalogues. I've got them all now."

She pointed again. "Your helmet there....I remember now.... it was in the 1951 Greenwich exhibition, but they put the wrong date on it. I've got that catalogue as well."

Her voice had faded, and she looked sad.

I said nothing, but I sensed what was coming.

"He was killed in Ireland you know....my Dad.... Undercover. Bloody Army....Bloody Politicians! Send folk anywhere, get anyone killed except themselves."

"What about Mum?" I asked, and then bit my tongue.

"Oh, She ran off years ago, and left us. Couldn't stand being an Army wife. I was brought up in a series of very fancy boarding schools for girls."

And then, suddenly, quite out of the blue, she burst into tears and threw herself into my arms.

I hugged her to me, and her tears soaked through my shirt and wet my chest. She just sobbed and sobbed, her whole body heaving.

After about five minutes it subsided. She looked up at me, her eyes were red, and her beautiful eye make up was running everywhere. Then she smiled. "That's never happened before Eddie. Maybe it's a long time overdue.

All of this," she gestured around, "it brought back so many happy memories, I just couldn't stand it." She sniffed. "I really needed to get that out of my system. Don't worry, it won't happen again."

But I felt awful. "I'm sorry, I had no idea, You don't need to come down here again."

She laughed, and it was like the sun coming back out. "Just you try and stop me!"

We climbed back up the stairs. I closed and locked the door, and slid the unit back in place.

I keep only one sword on display in my house. It was behind a glass panel in the centre of the bookcase. Kate went over, and looked at it with interest.

"Now that I've seen your "collection" Eddie, tell me, why do you display that one? I mean it doesn't look to be anything special."

I opened the glass, and took it off its stand. "I bought this years ago, in one of Christies' sales. It was thrown in with another sword, a late 18th century courtsword. But this was the special one."
I drew it from it's scabbard.

It was a plain steel hilted smallsword, third quarter of the eighteenth century, with a worn, and battle nicked blade. A three sided hollow ground blade, with not much weight in it at all.
I handed it to Kate. She looked at it, checked the balance.

"It's too short for the scabbard. It's either been broken, or cut down. What's so special about it?"

"Why would they cut it down?" I asked. And it dawned on her. "Naval use? So you could wield it in a small space?"

"Correct. Now look closely at the blade"

She turned the blade in her hand, and then she saw it. Three inches above the guard, inlaid into the steel in copper. Two small roses, with leaves. She smiled at me. "It's a Jacobite sword, I've seen this on drinking glasses. Two roses, one for the Old Pretender, and one for the Young. Except to the Jacobites they weren't Pretenders at all were they. They were the real thing, James the Eighth and his son, Bonnie Prince Charlie.

"Yep," I nodded. "And that's not just any old Jacobite sword. That there's a Jacobite naval sword. And that really is rare. I've not had the chance of another. They were defeated, the Jacobites, but they didn't give up their beliefs you know. Many of them were just absorbed into the British army, or in this case the Navy. That old battered sword, represents a great era of British Naval history, probably right through to Nelson's time. Jacobitism was alive long after the '45.

But the other thing I love about it, is that it went right past a major auction house, totally unrecognised! You lose some, but sometimes, not often perhaps, you do win some."

She slid it back into the scabbard, and noticed that as well. "Its loose in the scabbard too, just like a western gunfighters holster, ready for a quick draw."

She was quite a girl.

"Can't have this, you're too good. If I'm not careful you'll be turning up at auctions, and giving me some extra competition."

The next morning we went down to the gatehouse, and finished her stick.

We rounded off the rootwood into a comfortably shaped ball that fit her hand perfectly, and I smoothed over the "knuckles" where the thorns had been, so that no trace of the actual spikes remained.

Now, you could run your hand down the shaft of the stick, or grip it, without fear of injury. But the projecting "knuckles" still made it a formidable weapon.

I turned up a steel ferrule, and we fitted and filed it to match the elliptical shape of the stick. And then I varnished the entire thing, bringing out the colour of the bark. This one wasn't dark reddish brown like the average blackthorn, but a deep black. It would take a few more coats over several days before it was completely ready for use, but I think it was the best stick, I've ever worked on. No use to me, a bit on the light side for a man.

But perfect for Kate.

When the stick was varnished and dry, we went out onto the hillside behind the house, and practiced the few moves of single stick.

Most broadsword fencing consists of little more than seven or so basic practice cuts. Vertical, to the top of the head. Diagonals, delivered in the shape of a St. Andrews cross, the top two arms being delivered downwards the lower two upwards. And a horizontal from each side. Add in a really nasty eight. Upwards to the groin. The trick of it all, is in the suppleness of the wrist.

Kate took to it like a duck to water. Then, she shocked me again! Said it wasn't all that different from her whip and cane work at the Clinic, and that it would help keep her hand in. Said if I fancied a demonstration? ..... and then she laughed.

"Sorry Eddie, Just teasing!"

So I explained that striking with the stick was just part of it. And she surprised me again.

"I know," she said, "You have to draw the cut slightly with a sword, or a stick, to make it effective."

"Believe it or not," I told her, indicating her stick, "That stick you have there, although it isn't actually sharp, properly handled, it is quite capable of severing the main artery in the neck. It really is deadly."

We did a few more moves, this time from Indian stick fighting.

This involved reversing the stick, and using the hard round ball usually gripped by the hand, as the striking end. I added in a few thrusts, gripping the stick with both hands.

Then we moved on to parries. But I explained that if you are around to parrying, you are most likely up against an armed and trained opponent. So unless you are very good, just try and run away, and live to fight another day.

Or, if you've a gun, just shoot the bastard!

It may have been strange for me having a woman around the place. But I found that I quite liked it.

Although I would never admit it to anyone, I was growing fond of her. We both had the same odd sense of humour.

We sat for hours amongst the sunflowers on the grassy bank in front of my house.

I remember one glorious morning, walking around the side of the house and finding her bare breasted in the sunshine. I commenting that she reminded me of "Clytie" the sunflower maiden, who fell in love with Apollo. She loved that, and laughed aloud, making no effort to cover herself. She was totally without embarrassment.

I told her tales of my time in the Met. and later in Military Intelligence, and she regaled me with stories of the scandalous goings on at the Clinic. But she never mentioned any of her clients by name. That, she said, would be far outside the rules of

"Clytie"

Louis Welden Hawkins.

In classical mythology Clytie was an ocean nymph who fell in love with the god Apollo, (Helios), and was rejected

Each day thereafter she sat and watched the progress of the sun across the sky.

Eventually, she transformed into a sunflower, the blooms of which follow the path of the sun throughout the day.

professional behaviour.

Yes, that's right..... "professional behaviour." You see there's honour where you least expect it. (And very little where it ought to be, you say?)

We took to having long walks in the hills. An entire system of forestry roads link in with the track where I live. I carry a compass, and map just to be on the safe side, because if the fog comes down, one of these roads looks much like another. Just recently a couple of shooters out after deer lost their orientation, and disappeared for three days before anyone found them.

The safest way "off the hill," is to simply follow the flow of water. It can be tedious, and without doubt it will take you over rough country, but ultimately you will come to the main watercourse, and then you just follow it down to some form of civilisation.

It doesn't always work though. Even for locals.

A few years back one young lad trying to escape the law, (he'd literally ditched his car when he had a few too many beers on board,) tried to walk back out across the hills to get home.

The fog came down, so he decided to follow a stream and find his way off the hill. It wasn't even such a big hill, but he walked straight over a 60 ft. cliff. An experienced countryman.

It took weeks to find him, and by then, the foxes had spread his bones across the hillside.

I still had the uncomfortable feeling of being watched. We had our sticks, which were fair enough at close quarters, but just to be on the safe side, I took along Viktor's unnumbered Colt 45. Highly illegal, probably they would put me away forever if I was caught. But I felt better with it than without.

Kate looked shocked the first time she saw it. But I told her that since the incident with the Russian at the Cafe back in January, and the helicopter crash, it was perhaps better to be safe than sorry. I carried it in my old shoulder holster. Felt like I was back in the 'Stans.

In Britain no-one is used to seeing guns anymore, our Government has made sure of that...They've banned them.

Oh Sorry, not actually totally banned. Move in the right circles, know the right people, or come up with the right money, and you can still have a rifle capable of killing at a mile.

Take up deer hunting, then you can tote it around the countryside in the old Landrover. No real questions asked.

There seem to be a rising number of "part time gamekeepers" these days, and these so called "gamekeepers," have some very heavy firepower.

Quite frankly there are some right dodgy buggers amongst them, and I've no doubt that one day the wheel will come off, (again) and we'll have yet another round of "legislation."

But they'll never totally stop firearms. It's another "class" thing, and the so called "Gentry," both the real and the aspiring, will continue to be allowed to hand out shotguns to their guests at shooting parties like they're no more dangerous than tennis racquets, (they sometimes mix it with drink too!).

And, they'll invite a few politicians and senior police along to join in, just to make sure that everything stays sweet.

"Oh, I shoot with the Chief Constable." How many times do young policemen hear that one when certificates need renewing?"

One of our senior politicians actually peppered one of his "beaters" a few years back. All kept low profile of course, and that hasn't been the only case. Ask around in any country area, and you'll be surprised how many folk are carrying birdshot around in them, from earning a few quid (and a very few at that) as a "beater" for the Nobility.

But handguns? Strictly Verboten! Even the ubiquitous .22. So no more British Olympic shooting teams can train here in this country, and the only people who have handguns are criminals.

And they don't care.

Since they banned them back in 1997, there are now more illegal handguns floating around in Britain than ever before.They've become status symbols and objects of desire for our burgeoning drug gangs.

Since I suspected that I was now in the unofficial employ of some shady branch of M16, I wondered if perhaps they would allow me the gun anyway.

Depended on who I shot with it, I supposed.

I took Kate searching for blackthorn sticks, and she came to realise just how rare they really are. The leaves on the bushes were still green, with just a touch of yellow here and there, and the small hard sloe berries were taking on their purple hue now.

It was the wrong time to cut sticks really, but as the old saying goes, the best time to cut a stick is when you see it...... before someone else does!

Really they should be cut in the winter when the sap has dropped back down into the roots. They're easier to see as well, when the leaves are off.

We took along a couple of my camera's and we photographed deer, badgers, foxes, and other wildlife, but her real favourites were the hares.

We lay in the long grass on the hillside, down at ground level, and watched them float across the grass, as if their feet never even touched the earth.

There are all sorts of legends associated with the hare. Folk once believed that witches could transform themselves into hares, and travelled across the countryside in their likeness.

They're beautiful, harmless creatures, and I've heard that it's possible to domesticate them just like kittens if you get them young enough.....I don't know if it's true though, because I've never been able to catch one.... One day perhaps I will.

They are supposed to stare at the rising moon mesmerised, and we went out at night, and tried to see one actually at it. But we never did.

It was worth it though. Few in this day and age in Britain are lucky enough to see the sky with no light pollution. Almost everywhere the sky glows orange from city lights. But not out where I live.

Climb to the top of one of the hills, or drive up on one of the few narrow track roads, and all of the heavens are there in full view.

It's magnificent. A huge blue black sky, studded with brilliant stars. No artificial light, at all.

When the moon rises, it rolls in golden splendour along the profile of the hills. Later it shines like a silver crown in the sky, painting the hills and valleys with light and shadow. Reflecting off the rivers like quicksilver.

When the moon is down, the milky way stretches from horizon to horizon. Satellites and space debris float slowly across the sky. Shooting stars streak across the heavens, and at some times of year, there are showers of them.

Frequently, the aurora glows on the northern horizon.

After a while you learn to tell the time, by the lights of the aircraft passing across on the way to the United States. I'm just a kid at heart, I love watching aircraft. Kate did too.

Live in a city, you have pubs, entertainment, theatre. But out here nature has a theatre all of its own, and every night there is a different show.

But about eight each night, Kate would phone Pete Irvine on her mobile. He still had no idea where exactly she was, but they would talk for around an hour.

And it began to irritate me. Because, I knew I was growing ever fonder of her.

I was also becoming jealous.

And that was not a good idea.

It was a beautiful late afternoon, we'd eaten an early meal, and so Kate and I decided to walk out along the track beside the Teviot.

As we came out of the forest I noticed two guys around a couple of hundred yards away, just below the cottage at Merrylaw. They were sweeping the bankside with metal detectors.

Both were dressed in old army camouflage trousers, green body warmers, and had their headphones clamped on over the top of green baseball caps. Hard to see against the hillsides.

I gave them a wave, but they never even noticed me.

That's not unusual. With that game, you get so engrossed, that you lose awareness of everything. I remember one time when I was detecting, I switched the headphones off, to pack in for the day, turned around, and found myself face to face with a huge bull. About six inches away. He must have been following me for an age, and I'd never even noticed.

But that bankside they were on? It was a good spot that, there had been a settlement there for centuries, and further back on the hill behind, there were even signs of Pictish occupation.

Don't know why I hadn't been over that bit of land myself.

Strange lot, us detectorists, out in all weathers, at all hours of the day and night, grubbing about in the mud and cowshite. Usually for grotty little bits of scrap.

It's a bit like fishing though, it's not that you find much, especially out here in Teviotdale, where they never had much to lose anyway, but it's a way of totally switching off from the worries of the world.

These two had left their little green Suzuki Jimny parked down by the water. I'd seen that, way out on the hill, off and on for a few days now, and their tiny figures walking about by it, so maybe they'd had more luck than I ever had.

There was once a big Roman fort on Caerlanrig, and most of that ridge and the surrounding area has been gone over a thousand times. But every now and again another couple of lunatics will arrive, and do it all over again.

Some folk complain about them, but they're advancing our knowledge of history every single day. And in terms of labour, it could never be done if it had to be paid for. Hundreds of thousands of man hours. It would be a bit like asking the population of a small town, to go over the entire countryside of Britain, with vacuum cleaners, and then to sort through all of the dust in all of the bags.

Well,I thought, best of luck to them. We might just have a walk along and chat to them on the way back.

So off we trotted.

Knowing Kate's condition, I took it quite easy, trying to walk a bit slower than I was used to. She was around five months pregnant now, and it showed.

But she just strode along with her little blackthorn stick over one shoulder, occasionally swiping the tops off thistles, and sending the thistledown flying away on the light breeze. Just for the very fun of it.

We had been good for each other, and we laughed a lot these days. The depression I had felt after the crash of Donnie's helicopter had lifted. Errington Vardy had been forgotten, and it wouldn't be too long to the wedding, but I think she was the same as me. Unsure of the future, and not entirely looking forward to our time together coming to an end.

I think other folk were aware of our feelings too, because Shorty kept giving us odd looks, and when Abbie and Ros came to visit, there was always just the slightest "atmosphere."

As if something was better left unspoken.

We walked on, way up into the forest. Deer crossed the track in front of us, we watched a heron fishing by the waterside, but as the sun dipped lower we turned for home.

She slipped her hand into mine, and together we walked back down the track. Two young hares chased each other ahead of us, occasionally stopping and sitting side on to us as we approached, before taking off again for a run of another fifty yards.

I'd never felt happier. We rounded a bend in the track, and there were the two detectorists.

They'd moved upriver, and were between us and my "road end." Their backs were to us, and they were perched on a fallen log sharing a flask, and what looked like sandwiches.

Their detectors were lying on the ground nearby.

They didn't seem to hear us approach, and so, just before we came level with them, I called out......."Any luck lads".

They rose as one and turned to face us. And I realised my mistake.

They were Asians, and each held a knife with a long black blade close in by his right hip.

Professionals.

* * *

Parsa bared his teeth as he grinned.

Oh!......this was even better than he had imagined. Not just Graham, but Graham, hand in hand with his girl!

He'd seen that girl once with Vardy, and again out at the Cafe, up on the stage singing.

And now she was Graham's girl.....and pregnant too!

Pregnant with Graham's child!

Better and better!

Oh, How he would enjoy slitting *that* little belly open!

Graham could watch them bleed, before he died.

What a pity he didn't have more time. Work like this should be done slowly.

He closed in on the girl, moving the knife from side to side, the falling sun flashing redly from his blade

But the girl didn't move at all. She just stood there transfixed, right foot slightly forward, holding her hand on that silly little walking stick, with its end resting on the ground.

And she stared into his eyes, like a rabbit, caught in the stare of a stoat.

He moved even closer, and suddenly, he lunged at her belly with his long cruel knife.

* * *

As the one on the left moved towards Kate, my hand slipped beneath my jacket, and I began to draw the Colt. But the hammer snagged in my shirt.... I fought to drag it free, but as I saw him begin his lunge I already knew that I was too late.
His partner, had made no move, he just stood there seemingly paralysed, watching his companion attack a defenceless girl.

But Kate was far from defenceless, and as the knife flashed in towards her belly, she swept the stick up from the ground.
She took her assailant on the inside of his right wrist, completely numbing the hand, and sending the knife flying in a glittering arc through the air.
Kate's stick continued its upward sweep, as the man stared down in horror at his wrist, now gouting blood across the grass
And that was his fatal mistake. Because as he looked down, he exposed the side of his neck to the blackthorn.
Kate brought the stick back down in a perfect cut, just as we had practiced over the weeks.
The last six inches took him in the side of the neck. But this was not just a strike.
She drew the cut just as if it were a blade, and the hard knuckles cut through both skin and flesh.
I had heard it was possible. I had said it could be done, yet until that moment I had never been certain. But the stick cut onwards deeply through the flesh, severing the carotid artery.
Blood fountained into the air, and the man stumbled backwards, his hand clamped to his neck, disbelief in his eyes.
And then incredibly, near impossibly, considering her condition, Kate lunged forward.
I knew she had fought epee. But I didn't know how good she really was.
She dropped forward almost onto the ground, right foot extended, left hand flat on the track.
Her right hand now held the thin blackthorn like a rapier, and her arm shot forward like a rod of steel.
With massive force, the point of the stick with it's tiny steel tip, entered her opponents left eye. It punched the eyeball completely out of it's socket, and continued forwards, smashing through the sphenoid bone, forcing its way through the superior orbital fissure,

pushing fragments of bone before it, onwards, and upwards into the brain.

Kate heaved back on the stick, withdrawing it from the wound, with an audible, sucking pop.

The man was uttering a long, high, keening scream.

He staggered backwards a few paces, lost his balance on the rough ground of the rivers bank, and collapsed onto his back into the shallow water.

And there he lay, kicking and shuddering in the shallows, his head beneath the surface.

Drowning, bleeding to death, and at the same time, dying of a brain injury.

His feet were on the shingle of the shore, his body was in the river.

And a huge plume of blood, spread slowly downstream from his wounds

* * *

Shabaz rejoiced. It was unbelievable! That little girl had killed him, his hated uncle was now dead!

He turned knife in hand, and faced Eddie Graham. And he found himself staring straight into the single black eye of the Colt 45.

He knew then that he was dead.

His last thought was of Mehri, who he would never see again.

* * *

One down, one to go. And I had him!

I had him right in my sights. And at this range I couldn't miss.

Here was one of the men who had killed Donnie. One of the men who had tried to have Shorty and I killed at the Cafe. And now, he had come again to kill both Kate and myself out here in my very own woods.

My finger began to tighten on the trigger.

I could see the fear in his eyes. I could almost smell it on the light breeze.

I saw a single tear, trickle from his eye, and run slowly down his cheek.

And it was in that moment that I recognised him.

It was the boy from Sark. The boy I had seen that day, out by Kinmont Willie's Grave.

The boy with the beautiful Asian girl.

But still, I reasoned, he was the boy who had come here to kill us.

My finger tightened again on the trigger.

But try as I might, I couldn't shoot.

If I killed him, what would the result be?

What would happen to his girl?

What children perhaps, would never be born?

And infinitely slowly, all of its own accord, the gun dropped to my side.

* * *

Shabaz had no idea what had happened. Graham had him, there was no escape.

He had seen the knuckles of his finger whiten as he applied pressure to the trigger.

And then something had changed.

Something in his eyes, and the gun had simply fallen to his side.

And Eddie Graham, just waved him off and turned away.

Shabaz dropped the knife, and simply ran.

* * *

Kate was down by the waterside washing her stick when I turned.

The man's body lay where it had fallen. He was still now. He had more or less bled out, and lay on his back in the shallows staring at the sky with his single intact eye, whilst the other swung on its thread from the socket, drifting eerily in the small current in the shallows.

Kate dried her stick on his trouser leg, which was still on the shallow bankside.

"You were right Eddie," she said with a smile, "you can cut through the main artery in the neck. Just as well we practiced."

My God! I thought, She's got no nerves at all.
A voice spoke from behind us. "Thanks for leaving one alive Eddie, it was touch and go there for a few moments. Had it been me, I think I would have shot him anyway."
Another voice, a woman's his time. "Neat work Kate, couldn't have done it better myself! If you hadn't of moved, I'd have had to shoot him!"
Viktor and Ros. Both in camouflage suits, both with short take down rifles with telescopic sights.
Babysitters! Watchers, Looking out for us?
"You left it pretty Fucking late though didn't you!" I yelled, pointing at the body in the river.
"Oh don't worry so, I'd have got him before he killed her."
"Really?" I asked. "Of course," she replied, and behind her Viktor nodded.
"Or I would have."
"Oh, that's bloody nice to know!"
Kate hugged my arm. "Don't worry Eddie, I'm okay!"
"Well, Must be off." Viktor turned and walked back into the woods.
"Tidy up Ros? he called over his shoulder.
She was leaning over the body, taking photo's with a small camera. She just nodded.
A minute later, I heard his bike start up back in the woods.

So we "tidied up."
Ros stayed with the body, whilst Kate and I went back to my compound.
Despite her nonchalance, I thought she looked a little shaky. But I left her in the kitchen to make a bite to eat. Because, some things just have to be done.
So, I went out back into the workshops, and selected a length of heavy chain and a padlock. Then, I took Shorty's quad bike and trailer back up the trail.
Ros and I loaded the body into the trailer, covered it up with tarpaulin, and we drove back out onto the hillside to the south. About a mile out.
Ros rode in the trailer.

There are places out there that just look like green grass. But they're not. Try and walk on them, and the whole area quakes like the ocean. A heavy carpet of moss on top of peaty water.

I've tried to bottom them with a stick.......It just goes down and down.

We stripped him of all his clothes. Wrapped him in chain, and locked it on with the padlock.

I pierced his body with his long knife so the gases would escape as he rotted, and then? .....We made another "bog man."

You've seen those bodies that come out of the peat, thousands of years old? Well just perhaps, in three of four thousand years, when this bog had drained, then someone would find him.

They'd give him to the "experts."

"Ritual killing," they would say. "Religious Ceremony."

Or perhaps, "Human Sacrifice."

Some such load of bollocks.

But it's really just society getting rid of its dross.

I cut a slot in the heavy cover of moss, and we slid him in head first. The single eye stared at me accusingly as I did it. The other eye floated just beneath the surface on its fleshy string, as his head went under.

Then he vanished beneath the dark, peaty water. His bare feet disappearing like the stern of a sinking ship. And the moss just closed over him..... Gone, without trace.

We drove back down the hill.

Kate cooked us a huge ADB, and we opened a bottle of decent red wine. Kate deferred out of respect for her baby.

It may sound strange eating heartily after a day like that. But you've got to be alive to eat you know.

I did notice though, that we all went easy on the tomato sauce.

Ros hot wired the Suzuki Jimny which was still standing near the bottom of my track, and said she would dispose of it somewhere. There had been no keys on the man's body.

And I wondered where the driver had gone.

* * *

Shabaz sat in the armchair, and wept.

The cat, sensing his misery, leapt up onto his lap and rubbed itself on his chest, purring loudly.

He hugged the cat to him. What a fool he was. Why had Graham not just shot him. Put him out of his misery.

It had taken him hours to carefully work his way through the woods, out across the hills, and back down onto the road. He had lost direction several times, and it was pitch dark when he stumbled out onto the main A7, torn, muddy, and bleeding from the cuts he had sustained in clambering over almost invisible barbed wire fences in the dusk.

But he was fortunate, he had escaped. And he hadn't been on the roadside for more than five minutes, when a delivery driver, late and heading for Carlisle spotted him and pulled to a halt alongside.

He improvised a story about falling off his mountain bike back in the woods, and needing a lift.

45 minutes later, the man deposited him on the bridge over the river Eden on the North side of the City.

And that was when he made the worst decision of his life. Because, he should have gone back to the flat. He ought to have rested, and thought things through. But he didn't. And late though it now was, he'd turned, and walked slowly back to Stanwix.

Mehri, was in bed when he rang the doorbell, and it was several minutes before he heard her frightened voice asking who it was outside.

"Shabaz!" she cried flinging the door open "What is it?" She stared in horror at his stained and bloody clothing, and then she dragged him inside, and up the stairs into the flat.

He must have still been in shock. He never thought, he didn't reason, he just sat there on the sofa, with his head bowed, and everything simply poured out.

The death of his parents. His uncle. The school. The training.

Their Mission.

The need to kill Eddie Graham. The events of that afternoon. The death of Parsa.

Eddie Graham's refusal to kill him.

And lastly his love for her, and his wish that he could leave all of his old life behind him.

Finally, emotionally and physically exhausted, he looked up.

And that was when his entire world collapsed. He had thought that she might understand. That they might be able to have a life together.That now that his Uncle was gone, he could pick up the threads of his life and be happy.

But he was wrong.

Mehri just sat staring at him, utter horror on her face.

"You're a Terrorist? That's what you're saying? Here to bring down this country.....You're part of Al Qaeda!"

He nodded. "But that's all finished with now. Parsa has gone. He is dead. And now we can have a good life together you and I."

She rose to her feet, crossed the room, and flung the door open.

"Get Out!" She yelled. "Leave! Just go back to whatever stinking little hole that you and your uncle crawled out of!

All of these weeks, all of that time we spent together. Was it nothing but a lie, a deception? Was I just your little distraction, something to take your mind off your foul plans?"

Tears were streaming down her face.

"Leave now! Go! Get out of here, and leave this country.....I hate you people!"

"Now!" she pointed at the door. "Just get out of my life! I never want to see you again!"

Shocked....Horrified, Shabaz backed away from her, then he turned, fled down the stairs, and ran off into the night.

* * *

The cat still purred in his lap.

At least, he thought, someone loves me.

What could he do? The mission was finished. He was alone. There was no way to carry it out now.

He rose from the chair, and deposited the cat in its basket. He couldn't go back to Afghanistan. They may just kill him anyway, those people didn't care too much for failures.

He wandered aimlessly about the flat, picking up odds and ends, putting them back down again.

And then he began to pack his bags. He still had the Mercedes van. He would go down to London, that was a large and anonymous city. He would find work, a new identity, he would have a new beginning. But of course, that would require money, quite a lot of money.

Parsa, had always controlled the cash, but where was it? Where would Parsa hide his valuables?

He went through into his Uncle's bedroom, and his eye fell upon the large cases he had lugged up the stairs when Parsa had returned from Leeds.

He crossed and lifted the lid of the first case. Clothes, binoculars, night vision scopes, camera's and lenses. All of the equipment that they had used to track Graham and his friends.

But no money.

He tried the other case. It was securely locked.

What was it Parsa had said. "Fashionable clothing, you'll like it?" But then he'd laughed and given some sort of warning...... About being careful, and not touching it?

Problem.....He searched the entire flat. No keys anywhere.

He went back to the first trunk, and removed a small portable tool kit.

It took him he best part of an hour, to carefully remove all of the wood and metalwork surrounding the locks. But it was worth it, because as soon as he lifted the lid, he found the money. A thick wad of fifty pound notes, and a small but very heavy box, secured with a clasp.

Small and heavy, he didn't like that. Could be dangerous.

Slowly he lifted the lid.

But he needn't have worried, for inside nestled twelve small gold bars. Negotiable nywhere!

He also found codes books, contact numbers, and three mobile phones. He checked them. All were pre programmed with a series of telephone numbers. No chance of him using any of those. He was off.

But where was the clothing that had caused his uncle to laugh so much?

He lifted everything out, and placed it on the floor, and it was then that he realised that there was a lower level to the trunk, beneath a hinged lid.

Carefully, he raised the lid, and stared in horror at the contents.

It was his uncles true legacy.

Explosives! And in his mind, he heard Parsa's voice. A voice from beyond the grave.

"Fashionable clothing..... you'll like it."

Because this wasn't just a bomb, or even bomb making equipment.

It was a suicide vest. A flak jacket, equipped with vertical pockets to contain the explosives packages, batteries, a small box with detonators, and a sinister lead with a red button on the end.

His depression returned. Worse than ever.

His uncle had been right. And perhaps after all he did like it. For here was a way for one man, alone, to complete this mission. And *he was* that one man. He could change the world. Bring down a Nation. A nation which had oppressed his people for so long.

Who had he been fooling? What chance was there for him in this country after all.....He had lost the girl he loved.... He had no-one, he had nothing left to live for.

Why *not* go out in a blaze of glory?

He lifted the vest from its resting place, and slipped it on. It fit perfectly. But of course it would, wouldn't it?

It had been made for him.

* * *

Mehri lay in the bed.

It must be around 2 a.m.....But how could she sleep? She had wept and wept until she could weep no more.

Why had she sent him away? Perhaps she could have saved him? She believed that he could be a good man, and she knew in her heart that he loved her. Why had she not tried? Why had she not helped him in some way?

She slipped out from under the sheets, made her way into the small kitchen, and brewed some strong coffee. Perhaps it was not to late?

Although she had never been there because of that awful man Parsa Khan, she did know where the flat was. And now that Shabaz's uncle was dead....?

She must go there immediately. She must reason with him. She must try to help. Together they could find a way out of this.

Downstairs, the doorbell began to ring, urgently, on and on.

Shabaz! He'd come back!

Hair flying, still in her nightclothes, she ran down the stairs, fumbled with the lock, and flung the door opcn. And the smile died on her lips.

For it was not Shabaz.

He was all in black, black jeans, black jacket, black ski mask.

In his right hand was a long black gun. A gun with a huge silencer screwed into the end of the barrel.

She made to scream, but no scream came, for his left hand clamped across her mouth, and he forced his way inside.

His voice was no more than a whisper.

"Hello Mehri, expecting someone else were you?"

The door clicked shut behind him.

And she realised then, that she was alone with a killer.

* * *

October 1st 2003.

Anthony Errington Vardy, hummed quietly to himself, and tapped the steering wheel in time to the music playing in his head. "The Ode to Joy."

And why not, he thought, for he was truly...... Joyful!

Everything was now in place, and all that now remained was to rid the world of the irritation that was Eddie Graham.

But, his pet assassins, Shabaz and Parsa, had been dispatched, and by now they ought to have dealt with that little problem. There had been no need to get his own hands dirty.

Pity though in a way, he'd like to have got rid of Graham himself. But he'd given them instructions to make it as slow and as messy as possible, and they did like their sharp little knives these Afghans. World class experts they were.

No doubt he would hear about it in due course.

Once Graham was out of the way Pete Irvine was next on the list.

That would be pure artistry.

Irvine would be found dead of an overdose of heroin, in his grandfather's library. He would be surrounded by documents proving the old fellows involvement in the plot to kill Churchill, letters from Adolf Hitler, agreeing to his very senior role in the pro German Government which was to follow, and a list of his fellow conspirators.

Poor Peter! His suicide note was a masterpiece of the forgers art! Telling of his shame at the discovery of his grandfather's treachery, the remorse he felt over his family's abuse of the trust placed in them. Of his sorrow at his own weaknesses, his inability to take the reins after his father's death, and of his joy that he was able to hand the reins of power over to such a worthy successor as his loyal factor, Anthony Errington Vardy, to whom he wished to apologise most profusely for the embarrassment his death would undoubtedly cause. His last wish was that dear Anthony, as his successor, take upon himself both his name, and the title "Duke of

Marchbank."

Vardy laughed out loud!

This would be the culmination of all of his years of work, of all of the careful negotiations.

The contracts were in place, and once Pete was gone everything would swing into action.

Industry! Mining! Natural gas! Windfarms!

Lovely! Lovely! Money!

Oh Yes! ......His Future was Rosy! It was so bright, he was going to need sunglasses!

He despised them both, but those two Afghans had certainly come through with the documentation, and the last installment of his cash had arrived by courier that very morning.

Now that it was all nearly over, the older of the two, had offered him that old Landrover he drove, for an absolute song. The bloody idiot! It might be a bit battered, but there were hardly any miles on it. All he had to do was pick it up in Carlisle.

Ought to make five to ten grand on that at least!

But for now, he had work to do.

He'd had a wonderful idea. Kathy Pringle! She'd quite slipped his mind. He really must find Kathy Pringle, for one last session with Marchbank.

He'd thought she should be back in the Borders just about now, so he'd asked questions here and there, but bloody Kathy Pringle seemed to have dropped off the face of the earth, or at least of the Borders.

But then, Vardy thought, he must persevere, this was Tradition after all. One really should grant the condemned man one last wish.

Of course "Dear Peter" didn't know he was a condemned man did he? But, there isn't much on the telly these days. And I'm due for a bit of fun. It's been a long time after all.

So, he would find Mistress Pringle, and arrange a session. Then he would watch through the mirror, whilst she performed her little tricks. It would be delicious....He loved to watch a true artist at work.....And he'd record it all in high definition. Put it up on the Internet when Marchbank was dead? A sort of Obituary?

He burst out laughing again. What an icing on the cake that would make!

He was almost weeping with laughter now.

He'd tried Welldean, and the old idiot, Zhang, said that she'd been unexpectedly called back to London on urgent business. So, he'd rung the Clinic. All he could get out of them was that she'd be unavailable for some time. But he didn't believe that either.

She was hiding from him. They always ended up hiding from him.

Then, he remembered.

Parsa, who he considered to be a horny little fundamentalist with an eye for the women, Parsa of all people had said he'd seen her about three weeks ago at that bloody Cafe just out of Langholm, up on stage singing with an Elvis Presley impersonator.

Bloody incredible!

She'd been with that slag Rebecca, from Welldean, and a couple of other women. The entire business sounded odd.

He knew though. She was just trying to avoid him, get out of her obligations.

When this was over he might just have to get rid of her.

Oh, what a fine time he could have doing that. He knew some painful little tricks even she had never heard of. He wondered how long he could make it last?

He double declutched, changed down, and screeched through a corner. Careful he thought, This one's no Range Rover.

It was a black Porsche Cayenne, a present to himself.

Another month, when that despicable weakling Pete Irvine was gone, he would even be able to afford it.

His was a 4.5 litre V8. Turbo S 521 horses, over 170 mph, special paint job, "Pearl Black," tinted windows. Beautiful.... a car fit for a Duke.

But then, by next month he would *be* a Duke!

His old Range Rover was back at Marchbank House. Make a good little runabout.

Well!..... Here we are, and he swung the wheel left, arriving in the car park of the Last Chance in a flurry of gravel.

Shorty and Reb were off out for the night.

Chuck was in charge. He had a couple of girls coming in later to help out with the waitressing.

It was 7.30 p.m. and he was just about to go up on stage, and begin rehearsing.

Tonight, he was wearing his white Elvis suit with the flares. Personally, he preferred the black leather one, but Yvonne and Denise, his favourite twins, had especially requested this, so how could he say no? He had to keep them sweet, 'cause he had hopes that he could persuade them to join the band as backing singers. Kit them out in some 50's style dresses, and they'd be just perfect.

God! but those girls knew how to move in time to music. He smiled at the fond memories.

Just then gravel rattled against the side of the building, and a shiny new 4x4 slewed to a halt outside.

Another Flash Bastard, he thought, What now?

The door slammed back against the stop, and a tall fair haired man in tweeds, and a revolting yellow waistcoat strode in.

He walked straight across to the stage, and stared up at Chuck.

"Okay "Elvis," come clean. Where is she!"

"Who," asked Chuck, "Me Auntie Mary? She's out the back in the kitchen, working on her steak and kidney puds. If you want any, you're too late. Come back tomorrow."

"I don't give a shit what your bloody Auntie Mary, is concocting in the kitchen! Where's that bitch Kathy Pringle!" He pointed a finger at Chuck. "I know for a fact that she was up on that stage, singing with you! Where's the dwarf who runs this place, I'll wring it out of him, if you don't come clean. I owe that little bastard one."

Chuck said nothing, he just climbed down from the stage, walked over to the corner, and picked up his golf bag. Then, he simply walked out of the door.

Errington Vardy followed him. *"I'm Talking to You!"* he yelled. *"Now, where is that slovenly cow Pringle."*

But Chuck just nodded, and looked at him sideways. Very carefully, he placed the golf bag against the wall. Very carefully, he selected a heavy looking driver, and slid it from the bag. Slowly, he removed the cover from its head. Calm, and quite unperturbed, he turned to Vardy.

"Sir," he commenced. "You don't mind if I call you "Sir" do you? I know you like it. You see, I know of you, "Sir." And I know that you like to be shown proper respect.

But...... "Sir," he continued. "You have spoken ill of a Lady who stands high in my affection. And, what is more "Sir," he went on, "I also know exactly who you are." And he yelled. "YOU'RE THAT POSH WANKER ERRINGTON VARDY, WHO SHOT

DOWN ECKY CHARLTON'S SISTER'S LADDIE'S AEROPLANE!

And so saying, Chuck raised his club, and with a tremendous swing, he stove in the driver's window of the Porsche.

Errington Vardy let out a horrified scream. and rushed forward.

Too late! Chuck straight armed him in the chest, knocking him back onto the ground on his buttocks. Then, he reached through the window, took a firm hold of the metalwork of the door, and, using all of his considerable strength, he wrenched it completely from its hinges!

Carrying it high above his head. he walked around to the back of the vehicle, and hurled it through the rear window. Glass cascaded in a glittering shower. The car alarm was screaming.

Chuck was laughing aloud. He ran around to the front of the Porsche. With one great leap, he mounted the bonnet, and, stepping from there up onto the roof, he proceeded to pound up and down, like a demented orang outang, his huge feet hammering the roof into the semblance of the craters of the moon.

By now cars were pulling up on the road, and camera's were whirring.

At long last, Langholm had a major Tourist Attraction.

Perhaps one day, Chuck thought, there may be a statue. A bronze perhaps? Alongside the memorial to Hugh MacDiarmid?

For who could resist the sight of a six foot six, eighteen stone Elvis impersonator, dancing in a white suit with flares, on top of one of Porches most beautiful creations.

And Chuck rose to the challenge. For now, *his moment* had come. Fame beckoned. And he had his audience in the palm of his hand.

He threw his head back, pointed a finger at Errington Vardy, and bellowed out :-

"You ain't nothin' but a Hound Dog.
Cryin' all the time"
You ain't nothin' but a Hound Dog,
Cryin' all the time,
Well you ain't never caught a rabbit,
And you ain't no friend of mine!"

He drum rolled accompaniment, with his huge boots, on the roof of the Porsche.

Anthony Errington Vardy climbed slowly to his feet, and surveyed the wreck that was his car, just as Mary Kang, wielding a long wet mop erupted from the Cafe.

"Chuck" she yelled. "Get down off of there."

"But Auntie Mary," Chuck pointed. "He......He called Kathy Pringle a Bitch....and a Cow."

"WHAAAT," cried Mary. "POOR PREGNANT LITTLE KATHY?"

And she swung the mop at Vardy. Who ducked just in time.

A Dreadful Suspicion entered Vardys mind.

"PREGNANT!" he screamed, purple with rage. "WHAT DO YOU MEAN, PREGNANT!

SHE'S NOT SUPPOSED TO *BE* PREGNANT! WHERE IS SHE? WHO'S THE FATHER?

TELL ME,....THEN I CAN GO AND MURDER THE LITTLE SLAG!"

Mary swung at him again with the mop. "NEVER!" she cried, lunging artfully with the shaft.

Chuck jumped down from the roof, and loomed forward. Vardy, recovering his senses, dodged Mary's blows, leapt into the drivers seat, started the vehicle, and tore out of the car park.

Folk cheered. Car horns sounded, and the audience clapped in appreciation.

"ENCORE ELVIS!"...they yelled.... "LONG LIVE THE KING!"

Mary put her arm around Chuck, rested her head on his magnificent biceps and wept.

"Oh God" she whimpered. "What have I gone and done?"

* * *

Since becoming an unofficial agent of MI6, Detective Inspector Ecky Charlton had commandeered a corner office of Langholm's old Victorian Police Office in Buccleuch Square,

It was an imposing red sandstone edifice with the crow stepped gables and other detail picked out in lighter yellow stone.

Unfortunately the entire building was usually empty, so commandeering an office was not really any kind of triumph.

In fact, he fantasised, he could have taken possession of the entire place. Held wild parties with some of those hippie chicks, who wandered past on the way Samye Ling, the Buddhist Temple out at Eskdalemuir. Or, he could have sold the building before anyone realised, and moved abroad with the proceeds. But then property in Langholm never brought that much money anyway.

Frankly, before Eddie and Shorty moved here, there really had been no need for a police presence in the town at all.

Ecky leaned back with his feet on the desk, and idly flicked balls of screwed up paper into a basket on the other side of the room. Another half hour, and he'd wander over to the "Last Chance," have a plate of "Geordie burgers" and chips, and check on what was doing. "I wonder what the Hell they do put in them?" he mused.

His speculations were disturbed by the urgent ringing of the front door bell, followed immediately by a mad pounding on the wood.

Bloody drunk probably. Almost everyone knew that the station was not usually manned.

He peered out of the office window, but from there he couldn't actually see the front door. What he did see however, was the battered hulk of what appeared to be a black Porsche Cayenne, parked half on the pavement outside. The driver's door was missing completely, and the rear window was stove in. From the state of the roof, it looked as if the car had been rolled.

Still,.....uniform business, nothing to do with him.

But the pounding on the door resumed. In fact it got worse. It now sounded as if someone was actually kicking at the woodwork.

A loud and angry voice shouted, "Come out you idle bastards, I can see the lights are on, so I know you're in."

He knew that voice too, Anthony Errington Vardy.

Ecky smiled wickedly, and walked through to the front office.

Quietly, he released the lock on the main door and turned the knob, just as Vardy renewed his assault.

Totally unbalanced, Vardy flew in through the now open doorway.

Quite inadvertently, Ecky stuck out his foot. Vardy tripped, and sprawled across the floor.

Ecky gave an ironic salute, and grinned down at him. "Good Evening, "Captain" and how can we assist you today."

"Charlton!" Vardy yelled, climbing to his feet. I've been assaulted! My....My....Porsche has been trashed. White faced with anger, he pointed a shaking finger at Ecky.

"Charlton! This is an order! You will go now, and arrest Chuck Elliot, that lunatic Elvis Presley impersonator at the "Last Chance Cafe." And he poured out the entire sorry story of his humiliation.

But Ecky's smile simply grew wider. "Mr Vardy," he intoned. "I regret that, having been temporarily seconded to "other duties." I am no longer acting in the capacity of a Police Officer.

Were I in a position to do so, however, I would take the very greatest of pleasure in arresting you, for you are without doubt drunk, and moreover drunk in charge of a motor vehicle. A vehicle which has most obviously been involved in some variety of accident.

Further, "Captain" Vardy. You have caused a breach of the peace, and damaged the paintwork of the door to this ancient and venerable Police office. And to make matters worse, you have maligned the name of a respected and talented member of our Community. To whit....Chuck Elliot.

I suggest therefore that you take this opportunity to remove yourself from these premises, before my unaccustomed spell of good nature expires. But, since I suspect that you will not let this matter rest, and may wish at some point in the future to renew your complaint, then take this little thought with you."

And Ecky grabbed the mike from the ancient force radio in his right hand. He leapt onto the counter of the front office, stretching the cord to its very limit. Straddle legged he stood, towering above Errington Vardy, and warbled in best Elvis fashion.

"You're caught in a trap.
You can't get out,
And I don't love you baby"

Whoa, Whoa, Whoa,

I just can't see,
Why you're bringing this to me,
When I just don't believe a word you're Sayin"

Now, Just Fuck off,
And Complain about that!"

Ecky jumped down from the counter, and as he did so, his jacket fell open, revealing the butt of the Smith and Wesson automatic gleaming evilly in its shoulder holster.

Vardy stared at it in horror.....Scottish Policemen just weren't supposed to be armed!

He let out an inarticulate scream, and ran out of the door.

* * *

The Porsche may have been battered, but it was still sound.

The slipstream ripped at his tweed jacket, as he hurled the vehicle through the corners, en route to Marchbank House.

In his heart he knew already who the father of the child was, but he would take the greatest of pleasure in beating the truth out of that bastard Irvine. And when he had, he would find Kathy Pringle, and remove her from the picture entirely.

He reached the Border, and immediately swerved right onto the long drive to Marchbank.

He slowed, and struggled to regain his composure. He stopped the vehicle just out of sight, behind a stand of bushes.

He crossed to his bungalow, in the grounds, let himself in, went into the bathroom, brushed his hair, and splashed water onto his face.

He brushed down his tweeds, and then went to the stick rack just inside of the front door.

Carefully, he went through his selection of sticks, finally choosing a decent ashplant, one with a heavy polished rootball for a grip.

Jauntily, swinging the stick in his right hand, he crossed to the main house.

Using his personal key, he let himself in through the front door.

Music was playing softly in the library. "Albinoni's Adagio."

Oh, but he was looking forward to this. It had been so very long.

And.....the perfect music...... Music......to beat Dukes by!

"Hi Peter, I'm back," he called cheerfully.....Where are you........?

I've brought a little treat for you."

And he tapped the ball of the stick in his palm, as he walked into the library.

* * *

He knew he'd gone too far, much too far. All he'd really needed to know was if the child was Irvine's.

But then he'd blurted out that not only was the baby his, but he intended to marry the cow. And he'd just lost control.

But it always had been difficult to stop when he was having such fun!

If the bloody chauffeur hadn't come in, he reckoned he would have finished the job properly and killed him.

Bloody chauffeur! He guffawed. Well he certainly was that now!.......Bloody!

But he had to face the truth. It was over. The Law would be after him for certain.

So Charlton thought he would make a complaint did he?

Oh no....He had far more in store for Charlton and Graham than that.

Disgrace. He sniggered. Everlasting disgrace!

Because really there was only one thing for it. Only one thing a Gentleman could really do. Draw a line. End the matter like a man.

He looked down at the passenger seat of the Rangerover. Need a good gun for a good job, and the Dukes favourite Holland and Holland lay on the leatherwork, a box of 00 buckshot beside it. Not the right ammo for that gun, much too heavy, but so what?

He turned down the narrow road and headed for the forest.

Five minutes later, he deliberately put the vehicle off the road and into a ditch.

He took an envelope from the inside pocket of his tweed jacket, and laid it on the driver's seat. A little present for Eddie Graham and his friends,

He picked up the gun and the ammunition, took one last look at the car, and walked off into the trees with the shotgun under his arm.

He whistled, and then sang softly to himself as he marched along.

"The British Grenadiers."

"Some talk of Alexander,
And some of Hercules,
Of Hector and Lysander,
And such great names as these"

Must preserve the honour of the old regiment you know!
He giggled insanely as he disappeared beneath the branches.

"But of all the worlds great heroes..........
There's none that can Compare........

Minutes later, a single shot echoed through the woods,
And a cloud of dark crows rose from the branches

* * *

They found Vardy's Range Rover down by Kershopefoot, on the track out to Roadhead. It was nose down in the ditch, and there was a note on the driver's seat.

He was full of remorse over his attack on Pete Irvine. He said he couldn't stand it any longer, and intended to end his life. He laid the blame squarely at the door of Eddie Graham, who hated him, and had hounded him for years, blaming him for the murder of poor little Quentin James in London years ago.

Graham tried to fit him up for that murder, and failed.

Vardy claimed that I had tracked him down to the Borders, and that with my friends Septimus Higgins, Detective Inspector Ecky Charlton, and the lunatic Chuck Elliot, I'd started a campaign of harassment aimed at driving him to the murder of Peter Irvine.

We'd humiliated him, smashed his shotgun, and trashed his car.

We had almost succeeded. But at the last moment Vardy had come to his senses. He'd realised what had happened, and stopped his attack on Pete before he'd actually killed him.

Now he was off into his beloved forests to end it all.

The police, and a motley collection of volunteers were searching the surrounding woodland for his body.

It could just be that the Authorities would believe it.

Maybe he had topped himself.

* * *

Ecky Charlton's Last Stand.

He stood in the corridor, patted the left breast of his jacket, and felt the reassuring bulge.

It was safe.....My God, but Viktor and Ros certainly knew how to supply the right weapon for the right occasion.

Ecky turned, knocked on the dark panelled oak door, and that familiar, grating voice spoke a single word.

"Enter"

Ecky opened the door. And there he sat behind his desk, the light behind him, and only his silhouette visible. Superintendent William Mason, known and loathed throughout the force as "Free" Mason.

Not just because of his membership of that organisation, but because he truly believed that his position as a senior police officer, entitled him to receive almost everything for "free."

He ate free lunches at the local restaurants, drank free drinks in local hotels, and demanded huge discounts from all of the local stores. And God help anyone who tried to charge William Mason, for life could be made very trying indeed.

Promotion and preference, in Mason's police area were entirely dependant upon the number of favours received.

Any competent tradesman who joined the force, fell within his sphere of influence. Mason's house, and the homes of his near relatives were in pristine condition, maintained by an army of off duty police officers, blackmailed into it, either by threats, by hopes of promotion, or nice little nine 'til five office jobs, well out of the line of fire.

Mason's own promotions had been achieved by a mixture of gross incompetence, combined with a total lack of charisma.

No-one could stand to be around him, and to actually be locked in a vehicle with him for eight hours was pure torment.

But fortunately PC Mason had a small degree of intelligence, and consequently after three years of devoted study, he managed to pass all of his police exams.

And so, in the time honoured tradition of the police service, the loathed officer, was promoted to sergeant, and posted to a station as far away as possible. To a station where he was equally despised, and similarly disposed of. Thus, his rise through the ranks was meteoric, and only ten years after he was first dispatched upon his perambulations, he arrived back, exactly where his career had begun......Superintendent Mason, in charge of his very own little kingdom.

And there, he would forever remain. For no-one dared promote the officious little bastard further.

Now, he sat behind his magnificent desk, a little fat slug of a man, topped off with a dark and wavy wig.

All that remained of his lacklustre career, was retirement. But go willingly? He would not!

Because once retired....Then, nothing would be ever be free again. He would be plain Mr. Mason. No-one would show him the respect he deserved. And he had made enemies. Even within the Force, there were mutterings that his civilian life may well be less than easy.

Ecky looked at him with distaste. He knew that the sly bastard had had the legs of that chair especially raised, to make himself appear taller. PC Jimmy Henderson, who used to be a joiner, had been "persuaded" to do it. ("back out on the streets if you don't")

Just as he knew that the chair in front of the desk had slightly shortened legs

"Come in, "Inspector" Charlton. Do have a seat."

"No thanks Superintendent, I'd rather stand."

"Never mind the "Superintendant" Inspector. I expect "Sir" from the likes of you"

They were alone. No witnesses, and Ecky smiled in anticipation.

"Well, Okay then "Sir,".... But you do know what they say,..... "Sir?"....

Every time I say "Sir,"......"Sir,"...... I think......... "Shit!"

Mason's complexion turned purple. Ecky leaned over the desk.

"Now.... "Sir."..... What was it you wanted to see me about?"

"You're finished Charlton!" Mason exulted. "I've looked forward to this for years! Who wants a policeman who sings Country songs, and dresses like that sad loser Hank Williams!

A man whose weird friend's ride home built motorcycles, and run a broken down Cafe?

And now, you've played right into my hands, and I've got you!

Because now you and those idiots, have gone too far, and you have brought about the suicide of a fine man. Captain Anthony Errington Vardy!

You and your friends have driven him to it, and the body of the poor fellow now lies somewhere out in the woods at Kershopefoot.

Not only was Anthony a brave and honourable fellow, he was also my dear friend, and the associate of some very senior members of Police Forces on both sides of this Border. All of whom are insistent upon your instant dismissal. As we speak, disciplinary proceedings against you are imminent.....

So go! "Inspector." Clear your desk, and get out of this station! It's unlikely, but perhaps you can salvage a musical career for yourself and that wife of yours. But," and he smirked as he pointed a podgy little finger at Ecky, "If *you* avoid criminal prosecution I shall be very much surprised."

"Finished?" Ecky asked, smiling inwardly as he reached into his inside pocket.

At Last.........Showtime!

And mysteriously, quite unbidden, the first bar of Ennio Morricone's theme for "The Good, the Bad, and the Ugly," played inside of his head......Shorty, he thought, would be proud of him!

Ecky withdrew a yellowing sheet of paper.

Slowly, he unfolded it.

"Remember this William? The Official Secrets Act?" He tapped the ageing paper with a fingernail. "You signed this over 30 years ago, and it means that what you're about to learn, goes no further.

He reached into his pocket for a second time, extracting a thick folded document, together with a small leather billfold.

He placed the document carefully on the desk in front of Mason, opened the billfold, and held it in front of the Superintendent's eyes.

"Actually, I..... outrank you William. "Detective Inspector" I may be. But my rank in this "Organisation," places me above any officer in this force.

It was his M.I.6. identification.

"That there," he pointed, "on the desk, is a resume of the career of your good friend, "Captain" Anthony Errington Vardy, disgraced Guards Officer, liar, cheat, forger, murderer, and, Ecky paused for effect......KGB Agent!

Rumour has it "Sir," that he was also, a very senior member of your own little brotherhood.

Now William, we in the Service have reason to believe, that there is a distinct possibility, that in the immediate future, "The Shit", or the 'Sir" as I prefer to call it, "Will hit the fan". And it will not be possible within Police and Security circles to play down the "degree," if you will pardon the pun, of involvement of both yourself and your associates in this very sorry business.

I mean William,.... you have been providing shelter and succour to an Enemy of the State."

William Mason looked in horror at the document in front of him, and he saw his world crumbling.

Then his eye fell upon the Smith and Wesson just visible beneath Ecky's jacket, and his face drained of colour.

Ecky saw the glance, and smiled sadly.

"What do you want me to do.....Inspector Charlton.......Ecky? What do you expect of me?"

Remember.... Ecky thought.....He insulted Hank Williams!

He steeled himself. And for the first time in his life, kind, considerate, Ecky Charlton gave in to a truly evil thought.

He placed his hand on the butt of his pistol, slowly withdrew it from the holster, let it lie there on his palm, and contemplated it in silence for a moment.

"William," he intoned. "You know, and I know that there is only one way out for a Gentleman.

Think of poor Anthony, lying cold and dead out there in the forest. His body, gnawed by foxes, his very bones spread across the lonely hills. In life nothing more than a traitor.

But in Death?......... Well at least, he went out like a Man."

Mason was white and shaking.

Ecky put on his executioner's face, as he intoned. "It has been left to me, William to decide your fate." He weighed the pistol in his hand.

Then he smiled "Ugly things aren't they? Bloody uncomfortable to lug around too."

He returned the gun to it's holster, picked up Errington Vardy's file, and walked to the door.

"Just clear your desk William. It's time for you to retire. As to your ultimate fate?"

His mind clicked into "Clarke Gable" mode. "Well," he paused.... "Frankly Scarlet, I don't give a damn. Just make sure, that you're....“Gone with the Wind.”

Ecky closed the door behind him, and burst into hysterical laughter.

Odd.......But......He didn't feel guilty at all!

* * *

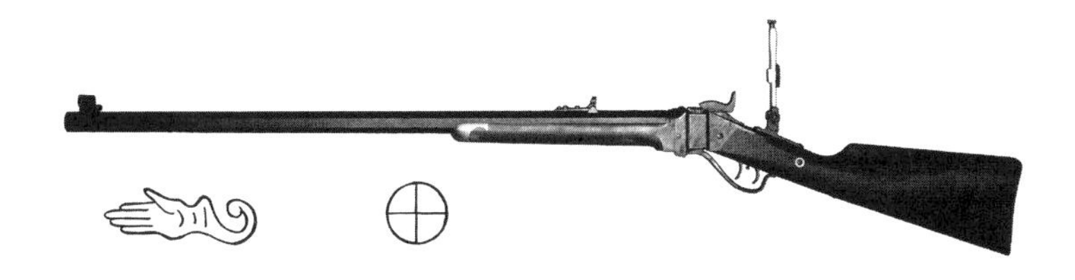

October 23rd 2003.

Shorty set up his heavy wooden stand, slackened off the universal mount, and lay down in the grass of the little knoll on the north flank of Bowan Hill.

It was beautiful, crystal clear, late afternoon, with the sun coming in low along the length of the valley, and illuminating to perfection the orange oil drum he had set up in the old quarry on the opposite hillside.

1290 yards,....not Billy Dixon, but a good long shot anyway.

He was getting better all of the time, and today the conditions were perfect, dry, still warm, and windless.

He took the heavy binoculars from their wooden case, set them on their stand, and adjusted the focus. Clear as a bell.

He'd filled the drum with water, and when he hit it, the result should be spectacular.

Eddie was off seeking some piece of wreckage, supposed to be part of Hess's plane, and Reb had taken the opportunity to nip out to Merrylaw to see Kathy Pringle about wedding arrangements.

Eddie wouldn't be back for an hour or two yet. John Tullie and his missus were off out from Bowanhill farm, and for a change there were no animals on the hillside.

Oh, life was great.

He drew the rifle from the leather guncase, and set it up on the wooden rest.

He swung the gun around, flipped up the vernier sight, and squinted across the valley.

No wind, air neither too hot nor too cold, make allowances for drift due to the spin on the bullet.

He opened his ammunition box, pulled the hammer to half cock, dropped the lever on the Sharps, and slid the huge round into place.

He closed the breech.

A familiar sound drifted to his ears. A bloody Toyota twin cab with a knackered exhaust, coming from the direction of Hawick. Eddie was back! .... Oh Christ..... He should have been away for hours!

Shorty saw the Toyota pass along the road below, and a few seconds later, he saw it make the turn onto Caerlanrig.

Then he saw the second vehicle, an old green Landrover, and something about it stirred memories....... "Oh Christ!"

He swung the binoculars around .... "Bloody Hell!"

That driver looked like Vardy!

He adjusted his focus slightly.

Shit!....It was Vardy!.... But he was supposed to be dead!

The Landrover turned right, following Eddie, but just far enough back to remain out of sight.

Shorty swore......What the Fuck was going on?

* * *

Waste of bloody time I thought, all the way over there, and the guy had nothing from the Hess crash site anyway, just another chancer trying to fob off a couple of fake pieces of Nazi memorabilia.

I passed Caerlanrig Farm, no sign of anyone about. Then I remembered....the Douglas's were folk fanatics, and they would be out, over at the "Cross Keys" in Denholm, where there was a session on.

I rattled over the cattle grid. Must take the old heap in and get a new exhaust, the noise was rattling my teeth.

A pair of hares ran across the road in front of me, and stopped about 70 yards away. Beautiful silly buggers, too close, someone will jug you if you don't take care.

I drove on to the old observer post, and pulled into the layby.

The setting sun was casting the shadow of the vehicle across the valley, and that odd halo of light was clearly visible around the shadow.

I cut the engine, climbed out, walked onto the grass, and stood admiring the view.

One day, if I could prise this place out of the hands of Buccleuch,

I would build a house here. Near 360 degree horizon, no light pollution, magnificent skies. Triple glazing of course, and well insulated.... the wind fair howled through here in the winter.

Gravel crunched behind me, a door slammed, and I turned,

"Captain" Anthony Errington Vardy was walking purposely towards me......Alive and well!

I should have known the bastard would never top himself!

On the grass verge behind him was an old green Landrover.

His face was flushed, he was shaking with rage, and he carried a double barrelled shotgun, clasped in both hands.

He slammed the weapon closed. "Got You, Graham!....Now... You're about to experience a tragic shooting accident!"

"Well, Anthony..... Nice to see you've brought the Holland and Holland, 'cause I'd hate to be shot with a Baikal".

He turned puce.

* * *

"Oh Shit!........Eddie, what have we done."

Through the Russian binoculars, Shorty could see the scene unfolding on the hillside with perfect clarity.

He dragged the rest around, and swung the rifle.

He checked his map with its concentric range circles.

Just over 1900 yards!

"Oh, My God!..... No-one could do that!"

He made the calculations....Adjusted the vernier sight.

Then he went back to the binoculars.

* * *

Vardy stopped ten paces away.

"I know, Graham, ... He told me .... Marchbank.... The smug little bastard laughed in my face.

He's getting Fucking Married.

Fucking Married!....Fucking Married!....FUCKING MARRIED!

AND IT'S ALL YOUR FAULT!

All the years I've spent on this, pandering to that weakling Irvine, setting everything up....

All down the drain, because you, that lunatic dwarf, and that burnt out hippy bitch, have convinced Marchbank that he's fathered a child!

Well at least I'm going to have the satisfaction of removing you from this earth."

Spittle ran down his chin, staining his tweed jacket, and soiling his yellow waistcoat.

He flipped the muzzle slightly.

"Two cartridges, double ought buckshot. What is it, six, seven balls in each cartridge. Each around 8mm. Could cut you in half that could!"

And then he snapped completely.

He laughed, high pitched, lunatic, almost a scream.

"First one in the guts, Eh, Eddie.

"That's the way to do it," he screeched.

"Mr Punch!" he yelled. "Now *He* knew how to deal with naughty children.

Then, I'll let you squirm a bit, and after a suitable interval......

KERBOOM!...... The second one in the head!

Now..... kneel down Eddie". He sniggered. "Be a good little boy."

* * *

So, I thought, this is it. Lights out. All of that time in the Stan's, all the risks. Not Al Qaeda. Not the Secret Services. Not the Russians......

Killed on a Border hillside, by a bloody Estate Manager!

I looked him in the eyes....."Sod off."

He raised the gun. Turned petulant

"Oh, have it your way then......Tell you what, I'll count to twenty, and then fire the first shot.

"But," he continued, "I'll count a bit funny.

OneTwoThree," He fired it all off in almost one word.

Five seconds or so passed.

"Five........Six". He giggled.

* * *

Through the binoculars, Shorty saw the shotgun come up.
Shit!
He reached for the rifle and sighted through the vernier peep sight.
He pulled the hammer back to full cock, and squeezed the first trigger,
He then rested his finger on the forward, "set" trigger.
Oh Christ!..... he couldn't get a clear view.
Tweed was made for hiding on hillsides.

* * *

"SevenEightNineTen," Vardy rattled.
"Eleven!"
He turned slightly to take the recoil of the shotgun, and his tweed jacked fell aside revealing his waistcoat.
The sun was almost in my eyes now, turning him into a black silhouette. I measured the distance between us.
Ten paces..... No chance. But I had no chance anyway.
I readied myself to make a run at him.
"TwelveThirteen," He guffawed.
"Thirteen's...... an unlucky number Eddie!"

* * *

Suddenly, in the tiny aperture, Shorty glimpsed a flash of yellow,
Tiny, minute, just to the right of the figure of Eddie,
He exhaled slowly, and ever so gently, he squeezed the trigger.
The Sharps erupted in a cloud of white powder smoke.
The recoil slammed his shoulder, and he was knocked back across the grass.
He grabbed the glasses, but could see nothing for smoke.
Shorty looked down at the gold symbols inlaid into the barrel of the Sharps,
The Sun Wheel....The Hand of God.
And for the first time in his life, Shorty prayed.

*   *   *

"Fourteen Eddie."

Out of the corner of my right eye, I saw a small white flower bloom near the peak of Bowanhill.

It hovered in the air.

Someone had fired a black powder rifle.

*   *   *

The bullet, exited the muzzle at over well over 1300 feet per second, 650 grains, close to an ounce and a half of spinning lead, faster than the speed of sound.

It soared, over 400 feet above the hilltops, a silver streak above the valley, losing velocity, going sub sonic, now falling at an ever steeper angle, it's speed reduced to 700 feet per second.

*   *   *

"FifteenSixteenSeventeen"

It could not be done. Even if it was the Sharps. Even if it was Shorty

No-one had ever made a shot like that. It was totally impossible.

But just as I tensed myself to run at Vardy, there came a rumble like thunder.

Sharps thunder!

Vardy half turned towards the noise, puzzled.

I looked into the clear blue vault of the sky, and I swear I saw it coming in.

The very thinnest of lines, a blink of red light in the setting sun.

Then came a hissing scream....... And the noise I will never forget.

Like the noise of a gigantic butcher's cleaver striking meat.

The bullet coming in from a high angle, took him below the left armpit. It travelled clean through him, knocking him sideways and down. Exiting through his lower back, and taking most of his innards with it in a mist of blood.

I saw earth spurt where it plowed into the hillside.

Echoes reverberated through the valleys. They took forever to die.

He was still alive when I got to him. He looked up at me, the light fading from his eyes.

"Higgins?"

I nodded.

"I always said dwarves were bad luck"

Adrenalin took over. "He's not a fucking dwarf!" I yelled.

He fell back

I lifted the shotgun from where it had fallen. Prodded him with my foot. His eyes were blank.

He looked as dead as the Dodo.

Maybe he was.

Just as well. Because, I put that shotgun up against the entry wound, and fired both barrels in quick succession.

The heavy projectiles ripped through the flesh, completely eradicating the path of the shot that had really killed him.

God, What a mess!

I walked over to the Toyota, took a spade from the tool box, and dug out the bullet from the Sharps. Carefully I replaced the divot.

Another tragic shooting accident.

I reached for my mobile phone.

* * *

All you need are the right contacts, and for once I had them.

Ecky, Ros and Abbie "arranged" it all.

Errington Vardy's "suicide note" was never made public.

Just as in the case of the helicopter crash which killed Donnie and Janet, "D" notices were issued, a cover story was prepared, and an "official statement" was released.

But for once, the "Establishment" was on the side of the angels.

Errington Vardy's body was "found" out in the woods at Kershopefoot. His death, the result of self inflicted shotgun wounds.

It was believed that he had committed suicide after assaulting his employer, the Duke of Marchbank, and seriously injuring the Duke's chauffeur, Martin Elliot.

An large quantity of jewellery and other valuables belonging to the Duke, were recovered from Errington Vardy's Rangerover.

The media carried a brief profile of Anthony Errington Vardy, outlining his "career" in the Guards, his trial for the murder of Quentin James, and his later employment as Estate Manager for Peter Irvine.

Ecky Charlton's nephew gave a short interview describing the destruction of his model Spitfire as a result of Vardy's gunfire.

Channel 4 News had a whip round and sent him a new one.

Several high profile companies with whom Vardy had had contacts, suddenly lost interest in the industrial development of the old Debateable Lands.

Although the Duke had been badly beaten, he was recovering well, and issued a statement to the effect that he would not allow the incident interfere with his marriage plans.

His chauffeur, although now out of intensive care, would be obliged to remain in hospital for some weeks, however his doctors expected that in the course of time he would make a full recovery.

There was no mention of any incident at Caerlanrig, or of the names Eddie Graham and Septimus Higgins.

* * *

Three Songs for Eddie.

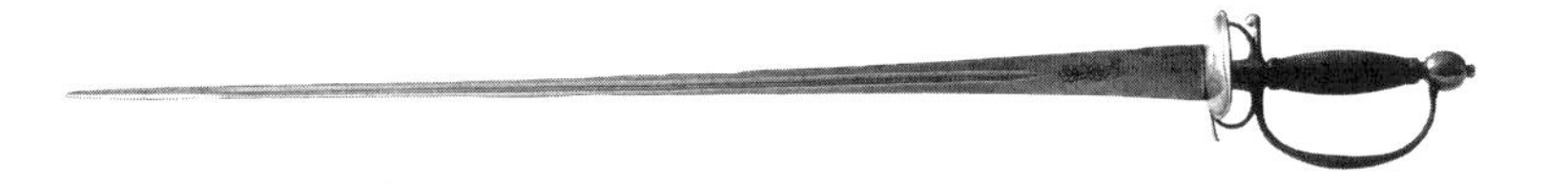

I carefully placed her luggage on the back seat of the Toyota.

My little Jacobite sword was safely wrapped in tissue, and packed in a long mailing tube.

A memento of our time together at Merrylaw.

She hadn't wanted to take it, but I knew she'd really did, and so I'd insisted.

She cried a little, and then she disappeared into her room. A minute later she returned, and handed me a small silver coin on a chain, a Victorian sixpence.

"It's a sort of talisman, I've had it since I was a child. Take it, it's for the sword. You know it's unlucky to take a blade without payment."

I undid my shirt, and fastened the chain around my neck.

"I'd forgotten about that, can't go giving you bad luck now can I?"

"Thanks again Eddie, this will be the start of my own little collection."

Now, she kept the sword with her in the front seat, clutching it to her like a doll.

We drove out through gate, and I locked it behind us.

She hardly looked at me as we drove out over the ford, then up and along the high ridge of Caerlanrig, through the enclosure of the old British fort, and past the place where Errington Vardy had died.

Then, past the farm, past Woodbrae, and back down into the valley.

Small rabbits scuttled across the road, high above a buzzard wheeled. Magpies flew from the trees just above the old graveyard.

Didn't used to see many of those, used to be the keepers kept them down. They take young chicks in the spring you see. But now they're coming back. Next, the jays will return.

I pulled in beside the church. Time for a small goodbye.

She climbed down from the cab, and together, we crossed to the old churchyard.

It was a fine sunny afternoon, and the weeping willow in the centre of the stones cast its long shadow over the old memorial to the Armstrongs.

I opened the bottle, passed it to her, she took a small sip, then raised the bottle in salute, and solemnly she poured the remainder onto the ground in front of the memorial.

We wandered around for while, reading the old inscriptions.

She paused by a small moss covered stone.

"Tibbie Bell, Wat's Housekeeper," I wonder who she was? Some girl who came out here to stay for a little while, and just never went away"

I just shook my head.

"I'll come back one day, and we'll do it again Eddie, I promise."

I wasn't quite sure that she meant the ritual with the beer.

She was silent almost all of the way to the cafe.

We hardly spoke.

But we did speak.

"I don't know if I can go through with this Eddie. Things have changed. I've enjoyed myself more being out at Merrylaw," she smiled, wistfully, "that is, out at Cockplay, than I have for years. I don't know if I still want to marry Pete."

I couldn't look at her.

Fortunately driving covers most things.

"There's not really any option Kate. I truly wish there were. You're pregnant, you're engaged to be married, and you're going to be a Duchess. But don't go thinking that you've seen the last of Eddie Graham. Because you haven't. And I promise you this....Any time you need me, for anything at all, just ask."

And I thought, Okay....Well done....Noble Eddie. That's it then.....you've said your piece.

And we drove on.

But I couldn't do it. I couldn't just leave it at that.

So I pulled in to the layby just north of the bridge, opposite tourney holm, where the old Reivers used to fight their single combats.

Because I'd lost my own battle, and try as I might not to..... I had to say it.

There was no-one else there. We were hidden from view. Hidden amongst that ancient grove of trees. Trees now red with hawthorn berries.

And I turned to her.

"I've thought this through fully Kate. It's been on my mind for the last two weeks, and I have to tell you. If you want to drop out of your "arrangement."..... I paused, and took a deep breath.

"Then I'll marry you, and we'll bring the child up as our own."

Just say "Yes,".....And I think we'll both be happier".

But of course, she didn't just say "Yes."

She burst into tears and threw herself across the cab into my arms.Thank God no-one could see us.

"I knew you would say that, I hoped you would, and I want to say "Yes," But I can't.

I think we both know that we can't really do it.

Despite all of his problems, Pete is a good man. It is his child, he needs an heir, and I ought to be his wife when my baby is born. So I'll go through with it. But it's not what my heart is telling me to do."

Tears ran down her cheeks.

"And I've told you Eddie, I won't be married forever. We might still have another chance?"

I couldn't speak, so I just nodded. So much for tough, hardboiled Eddie Graham.

It took us ten minutes to recover.

Kate cleaned off her ruined make-up, and used the mirror to re-apply her eye shadow.

I watched her in fascination. It must be the pregnancy I thought, but perhaps it was me. She simply glowed,.....and at that moment I knew that I had never loved any woman more.

Five minutes later, and she was smiling as we walked into the "Last Chance."

It was 4.15 p.m. but it felt like "High Noon."

I could actually hear the clock on the wall.......ticking our last seconds away.

"Do not forsake me......Oh my Darling."

The Duke of Marchbank's car was collecting her at 4.30.p.m.
Yet all was normal at the "Last Chance," Shorty and Reb were behind the bar, there were quite a few couples in, Ros and Abbie had commandeered the management table, and Chuck was up on the stage, messing around with the speakers.
The centre of the floor was clear, forming a minute dance floor for anyone feeling romantic.
On the sound system, Hank Williams was extolling the virtues of "Jambalaya."
All that wasn't normal was me.
Kate walked across and conferred with Shorty and Reb. Shorty fiddled with his sound system. I chatted with Chuck.
Then she came back to me holding out her hand.
She led me to the centre of the room.
"Last Dance Eddie?"
Now I don't dance, and I thought everyone knew that. But what else could I do?
Shorty and Reb were grinning away behind the counter. Abbie and Ros sensed something was about to happen, and looked across.
Hank Williams faded away, and......The music changed.........

Just....Three records.
Only.....Ten minutes and eighteen seconds.

Elvis..."Can't help falling in love with you".

"Wise men say,
Only fools rush in"

We clung to each other, moving together with the rhythm of the song.
Her belly was tight against me, and I swear I felt the baby moving....My shoulder was wet with her tears.

"But I can't help,
falling in love with You."

Then Elvis segued, seamlessly into Gladys Knight.
One of the saddest and most beautiful songs ever written.

"Help me make it through the night".

We swayed together in unison, lost in the words.
She'd rounded it off with Ella Fitzgerald.
The most perfect version ever of,

"Every time we say Goodbye"

Ten minutes and eighteen seconds......It wasn't really that long.
But pcrhaps it had been the rest of our lives together.
Would that it could have gone on forever.
But her timing had been perfect.
The music ceased.
There was total silence in the room.

All eyes were upon us.

And I heard the gravel crunch, as the old, long Bentley pulled up outside.

A uniformed chauffeur, stepped out and opened the rear door.

Shorty came to my rescue. He parted us, and took Kate by the hand. She turned, giving me one last long lingering look, as he led her to the door.

I watched as he handed her into the back of the limousine.

The chauffeur placed her luggage in the trunk. But she wouldn't to give up the tube with the sword, clinging to it like a small child seeking comfort from a worn and much loved toy.

Shorty bowed, gave a small salute, and gently he closed the door.

Almost noiselessly the car started.

And then the Bentley, now carrying the Duchess of Marchbank, swept out of the car park and turned south for the Border.

I wouldn't see her again until the wedding.

There was light applause, as I walked back through the cafe.

I looked over at Reb. She was in tears.

But I wanted no company, no conversation. So I walked straight through the to the back, and the seclusion of the office.

I could still feel her warmth, smell her perfume. It did not seem possible that she was really gone.

I collapsed behind the desk, opened the top drawer, took out the bottle, and poured myself a large whisky.

Shorty came and leaned against the doorframe. "Oh Christ Eddie, I'm so Sorry."

But I couldn't speak, so he just turned and went back behind the counter.

The sound system came back in, "Creedence," "Proud Mary," Thank God Shorty had played a happy one. Couples were out on the floor dancing.

Then Dire Straits, "Walk of Life."

Maybe I *would* survive after all.

* * *

I drove down to Teviothead. Pulled up in front of the workshop....."The Celtic Goldsmith."

I could see Ken through the window, bent over his workbench. He looked up, smiled, and came around to the door.

"Okay, if I borrow a workbench for the day Ken? Plus I may need a little bit of advice."

"Aye fine, what do you have in mind?" I took the small package from my pocket, opened it up, and explained what I needed to do.

* * *

Abbie arrived the next day.

I was knocking hell out of the bankside with a pickaxe, making space for an oil bunker, when I heard the bell on the front gate ringing.

I could have used the mechanical digger, but my mood was such that I needed to hit something hard. I'd been that way since Kate left. That's what women can do to you.

She took one look at me, and smiled hugely.

"Oooh, a hot sweaty man! I can smell the testosterone from here! Are you going to open the gate for me?"

I hit the electronic release on my keyring, dragged the gate open, and she drove the small Suzuki through. I looked for Ros, but she was alone in the vehicle.

She parked right outside of my door. Just as well, 'cause she'd never have managed the compound in those heels.

She called over to me and beckoned. “Come along Eddie. Thought you might need a bit of company, don’t want you brooding out here, all on your own. Aren’t you going to offer a lady some hospitality.”

She was definitely *not* dressed for the country. Tight pink skirt and jacket, white blouse, open three buttons down. Full make up.

So off I went....Innocent little Eddie....Right into the spider’s web!

I poured her a drink, found some savoury biscuits, made my excuses and went off for a shower.

One minute later the door to the cubicle opened, and she joined me.

“That’s right Eddie, stand to attention for the Lady!”

What could I do? I’m only human after all!

Afterwards we lay on my bed, exhausted.

“So, Miss Ffanshawe..... That’s what they call being pumped for information? I’ve always wondered what it meant?”

She giggled. “Knew first time I saw you that we’d get round to it eventually!

Poor Eddie.....stranded out here for all of those weeks.... It must have been....Sooo very difficult for you, all alone here in the hills, with only a beautiful woman for company. But they do say that “abstinence makes the heart grow fonder,” and I can vouch for that!

She stayed for several days. But eventually she had to leave.

* * *

“Resign......Be my Secretary....., You can be Velda, and I’ll be Mike,”(Novices...see Mickey Spillane). “We’ll solve cases together....Save the world from Tyranny. ...... Kill Baddies......Bring Justice.... Free the Common man from Bondage.

But first..... “Miss Ffanshawe”...... tell me....what’s your real name”,

A mischievous smile spread across her face, “Just call me Bond, ...Jemima Bond.”

“Oh...I much prefer Abigail with the two “F’s”

She laughed out loud, and walked towards me. "What was that about "Bondage?"

"Oh Jesus," I thought, "not another one!"

I looked into those deep blue eyes.

"You know, I was so alone here but......I laughed. "I knew you'd come eventually."

She met my gaze,

Telepathy!.......I knew exactly what she would say next.

"That"......she paused....... "is one of my lines."

She reached down, and began to slowly unbutton her skirt.

An hour later she left.

* * *

Why did she start our relationship?......I don't know.

Maybe she *was* seeking information?

For certain, during those days, in what she thought were unguarded moments, she did ask me questions about Hess. But if that is interrogation "M.I.6. lady" style, then suspects must be giving themselves up in hordes.

I tried flattering myself into thinking that I must simply be irresistible, but that didn't work, and I ended up suspecting what was probably the truth. She really did feel sorry for me.

But I'd be a liar if I told you that I didn't feel better for it all.

The downside of those memorable days though, was the guilt.

The woman I loved was about to marry another, and we'd never exactly had a physical relationship anyway.

I told myself that I was a free man.

But it didn't help, I still had a nagging feeling that I'd betrayed Kate.

* * *

I passed him the buckle.

Hammered silver, with the gold Sharps 50/90 in half relief.

"Its a reliquary buckle. It opens with a small catch on the left side."

He slid the catch, and opened it up. Inside, in the centre, was mounted the distorted 50 calibre bullet that I had dug out of the ground on Caerlanrig.

Around it was inscribed "Septimus "Shorty" Higgins," one dead Indian, 1910 yards, best never recorded shot."

"Problem, Shorty, is you can never show it to anyone."

"Who cares," he replied, "Thanks Eddie." He sniffed, and I swear a tear ran down his cheek,

Loveable, ludicrous, murderous, little Lunatic.

And the best friend I have.

* * *

October 31st 2003

Wedding day.

The long black Rolls with the crest on the door, swept in off the main road, and glided with just the slightest swish along the gravel drive.

It pulled to a halt before the main door of Marchbank House. A chauffeur in a beautifully tailored, "regal red" uniform, climbed out, gave a tug to straighten his jacket, and then opened first one, and then the other of the rear doors.

Two men emerged, one from either side of the vehicle.

Immaculately groomed, they were obviously father and son. Both were tall, slim, and fair haired, although the elder of the two was slightly receding. Both looked fit and tanned. They were dressed near identically, in dark business suits, but the older man wore a black "Crombie" overcoat draped over his shoulders, hands out of the sleeves, like some Hollywood version of a Mafia Don.

Peter Irvine, Lady Rebecca, and Shorty stood ready to greet them on the steps.

Peter was immaculate, dark trousers and white jacket complete with red carnation. Very Brian Ferry.

Lady Rebecca was in white jeans, and a matching polo necked jumper.

Shorty also had risen to the occasion, and wore khaki cargo trousers and a black T shirt, combined with a cut off denim jacket which was emblazoned on the back with a large "Border Alliance" badge. His leathers were draped over the saddle of a heavily chromed Harley bobber parked nearby.

The two men advanced from the car smiling, and approached the group, right hands extended in friendship.

They nodded curtly to Reb, completely ignored Shorty, and closed rapidly in on the Duke of Marchbank.

"Peter old chap!" the younger of the two cried in delight, "so very good to see you. Haven't had the chance of a chinwag since the last school reunion. And now here you are, about to tie the knot."

The elder chimed in, "Must be years Marchbank.... last I saw of you was out at Eton, when I dropped Peregrine here off at the beginning of term."

The younger of the two, Peregrine, turned to Reb.

"Rebecca!" he snapped, "Come inside, and have the dwarf there bring our bags!.... Jaldi!

Shorty smiled and followed a pace behind, as Reb advanced upon her brother.

She extended *her* right hand, took hold of the front of his immaculate Saville Row trousers, and exerting all of her strength, she heaved upwards.

"Doesn't matter which side you dress on bruv. This is called a "Melvin"....she paused....."and it can be painful."

And he twisted her wrist to increase the pressure.

"Now listen....He's *not* a DWARF!

HE'S MY FUCKING HUSBAND!"

WHAT! YOU'RE MARRYING A MIDGET! yelped her father as Shorty clasped his arms around his waist, grinned up into his face, and exclaimed....... "Hello Daddy!"

.....And Kathy Pringle, radiant in a short black satin dress and pearl necklace emerged from the house.

Pete Irvine proffered a palm, "Allow me to present my bride to be. This is Miss Katherine Pringle, soon to be the Duchess of Marchbank."

Kathy extended her hand. "Hello Monty! Long time no see."

"Monty," reeled back Shorty still clinging to him.

"Mistress....Kat...ehhhrrr..... Nice to see you Katherine."

"Likewise......Pleased to see you and Shorty are getting on so well Monty. Rebecca was a little worried that you may not care for bikers."

"You two know each other then Monty," asked Pete Irvine, "I'd no idea you were old friends."

"Not so much friends Darling," Kathy replied, "More associates. Monty tends to get a bit tied up in some of my business ventures, now and again."

Rebecca lowered her brother to the ground. Shorty released her father's waist, and extended a hand. "Nice to meet the family at last." He linked the two men arm in arm.

"Monty, Perry..... Fancy a pint? I've got a crate of "Nukey Brown" in just especially for you.

Tell me, when I marry the Lady Rebecca, well, I was wondering, will I become an "Honourable"? You know..... "The Honourable Shorty Higgins," 'cause I'd quite like that. I could put it on the back of me leathers. The two men looked blankly at each other as Shorty led them off.

He winked "Thank you" to Kathy, and she winked back.

Pete Irvine, The Duke of Marchbank, looked puzzled.

* * *

I was Shorty's best man. Ecky was Pete Irvine's.

The weddings took place at Arthuret Church, at three in the afternoon, and as Shorty had predicted, it was a most unusual guest list.

Around thirty bikers attended, mostly on heavily "customised" Harley's. There was a fair sprinkling of Border "Nobility," and Master Zhang attended with around ten of his "disciples."

Mary Kang was there with Chuck, who'd brought the twins, Yvonne and Denise, the three of them decked out in late 1950's style. Perhaps, I thought, Chuck could convert to Islam, and have two wives?

Viktor came, together with Ros. Archie Armstrong was home for a week or two, and arrived in uniform, with a spectacular Asian girl called Aleysha on his arm.

Close friends were able to stay overnight at Marchbank House, which had a large number of available bedrooms, and some of the bikers had arranged camping facilities down by Canonbie.

Somehow, whilst we waited for the Brides to arrive, Shorty, Ecky and I ended up sitting on the grass out behind the old broken cross.

Aleysha was chatting to Mary Kang, and Archie wandered over.

Then, Chuck arrived.

Luckily I'd prepared for this, and had a couple of bottles of "Hooky" behind the passenger seat of my truck. We sat in the sunshine, and passed them from hand to hand.

It was a strange moment, and we all felt it, Graham, Armstrong, Charlton, Elliot, and Higgins. The old names. All sitting there, surrounded by the dead.

I had the last of the bottle, and Shorty had the other. I raised mine to the old cross, and I was aware of Shorty doing the same.

"Here's tae us,
Wha's Like us.
Gae Few,
And they're all deid."

What my grandfather used to call the "Gilknockie Toast."

Ecky spoke softly....."Absent Friends." And together Shorty and I poured the remainder of the beer into the ground at the foot of the cross.

Then the cars arrived at the gate of the church, we all climbed to our feet, and made our way inside.

* * *

I sat with Ecky Charlton, his wife Judith, and Brian Moffatt and his family.

For once Brian was without his laptop, although I did notice that throughout the evening, he would take a small red book from his inside pocket and make a note or two, at least until Maureen saw him and nudged him with her elbow.

We were seated in the ballroom of Marchbank House.

Tables had been arranged around the walls, the lighting was subdued, and the main source of illumination were the lights trained on the small stage at the north end of the room.

Rumour had it that although the ballroom was in England, the stage was in fact in Scotland. It made for interesting licensing arrangements.

Hank Wangford, and the Lost Cowboys, had just completed their first set up on stage, and would return later in the evening.

I knew Sam Hutt, that's Hank's real name, from years ago in London, when we'd had a sort of nodding acquaintance around some of the Country and Western Clubs.

Kate thought it a great joke when Hank and Co. arrived. All that we'd said was that we would arrange the band for the wedding. And, you see, in his other persona, "Hank" is a gynaecologist.

Shorty told her that in view of her condition, he thought that it might be handy to have one on call. I just hoped that Pete Irvine liked Country and Western.

I hadn't really met the Duke of Marchbank before. I'd seen photo's and now and again, I'd seen him at the local agricultural shows, but we'd never spoken.

It was about half an hour before Hank was due back on stage, that "Pete" wandered over.

He was still heavily bruised, and rested his right side on a stick, but he was holding up well considering.

He was shorter than I'd imagined. Looked a bit like Richard Nixon gone right. Dark haired, with that widow's peak, which is more characteristic of the Armstrongs than the Irvines. But then the bloodlines are all mixed up in this part of the world. Ecky said he looked slightly like me.

I hoped not.

Ecky, who was his old friend did the introductions. Judith of course he already knew, then Brian and his family.

He looked curiously at Brian, they all do, ever since that book of his "The Devil and King James." He trod on a few powerful toes with that one.

And finally Ecky introduced me.

He extended his hand. "Good to meet you at last Eddie, just call me Pete, everyone else does. I've heard a lot about you lately, and I've not had the chance to thank you for everything you did for Kate."

I just shrugged, "I was pleased to assist, I'm just sorry about the violence that was involved. She should never have been placed in that kind of danger, but there was no way of knowing what was about to happen. She saved my life you know."

He gestured to my drink, "Come on let's go over to the bar, and get another."

I rose and followed him, but he didn't go to the bar, he just waved to a waiter, collected a couple of large whisky and soda's from a tray, and led the way outside.

We stood in an awkward silence on the balcony looking out over the valley.

"I suspect Eddie, that you know far more about me, than I am comfortable with anyone knowing, and even a few things relating to this business that I have no idea about." I shrugged again, and he continued, "I know I can't thank you enough, both for what you have done, and also perhaps for what you have not done. Kate trusts you utterly, and she tells me that I can as well. If there is anything further that I can do, you only have to ask. Anytime, anywhere."

I looked out across the valley. To what had once been part of the land of the Graham's

"Just look after her Pete, and look after the baby when it comes." I let the silence stretch. "And look after this land, I know it's yours in name, but really it belongs to us all. It's soaked with the blood of countless generations of Borderers. All gone now.....Spread about the world.

But this..... It's still one of the untouched treasures, so don't just take the money, and let them ruin it."

He held out his hand, and we shook again. "Deal," he said. And I believed him. Shorty has always said that's a weakness of mine. I try to see the best in people.

He turned away, and opened the door. Then he called back over his shoulder. "Kate's waiting for you in the library. She has something for you."

* * *

I walked around the outside of the house, to the south elevation.

The curtains were open, and the lights were on in the windows to the left of the stone staircase.

The library.....I could see her through the glass.

She had changed out of the white wedding dress, and was wearing a full length green silk gown, cut low. Her long dark hair cascaded over her shoulders. The pregnancy was starting to show properly now, and I'd never seen her look more beautiful.

I tapped gently on a pane of the french doors, and she started.

She crossed, opened the door, and we embraced. Reluctantly we parted, and I held onto both of her hands. "You're a Duchess."

She laughed. "I was already a "Lady" before."

"Pete said you wanted to see me. He must be mad, in his position I would keep us as far apart as possible."

"He trusts me Eddie, he wants to show his gratitude, and he asked me how we could thank you."

She led me across to a table. Lying on it was an ancient walnut case, with dark wrought iron fittings, not unlike a guncase, but older, deeper.

"Open it," she instructed.

I lifted the catch on the lockplate, and lifted the lid.

I would say I've never seen anything like them, but I had. They were also described in detail in Brian's latest book, but as far as I was aware, nothing else like them had survived intact.

It was an early English basket hilt, with a huge gilded globe pommel. A pommel segmented like an orange, with the segments separated by applied silver wires, and with it, was it's matching dagger. I'd never actually seen a pair.

It was the holy grail of basket hilted swords, and I knew where I had seen these before......"The Hampton Court Portrait." The one suspected of being an early portrait of the young William Shakespeare.

Then she walked over to the wall, where dark red velvet curtains concealed what I had thought was a small window. Her hand reached up, she pulled on a silken cord, and the curtains slid aside.

Automatically, subdued lighting glowed.

"It's in London and in storage," I breathed. She smiled.

"The copy is Eddie. This.... is the original. Painted from life, painted here, and that, over there on the table, is Will's sword and dagger. Look after them......because now, they're yours."

"Jesus, Kate. I can't take these."

She laughed. "Oh yes you can Eddie, and one day perhaps, you'll find out why."

So, I unclipped the chain from around my neck, turned her around, and refastened the necklet with its old Victorian sixpence back where it really belonged.

"Unlucky....Can't take blades without payment, and this is really yours anyway."

And right then, totally out of the blue, she dropped the bombshell......

"How's Elspeth been taking care of you then?"

"Elspeth? Who the hell is Elspeth?"

"Oh...! Sorry Eddie. Slip of the tongue, I mean Abbie, I'm not supposed to use her real name. But it's best that you know.

You always knew that she wasn't called Abigail Ffanshawe didn't you?..... Well.....She's my sister!

She smiled sadly....."And she always did enjoy playing with my

The "Marchbank Portrait" of William Shakespeare.

The so called "Hampton Court Portrait" allegedly of Shakespeare, was purchased by King William 1V from the de L'Isles of Penhurst.

No good modern photographs exist, and the portrait is now believed to be in poor condition. A number of copies were, it appears made during the 19th century, one by an "H. Duke" in 1860.

It has been argued that the style of clothing of the sitter is too late for the apparent date of the portrait (1598), but it must be commented upon that the sword so prominently displayed, with its large segmented globe pommel is of a rare British type, which would be consistent with the third quarter of the 16th century, whilst the matching dagger would seem to be a product of the 1590's.

toys."

I was speechless, stunned, I collapsed into an armchair.

"That's the reason she begged to come up on this investigation. Not because of Hess, not because of you, and not because MI6 sent her. But because her little sister, had got involved with Anthony Errington Vardy."

My mind was reeling.

"Take your time Eddie, I know it's a lot to take in."

"Does Ros know."

She laughed. "Who can tell what Ros knows, or Ros guesses. Ros is distracted, Ros is tired of her job. She's looking for a way out, and I think Ros has her own agenda to take care of now."

She walked to the door of the library. "I must go back to my guests now Eddie, or Pete will wonder what is going on. Take your time. Enjoy your swords."

She blew me a kiss, and closed the door behind her on the way out.

I sat there for half an hour, then I went over to a drinks cabinet, opened the door, and poured myself a good measure of the Duke's finest single malt. I didn't think he would mind.

I heard Hank and the boys start their second session.

Then I rose to my feet, picked up the case with the sword and dagger, and went back to the ballroom.

I really needed to talk to Brian.

We sat in the Dukes private office, myself, Brian and Maureen, "Abbie" and Kate.

Abbie was wearing a short, green satin 50's style dress, with a white flared petticoat. Her blond hair was in ringlets, tied back with a green ribbon. Rock and roll chic. She held Kate by the hand.

How had I missed it? Now that I knew, it seemed obvious, I even remembered actually thinking it, the first time I saw them sitting side by side in the Cafe. And now here they were, together again.

Two sisters, two loves, one dark, one blonde, both wearing green satin.

31st of October...All Hallows Eve...The night the Witches come out?

Jesus, was I going mad?

Hank's voice drifted through from the ballroom......"Falling Angels"...Beautiful.....one of their latest, and a favourite of Kate's and mine.......Our song. We'd played it again and again during her time out at my place.

Another long coincidence?

I caught her eye, and saw a lone tear run down her cheek...

Abbie...... Elspeth, opened the proceedings.

"She told you then, I knew she would eventually."

And I turned to Brian. "The proof copy of your book, the one you lent me? "The Watchers of Enoch." He nodded.

"Let me introduce you to Kate......and Elspeth."

He frowned. "Who's Elspeth."

Abbie answered. "I am, I changed it to "Abigail Ffanshawe" years ago, back when I first joined the Service.

"You" .....She pointed at the three of us, "are not supposed to know my real name. However, it's "Elspeth Pringle." She paused.... "And Kate is my sister."

Brian looked uncomfortable. "Coincidence Eddie. They're sisters, and they have a couple of names from my book.....

It happens."

I picked up the case from the floor. "That would be fair enough, if that was all of it."

And so, I told him. "My name's not really Eddie Graham.
At least it is, but it shouldn't have been. My full name is Edward Christie Graham. The Christie is an old family name, very old, and I'm named after my grandfather, the one who saw the Hess crash. You see, because he was killed in the war, my grandfather never actually married my grandmother. He didn't even know she was pregnant, and my grandmother was a Graham, hence my name.

But Christie was an Armstrong, "Christie Armstrong," and that should have been my name....And, Archie Armstrong is dancing out there in the ballroom.

He was pale. "I've no idea Eddie. I just wrote it as it came into my mind."

I placed the case on the desk, opened it, and Maureen drew in a quick breath. "Shakespeare's sword and dagger?"

"Kate and Pete gave them to me. They also own the original of the Hampton Court Portrait.It was painted here."

Kate and Elspeth turned to Brian and Maureen, smiling. Elspeth spoke, "Oh....You've written a book!... An interesting book? And we are in it? How charming, we'll look forward to reading that." Then they laughed, turned, and walked hand in hand out through

the door, back towards the ballroom.
Back towards sanity.
Brian was in shirtsleeves, and I saw the goosebumps rise on his arms, the hairs actually standing on end. I was cold.
Maureen shivered involuntarily.
And somewhere in the depths of the ancient house, a clock chimed midnight.

* * *

Zhang helped her down the corridor, arm around her waist.
"Sorry about this," she whispered, staggering slightly and brushing him with her breast. "Must be the champagne, don't drink you see, not approved of in my line of work."
They came to the room. She reached forward, stumbled slightly and turned the handle.
"Ooh look.....It's unlocked, must have forgotten," she slurred. She entered unsteadily, placed her brown leather purse on the table and sat on the edge of the bed.
Zhang's breath grew short. When he had first met her he hadn't fancied her at all. Scruffy, mousy, far too much to say for herself. But since then, she seemed to have tidied herself up a bit. Lost some weight. Done something with her hair. Better dressed.
Now perhaps he thought, she was rather attractive in an unusual sort of way. Could just be the thought of all that money though.
"Wow,"......he thought, "I wonder why they call her "Dirty"? His brain shifted into Neutral.
Imagination, Fantasy, took over.
She must be a mind reader. She undid the top button of her blouse.
"Phew, it is rather hot in here, isn't it?" She lay back on the bed, her legs over the edge, and her feet still on the floor. Her skirt rode up slightly.
My God, this was unexpected. His breath caught.
"Ah, ...Erm,....Eh,...Miss Molesworthy,....Erm, May I ask you a rather impertinent question?"
"Oh, anything at all "Master Zhang," she replied dreamily, her legs, parting ever so slightly.
"Well,..... its about your nickname."

“Oh that silly business.” She smiled, “Dirty” you mean?
Why, you naughty Tantric Master! Hand me my purse, and I’ll show you what that’s all about.”

Zhang reached across to the table. Now here was a lady knew on which side her bun should be buttered.

The brown alligator purse was heavy in his sweaty grasp. His heart pounded.

“Pwhoar!” What could be in there. This was one hot lady!

She must carry “equipment” with her.

She raised herself to sitting position. “Now, just pass it over.”

There was a metallic click, as she released the clasp. She took a pillow and placed it behind her hips.

“I’ll just get comfy.” She indicated the floor in front of her.

“Right, kneel down there,..... and I’ll show you my little secret.”

Zhang knelt.

“It’s really all Clint Eastwood’s fault.”

“Eastwood?” Zhang thought. “What the Hell’s Clint Eastwood got to do with it?”

“You see,” she continued, “Roselinde is my middle name. My first name’s Harriet. Get it?.....“Dirty Harriet.”

And her right hand came out of the purse. Holding a huge revolver.

“Pretty isn’t it? “Smith and Wesson,” a Model 29, 44 Magnum, with a 4 inch barrel.
Harry Callaghan’s favourite.”

The soft lights of the room glowed on the blue of the frame.

God, it was so big he could actually see down the barrel.

He could see the bullet.

“Now,” she purred lying back against the pillow, hips raised, gun in hand, legs parted.

“Now,” She said, pointing downwards.

“Go ahead Punk,....... Make my Day.”

* * *

We sat together in the ballroom, myself, Abbie and Kate, Brian and Maureen.

“So how did our names get in your book then.”

"No idea Eddie. Coincidence, telepathy? Unlikely, I mean.... but think about it. Most names in these parts are family names. How many "John Armstrongs" have you met, how many "Walter Elliots." And I've been reading Border history for years.

I simply plucked those names out of the air. Coincidence that's all it can be. Anyway its a bit of fun isn't it, after all it is Halloween, and everyone likes a mystery."

But I thought of Shakespeare's sword and dagger lying in their case, and I wasn't so sure. And Abbie and Kate just sat there smiling, saying nothing.

Then Shorty wandered over, laughing and joking, and everything seemed normal once more.

Kate went off, and joined Pete Irvine, and a couple of minutes later, Ecky was up on stage to do his Hank Williams numbers.

We were sitting by the long french windows, and I could see a bright moon shining outside.

Way down the drive, I thought I could see a small figure moving.

Must be a latecomer. And I turned back to listen to Ecky.

* * *

Shabaz.

Half an hour past Midnight.
What was it they called Midnight here?...... "The Witching Hour"
The driveway up to Marchbank House was longer than he had expected.
He realised that he was standing on the Border.
He had one foot in England, and one foot in Scotland.
One foot in Heaven, and the other..... in Hell?
One foot in life, and the other.....?
Because on this night in this place.They said that the dead, could walk.
And perhaps they were right.
Because......perhaps...... He *was* the dead.

He had left the van behind a large camper, out by the road, on the end of a long line of parked vehicles.
It was a big wedding, but there had been no security, no-one about at all.
It was late.
The driveway was lined with huge and ancient holly trees, and the bright full moon cast the shadows of their trunks across his path.
He moved slowly from darkness to light, darkness to light.
The jacket, with its pockets of explosives was heavy and uncomfortable beneath his overcoat, and already he was sweating profusely.
He held the trigger in his right hand inside of his pocket, but he took care to keep his thumb well clear of the red button.
"How many virgins a day did they say he would have in paradise?" He giggled. "What rubbish had they filled his head with?" What fun would eternal virgins be anyway? An eternity, spent with frightened little girls?What sort of heaven was that?" So, Shabaz decided he would think about some other heaven.
And it would be a heaven of his own choosing.
Now he could see the lights of the big house, and the long line

of illuminated french windows.

He could hear the music. Someone was singing an old Hank Williams number. Before he came to this country he'd never heard of Hank, but all of that time tracking Eddie Graham, sitting in the cafe, or in the carpark outside, he'd heard this tune over and over again.

"So Lonesome I could Die"

Strange music for a wedding. One of these days, he would buy it for himself on CD.

And then he remembered. There would be no more days, at least not for him. This was it. The end. The end for him. The end for them. And perhaps the end of "Great" Britain?

Mission accomplished!

Now he could see all of them inside of the ballroom. Dukes, Lords, Bikers. What a strange mix. And at a long table, right beside of the window......Eddie Graham, Shorty, those two women from the hotel in Canonbie, and that other couple, those friends of theirs from Teviothead.

All just sitting there laughing and enjoying themselves.

It was almost time.

He would walk across the grass, up the steps, and onto the veranda.

He would cross to the french windows. If possible he would enter, but if not... then he would simply press the button right outside.The blast, and the glass from the windows would do the rest.

He started to turn off the drive towards the house.

And a quiet voice spoke from the shadows.

"Shabaz Ghalzai."

He turned. Two figures stood beside one of the trees, a man, and a woman. But the moon was behind them, and he couldn't see their faces.

"No need Shabaz. It is over, your mission is unnecessary. They know about the plan."

And Shabaz realised that the man was speaking to him in Pashto.

Shabaz lifted his right hand from his pocket, and placed his thumb on the red button. He wasn't going to stop now.

"I don't believe you," he called, "Just keep back."

The man stepped back into the shadow of the trees. But the

woman didn't.

The woman moved right out into the track, and spoke to him in English.

And the bright moonlight shone on her face. She was very beautiful.

But of course she was beautiful, he thought.

She was Mehri.

"Hello Shabaz."

She walked towards him.

And, all will to die gone, his hand fell from the trigger. The cable hung useless by his side.

They embraced, and he was aware of nothing...... but Joy.

He barely felt the needle as it entered his right arm.

* * *

Viktor lowered the unconscious body to the ground. He loosened the overcoat, and disconnected the trigger mechanism.

"Stay here with him Mehri, I'll go and get the van."

* * *

I saw Viktor enter through the main door of the ballroom. We'd not seen much of him for weeks. Working out at his house we supposed, Ros seemed to have been helping him.

Kate had sent him an invitation to the wedding, and had been rather upset when a reply came back stating that due to circumstances, he may not be able to attend. And now here he was, beckoning urgently to me across the floor of the ballroom.

And who came to a wedding in a camouflaged combat jacket, heavy cord trousers, and army boots? I excused myself, and went over to join him.

Kate had spotted him too. She arrived just before me, flung her arms around his neck, and hugged him. "Better late than never Viktor?"

Viktor held her at arms length, and looked at her in admiration.

"The most beautiful lady in the world. I love the green dress."

She laughed, "I selected it especially for you Viktor, just to match your jacket! What have you been up to? Where have you been?"

"Oh," he replied. "I'll tell you all my little adventures later, but for now, I must borrow Eddie here for half an hour or so."

"What's exactly is this all about Viktor?"

But he just shook his head, "Not now," and he took me by the arm, and led me out of the door.

His camper van was parked 50 yards away, just off the drive in a gap between two trees.

The lights were on inside.

Viktor first unlocked, and then opened the door. He waved me through, but I was totally unprepared for what I found inside.

The Afghan youth who I had last seen in the forest, was lying barely conscious on one of the fold down bunks. he was handcuffed to one of the supports, and kneeling by his side was the beautiful girl I had seen with him out at Sark.

Lying on the floor at the rear of the camper, was a "suicide" vest, its rectangular pockets still packed with explosives.

Viktor spoke, "Don't worry Eddie, it's safe." and he withdrew a cable and trigger device from the pocket of his combat jacket.

He nodded to young couple. "Meet Mehri, and Shabaz."

She looked up at me, fear in her eyes.

"Shabaz can hear us, but he can't move too much at the moment. Now, I really do need to decide just what to do with him, or at least you do Eddie, because I'm going to leave his fate entirely in your hands.

You see, Shabaz Ghalzai here is not really such a bad fellow, he just doesn't know it. Ros and I have been doing quite a bit of research on both him and his partner, the one that Kate killed. That one went by the name of Parsa Khan.

Now Parsa was a really nasty piece of work. A bit like.... what was his name? That fellow in Charles Dickens? Oliver Twist .....Fagan!....That was him!

He procured young boys, but not to act as thieves. He sold them on, to be trained as terrorists. War orphans were his speciality. Built in hatred was what he looked for, and he told any old tale to make them hate the West.

"But Shabaz here," he nodded to the bunk, "Now Shabaz was a special prize. Because his parents were teachers, he's well educated, and he was brought up speaking fluent English.

We've been in touch with some of our old contacts back in Afghanistan, and it turns out that Shabaz is an orphan as well. Both of his parents were killed in a tragic car accident. Forced off the road by a lorry which didn't stop. A lorry which was abandoned ten miles down the road.

A number of witnesses saw the driver walk away from that lorry, and it turns out that he looked a lot like Parsa Khan.

You see Parsa killed them, and then he contacted Shabaz. He told the boy that he was his father's cousin, and his grandfather did in fact have a lot of brothers, who did have a large number of children. But Parsa Khan was not one of them.

He took him "under his wing," sent him off to one of those schools in Pakistan, and then on to a training camp.

He was a valuable asset was Shabaz, and when Bin Laden's lot hatched the plan to use the Hess documents, he was the obvious choice of agent, since, with no difficulty at all, he could pass as a UK Asian.

So, in January of this year they arrived in Scotland.

I knew about Parsa, and that he worked recruiting for Al Qaeda.... that was how I tracked them. But this young fellow," he nodded sidelong at the boy on the bunk, "he has no record of any kind."

They hired the assassin from Glasgow. Parsa arranged the helicopter crash, and when neither of those plans worked, he came up with a third.

They'd been watching you for weeks, out there on the hills with their metal detectors.

Good plan that by the way, but Ros and I had been watching them. So we knew where they were operating from, and I also found out about the lovely Mehri here.

You see, after Parsa Khan got himself killed, I tracked young Shabaz here," he nodded towards the boy lying prone on the bunk, "I watched him with my night vision glasses, as he crossed the hills, and I followed him back to Carlisle on my bike.

Then I went to see Mehri.

I thought that it was all over. And perhaps it would have been, if only Shabaz had managed to keep his mouth shut, and disappear forever. But, of course, he had gone and told Mehri everything, and naturally, being a fine and well brought up young lady, she threw him out.

And then, he must have found that." He pointed at the suicide vest. "A little present left for him, by his "Wicked Uncle."

Now.... I didn't know about that.

He must have heard about the wedding, and decided if it was to be "Goodbye, Cruel World," then why not complete his mission, and take Eddie Graham and Co. with him?

I wondered why he was still around, so I just kept on watching. I've been running around like a crazy man, trying to check all options.

And then we had a stroke of luck, because Shabaz sent Mehri a little present. Not actually so little at all, around £10,000 in cash, and twelve lovely little gold bars. With a note saying how sorry he was about everything. That was how I knew he would be up to something...And soon at that.

I guessed the target may be the wedding, so I took a chance. I called Mehri, we met out here, and it's just as well that we did.

Now Eddie, what would you like me to do with him? Because this one is up to you.

Just say the word, and I'll send him off to join Mr. Khan. We've talked it all over Ros, Abbie and I, and no-one will ever miss him. He will just never have existed. In fact, as far as the "Authorities" are concerned, no-one wants to know about any of this.....And no-one ever will."

I looked down at the boy. He may not have been able to move, but he could obviously hear.

Tears were streaming down his face, and sweat stood out on his brow.

The girl Mehri, was sobbing head down on her boyfriend's chest.

What was I to do? Whatever else he was, he was a trained killer, a member of Al Qaeda, an organisation I had spent a fair part of my adult life hunting down. On four occasions he had directly tried to kill me and my friends.

Perhaps it *would* be better if he *did* just disappear.

But what about the girl?

Silently, I nodded towards her. Viktor just shrugged, and murmered.....

"Collateral damage."

* * *

Shabaz couldn't move. He couldn't speak. Mehri was kneeling beside him, sobbing uncontrollably against his chest, but he could make no move to comfort her. Tears of frustration ran down his cheeks.

His entire life had been turned upside down. He had heard it all......That Bastard!

Parsa Khan had coldly and ruthlessly killed his parents. He had lied to him. And then he had stolen the last four years of his life. They had sent him to that school, and then on to the training camps. They had poisoned his mind. Tried to turn him into nothing more than a mindless fanatic, a weapon, to be aimed at whatever target they chose. And despite his doubts, even against his will, they had succeeded!

For even after Graham had spared him that day in the forest, he had still returned tonight, to try and kill them all.

How many times had they tried to kill him. The assassin at the cafe. The helicopter crash. Out in the woods with the knives?

And here again tonight....alone, he had tried once more. He had heard the other man, the one who spoke his language, tell Graham that it was his decision what happened next.

He had seen that look towards Mehri, and had heard the murmer of "collateral damage."

He knew exactly what that meant. If Graham decided that he must die, then Mehri would die also!

And why should he be spared? He had been allowed to go once before. And what had the result been?

Graham would be a fool not to kill him. And he realised that he didn't care any longer.

Really, he had nothing to live for. Who knew what the British would do to him, to extract information, and afterwards....?

His future would be nothing but a lifetime spent in some vile prison.

But Mehri. He must save Mehri!

His chest heaved, and with a huge effort, he slowly turned his head.

Towards Eddie Graham.

And looked deep into his eyes.

* * *

The boys head turned to me, and I read the unspoken plea.

The Girl!

But what could I do? Whatever he had suffered, whatever they had done to him, he was really no more than a weapon.

A weapon that had returned again and again to complete it's mission.

And his mission was to kill me and mine, and then to damage my country.

But if he died, then so must the girl. For if he did die, then no-one could be allowed to live to tell this tale.

Then from out of nowhere......a loop began to play in my mind.

The site of Kinmont's Tower out at Sark.

And over and over again, I saw them together, walking.

Walking happily, hand in hand, along that old green track. Out through the trees.

Disappearing into that strange mist.

Out there in that lonely graveyard, where the bones of my own forebears lay deep in the cold damp earth. And I knew then, that I could never send them down there to join them.

"Mehri?" She looked up at me, her huge dark eyes brimming with tears.......And a question.

"Do you still want him?" I asked. She nodded, and broke down, sobbing uncontrollably.

Viktor saw my look, and smiled exultantly "Knew you wouldn't do it! I can read you like a book!"

I collapsed into a chair. "Okay, Smart Arse, then what the Hell should I do!"

Viktor pulled a chair around, sat on it backwards, and looked into my eyes.

"What we are going to do Eddie, just you and me.... Is this.... We are going to write a story.

That will be the story we will stick to, and that story will become the truth."

"Fine," I replied, "but, just one last thing. If Mehri knew that it may have ended badly. Both for Shabaz, and herself, then why did she agree to come here with you? She must have known the risk she was running."

"What risk Eddie? I told her that everything would be alright."

"Alright how?" I asked. "She might have died."
"I just told her that you were a good man, and she believed me. She said she'd met you once before. She'd thought you were nice, and that you had kind eyes."
"Bloody Stupid! .....Bloody Irrational! ....Bloody Woman!"
Because.......I'd nearly told Viktor to kill the pair of them!

* * *

"Can you bring him back around" I asked.
"Of course I can," Viktor replied, rising from his chair.
I followed him through into the small kitchen.
He opened one of the wall cupboards, rummaged about, discarded a few items, and then removed a small case, and a tiny bottle with a rubber cap.
He took a pair of glasses from his top pocket, slipped them onto his nose, and examined the bottle under the light.
"Mmm," he mumbled, "This should do the job, only just past its sell by date. But they always allow quite a bit of leeway you know. Must remember to get some more, never can tell when I might need it."
He unlatched the case, removed a hypodermic syringe, expertly inserted the needle through the cap of the small bottle, and withdrew a small amount of clear liquid.
He held the syringe to the light, flicked it with his finger, and removed the air.
I hate the damned things. I've had to use them in the past, but they still give me the creeps.
"Are you certain that stuff is safe?"
"Oh just trust Doctor Viktor. Eddie, you worry far too much you know. He'll be fine, foul headache of course.
Anyway," he laughed. "He'll feel far better than he would be feeling if he was dead."
"You certain you can sort this out?"
He reached back into the cupboard, and removed a pack of antiseptic wipes.
"Oh sure, just sit through there and say nothing."
Back in the room, Viktor rolled up Shabaz's sleeve, wiped the

flesh of his upper arm, and expertly inserted the needle.

"There!.....he'll be back with us in about ten minutes.

Right, now to business.

You must have realised Eddie, that a great deal of this "investigation" has been on a very informal, and not quite official basis?"

I nodded.

"Ros in fact, is on the point of retiring, actually she's resigning and this will be her last assignment. I do believe that she has a career change in mind.

Abbie, it appears, may have had reasons of her own for being here, reasons in addition to the parameters of her investigation. And as for myself? Well, I was never here in any "official" capacity at all. Officially, I'm semi-retired.

The upshot of all of that, is that there is no real record anywhere of the existence of this young man, Shabaz Ghalzai."

Shabaz stirred.

"And so we must create a record. Ros and Abbie?....... They will go along with whatever we decide.

So, this is it. This is what I suggest.....

Shabaz is to be a hero, an agent placed by me, deep within the structure of Al Qaeda....An agent reporting only to me.

At the end of last year, he informed me of the impending implementation of the Hess plan, and at great personal risk to himself, he came to Britain. He contacted Parsa Khan, and acted as a courier for him, between himself, and certain contacts in Leeds. But all of that time, he was passing information back to Ros and I.

Parsa Khan acted alone in all of the attempts upon your life, and also in the matter of the Longtown car bomb.

Now that Parsa has disappeared, Shabaz believes that his cover has been effectively blown, that suspicion may well fall upon him, and so, he cannot under any circumstances be allowed to return to Al Qaeda. He will require official protection, and to be permitted to remain in this country."

Shabaz moaned, and managed to sit up, although he remained handcuffed to the bunk.

Mehri, rose from the floor, and sat beside him.

"In exchange for all of this, Shabaz, will agree to provide me with full details of all of his time with Al Qaeda, and details of all of the contacts he made in Afghanistan, Pakistan, and here.

He will be interviewed at length by both myself, and Ros and Abbie.

He will spend the next two weeks at a secret location. In other words at my house, out at Glentarras. After that he will be released into the custody of Mehri here.

All of this of course, is dependent upon his and Mehri's agreement......You happy with that Eddie?"

What could I say? so I just shrugged, and raised my palms.

Mehri threw herself into my arms, and hugged me tightly. It was rather pleasant!

"I knew when I first saw you that you were a nice man".

Viktor turned to Shabaz, and fixed him with his eyes. "Did you get all of that?"

He nodded.

"Any questions," I asked.

"Just one, Please, Please, it's been torture. Can I use the bathroom, I've not been able to move for two hours."

I couldn't help but smile.

Mehri was exultant, "Can I go and get it now Viktor."

"Of course you can Pet."

"Pet?" I thought, "Oh God, He's turning into a Geordie."

She laughed, and raced out of the door.

Viktor shook his head. "You'll see."

Shabaz was back, and sitting on the bunk, when Mehri returned.

In her right hand, was a small case with a mesh front, and as she entered the door, she released the catch.

A huge ginger cat emerged. It stared around in bewilderment, and then leapt onto the bunk, rubbing itself all over Shabaz.

"Guinevere!" He yelled, hugging the beast to him.

"Jesus," I thought. "What next! Now we've got bloody Guinevere the Terrorist's Cat."

Gwen, jumped down and rubbed herself against my legs, purring loudly.

Shabaz smiled for the first time. "She likes you, Mr Graham".

* * *

We commandeered Ecky Charlton. I handed him my car keys, and dispatched him, together with Shabaz and Mehri, off to Viktor's house.

Then we began our search.

We found the original Hess file, together with its additional faked documents right where he had told us they would be. They were in their original leather briefcase, embossed with the eagle and swastika, on the front passenger seat of Shabaz's Mercedes van, parked out at the end of the driveway of Marchbank House, just waiting to be found.

And then Viktor and I committed a little burglary.

It took us no more than five minutes to enter the bungalow once occupied by Anthony Errington Vardy, but it took us the best part of an hour to get into his safe.

Fortunately, Viktor's van came equipped with all of the "tools of the trade" necessary for the task. Inside of the safe, we found dozens of fake documents implicating Peter Irvine's grandfather in the proposed plot to assassinate Churchill, together with lists of all of his alleged associates. They were first rate forgeries, paper, ink, everything, matching 1941. We removed them all, placed them in a separate file, and added them to the contents of the briefcase.

We also found a large amount of cash in £50 notes.

I handed it to Viktor. "Expenses?"

He smiled, split it roughly into two, and handed me half back. "Partners?"

I shrugged, "Fine with me."

"Careless laddie that Shabaz," he commented.

"How's that then?"

"Oh, he dumped a load of papers in his household rubbish. Stuff Parsa Khan must have had. Mobile numbers, contacts, all that sort of stuff. It'll take us a while, Ros and I, to sort through everything, but we ought to be able to roll up a couple of terrorist cells working out of Leeds.....British bloody Asians! Brought up and educated here. What's wrong with them? This is not such a bad country you know, certainly better than where their parents came from. I mean this place has its faults, and the worst of them is your class system. But that could be put right."

He hefted the briefcase, and I guessed what was coming.

"Now Eddie..... I'm giving *you* the means to change things. No-one except Shabaz, knows the whereabouts of these original documents, and I can assure you that he isn't going to say anything. Not after I've had a few words with him.

"So here you are." And he handed me the case. "If that belongs to anyone it belongs to you. Your grandfather saw it fall. You tracked it down. Four times they tried to kill you. And now you must decide what you want to do with it, because........It's *your* problem.

You're going to be seeing quite a bit of me Eddie, because I'm not going back. I'm just going to dig myself in, out at my little house at Glentarras. I like it here. All of those years in the service of my country. All those years working towards an ideal, something I believed in fervently. And look at *my* country.......It's fallen apart.

You used to be my enemy, and now you're my friend. Both you, and yours. So I'm staying. Where there are folk I can talk to, in a place where I can put down roots.

Mehri is right. You are a good man Eddie Graham, but you're a dreamer, an anachronism. In truth, you're more of a Communist than I am. Somehow, you still manage to believe in the Common Man. Even though you know that it's just greed that makes the world go round.

You know that them that's got it's keeping it. They always have, and they always will.

People....? To them, they are just another cash crop, and every few years that crop is ready for harvesting.

Our so called "Masters?" They lie, they twist the truth, they keep people stupid. Feed them on a diet of rubbish. Mindless television, vacuous music, and a culture of idiot "celebrities."

They make their fortunes out of recessions, manipulation, and the misery of others.

Get rid of them?....There's more, just waiting in the wings.

"Roll on the Revolution?" We had one, and look what happened.

But now..... You have that file. So go on.....Publish it. Or....blackmail them with it, bring them to heel. Make them pay for all of those years of "Lording It" over you all.

I mean....Why not? You can destroy the system, you can have a fresh start. I won't to stop you. If you tell what you know, you will bring the class system crashing down. And you can dance in the ruins.

"The Triumph of Everyman!"

But I don't believe that you'll do it. Because, you still love this country don't you? Or at least, you love the image of what it ought to have been. Of what perhaps it still can be.

"Green and Pleasant Land," "Stiff Upper Lips," All of that......?

You and those like you Eddie?.... You're just fossils. Noble Fossils. You're all mixed up, you think that it just might be possible to talk those rich bastards round.

Fair do's for all, Eh Eddie? Happy workers? Shares in the Company....All for one and one for all!

But........?" He raised his hands in a gesture of helplessness. "It'll never happen, will it?.....And deep down you know it.

Forget all of that, Eddie Graham. Become a realist. Exactly as I have.

Just Survive.

Do what you like with that briefcase.

But......Why not simply look after yourself, and protect your friends?"

It hurt, but Viktor was right. The good guys don't often win.

But that doesn't mean that they should stop trying!

* * *

Remember, Remember.

Guy Fawkes Night.

We had a bonfire out behind the Cafe. A bit of a private do for a change.

Abbie had announced that now that it was all over, she would be returning to London.

We'd continued our relationship after Kate's wedding. It was pleasant in a friendly sort of way, but we had a tacit understanding, that it was coming to an end.

She was off in the morning, and this would be our last night together. She said she would be back up now and again to visit me, but I think we both knew that it was not really very likely. We liked each other well enough, and it had been fun. In another time and place it might have been different. But Kate's shadow would always be there between us, and though it was never spoken of, we both knew it.

Ros was the big surprise. Not only was she retiring from the Service, but she was staying in the Borders. And to my amazement, she arrived at the Cafe hand in hand with an escort. Master Zhang, of all people!

Inexplicably, Shorty greeted them both fondly!

I was sitting back in a secluded corner of the cafe, with Abbie, and I nudged her gently with my elbow.

"What gives with those three, Oh Beautiful One?"

She watched them for a while, and smiled.

"Ros, is a very unusual and determined lady Eddie. She won't settle down easily. She will have to have a project. So Shorty....He told her all about "Master Zhang," and his origins. Hadn't you noticed? Those little private conversations they've been having. Well, "Master Zhang," and his "Temple," back there in the hills are to be Ros's project."

"What! She's blackmailing him!"

"Oh no Eddie, she's much more subtle than that. You see Ros, is highly qualified. Martial Arts, Yoga, Meditation, all of that weird Eastern philosophy. She even has a set of titles to match

Zhang's......Except of course, that hers are real.
She's been "visiting him," on a regular basis for quite some time now, and the upshot of it all is.... She is now a partner in Welldean House.
She's rather well off since her father died, and she's put a little bit of her wealth into the project. All nice and legal too. She's a half owner, and if I know Ros it won't be long before she moves up to 51%.....Zhang won't know what's hit him!
She's now "The Abbess of Welldean." She nudged me with *her* elbow. "I've no idea how you address an Abbess...Have you?"
We burst into laughter, just as Chuck arrived and plonked down a couple of forks, and a plate of what looked like small fried dumplings in front of us.
"Give us your opinion of those folks?"
We spiked one each, and then worked our way through the plate.
Each one was different. They were a bit like Chinese wontons, but better, in fact they were absolutely delicious. They appeared to have been boiled to cook them, then lightly fried to a golden crispness, and each one had a slightly different filling, meaty, spicy, unlike anything I'd tasted before.
So I waved my hand in the air, palm downwards in a "not too sure" gesture.
"Mmmm.... Can't tell Chuck......Tell you what, go back and get us another couple of plates, and then we might be able to make our minds up. Auntie Mary invent them?"
He grinned. "Oh No Eddie, It was Vic. They're called Pelmini or something."
"Vic?" I asked, "Who the Hell is Vic?"
"Your pal Viktor Eddie, he's been showing me Auntie how to do things Russian style. She's been going out to his place on her nights off.
Actually .....Errrmm....Eddie.... Errr.... I've been meaning to ask you about that.
I mean.....Vic is okay isn't he?
It's just that......Well..... Auntie Mary doesn't come back some night's, and I wouldn't like to think.....you know.....that he's been....you know."
Chuck blushed bright red. "I mean Eddie. He wouldn't take advantage of her would he?"
We both burst out laughing again.

"What's so funny?" Chuck asked. "I'm worried that's all!"
"Forget it! She's fine, just go and grab your two twins, Yvonne and Denise, you're due on in five minutes.

The entire band was up on stage, when they walked in.
Which is how we missed seeing them.
Shorty, and Reb were on guitars, Chuck fronting, backed by Yvonne and Denise. Lonnie of all people was on drums, and Avril on fiddle.
They were belting out Reb's favourite, "Broken down Angel," the old Nazareth classic. They'd added in the sound of Reb's Harley, just to give it a bit more bite.
Viktor slipped quietly onto the bench opposite us.
"Liked the dumplings.... "Vic"....What's in them?"
He looked amused. "Oh, the pelmini? Pretty much the same mix as you put in your "Geordie Burgers". Mary's going to add them to the menu."
"Oh Aye...."Mary"....of course.....You sly bugger! You're part of the family now!"
He pretended to be abashed. "Don't mind, do you Eddie?" I punched him gently on the shoulder.
"Course not, Chuck's a bit worried though"
"I know," he replied, "Mary says he should call me "Uncle Vic" what do you think?"
"Ahh.... just let it be, he'll soon get used to the idea."
Viktor waved his hand, and Mehri and Shabaz emerged from one of the booths near the door.
"Must be slipping Eddie," I thought. "You didn't see them enter."
She was leading him by the hand, and he couldn't seem to meet my eye.
They stood by the table. Slowly, he raised his right hand, and extended it to me. Then he looked up. "Sorry's not good enough is it Mr. Graham?" I took his hand and we shook.
"It's a start Shabaz, for God's sake, go get your lady a chair, and join us." He reached over, and slid a chair across the floor.
"I like it here you know, I used to come in when you were away. I like the music, and Mrs Kang was always nice to me."
Mehri, passed me an envelope.
"What's this?"
She took Shabaz's hand, and looked shyly at him. "I know it's

quick, but it's a wedding invitation. We're to be married. In three weeks time. Please say you'll come Mr. Graham, it would mean a lot to me."

"It would mean a lot to us both." Shabaz added.

What could I say?

So I said "Yes."

* * *

November 6th 2003.

Manuscript.

Abbie was gone, Kate was married, and it was winter.

I called in at the newsagents in the centre of town, and picked up a paper.

Then I bought an old loaf at the bakers. The only place that I've ever heard of that can sell old stale bread for decent money.

I walked back to the cafe through the car park, and along the river bank.

All of the ducks had gone. I tore the bread up and left it anyway. Black crows dropped from the trees. Noisily and greedly, they began to feed.

I thought again about, "The Watchers of Enoch," Brian's book.

The castle ruin loomed across the river, washed out and colourless. Trick of the light.

Faint blue smoke hung in the air. Floating, drifting wraiths, that mourned the death of the only decent man ever to enter Parliament.

Odours of burned out bonfires, old, dead, damp fireworks.

Now we faced those long dark days before Christmas.

I thought of bright sun, the heat of Afghanistan. Never would have believed I could miss that. I shook myself. Snap out of it Eddie, there's a bright side to everything.

He was there when I reached the cafe. His Audi TT was parked outside.

So I collected the briefcase from my Toyota. Went in, and saw the Apple logo glowing.

He was in his usual place, in the shadows, percolator of coffee on the table, laptop on his knees, his personal cup in front of him, the one with the rabbit in the blue trousers on it. “Li’l Bri.”

I ambled over, and sat opposite.

“Anyone interesting in this one?”

He laughed, and looked up from his keyboard. “Hi Eddie, I really don’t know, I’ve told you I just write what comes into my head.

I nodded towards the percolator on the table. “It can kill you, drinking too much of that stuff you know.”

But he just laughed again. “So that’s what worries you most Eddie is it? Death by coffee?”

He smiled knowingly. and looked down at what I was carrying. I don’t think he misses much.

I put my empty cup down on the table.

“Help Yourself,” he continued, nodding at the brew, still more than half full.

“Got something for me have you.”

I slapped the briefcase onto the table.

It contained the Hess file, all the forged papers, and all of my notes.

“Nothing but trouble, do what you like with it.”

And so....... He has!

* * *

Epilogue.

Kate's baby was born on the 10th of February 2004, and it was a boy.

I should have been happy, but I was jealous. I ought to have been pleased for them, but I was envious. Envious of Pete Irvine.

These were new emotions for me.

And then, I felt ashamed, because they called their boy Edward.

Eddie....after me. And they asked me to be his Godfather.

He was christened in April, on a fine morning, at Arthuret Church.

After the official ceremony, Kate insisted on a second baptism, down at the old holy well way back behind the church. Back behind the old broken Dark Age cross.

It was that same well that St. Kentigern had consecrated back in 573. He had dedicated to St Michael......Patron saint of battles.

And somehow that seemed appropriate.

Kate stayed with them six months longer, and then, just as she had told me she would do, she left him. Six months later, and the divorce was well under way.

She visited them both on a regular basis.

Shabaz and Mehri were happily married, and helping with the running of her father's business in Carlisle. But Shabaz was now Shabaz Mohammed. Abbie had arranged the paperwork for that.

And Mehri's father believed that Shabaz was an ex intelligence officer.

Abbie also arranged for a story to be circulated in the press in Pakistan.

The official line was that the British Police were seeking an Afghan national named Parsa Khan, who was wanted in connection with the death of a young "escort girl" in Carlisle.

He was also suspected of the murder of his nephew, Shabaz Galzai, whose body was believed to have been disposed of in the Irish Sea.

Ecky Charlton, had been quite taken aback when he'd tried to return the Smith and Wesson to Abbie.

"Oh no you don't Inspector, you see, you're one of us now, and there's no backing out."

Ecky had been lumbered with the task of tidying up all of the loose ends. Liaising with Cumbria Police over Parsa Khan's involvement in the murder of the girl in Botchergate. And helping to arrange Shabaz's new identity.

And after all of that, unexpectedly, and quite out of the blue he suddenly found that he'd moved up a rank to Detective Chief Inspector. The catch though, as Abbie explained to him, was that he was now also M.I.6.'s "Man in the Borders"....."So Ecky, you get to keep the gun."

"The Job," also had to tolerate a Detective Chief Inspector, who moonlighted as Hank Williams, in a band that included the dreaded "Lonnie" from Canonbie as it's drummer.

Ecky claimed it as overtime. Said he was "Working undercover"

"Lady Rebecca and the Electric Willie Band" were sounding more and more professional, and there was talk of a recording deal.

Viktor and Mary Kang, now seemed to be a permanent "item."

They had created a unique menu, and the Cafe was building a fine reputation for good wholesome food.

A. A. Gill had even dined there, and had written a fine article in the Sunday Times. Unfortunately though he must have been lost, for the article referred to Langholm as "a wonderful little town in Cumberland." We all laughed.

Everyone was more or less happy.

Everyone that is, except perhaps for me.

I was producing a reasonable flow of small articles on local history, doing a bit of dealing,and working on my project to record the "forgotten sites" of the Border.

But there was unfinished business, and I knew that it wouldn't simply go away.

I left it a respectable six months. But then I just gave in.

I told myself that it was Andy Hall that did it. Another of the "forgotten men" from Liddesdale.

Andy came from Copshawholm, emigrated to America, and was one of the first men to navigate the Colorado River, right through the Grand Canyon.

Then he became a Wells Fargo agent, and was eventually killed in a gunfight with outlaws.The archetypical Western Hero.

Not known or remembered at all over here. So my only answer must be?...Go to the USA! Take a break. Catch some sunshine. Do a little investigating.

I could fly out of Heathrow.... And I reasoned that if you're flying out of Heathrow.....

Then why not call on a friend?

*   *   *

The Despoine Clinic.

I'd bought Brian's silver Audi TT.

But it was useless out at my place, too low for the forest roads, so I kept it down at the "Last Chance."

I dropped off the Toyota, and arranged for Shorty to keep an eye on Merrylaw.

That wasn't too much of a problem, 'cause, we were building another Van's RV6. Myself, Archie, and Shorty. And Shorty just loved working on that plane.

This time it was for me, because, three months earlier I'd got my pilot's licences for both helicopters and fixed wing.

Shorty, laughed at me when I said I would be away in Arizona.

"Bet you think I don't know what you're up to?....Just going off to look for Andy Hall? What a Cock and Bull story. And, I'm not so sure about the Bull. Say hello to her from me!"

Reb stuck her head through from the kitchen. "And from me!"

Was I really that transparent?

The TT might be no good on forest roads, but it was a joy on the motorway, and economical too. I set off at 8 a.m., stopped off for lunch at Edward Moon's in Stratford upon Avon, and arrived at three in the afternoon.

It was impressive.... Just off the M40, a mile or two north of the M25. Set in old woodland. Invisible from the road. Just a large pair of wrought iron gates, between two old moss covered stone pillars, and a discrete brass plate.

"The Despoine Clinic."

A bell and speaker box were attached to stonework on the right hand side, and I noted the cameras just visible between the branches of the trees.

I pulled the car up in front of the gates, got out, and pressed the bell.

"Yes, Can I help you?"

"Mr Edward Graham, for Miss Katherine Pringle."

A long pause, and then...."I'm sorry, Mr Graham, but you do not appear to have an appointment."

"Tell her it's with regard to a small Jacobite sword."

There was a longer pause, and then the gates swung silently inwards.

I drove through, and immediately they closed behind me.

The drive curved through the trees, effectively shielding the house from view.

It was imposing. Large, Georgian, and built of red sandstone, it glowed warmly in the afternoon sunshine.

The driveway swept in to the foot of a crescent formed by two sets stone stairs, each of which climbed towards a meeting point at the front door.

I was pleased I had brought the TT, because the Toyota would have looked well out of place alongside the vintage Aston Martin, and the long black Rolls with the diplomatic plates.

The door opened before I reached it, and I was greeted by a tall blonde, in a very short French Maids uniform.

Her hair and make up were impeccable. Her voice was refined, and just slightly husky.

"Good Afternoon Mr. Graham. Follow me please, Mistress Katrina will see you now."

She turned, and walked off, high heels clicking. Her legs were magnificent.

She led me up a flight of stairs, and along an oak panelled corridor. The walls were hung with mildly erotic art. Beautiful, late 19th early 20th centuries.....Louis Welden Hawkins'......Originals.

Kate had always reminded me of his depiction of "Clytie."

The "maid," stopped at the far end, knocked lightly on a dark panelled door, and a familiar voice commanded. "Enter".

She held the door for me, bowed slightly and stood to one side as I walked past her into the room.

It was all dark oak panelling, on one wall was a fireplace, and above the mantle on a small rack, hung my little Jacobite sword, and Kate's blackthorn.

She was standing behind a desk, with her back to us, staring out of the window.

She turned, and spoke curtly to the maid.

"That will be all Priscilla. Now! Go down to the basement, and present yourself to Dominique. You will be late, and you know she doesn't take well to being kept waiting."

She turned. "Yes Mistress, I'm so sorry."

The door closed behind her.

Kate smiled. "He will be sorry too."

He! I must have looked stunned. She burst out laughing.

"Oh Eddie! You weren't starting to fancy the Ambassador were you! He'd be delighted!....Just remember, nothing around here is quite what it seems."

She was dressed in a rather severe pinstriped business suit, over a low cut white blouse. Her dark hair was pinned high on her head. Her make up was perfect. Black eyeliner, dark blue eye shadow, full lips emphasised in dark red.

With her hair like that, and her black stilletto heels, she was taller than I am.

If I didn't know her, she would have looked intimidating. But of course, as she would no doubt have told me, that was the intention.

I thought she looked just great.

"I've been expecting you. Have you come down to sample the delights of my little establishment?"

I shook my head.

"No, I didn't think so. What is it then?"

"Andy Hall," and I told her all about my search for the "Liddesdale Cowboy."

"So this is just a little social call? You were just passing by?"

I shook my head again.

"What then?"

I slapped the envelope down on her desk.

"Two tickets. Tonights flight. You're coming with me. And I won't take no for an answer."

She held one hand to her mouth, and feigned shock.

"Ooooh.....a dominant one! How delightful! I haven't tried one of them. How long will it be?

No!.. wait!.. Don't answer that!... I know exactly how your mind works."

She walked over to a cupboard in the corner, opened the door, and removed a suitcase.

"Ready to go. Guessed you'd be here. Packed last week.

Just hope customs don't look inside. There are a few interesting little surprises in there. They'd be *so* shocked."

God! How I'd missed her. And I loved her teasing. Just like old times.

But she wasn't finished with her mischievous little games.

"Can you manage four weeks" I asked.

"Oh, no problem." Then, she pressed a button on the wall.

As if by magic the office door opened, and two of the most stunning women I'd ever seen walked in.

"Meet my "Business Associates," Claudia and Jeanette."

Claudia, was dark complexioned, dark eyed, with the longest black hair I had ever seen tied up in a pony tail high on her head, and cascading down her back.

She was dressed in a tight black leather mini skirt, a matching lace up black leather top, and shoes with five inch heels. In her right had she carried a short riding crop.

Her companion, Jeanette, was blonde, medium height, pale complexioned with lovely bright blue eyes. She wore a very feminine white lace dress, all frills and ribbons. She looked totally innocent.

Claudia, walked around me. Kate just stood smiling.

"Oh, I like this one Katrina. New is he? Can we have him to play with." The riding crop came up, and rested itself beneath my chin.

"Say Hello"

I smiled at her. "Hello"

"Now say it properly!" she snapped. "Hello Mistress!"

She slapped the crop loudly onto the desktop.

Jeanette laughed delightedly.

"Oooh he's going to be fun!"

"Behave girls, this is Eddie. And he's not a client, he's my friend."

Claudia, stepped back. "Sorry Katrina." Then she smiled at me.

"Sure you don't fancy an hour or two's fun Eddie? Katrina can come and join in as well? We don't mind."

"Be serious Claudia, and stop teasing him!

Now....Can you take charge of this place for a few weeks.

Rearrange some of my appointments. I'm taking a little break. I'll keep in touch by phone."

Claudia inclined her head.

"Okay, But.... Promise....You won't be away as long as last time will you?"

She turned to face me. Serious now.

"Look after her Eddie. She's really very precious."

And Claudia was right.

Because.....She is.

*   *   *

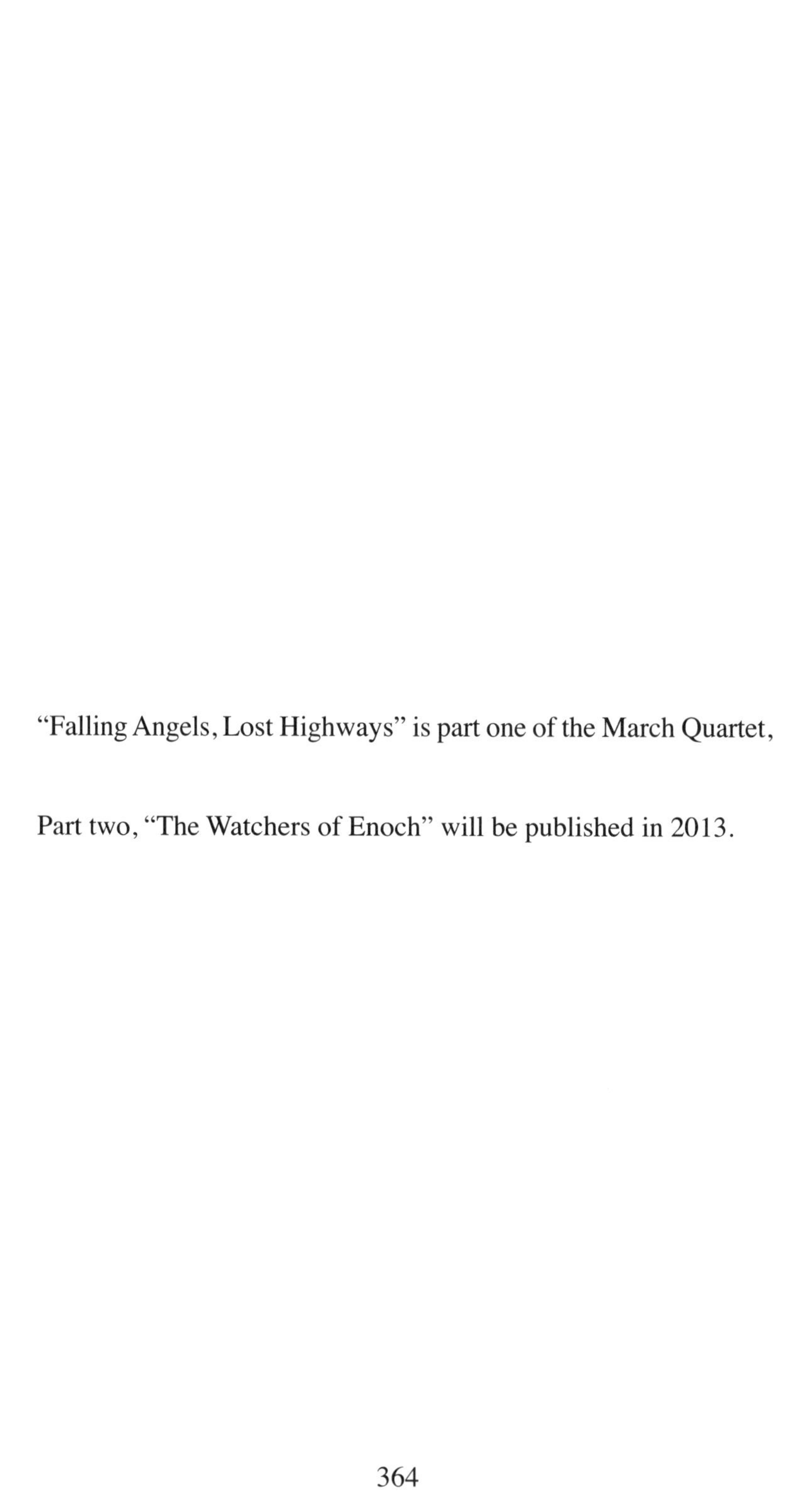

"Falling Angels, Lost Highways" is part one of the March Quartet,

Part two, "The Watchers of Enoch" will be published in 2013.

Author's Note.

I'm *not* Eddie Graham.

Although we do share a similar early life, both having been brought up in Blyth, Northumberland, and both having attended the same school.

In fact I actually did once live in Shorty's house in Sussex Street, and when young, I worked for a plastering contractor in Eddie and Shorty's workshop below his Auntie Bella's flat.

Friends of mine operated fishing cobles along that stretch of coast, and just like Eddie, I was once in the Metropolitan Police. But I transferred back "up North," whilst Eddie stayed on a little longer, before returning North, and then joining the Army.

Also like Eddie, I have a close knowledge of the London Auction Market. But the rest of this story is Eddie's and Eddies alone.

Researching the background for this book has been a bit of a revelation. The material on the Hess crash in 1941, is as accurate as I can make it, and for anyone wishing to look into it all further, I would strongly recommend "Double Standards, The Rudolf Hess Cover-Up" (Lynn Picknett, Clive Prince and Stephen Prior), and The Red Book, The Membership of the Right Club - 1939, edited by Robin Saskia, as starting points. And then a perhaps, good trawl of the Internet.

Certain "sensitive" information although hinted at in various publications, has apparently become "unobtainable" in the last 15 years or so, and seems to have been removed from what records there are. But no matter what, there appears as late as 1941, to have been a considerable covert lobby in England, and in particular in Scotland, for a negotiated peace with Hitler's Germany.

All of which is in complete contradiction to the information which has been fed and still is being fed to the general public over the last sixty or seventy years.

As Shorty would put it.....

"The Hess flight is the equivalent of the Deputy Prime Minister, John Prescott, baling out of an unarmed Phantom over Baghdad, at the height of the Iraqi War, and attempting to negotiate a peace settlement with Saddam Hussein!.... Now *that* would have been *really* interesting."

And I doubt that it would have been so quickly "forgotten."

The Bin Laden information is also accurate, and well worth a little time on the web. Ariana Airlines certainly came as something of a surprise to me.

I can endorse Eddie's liking for both Theakston's and Hook Norton ales, as well as his taste in pasties.

The ultra practical Toyota Hilux, is now probably the most popular 4 x 4 mode of transport in the rural areas of the Borders.

And if the old Reivers *were* still around, I've no doubt at all that they'd mostly be driving Hiluxs.'

The small ritual with the beer, first came to my attention many years ago when I met an elderly gentleman (at least he seemed elderly to me at the time,) who was half British, and half Apache. He was tracing his ancestry in the British Isles, and this was his way of making contact with the spirits of his ancestors.

Ros was quite correct in thinking of her arrows as "little boys and little girls." In "Kyudo," the Japanese form of archery, arrows, (ya) are in fact classified as both male and female, and are fletched with feathers from alternate sides of the bird. Male arrows, (haya) rotate clockwise, whilst female arrows, (otoya), spin counter clockwise.

Kate's "Despoine Clinic" is named after "Despoine," or "Despoina, " Goddess of the mysteries of certain of the Arcadian cults. Despoine translates only as "The Mistress." Her *real* name, could be revealed only to initiates, and thus is unknown. Hence Eddie's amusement, and his reference to Kate as "The Mistress with No Name."

All of the locations used in this book are genuine.... but don't go looking for "Eddie" out at Merrylaw. He doesn't live there. And whilst there actually *is* a Cafe at the point where the road to Copshawholm turns off from the A7.... it is *not* the "Last Chance."

Eddie, Shorty, and their friends' story is very far from over, and I have the outlines laid down for three more books concerning both themselves, and their forbears.

This book has been entirely my own work, so there is no-one else to blame for any errors which have crept in.

The writing style and the diction are pure "Eddie," and probably the product of a "Newlands" Education.

To paraphrase David Cameron "I wish everyone could go to a

good school, like the one we attended."(sic.)

Hank Williams has a great deal to answer for, since his songs, and in particular "Lost Highway" sowed the initial seeds of this narrative. Hank's Greatest Hits is one of the bargain CDs of all time, and anyone who thinks that Elvis and Co. invented Rock 'n Roll, really ought to make themselves familiar with his 1947 recording of "Move it on over."

Thanks must go to my wife Maureen, and my family, who have had to suffer my ramblings for the last very many months. And hopefully will have to do so again in the years to come. Further thanks to Ken for the help and advice on the computer.

And lastly, thanks again to "Eddie," without whom all of this would not have been possible

Hope you have enjoyed this little outing in the Borders.

And remember Viktor's credo "Look after yourselves, Protect your friends, and...... Just Survive!"

All the Best,
Brian Moffatt
November 2012.

Photographs.

Almost all of the photo's within this book are photo manipulations of photographs and artwork in the authors personal collection, or are of his own making, and are copyright of the author.

The cover image, is the work of the author, with the kind assistance of NASA, and the Hubble Space Telescope, (Milky Way, and the Angel Nebula.) The road on the back cover, is the road from Caerlanrig to Merrylaw, whilst the sword on the front cover, genuinely is "Kate's" Jacobite naval smallsword. The resulting montage and wording, however, are copyright of the author.

The photo of Hank Williams, was made for publicity purposes at an unknown date in the 1940's, and is in the public domain.

"Clytie," by Louis Welden Hawkins, is copyright free, and is in the public domain. The current ownership of the original is apparently unknown.

The "Marchbank Shakespeare," is in a private collection in the Borders, and the author thanks the owner who wishes to remain anonymous, for kind permission to use the image.